Sparrows

A novel

Rose Betit

The author, Rose Betit (far right), at age 6 with her siblings in the backyard of their apartment on Society Avenue.

for my children, the loves of my life,
without whose encouragement
i might not have written this story

to my mom, whose spirit threads through
from start to finish

to my siblings, who are always part of my soul

Chapter One

February 1985

I'm jolted awake by the bus lurching forward. "Waaaow!" I exclaim, bleary-eyed, about the snow hanging in clumps on the pine trees that line the highway. I haven't seen snow like this since I was four, so I've forgotten how thoroughly it blankets a landscape.

Several of my fellow passengers on the Trailways bus turn quickly to look at me and smile. Embarrassed by my dreamy outcry at the sight of snow, I smile back, and rest my head on my arm against the cold window. I fix my gaze on the wintery scenery just as we're passing a sign welcoming us to Virginia. "Virginia is for lovers," it declares.

"Oh, honey, something done fell out your bag," says an elderly lady who is leaning over from across the aisle and tapping my arm. She's handing me the small Tupperware container with a label taped on it that reads, "Rest in Peace".

"Thank you, ma'am! I'd have died if I lost this!" I reach over and take it from her and clutch it in both of my hands, close to my chest.

"Must be something special," the lady says, looking at me as if she's expecting an explanation. I'm wondering if she guessed from the label that it was someone's ashes I'm carrying. I wonder if it's okay to carry such a thing on a Trailways bus in the first place.

"Yes'm. It *is* special," I say politely to her and put the container back in my bag, making sure to zip it up this time. I tuck the bag in between my head and the window, close my eyes and pretend I'm going to sleep, so maybe she won't ask me any questions.

My sleeping act is working. The lady is leaning back in her seat, drifting off in her own sleep with her silver hair falling across her satiny brown face, with several strands hanging loose, following the line of her fierce cheek bone.

Chapter Two

Winter 1972
Augusta, Maine

Mama says for us to keep our hats and mittens on inside until she gets the fire going in the wood stove. That way we won't get frostbite. I wonder if I have frostbite anyway because my fingers are burning. I don't want to tell Mama. She'll get mad at me. I don't know why she'll get mad at me for having fingers that burn in the cold, but she always gets mad at me or my brother when we tell her we don't feel good.

My big brother, Stevie, is helping Mama break up the chairs from the kitchen to burn them in the wood stove.

"We don't have no choice," Mama says when Stevie asks her why we're breaking up the furniture.

Mama was outside all morning going up and down the alley looking on the ground for wood. She brought in some sticks, but they were wet with snow and ice and wouldn't burn and just got the house all smoky. So, we had to open some windows to let the smoke out and more cold air in.

I sit and watch and don't say anything because Mama says I can't help since I'm too little. I would just slow things down. I'm only four. Mama says four-year-old little girls shouldn't be working but playing with dolls instead. Stevie is eight and a boy, so he can do some work, she says.

"What are we gonna sit on now, Mama?" Stevie asks.

"We'll sit on the floor around the fire," she says and slams the chair hard against the floor. The wooden legs break into pieces flying all over.

"There," she says.

"But, Mama," Stevie says. He tries to break his chair the same way, but he can't do it so fast because he's not a grown up, "won't Papa get mad about the furniture?"

"Well, he ain't here putting wood in this stove, now, is he? Is he?" Mama's voice gets louder on the second "is he?" Stevie answers her, "No ma'am."

He says "ma'am" and I say "ma'am" to our mama because she's from the South and that's how they talk to their mamas in the South. They don't say "ma'am" up North, so people laugh at us when we say it. We have to say it anyway. Mama gets mad if we don't.

We don't like when people laugh at us, but we really don't like it when she's mad at us. Then, we can't have any hugs or kisses or even a smile from her. She turns her back right at us and if we scrape our knees or if we're hungry, she acts like she can't even hear us when we cry or ask for something to eat. She sits stiff and quiet and cold in her gray sweater with her back straight up and her arms bent and stiff at her sides like a metal chair that won't be warm or soft to sit in.

Stevie and Mama pile the wooden legs and other parts of the chairs over to the side. Mama says we can't use it all at once. She says I can crumple some newspaper if I want to because that's easy enough and put it in the wood stove.

I crumple the newspaper and put it in the stove. Mama lights some sticks in there and we sit and watch it burn before Mama closes the little metal door and tells us to step back, don't play around it or we could get burned. We shut all the doors to the living room to keep the heat in. Mama walks around shaking her head back and forth. She's saying something down low about what a fool she is for moving north to "freeze her ass off every year."

My papa was in the Army. The Army made him go to Georgia. He met my mama when she worked at the movie place. She says he was the most handsome man in town, and he promised her a house in Maine if she would marry him and move there. Her mama said she was going to shoot Papa if he thought he was taking her daughter north. Papa took her anyway when they ran away and got married. Mama told us that's why we live here. She says after nine and a half years she's tired of waiting for a house she's never going to get from Papa.

"If we lived down South, we might be poor and we might be hungry, but at least we wouldn't freeze to death," is what she says with her head down and shaking.

Mama tells us that she's had enough of the north. "We're going South," she says, and grabs a pencil and tears a piece of paper from Stevie's school writing pad. She sits down on the floor in front of the fire all hunched over with a cigarette hanging from her mouth while she writes on the paper. She doesn't hear me ask if I can write on some paper too and Stevie takes my hand and leads me to sit with him, curled up in the corner on the cloth chair with a story book.

The next day Papa's sister, our Aunt Monique, comes by and can't believe when she sees that the furniture is gone from the kitchen and in a pile in the corner of the living room.

"What on earth? Where's your Papa?" she asks me and my brother, but she looks at Mama before we can say anything and asks, "Where on earth is

Leo?" That's Papa's name, Leo.

"I don't know. He's been gone for days. He's run off again. Cattin' around, I guess."

I wonder what "cattin' around" is and I think it must mean he's out playing with cats somewhere. I don't know why Papa would be out playing with cats when we're here freezing to death and hungry.

"We had to burn the chairs for heat. We didn't have no choice. I was afraid the kids would get frostbite. Don't go tell Mémère about the chairs. It'll break her heart since she gave us these when we first got married. I saved one of them just to try to keep a part of it."

"You know she'll find out anyway. You can't keep anythin' from her," my aunt says about my Mémère, who is my papa's mama, and my northern grandma.

"Oh, my goodness. It's truly a cryin' shame!" Aunt Monique says and walks around the edges of the living room. Her fingers are clamped together on her belly like she's praying.

"You got to do something, Jolene. You can't keep living like this with these children. If my brother won't take care of them the right way, then you're gonna have to do something. I know he's my brother an' all," she says about my papa, "but I'm ashamed of the way he doesn't even try to take care of his children. Out cattin' around! It's a disgrace!" Now, Aunt Monique is shaking her head like Mama does and talking about Papa out there playing with cats.

Mama tells Aunt Monique that she wrote to her family to see if they could help her move back South. My aunt thinks that would be for the best.

"Well, I'm sure we'd miss you, but you gotta do what's best for these children." She looks at us and smiles.

"Oh, I almost forgot!" she says. "I brought you kids some goodies!" She turns quick, runs out to her car and comes back in with a brown bag full of jelly doughnuts.

Me and Stevie grab one and start eating too fast when Mama says, "Slow down. You'll choke on it, for God's sake! And don't forget to thank your Aunt Monique."

"Thank you," we say with our cheeks filled with doughnut.

Aunt Monique says, "That's okay," and laughs at me because I have red jelly all around my mouth. She hands me a napkin and reaches out and touches the tops of our heads and messes up our hair.

"I have to get going," she says, leaving the bag with more doughnuts on the table that doesn't have any chairs left around it.

Mama waits until Aunt Monique is gone before she gets a doughnut for herself. When she eats it, she eats slow and wipes the corners of her mouth a lot with a napkin to keep the jelly off. Her little pinky finger sticks out while she's doing this, and she says it's because that's also a thing they do in the South.

"Southern ladies do it, I mean, it's like saying ma'am. It shows you got manners," she says.

I try to do like she does when I wipe my mouth. I ask," Mama, am I a Southern lady?"

"No," Mama says, "you'll always be a Northerner deep inside because you were born here. Even if I take you down to Georgia, you'll always want for the North the same way I always want for the South because I was born there."

"Oh," I say and let my little finger curl up with the rest of them.

My Aunt Monique didn't tell Mémère about the chairs. Stevie said she told her church instead. One of the men at her church works for the newspaper and he's at our door asking Mama if he can do a story about us and our furniture burned up for firewood. Mama says, "Well, I don't know."

"With that kind of publicity, Mrs. Letourneau, I'm sure the kind people of Augusta would step forward and assist your family in heating your home this winter."

"Well, I guess that might be true," Mama agreed.

The man sat in the chair that Mama saved from the wood stove and wrote notes in his notebook while he talked to her.

Mama's perched up on the window ledge talking away, telling the newspaper man our story. The sun coming in the window is bright across her face and she lights up a cigarette.

"Oh, pardon me, do you mind if I smoke?" she asks the newspaper man.

He says, "No, go ahead," and laughs a little bit while he pushes his glasses back up on his nose.

When they finish talking, he says he'd like to take a picture of us three next to our pile of broken chairs that were going away fast in the wood stove.

On Saturday, the newspaper has the story and Stevie reads it out loud to us. The big black words at the top of the story say, "Destitute Family Burns Furniture for Firewood." There's our picture with me in the front, Stevie standing behind me looking at the floor, and Mama with a sad look on her face and one hand on Stevie's shoulder.

"What's destitute mean?" Stevie stopped reading to ask Mama.

"It means poor," She says.

"What's poor?" I ask.

"Poor is when you don't have money to buy firewood," Mama says.

Stevie reads the rest of the story that tells how we had to break our chairs that Mémère gave us and how we don't know where our papa went off to. It told how Mama doesn't got a job to make money to buy wood and how she's from the South and wants to move back in the spring.

"*If* they can make it through this last winter here," it says.

Stevie finishes reading and looks up at Mama with his eyes big.

"Why does it say *if* we make it through this winter? Are we gonna die?"

We both look at her waiting for the answer. Mama is quiet, but then says,

"Why, no...we ain't gonna die."

"Then, why do they say 'if'," Stevie asks again and I feel scared because I can see that he's getting scared until Mama says, "Oh it's just for the effect that they say it like that, so people will care more. A lot of times people don't care unless they know someone could die, so the newsman just wrote it like that, so folks would care. Okay? No, we ain't gonna die. Put the paper away and go play."

The newspaper man was right about how people will help if we put the story in the paper. When we only have a couple more sticks of chair left to burn, a firewood company gives us so much wood Mama says she thinks it will last us the rest of the winter.

In February, Mama gets a letter from my grandma from the South and hangs her head low and cries.

"Can I see it? What does it say?" Stevie wants to know.

"You don't need to read it. Grandma says she'll help, but she says she can't pay for all of us. I'll have to get help from some kinfolk up here for the airplane fare, that's all."

Mama stuck it on a shelf. Stevie snuck and read it later. He says that Grandma doesn't want Mama to bring me and Stevie and that must be what made her cry.

He read it out loud:

"I told you not to run off up North with that nasty French Catholic that doesn't think of anything but laying up in bed and making babies or running off with some French whore. You want me to pay for those little snotty nose young'uns? You shouldn't have had them

if you can't take care of them.

Well, I guess since I'm your mama I'll help you anyway, even if I don't agree with what you did with your life. Y'all can come down, but when you're at my house, you'll live by my rules.

Next month, I'll send enough money for two of y'all. You'll have to get help from your kinfolk up there with the rest. Sorry, but I'm not made of money.

Bye for now.
Mama."

I ask Stevie what a "French whore" is. He says he doesn't know, but he thinks it ain't something good.

Chapter Three

It snowed all night last night so Mama said Stevie and me can go sledding on the hill down the street. She said Stevie is so responsible for an eight-year-old that she knows he won't let me get hurt while we're out. I think my brother is like Super boy because he can pick me up and carry me if I need him to. He puts me on his back and gives me a piggyback ride when my legs are tired.

We pull Stevie's wooden sled that Mémère gave him for Christmas once, from the closet. Mama jokes that we could have burned that in the wood stove when we needed wood. I know it's a joke because she's smiling, and Stevie is smiling back, and I know she would never burn this sled because it's Stevie's favorite thing in the world to play with in the wintertime.

Mama tucks my shirt in my pants, makes me put on a sweater that makes me itch and puts on my jacket with the snaps all the way up my neck. She makes me put on two pairs of pants to keep myself dry and I feel like I can hardly bend over because my clothes are so thick on me. I slide my feet into my boots that are big and floppy. They were my cousin's boots once. Now they're mine. When she puts on my hat and mittens, she warns me not to take them off and leave them at the snow hill.

"Your Mémère can only knit so many pairs of mittens and hats, you know, so you need to keep up with these ones, you hear me?" she says.

"Yes ma'am," I say, and I squirm away from her toward the door where Stevie waits with the sled. He has his hat on too, but he always takes it off as soon as we get around the corner where Mama can't see him.

"It makes my head itch," he says, but he tells me I have to keep mine on because Mama will get mad at him if I lose it.

I climb in the sled and he pulls it by the rope while I ride.

"Stevie, Stevie, you're a sled doggie. Okay, Stevie? Okay?" I say.

"Okay, hold on tight. I'm the fastest sled dog there ever was!" he says and runs as fast as he can dragging me and the sled behind him.

He even pulls me to the top of the snow hill and that's another reason why I think he's a Super boy. Because I don't see any other little sisters being pulled by their big brothers up the hill. The rest of them are crawling up the hill behind their big brother or sister, crying all the way up that the hill is too high.

When we get to the top of the hill it feels like we are on top of the world because we see the tops of trees near the bottom of the hill. I like seeing the tops of the trees because I can pretend that I'm a bird up high somewhere.

On the sled I sit behind Stevie and hang on tight and lay my head on his back. When we start to slide, I let go to spread my arms out straight like wings. The wind is cold in my face and my eyes get watery. It's hard to breathe because the air is blowing too fast in my mouth.

"Hold on, Isabelle!" I hear Stevie yell at me, but he can't stop the sled, it's going so fast, so he can't make me hold on.

"No, I'm a big hawk bird!" I holler. "I won't fall!"

"Hold on, Isabelle!" he makes a screechy sound almost like a cry at me, so I hold on to his shoulders and we slide fast past kids who are climbing up.

"Out of my way!" Stevie yells at some kids at the bottom of the hill when we are almost at the bottom of it. They scatter, and Stevie is laughing so I start laughing and the sled turns sideways. We both slip off of it, onto the ground. We are both still laughing because we didn't get hurt at all. It's fun to fly and land crashing in the snow when you don't get hurt doing it.

We jump up and Stevie pulls me up the hill again.

"You hold on this time. Because if you don't, this will be our last time down. Okay?" I tell him I will, but I think he knows that I'm going to let go again.

"Promise, Isabelle, and cross your heart and you can't lie if you cross your heart because it's a sin for sure."

"Okay, I promise and cross my heart," so I make a cross on my heart with my fingers, and he believes me. We go down and I hold on tight because when you promise with a cross on your heart you have to keep that promise and I didn't like that his voice made that cry sound.

When the sun is starting to go down over the hill Stevie says we have to go, or Mama will worry. I climb on the sled and Stevie's a sled dog again. We stop on the way when we see snow that nobody walked on yet and Stevie says it's a perfect place to make some snow angels. We lay in the snow beside each other and wave our arms and legs back and forth to make the wings and gown shape in the snow.

An old lady walks by and says our snow angels are the best snow angels she has ever seen, and don't we think so too? We say, "Yes, ma'am, we do," and she laughs and repeats the "ma'am" part like northern people always do.

We don't know what else to say to this old lady who thinks it's funny to say "ma'am" and we are happy when she walks on down the sidewalk. She walks slow and bent over. Stevie says he hopes she doesn't fall on the ice.

"Get on. The sled dog is ready again," he says. He's puffing hard when we get home. I can see the air moving fast like smoke out of his mouth because it's so cold you can see it.

"Glad we're home. You must be growing Isabelle; it's getting harder for me to pull you," he says.

Aunt Monique's car is parked in the driveway, so we know she's visiting Mama. We can see them through the kitchen window sitting on some old chairs that Mémère got from her cellar and gave us after she found out that we had to burn ours. Just when we open the door, we hear Mama say to Aunt Monique, "Well, Isabelle can stay here for a while and Stevie and I will go on down to Georgia."

They both turn to look at us like they're surprised to see us back. I start screaming at Mama before she can say anything else.

"I don't want to stay, Mama! No! I want to be with Stevie and you, Mama!" I clunk over in my big boots and track snow and mud all over.

I pull on Mama's shirt and cry more. Aunt Monique gets up quick and tries to hug me. She tells me to calm down and that she and Mémère will take care of me.

"No!" I scream.

"I want Stevie and Mama! Stevie, tell Mama I don't want to stay!"

Stevie tells Mama that I don't want to stay and asks her why I have to.

Mama says it's the money for the airplane fare that she don't have right now and that she needs me to stay here so she can get a job down South and not worry about me or where I can go to be babysat while she works.

"Stevie," she says, "is old enough to take care of himself and he's old enough to be of some help, but Isabelle, she'll just get in the way."

Stevie stops asking Mama anything else about it and starts helping me take off my wet jacket and muddy boots. I just sit lumped up, crying in his lap. They're leaving in the spring and I'm staying. Mama says she's sorry, but that's just how things are right now, and I should be mad at my papa if I'm mad at anybody because he's the one that ran off and left us like this. But I don't feel like I'm mad. I'm just sad and I don't know what I'll do when next winter comes and I have to make snow angels alone in the snow without Stevie.

Chapter Four

It's May, close to the end. I know it is because Mama has a little calendar that she puts "X's" on each day passing. The last one she put this morning says 20 on it. Stevie is reading a story to me on Mémère's sun porch. I'm listening, but I can see the drops of water from last night's snow melting off the roof. Last night, I asked Jesus to wait to bring spring. I thought when it snowed, that was his way of saying, "Okay."

But all that snow is dripping down, and I know that means it's spring. The sun through the window is hot on my face and I'm so warm on Mémère's couch with Stevie's story that I could fall asleep. I wonder if falling asleep would keep the spring away and I ask Stevie. He says, "No" and, "You're not making any sense, Isabelle. Are you listening to the story or what?"

"Yes, I'm listening, but I don't want spring to come yet, Stevie. Can we stop it?"

"No, silly. We can't stop it. Just listen to the story and forget about bad things. Listen to stories and when you get big, like me, you can read them, and you can be in a different world when you feel sad. That's what I do."

"But when you go South who will read stories to me then?" I ask him.

"Well, I'm sure Mémère will read to you and Aunt Monique. Then before too long Mama will send for you. Won't that be nice? Think of that. Okay?"

"Will I go on a big plane?"

"Yes."

"Will you and Mama be on the plane with me too?"

"I think so," Stevie says.

"Well, I hate spring," I say, "and I wish it would never come."

"Oh, don't say that … because then how would flowers and trees grow? And birds would never fly back up North either. Now wouldn't that be a sad thing? I'll write to you every week. Okay? Won't that be fun to get your own mail?"

I don't want spring to come even if the birds could never come back, but even if I wish real hard for it not to, the snow melts and I hear Mama talking more and more about going South.

She tells me that I have nothing to worry about, that she won't forget me, and Stevie won't either and as soon as she can, she will send for me.

"When will that be, Mama?" I ask.

"I don't know," she says, "as soon as I can, that's all. Don't keep asking because I just ain't sure right now. Okay? You're going to make it worse than it has to be, Isabelle, by asking too many questions."

Aunt Monique is sitting at the table with us and she turns to Mama and says, "My goodness, Jolene, she only asked one question and you're telling her it's too many. A child needs to know she's secure, you know."

"Well, Monique, since you seem to have all the answers you can just teach her everything when I leave her to you then. How about that?" Mama snapped at my aunt and stomped away huffing.

I wonder if I just heard my mama say she was giving me away to Aunt Monique.

"Aunt Monique, did Mama say you can have me for good?" I ask.

"No, no it's not that at all, dear. I'm just going to look after you for a while, with Mémère ... remember? Why don't you and Stevie go play outside since the weather is good and I'm going to talk to your mother a while. I think she might be a little upset."

So out we go and sit in the grass out front. It's cool and green and I like the way it feels on my skin. The lilac bushes are growing flowers everywhere and I breathe the smell of them in deep. I want to pick some of those flowers for Mama, then maybe she will be so happy with me that she decides to bring me with her to Georgia where all the birds go in the winter when they go away from here.

It's a warm Saturday and Mama and Uncle James, who is Aunt Monique's husband, are moving our furniture out of our apartment and into a storage shed in the back of their house. Mama jokes that that's one good thing about not having much of anything.

"It don't take no time to move it," and she laughs.

I hate that she's laughing right now, and I want to go up and punch her legs because she's leaving me and laughing just the same. I don't, though, because you can't go up and punch your mama about laughing over not having much furniture.

Instead, I just hop up and run down the back alley as fast as I can. I don't know where I'm going, but I'm running, and I can't stop myself. I'm running...running...and splashing mud in my face from the melted snow. I'm running and crying and soon I hear Mama and Aunt Monique calling to me.

"Isabelle, come back! Have you gone plum crazy?" my mama screams.

Mama says that to me a lot. That's why she took me to the doctor for talking to the moon.

"Your daughter has a big imagination," the doctor said.

"But she's talking to herself and her friends that I can't see. And she tells people stories that can't be true, like she can fly and stuff like that," Mama went on, all worried.

"Oh my, Isabelle, you do know that you can't truly fly, don't you?" the doctor's forehead wrinkled up.

"But I can," I said, and the doctor looked at Mama, who was still worried about my "imagination."

"Well, Mrs. Letourneau, I believe she'll grow out of these fantasies."

Mama said she hopes so, but I don't think she believed it.

So, I'm running, I put my arms out in wide wings. I see my feet lifting and the ground is moving fast under me.

I look back and I can see Mama, and Stevie and everybody getting smaller. I keep going but then they send Stevie to fetch me and he's faster than me.

"Isabelle! Stop running ... wait for me!" he's yelling, and I see he's splashing mud all over.

I can't stop going and crying though, and soon he catches up to me and grabs me under the arms and swings me around ... and around and around. I start to laugh and he's laughing, and we fall into a puddle right in the middle of the alley.

"Mama's going to have a fit at how dirty we are. Why were you running?" he wants to know.

"I don't know ... my feet just started going this way."

"Well, come on ... get a piggyback. Let's go get cleaned up" He lets me climb on his back and he carries me all the way back down the alley and tells me a story about the three little pigs who build houses. A wolf comes and blows two of them away because they weren't strong enough and they built them in a hurry. Except this time the wolf explains that he didn't mean to blow down the house that he sneezed on account of he has a cold. And it was raining out and the pigs invited him in for a nice tea," Stevie says.

"And so, he doesn't eat them?" I ask.

"No, they give him a bathrobe, a bonnet to wear, and a teddy bear. So, the wolf falls asleep on the couch sucking his thumb like a baby."

This makes me laugh more and I love how Stevie can think up a story that's different from every other story any time.

Chapter Five

There are too many of us piled in Aunt Monique's Beetle bug car that's round and has a top that's made of plastic and opens and closes if she wants it to. It's raining hard and making tick, tick, tick noises on the little plastic windows and dripping into the back of the car and making a little river down the side of the seat and onto the floor next to Stevie. We're squeezed in too tight on the way to the airport, but Mémère said we all have to be there to see Mama and Stevie off in a proper way. I'm sitting on Stevie's lap. He says that I'm getting a little heavy sitting there on his bladder and Mama scoops me up and sits me on her lap. Mama jokes about us looking like a pack of sardines and laughs all shaky.

The airport is busy with people all in bunches saying their goodbyes and giving hugs. There's a family next to us with a lot of kids playing chase around the seats in the waiting area.

"That there is how *not* to act in an airport," Mama says down low and "I hope they won't be on the same plane with us."

Then the announcer man calls out that a plane to Chicago is loading and the family with the kids picks up everything in a hurry and rushes off to Chicago.

It's not long before the announcer man calls out Mama and Stevie's flight number.

We all stand up in a circle and look at each other. I hold on to Stevie's hand and feel like I might choke on the lump in my throat.

"How about one more piggyback?" Stevie asks, and I climb on and wish I hadn't promised that I would try not to cry.

"I'll send you a post card right when I get there okay?" Stevie says.

Aunt Monique says, "We'll say our goodbyes here."

Just then a dark-haired priest walks by and Mama says how handsome he is, especially in the collar.

My Mémère reminds her that he *is* a priest and she's wasting her time looking at a man of the cloth. I wonder what she means "a man of the cloth," but I'm too sad about saying goodbye to ask.

"I do declare, I believe he's getting on our flight. How nice," My mama says and Mémère and Aunt Monique look at each other and roll their eyes.

Stevie puts me down beside him and I'm tangling my fingers in his shirt and hugging him. He hugs me tight. We're still hanging on to each other when Mama steps in to hug me. She grabs me tight, but she's looking out of the corner of her eye at the handsome priest. She kisses me quick on the cheek and promises to write to me and she'll send for me as soon as she can. Then she stands up straight and walks toward the plane with her high heeled shoes making tapping sounds on the floor. My aunt and Mémère step closer to me and Stevie reaches out and grabs another hug.

"Mama's just afraid she'll cry," he says. "That's why she's in a hurry."

I hold on around him, closing my eyes and swallowing the crying that's in my throat.

Mama stops walking, turns around and calls to Stevie that he needs to come on now or they'll miss their plane.

"Yes ma'am," he says and Mémère steps up to pull me away from him. I break away still holding his shirt and Mémère unfolds my fingers. She whispers that it's time for them to go.

I let go and I watch him walk toward the plane and catch up to Mama, who is standing in line just behind the priest. She's throwing her head back and laughing while she pats him on the shoulder.

I watch my brother and mother climbing onto the steps to the airplane. Stevie turns and waves one more time before he gets on. I cry now and Mémère picks me up. We stand in the window watching the plane take off and fly away until it is a speck in the sky.

Chapter Six

Mémère holds my hand when we go through the market. This is the third store we went to looking for chocolate covered ants. I wonder why anyone would want to eat ants, even if they *are* covered with chocolate. I ask her, and she says, "It's a delicacy...an acquired taste like blood pudding is." I especially don't know why someone would want to eat pudding made from blood. My stomach feels mixed up just thinking about it.

We don't find any chocolate covered ants, but she leads me over to the lobster tank and lets me pick out a lobster. I think I'm picking one to be my pet when she tells me, "No, silly, it's for eating." I scream and cry all the way home and say I'll run away if she cooks the poor lobster. She cooks it and I don't run away because I don't have anywhere to run to, except I go hide under the stairs in the dusty hallway until I'm chased away by a scary looking spider.

"I won't eat it!" I yell at Mémère. "And you can't make me!"

"Ok," she sings and hums a little tune while she pulls the lobster dead from a pot of boiling water.

"Oh my! Imagine that; a native-born Mainer who don't even know the taste of lobster," she continues like she's singing it. "You can't be a true Mainer if you haven't even had a lobster cross your lips."

"I don't want to be a Mainer!" I snap back. I'm mad that she's having fun eating the dead lobster. "You killed it!" I scream and push my plate away. I want to get up and stomp off to the bathroom like my mama would in a case like this, but I don't because I don't know what Mémère would do if I do that. Stevie said Mémère is the nicest grandmother in the world until you cross her the wrong way. Once he sassed her and she pulled him by the ear all the way up the block to the confessional at St. Augustine's Church and made him tell the priest what he did. Since then, he just couldn't bring himself to cross her that way again.

"Would you rather I eat it alive?" she's laughing at me.

"Oh, Isabelle, what am I going to do with you?" I shrug my shoulders to show her I don't care.

"Then eat your mashed potatoes and stop complaining," is all she says. We eat without saying a word. I try not to look when she cracks open the lobster and puts little bits of meat on her plate in a neat little pile. She gets out all the meat she can and says, "There, I'll get rid of the outside part and you can pretend it's chicken."

When she gets up to toss the outside part in the garbage, I sneak a tiny piece just to taste it. It tastes strange to me and I don't really like it but I want to be a real Mainer like Mémère and Aunt Monique.

I like being here at Mémère's house because there is always electricity and warm blankets for when the nights get cold. The bathroom closet is piled high with towels that were dried in the sun and when I get out of the tub, I can wrap myself in one of them. I feel like I'm wrapped up in sunshine because of the smell of the towels.

There is always enough food for the two of us and her apartment always smells like food cooking. I wonder why we couldn't all three, my mama, brother, and me move in with Mémère since she has so much food. Mémère says we'd be packed in pretty tight with her one bedroom and certainly the food would get scarce from trying to feed four with enough food for two.

Mémère buys me a doll that's my first new doll and she helps me name it. We call her Soleil because that's the French word for sunshine and my doll's hair is yellow like the sun. Soleil goes with me everywhere, even to Mass on Sunday and Saturday and Monday and Tuesday and Wednesday and every day of the week because Mémère takes me every day in the morning to Mass. She says she needs to have her body and blood of Christ.

In Mass we sit quiet while the priest says a prayer over little flat pieces of bread on a plate and wine that he pours in a big gold cup. Mémère has her head bowed down. She looks all serious dressed in black with a little black hat on her head. When I see her like this, all dressed in black with her black hair, she makes me think of a crow and I know that's a strange thing to think about your Mémère in Mass all dressed up in black. The priest announces that the bread and wine are now the body and blood of Jesus Christ. I'm squinting my eyes, looking at the bread so I can see if the body of Christ looks anything like the body of lobster. It looks like flat pieces of bread to me, so I poke Mémère on the shoulder and whisper to her that I don't think the priest's trick worked.

She gives me an angry look and whispers loud at me, "Shhh! It's not a trick." People turn and look at us.

I shut my mouth because I don't want Mémère to pull me by the ear to the confessional like she did my brother. When our turn comes, we stand in line and Mémère closes her eyes while the priest puts bread on her tongue.

"Body of Christ," he says in a low voice and Mémère makes a cross on herself.

I stand on my toes beside Mémère to see if I can get a closer look at the body of Christ. I want to tell the priest that it's still bread, and not flesh like he said it should be, but then he reaches down at me with a smile and draws a cross on my forehead with his thumb, so I don't say anything.

We step over so Mémère can take a sip from the blood of Christ and I can't see if it is blood or still wine, but I think it was still wine because when we get back to our seat and kneel to pray, I can smell it on Mémère. It smells just like the wine that Aunt Monique brought to drink with Mama that time on Christmas Eve when she brought a little silver pretend Christmas tree for us to put paper decorations on. Mama didn't like it much since it wasn't even green, but it must have been okay since Santa left Stevie and me a toy.

After Mass we shake the priest's hand. Mémère talks to him in French and he talks back to her in French and I wish I knew what they were saying. I wonder if she's telling him that the bread was still bread and the wine was still wine. I wonder if I can say something about it now that we are out of the church.

"How come the bread didn't turn to Jesus' body?" I ask.

"Isabelle! Don't ask such things!" Mémère says and laughs because I can tell she's embarrassed.

"It's okay," the priest says, "it's a mystery, child. We can't see it change, but we believe it does. We have faith," and he smiles down at me and I wonder if he can be my papa since we call him Father anyway.

While we walk home, I ask Mémère if the priest could adopt me and be my father maybe since we call him Father anyway. She laughs and says, "Oh my! I'm glad you didn't ask him that like you asked him about the body of Christ!" And that's the only answer she gave me about that, so I think that means no.

Chapter Seven

It's getting cold outside and the days are getting shorter. Leaves are turning all orange and red. It's fall and Mémère says it's time for me to go to pre-school, so she takes me down to the Head Start center and registers me. I'm going to be in Mrs. Jakes' class with ten other children my age.

My Aunt Monique takes me to buy some new clothes for school. I'm excited to get new clothes, but I don't want to go to school away from Mémère and Soleil and my drawing desk all to myself. I tell my aunt that I don't want to play with other children. She tells me she knows I'm afraid and that's okay. I tell her I'm not afraid and that I just don't like other children.

"Sometimes, Isabelle, I think you *are* a bit peculiar." I don't know what peculiar means, but I don't think it's a good thing because Aunt Monique has her forehead wrinkled like she's in pain or something.

We're looking at jackets and the one I like is red and blue checkered and soft on the inside. It has a hood on it that is very big, though, and we laugh at the size of it. My aunt says it must be made for a child with a very large head and we laugh so hard that I fall right on the floor in the coat department at

Sears. I like laughing like that so that is the one I choose, but Aunt Monique says that everyone else will get a laugh out of it too and I wonder if I really want everyone getting a laugh out of my jacket. I put it back and choose one that is not so funny.

At Head Start I like playing in the sand box. I like building with blocks, but I like playing by myself and Mrs. Jakes says I have to share, so I do. The other kids don't want to build what I want to build with the blocks. Instead of fighting, I just stand on the side with a pile of my own blocks and build little buildings. When we are playing in the sandbox, a boy named Tommy doesn't think my castle looks good, so he crashes it with his fist. I crash his. He picks up a handful of sand and throws it in my face. My eyes sting with sand in them and I scream and cry with my eyes shut and I can't see where I'm going, and I trip over a chair that is next to me. I can feel the teacher pick me up fast off the ground and she rushes me inside to the sink and soaks my eyes with water. Tommy has to sit in the corner. He's crying out loud like he's the one hurt. After that, I won't play in the sand box at all because that means I have to share it with someone who might throw sand in my face again.

After lunch we all have to lay on our mats and take a nap, but I don't want to. I never took naps before and I don't see why I have to now. The teacher told me that if I don't take my nap, I won't have an Indian cookie. That's like a cracker that's more like a dry piece of bread than a cookie. It's not sweet at all and I wonder if this is what little Indian children are stuck with instead of real cookies. "I don't care," I sass the teacher's helper. "I don't like those cookies anyway."

"You have to at least lay on your mat," she sighs.

I ask if I can have a book to look at. She sighs again and brings me a book. It's a story called *The Jungle Book.* I can't read it, but I can tell by the pictures on the front what it is because I've heard the story before. I lay there looking at the pictures, trying to make out some of the words, so I can tell what's going on in the story.

After nap time when everyone else is eating their cookies that are more like bread that's dry, I ask Mrs. Jakes if she will teach me how to read *The Jungle Book*. I have the book open to the first page, ready to learn.

"Oh, you are still too young yet, Isabelle. You'll learn all that in kindergarten or first grade. You don't have to rush," she says. I close the book. I wish Stevie was here. He wouldn't tell me I'm too young. He would show me how to read for sure.

After school I ask Mémère to teach me to read and she's happy that I would ask her such a thing. She tells me that I might well be the smartest of all her grandchildren "even smarter than Stevie, who is really very smart," she says. I don't think I could be smarter than Stevie because he knows almost everything.

Mémère takes me to the public library. I love the smell of the books all lined up on the shelves. I'm so excited I run up and down the rows of books until Mémère grabs hold of my shirt and says, "Whoah! You can't go running in here. This is a library."

The library lady comes over smiling and says she can show us where the children's section is. We go into another room and I see rows and rows of picture books. I want to run to them and pull them off the shelves to look at them all at once. The library lady tells us that we can borrow six of them for two weeks. Then we can come back and borrow more when we bring those back. I ask Mémère if we can come back every week and get some new books to read. She winks at me and smiles and that means "yes".

I picked out some books by a man named Dr. Seuss who Mémère says is not really a doctor and I found *The Jungle Book,* so Mémère can teach me how to read it. Then, I can go to school and read the one there and Mrs. Jakes will be surprised to see I can read it.

It's almost dark out and Aunt Monique and Uncle James come by. I'm so excited to tell them about my library books I run to meet them at the door with my arms loaded with my books. Uncle James reads *Hop on Pop* to me and I laugh because it's silly and that's what I like about Dr. Seuss, who isn't really a doctor.

Aunt Monique said I chose some good books, some of her favorites and I have good taste in literature. I never heard that word before, literature. She says it means stories.

"Have you heard from Jolene?" Aunt Monique asks Mémère. Mémère says no, but Stevie writes just about every week like he promised, so she guesses they're doing alright.

Aunt Monique says, "It's a crying shame she doesn't stay in touch with her daughter," and she shakes her head like she did that day in the airport when Mama was laughing with the priest and touching his shoulder.

I go get my letters from Stevie and set them on the table for Aunt Monique to see and she reads them all out loud to me. Mémère has already read them to me a bunch of times, but I like to hear them again and again. Aunt Monique reads my favorite one.

"Dear Isabelle,

I don't think it will be too long before Mama sends for you, maybe when spring comes. We moved out of grandma's house a week ago and there are two extra rooms in our new apartment. I'm sure one will be yours when you come. I'm sorry I can't tell you for sure when, but Mama doesn't want to talk about it when I ask her. I'm sure it's because she's afraid that if she talks about it, it won't come true, kind of like a jinx.

I sure do miss you. This winter I will miss the snow, so you will have to make a snow angel for me whenever you make one for yourself. Promise?

Love,
Your big brother."

Mémère says Stevie's letters are pure angelic and she's sure her grandson is destined to be a fine priest someday, if his mother would let him keep the faith. Aunt Monique says it won't happen because they're now in the land of the Baptists. Stevie's bound to lose his Catholic faith before too long if he hasn't already. Mémère says, "Once a Catholic, always a Catholic. There's no changing it."

I ask Mémère if I'll always be a Catholic and she says, "Yes, of course."

"Even when I go to Georgia?"

"Even then," she says. "Now go get ready for bed and we'll look at your books some more before you sleep."

After Aunt Monique and Uncle James leave, I curl up with Mémère in her bed where she lets me sleep every night. She reads *The Jungle Book* about halfway through and tells me it's time for me to close my eyes and try to sleep.

She turns out the light and the curtains are still open a little making slices of moon light on the wall. It's not a full moon so I can't see its face, but I can see the slice of moon light on Mémère's folded hands while she says her prayers. It makes me feel peaceful to think that the moon has a smile even if I can't see it.

Chapter Eight

The sun is big and yellow in the sky. It's melting the snow from the roof of Mémère's apartment. I remember the way it melted last spring. I wanted it to stop because I knew Stevie and Mama were leaving. I'm glad it's melting now. Spring is almost here. Mama will send for me soon.

The days are going by, though, and Mama still didn't send for me. I get letters from Stevie, but he doesn't say anything about my room anymore. I think Mama will never send for me and that makes me cry a lot and slam doors.

Mémère says she's had it with me slamming doors and she slaps me across my backside. Mémère never hit me before.

I scream at her, "You're not my Mama!" and she sits back on the couch with her mouth hanging open.

That day she writes a letter to my Mama. She tells her that she needs to send for me on account of my crying and on because I said she's not my mama. Mémère said. "A little girl needs her mother."

Mama sent a letter and Mémère reads it to me out loud.

"Dear Mémère,

It's time for Isabelle to come South. I fixed it up so a social worker can fly down with her. On June 1ˢᵗ y'all will take a flight from Augusta to Boston. Then her flight will be leaving from Boston to Georgia. The social worker will meet you at the airport in Augusta to go with her. His name is Joe Farley. Tell Isabelle she don't need to be afraid of him because he's a social worker from the Government."

On the last night in May, I sleep holding on to Mémère's arm. I'm afraid because I'm leaving her in the morning. Maybe I should just stay here with her.

Mémère says to think of the good things. This time tomorrow I'll be sitting with Stevie, reading a story. I try to think of those things, but I feel sorry for what I said to Mémère before she wrote the note to Mama to come get me. I feel sorry for slamming her doors. I'm afraid now she doesn't love me anymore.

I don't know how to tell her I'm sorry. Maybe I could just say, "I'm sorry, Mémère." But for some reason I just can't say it. I just hang on tight to her arm and sleep until she wakes me in the morning to leave for the airport. I try not to talk much because my words will let some crying out if I open my mouth.

We meet Mr. Foley at the airport. He's very nice, like Mama said. He has some coloring books and crayons for me to play with on the plane. I remember I left Soleil sitting in my little red rocking chair in Mémère's room and I want to go back and get her.

"Oh, dear, we don't have time. Your flight is leaving any minute."

I howl that I want my doll and I'm not getting on the plane without her.

"Shush... shush," says Mémère. "I'll send her to you in a package. Okay? Now be a big girl, shush."

We sit down and I'm on Mémère's lap. Mr. Foley is all smiles sitting next to us and trying to make me laugh by making a silly face. I smile at him, but I don't want to laugh.

The announcer calls out our flight number and Mémère asks for a moment alone with me so Mr. Foley steps aside.

"Listen to me, Isabelle." She puts her hand on my chin and looks right at my eyes. "You're a good girl. Mémère loves you. You *are* going to be alright." It's then that I say, "I'm sorry for slamming your doors, Mémère. I'm sorry I made you sad when I said you aren't my mama."

"Oh, shhhh... hush now. Think nothing of it," she says, and she wraps herself around me. I breathe in her smell, incense from Mass and food cooking. They're calling the last boarding call. Mémère unwraps herself from around me and lifts up my fingers that are holding onto her blouse.

"Let's go now," she says and walks me over to the runway with Mr. Foley holding my bags for me. Just before I take Mr. Foley's hand, Mémère draws a cross on my forehead and says she will ask the Blessed Mother to pray for me. She's talking about Mary, the mother of the baby Jesus. I remember that she told me once that she always asks Mary to pray for her when she's afraid. I wonder if she's afraid now and if I should I be too and it's like she knows what I'm thinking because she says, "don't be afraid." I promise to try not to.

"Good girl. Go on, now ... go on." Her hand is on my shoulder and I turn with Mr. Foley and walk onto the plane.

We take our seats and I look out the window and see Mémère standing alone, looking small and wiping her face with a tissue.

Chapter Nine

The plane is shaking like an earthquake and even my teeth feel like they're rattling in my mouth and my tummy feels upside down. I feel scared and sick at the same time, but Mr. Foley tells me that's normal when the plane first takes off.

"I'm sorry, I should have told you about that," he says and holds my hand. He gives me a bag in case I'm going to be sick. I take the bag, but that sick feeling goes away when the plane stops rattling us around.

I lean over and look out the window and everything on the ground is getting tiny. That's when I think that it must be what it looks like to birds when they fly up over us when we're on the ground. I like that I can pretend I'm a bird now and I don't have to imagine because I know what it looks like from up high.

Mr. Foley takes my hand and leads me off the plane. The airport in Atlanta is crowded with so many people I'm afraid to let go because I might get lost. There is a Black family sitting together on a bench and I'm looking at them hard because I only ever saw one Black person in real life.

"It's not polite to stare," Mr. Foley whispers to me and jiggles my hand as we walk by them.

We have to catch another airplane that will take us to Albany. That's where Stevie and Mama will be waiting for me. I'm so excited I don't know what to do with myself.

"Are we almost there?" I ask Mr. Foley.

"That's the third time in the last five minutes that you asked me that. I tell you what; I promise I'll tell you when we're almost there okay?" He seems a little mad at me for asking so many times but he's still nice and says we should play a game with the cards he has in his pocket. It's called "Go Fish" and I played it before with Stevie and Aunt Monique, so I know how to play.

I like Mr. Foley and I wonder if he might stay in Georgia and be my papa since Mémère said mine left and won't be coming back. I ask him if he could marry my Mama and he laughs and says he already has a wife and two kids who are 12 and 14.

"Oh," I say, and we play cards and I win. Mr. Foley pretends to be sad because he lost the game. I know he's pretending because grownups don't ever care if a kid beats them at any game.

"Oh well, you are just an ace card player, I guess. That's the first card game I ever lost. That makes you the champion." It makes me happy to be a champion.

When we land in Albany, the plane makes that same scary landing sound, but now I know it's okay and Mr. Foley holds my hand just in case.

I stretch my neck to see out the window when the plane comes to a stop on the runway. I don't see Stevie. I don't see Mama. What if they don't come get me after all? What if I'm left alone here in the airport in Georgia, far away from Mémère, and Mama and Stevie never come get me?

Mr. Foley says he will wait with me until my family comes. I wonder if they don't come will he take me home with him and I can live with him and his wife and two big kids instead.

But then, I see a boy who looks like Stevie, only taller and a lady who looks like my Mama and a lady that I never saw before with them. They're walking toward us. I know it's Stevie when he calls out, "Isabelle!" and starts running toward me with his arms out. I run toward him, forgetting Mr. Foley and my suitcases and everything except Stevie there with his arms out in his T-shirt with Flipper the dolphin on it.

He's almost as tall as Mama. I feel real small next to him when he picks me up and swings me around. Mama comes up quick.

"This ain't the place to be swinging people. Hugs will do just fine here, thank you," she says.

So, he picks me up and says I'm light as a feather. I ask him if he's grown up now because he's so tall.

He says, "No, silly, it's only been a year so, I'm only nine and a half. I just sprouted up last year."

"Hand me over my baby," my mama says, reaching toward me. I climb onto her.

"My, my you're light as a feather! Didn't Mémère feed you?"

"Yeah, she fed me good," I answer.

"What's this 'yeah' business? I leave you up North for a little while and you forget your manners? You say, 'yes ma'am,'" Mama says like she's scolding me, but she's not mad. I can tell by the way she's hugging me the same time she tells me to say "ma'am."

"Yes ma'am," I say, so she'll be happy.

"Isabelle, this here is your Aunt Gracie. She's my sister," Mama says about the lady standing next to her. I look at her and think she's not at all like my aunt Monique. She's smiling at me and she has red lipstick thick on her lips and her hair is curled up in round shapes on her head. I feel like I can't touch this aunt, even for a hug, because I might mess her up.

"Hello there, Isabelle. Did you like the airplane ride?" I think she talks funny. When she says 'ride' I think she says 'rad' and I look at my mama for an answer as to whether I would like a 'rad' or not since I don't know what one is. Mama says, "Well, Isabelle, your aunt asked you a question. How did you like the ride in the plane?" Then I can tell what my aunt was saying.

"It was fun, except for the scary part. But I played games with Mr. Foley."

The whole time Mr. Foley was standing on the side with my suitcase in his hand. We forgot he was there.

"Oh Lordy! Mr. Foley, sorry about my manners! Nice to meet you in person!" Mama says. "How did Isabelle behave on the plane? Fine, I hope." She doesn't give him time to answer.

"Gracie, this is Mr. Foley, the social worker who come all this way to escort Isabelle here. Ain't that nice of him?"

"Well, it was right nice of him. I'm sure the agency will pay him for it, though. Well, I guess that's what we pay taxes for, right? Well, most of us pay taxes," my aunt says. I don't' understand what she's talking about, but there's a squirmy feeling around us and Mama is looking down at her shoes, not saying a thing.

Mr. Foley clears his throat and says he better get going. He has to go to check in at a hotel, so he can be right for an early flight next morning to go back up North, he tells us. Mama thanks him for taking care of me on the way down and he walks off. We pile in Aunt Gracie's car that's big and not crowded like Aunt Monique's little car. I think my aunt must be rich to have a car like this and I wonder what my room looks like at home and will it be nice.

We are not going right home, though. First, we are going to my grandmother's house so I can meet her, and she can meet me. She's my mama's mama and I wonder if she will be anything like Mémère. I hope she will.

When we get there, I can see right away that she's nothing like Mémère. We go inside, into a hall and I see that everything is set up perfect and neat, with a fancy table at the end of it with glass things on it. These things are a lot like my aunt that you can't touch because you'll mess her up.

"Mama, we're back!" my aunt calls out to her Mama.

"I'm coming! I'm coming! I can only move so fast, you know!"

We go to the kitchen at the end of the hall and she comes into the kitchen from a door on the other side of the room. When I first see her, I think she must be a hundred years old. Her back is humped over, and she carries a cane to help her walk. My mama steps up beside me, ringing her hands around each other, "Mama, this is Isabelle. Isabelle, this is your grandmama."

"Are you a hundred years old?" I ask.

Aunt Gracie gasps and snaps at me, "What kind of thing is that to ask your grandmama when you're first meeting her?! Just like a Northerner, saying the first thing that comes to mind with no thought to manners."

"Isabelle, say you're sorry. That ain't polite to say to your grandmama," Mama says. I don't know why I have to say I'm sorry for wondering how old my grandmother is, but I say it anyway to make them happy.

My grandmother comes over and gives me a hug that feels stiff like she didn't really want to. I hug her back, but I don't like the way she feels bony and cold and she smells like some perfume that makes me want to sneeze.

"Well, y'all come on in here and sit down," she says like she's growling. I don't think I want to go sit down wherever she's going, but I follow her into the living room because that's what Stevie's doing. Mama and Aunt Gracie stay sitting at the kitchen table drinking coffee and talking.

I look over at Stevie who hasn't said a word since we got here, and I want to ask him if there is a rule against talking in this house if you're a young'un. I don't ask him though because I don't know if it would be against the rules to ask if something is against the rules.

We follow our grandmother into the living room, and she points at the couch and tells us, "Y'all sit right there, ya he-ah? This here chair is *maa* chair. Don't any young'uns sit in it." I'm listening, but I can't take my eyes off her finger that's so skinny except for the knuckle that looks like a little knob. She plops down in a chair that's nice and big and has pretty flowers on all it. I want to sit in that chair just once because it looks soft and sinky, like if I sit on it, it would hug around me. The couch is fine and comfortable too, but just because grandmama told us we can't sit in her chair, it makes me want to sneak and do it. She's not finished telling us about how it's *her* chair and *only* her chair. "Now, I have my yard stick raat he-ah." And I'm looking for a rat somewhere because that's what it sounds like she just said until I see her pointing to a yard stick leaning on the table next to her. I sit and listen good, "And the first time I catch a young'un in my chair he'll get a good swift pop with this here yard stick. Is that clear?"

"Yes ma'am," Stevie says something finally.

"Yes... ma'am," I say too. I'm afraid if I forget the 'ma'am' she might pop me with the yard stick.

"Mémère, I need to go to the bathroom," I say and hope there isn't a rule against kids using her bathroom.

"Mémère?! I ain't your mémère. I ain't French. You call me Grandmama."

"Grandmama, can I go to the bathroom?"

"Well, hurry up! Don't be having no accident on my couch!" she growls. "The bathroom is down the hall to the left. Do you know which way is left? That's another thing about young'uns, there's always a chance they'll mess on your furniture." I think 'mess' means to do pee or even poop and it's hard not to laugh at the word.

Sometimes I forget what is left or right, but I just look for the room with the toilet in it. The seat is up, and I don't know if I'm allowed to put it down or if I'll get popped for touching it, so I just sit on it with the seat up and fall in backwards just as I'm about to stand up when I'm done. It makes a big splashing sound and my back is wet with toilet water. I pull myself up and I'm glad my shirt didn't get wet because I had it pulled up and there is no water on the floor.

"What you doing in there, Isabelle? "Grandmama calls out. "Don't you be messin' up my bathroom now!"

"No ma'am, I ain't," I say.

"Hurry up, you're taking too long and making me nervous. Don't you get into anything, ya heah?"

"No ma'am, I won't," I say, and I dry my back with tissue and wash my hands and dry them on the towel that's hanging by the sink. I try to hang it just like it was when I'm finished with it. I hope Grandmama doesn't get mad at the wet marks where my hands were.

"Don't forget to flush the commode!" The commode. I take a second to understand that a commode is a toilet and I flush it.

I go back out into the living room and sit beside Stevie who doesn't say anything unless he's spoken to first.

"Stevie, how is school? Are you making good marks?"

"Yes ma'am. Straight A's."

"Hmmm...well maybe something good will come out of that union between your father and mother. Although that's hard to imagine, I reckon it could be so. Isabelle, you going to kindergarten next year, right?"

"Yes ma'am. And I can read already ... even if I ain't supposed to yet."

"Well, don't get too big headed. It's not polite to brag on yourself." I don't know why she tells me not to get a big head because I don't see what that has to do with reading. When she says "big headed" I remember that jacket that Aunt Monique and me saw in the store and I feel like laughing at that, but somehow, I feel that laughing here at Grandmama's house might not be allowed.

Above the couch, I see a painting of a girl dressed in blue pants that go to the knees. She has stockings that go up to the pants and she holds a blue hat with a feather in it.

"I like that hat that girl is holding," I say.

"Girl? That's no girl! That's a boy. Can't you tell? The name of that painting is Blue Boy. I guess you wouldn't know that though because I don't reckon your northern grandmama would have had culture enough to know about great art." My grandmama scowls at me and laughs and I think she's laughing at my Mémère for not knowing about the Blue Boy painting that looks like a girl.

I don't like this grandmama and I decide that I'll do like Stevie and don't say a word unless I'm spoken to. It's hard to know what is okay to say or do, anyway, when you just meet your Southern grandmama for the first time and she says she'll hit you with her yard stick if you sit in her chair that looks comfortable and is all covered with pretty flowers.

Chapter Ten

Aunt Gracie is driving us home and I'm excited to see my room. "Don't get too excited, now, Isabelle. You're going to make yourself a disappointment," Mama says.

We're driving along and suddenly Stevie lets out a fart and everybody starts laughing except for Aunt Gracie who starts right away yelling, "Don't you mess in my car! Did you mess?! You better *not* mess in my car!" She's looking back at us and we're laughing even harder that she thinks a fart is "mess" and there's that word again. I don't know why Grandmama and Aunt Gracie think everybody is going to mess on their stuff.

"No ma'am. I didn't mess. I just pooted. I'm sorry," Stevie answered in between his laughing. Then, we had to laugh at the word "pooted." Everyone except Aunt Gracie who just shook her head and sighed, "I declare. I do declare. I swannie!"

Finally, we go down a long alley with dirt that's red. I say to Stevie that I didn't know that dirt could be that color and did it come from a volcano or something? He tells me it's Georgia clay and that you can make pretend dishes from it if you want. I think the alley is so long and there is so much red dirt that I could make dishes all day long and not use it all up, so I plan to do that first chance I get.

Soon we're slowing down next to a big fenced in square of grass where some kids are playing baseball. We are turning down a long driveway with a light post at the end of it.

"Are those boys your friends?" I ask Stevie.

"Well, kind of. But they aren't always nice to me for some reason ... except for that little one with the limp; his name is Ricky," he says and points to a boy with a crew cut who is limping as fast as he can to home base. He makes it safe to home and his teammates run up all happy and pat him on the back.

Stevie continues, "He *has* to be nice, though, because his family is Baptist Christians. His mama and daddy don't tolerate him not treating people like the Lord would treat folks."

I look out the window and strain to get a good look at the boy because I don't remember ever seeing someone who is a Baptist Christian and I don't even know what that means anyway. The car stops. We all pour out and Stevie grabs my suitcases from the trunk. Mama and Aunt Gracie are steps ahead of us.

We are going up some cement steps onto a concrete porch that has black metal railings along the sides of it. Next to the porch is a great tree with pink fluffy flowers all over. It smells sweet like peaches.

Mama sees me looking up at the tree and says, "That's some tree, ain't it? That's called a mimosa tree. You won't find those up North. Or pecan trees neither. That's one thing I missed about the South when I was up North ... we got all the best kinds of trees down here." I'm looking at how strong the branches look and thinking maybe Stevie and me can climb this tree to the top and sit in the middle of the flowers.

We go into the kitchen and there's a table with a yellow top and metal legs with chairs that match. Aunt Gracie says that Grandma was kind enough to donate that to my mama when she got herself the new one.

In the living room there's a green carpet and a green couch the color of split pea soup. I think it's an ugly color for a couch and a carpet, but I won't say anything because I think it might make Mama or Aunt Gracie mad.

Aunt Gracie says that I can't be picky about my furniture, and I need to unwrinkle my nose at that couch that also was a generous donation from our grandmama. She tells me that every time I sit on that couch or at that table, I need to think about how grateful I should be to my grandmama, who gave that to us from the bottom of her heart, her with her arthritis making her crippled. "Even so, she's still willing to help your mama after she wasted her life up North like she did," Aunt Gracie goes on.

I look at Stevie who doesn't say anything. Then I look at Mama who's looking at the floor again like she did when we were in the airport. I wonder why Mama doesn't say something to her back instead of just looking at the floor. When Mama stares at the floor like this she makes me think of something wilting like a flower dying. I don't like Aunt Gracie or my Southern grandmama. I wish we could all be back up North with Aunt Monique, with her loud laughing and messy doughnuts in a paper bag and Mémère with her hugs that smell like incense from church and her chairs that aren't that fancy, but any kid can sit in them any time they like.

Stevie shows me his room and I like it because it's cluttered with books all over in every corner, even on the bed. Mama tells him he needs to pick up the books from all over and that no one boy needs that many books any way. He says, "Yes ma'am." But he leaves them all over anyway and I like that about him. I don't dare decide I'm not going to do what Mama says, but I like the way Stevie lets Mama's words just roll right over him and down his back when she's saying mean things about how he likes to read so much. There's a knock at the door and Stevie says, "Oh, that's probably Ricky." And he's out the door before Mama can say anything else.

My room is the last room at the end of a long hallway with gray walls with the paint chipped in places. The floor in the hall is made of tan squares with black splashes and swirls in the tan. Some of the squares are loose and move when you step on them.

Across from my room there's an empty room that Mama calls "the back room." There's nothing in it except a box with mix match shoes in it.

In my room I'm looking at every corner and I don't see a bed, only some boxes tucked away in a closet space.

"Where's my bed, Mama?" I ask.

"Oh well, Isabelle, you ain't got one...yet. For now, you'll sleep with me in my bed."

"Oh," I say, and I look again around the corners of the room. I think it's the grayest room I ever saw with the walls like the ones in the hall and a floor that's bare, with no squares at all, but dark gray and like metal.

I can see that one of the boxes in the closet has toys in it. I rush over to look inside. There's an old brown bear and a doll who has open and shut eyes with one of the eyes stuck in a wink. She's naked. I think she's the saddest doll ever with no clothes and her eye stuck shut like that.

"Mama, does she have any clothes?" I ask, and Mama says no and to just wrap her up in a little blanket that I'll find in the box if I keep on digging to the bottom. I find the blanket and wrap her up tight and lay her across my arms.

"You'd think it was a real baby the way she's carrying on about it, wouldn't you?" my aunt says to Mama. Mama laughs, and I don't like it because she's laughing at me with my aunt who I decided I don't like for making my mama wilt up like a dying flower with the things she says.

I ask Mama if we can send for my doll that Mémère bought me, the one with the yellow hair so we named her Soleil, "because that's the French word for sunshine," I tell my aunt and my mama.

"Is that so?" my aunt asks.

"Yeah," I say, and my aunt tells me I need to spend more time learning manners and less time with French.

"I can see you're going to have a hard time teaching this young'un to use proper Southern manners," She says, and Mama tells me that I should say "Yes ma'am" instead of "yeah".

"Yes ma'am," I say and ask again about sending for my doll.

"Oh, y'all won't have money for such silliness. Sending packages through the mail isn't free, you know," my aunt jumps in with the answer even though I was asking my Mama and not her.

"I was asking my Mama," I say, and my aunt wrinkles up her face and squints her eyes at me.

"How dare you talk to me that way! Jolene, you need to wash this young'un's mouth out with soap. You do! If she isn't the sassiest little thing I ever saw!" she said to my mama and at that moment I wished I hadn't said anything about Soleil in the first place but kept my mouth shut and stayed happy with my sad doll with no clothes and hair that's in knots on the back of her head. My aunt turns quick on the heels of her high shoes and I can hear her tapping all the way down the hall until she gets to the pea green carpet in the living room. We hear the backdoor slam and Aunt Gracie is off in her car. My mama has her hand over her mouth and at first, I can't tell if she's mad or not until I see the corners of her mouth turned upward behind her hand. She lets out a laugh and I laugh too.

"Can we send for Soleil?" I ask my mama again.

"I wish we could, Isabelle. But we just ain't got the money right now. Maybe Mémère will send it for you anyway." She reaches out and touches my hair to tuck it back behind my ear. I like her hand here because her fingers are soft on my ear, but she pulls it back fast and looks away.

"Sorry about your doll … and that you ain't got a bed right now," she says like a whisper and walks down the hall fast. It looks like she's carrying something invisible and heavy on her back.

I don't know what I'm supposed to do here in this room since I never had a room of my own before. I sit on the floor and lean against the wall, holding my doll, that I name Lucy. I'll just sit here and read my *Hop on Pop* book that Uncle James gave me.

I'm reading, and I look over at her and she's winking away at me. I reach over and open the eye. "Sorry about your eye and that you ain't got any clothes right now," I say and try to tuck her knotty hair behind her ear... but it won't stay put so I just smooth it down and promise to find some hair bows that I can clip her hair back with.

Chapter Eleven

Mama tells me it's a good thing she got laid off from her job waiting tables because now she can stay home with me while Stevie is in school. She says I could go to Head Start like I did in Maine, but down South the Head Start is packed full to the doors with Black folks and I wouldn't fit in, since I'm white. I don't understand what she means because when I was in Maine all the kids in Head Start were white, except for one boy who was Black, and it looked like he fit fine with all the white kids and was a lot like me since he never wanted to take his nap either.

So, in the morning I sit backwards in the rocking chair in the living room to watch Stevie while he gets his stuff together for school. Mama yells at me that I need to sit right in the chair before I fall and break my neck, so I slide off the chair and lay on the floor on my back with my feet on the rockers, rocking the chair back and forth with my feet.

"Maybe you *ain't* quite right in the head," she says and snaps, "I don't understand why you do the same thing every morning with the rocking chair, even though I tell you every single morning how you ought to sit in it proper or you might fall and break your neck."

When Stevie goes, it's very quiet with just me and Mama. She's sitting at the yellow table in the kitchen, drinking her coffee and smoking a cigarette. I'm not sure if I should say anything to her or not when she's sitting there so quiet, so I just walk up and sit in a chair next to her at the table.

"There's some cereal, if you want some breakfast," she says.

I do. So, she gets up to get a bowl for me from the cupboard. It's a plastic bowl that used to have margarine in it. She takes it over to the sink to run hot water over it.

"Never know if one of them nasty roach bugs have been crawling over it, so we better wash it. Same with the spoon. Hand it here...Oh my! Look at that black cloud hanging overhead!" Mama says when she looks out the window.

"Hope we don't have no tornado!" she wrinkles her forehead. "Down South we have to watch the sky for tornados when it gets this dark in the middle of the day."

This made me scared because I remember how the tornado in *The Wizard of Oz* sent Dorothy and her dog spinning around 'til they weren't in Kansas anymore. I watch Mama, though, and see that she forgets about the cloud, so I try to do the same.

She washes my plastic dishes and puts them in front of me on the table and gets out a box of Cheerios and a box of Raisin Bran from the refrigerator. She tells me I'm lucky because I have a choice today.

"How come the cereal is in the 'frigerator?" I ask, wondering if that's where Southern people like to keep their cereal because it's too hot in the cupboard for it.

"The roach bugs I told you about," she says, "they like to climb up in the cereal boxes if I put them in the cupboard. Oh, they're terr'ble. And they make a nest near 'bout anywhere. You'll tip the box and next thing you know you got a parade of little brown roach bugs crawling out. Oh, they run and hide in the light of day, but they come out at night and crawl all over everything and spread sickness. They might well even crawl up in your mouth if you sleep with it open." She's smiling while she's telling me this, but I don't know what's to smile about when roach bugs can climb up in your mouth while you sleep.

I choose the Cheerios because I don't like the way the raisins look like bugs and I decide that I don't think I'm going to like the South where you have to worry about roaches crawling in your mouth and tornados sucking you up while you're sitting at the kitchen table eating a bowl of Cheerios.

The dark clouds go away, and Mama says we have to take a walk downtown to pay the light bill if we don't want to lose our electricity. I remember when we all lived in Maine and sometimes, we didn't have lights. Sometimes we wouldn't have firewood for the woodstove, so we burned our furniture instead. I almost forgot about that because at Mémère's house we always had lights and running water and baseboard heat that made pinging noises and kept the place warm.

We walk downtown and it seems like a long way because my legs are achy and I'm wondering if we'll ever get to the light company.

We're walking along on the sidewalk with the sun beating down on us and Mama says it feels like we're in a giant roaster oven.

"Are we gonna cook, Mama?" I ask because I never felt heat like this before and I don't think I want to be cooked while I'm walking along with my mama on our way to pay our light bill.

"No, we ain't gonna cook. But we might sweat to death," she says.

"Are we gonna ... ,"

"Die? No, Isabelle. It's just a figure of speech."

I don't ask anything else even though I don't know what a "figure of speech" is because I think Mama isn't happy that I keep asking questions about whether we're gonna cook like a couple of chickens in an oven or sweat so much we die and I wonder if that means we'll drown since sweat is made of water.

We just walk quiet until finally we can see the big stone light company building looking squiggly in the heat from the ground ahead of us.

We go inside to pay.

"Wooh! It's nice and cool in here! This air conditioning sure is nice!" Mama says and counts her money and wrinkles up her forehead. I know this means she's worrying about something. She steps down from the payment window and whistles through her teeth.

"Sheeew! I hardly got nothing left, barely enough to get by."

She leans against the wall and separates dollar bills.

"This will get some bread, margarine and some mac and cheese," she says, holding up a five-dollar-bill. She holds up another five. "This, we'll go over to Woolworth and get my cigarettes and if we got any change, we'll get something at the diner there."

I hope we have some change because I'm getting hungry from all the walking.

In the Woolworth store I can smell French fries cooking and it makes my stomach growl out loud.

"Can we get something, Mama, can we?" I ask when the cash register lady counts back Mama's change.

"Reckon we can," she says, and we go over and climb up on the swivel chairs at the counter. A lady is on the radio singing about someone killing her softly and it makes me think she's talking about being smothered by a pillow. My feet dangle down, and I swing the chair around in a circle until Mama tells me to stop that before I break my neck. I wonder why it's always my neck that might get broken and not my arm or leg.

A lady comes up with a little book, so she can write down what we want.

She's short and round and has a little mustache. Mama taps at me under the counter with her foot when she sees how hard I'm looking. The waitress smiles at me and Mama and hands us the menus.

"Hey there, Jolene. How y'all doing?" she asks.

"Fine, Rhonda," Mama says, "but broke as ever."

"I know how that is." Rhonda's shaking her round head up and down hard and some curls of hair that are sticking out of her hair net are flopping around on her head.

Mama takes out a cigarette from her new pack and Rhonda digs a lighter from her pocket.

"Hell, I can barely afford my Winstons," Mama says, and Rhonda wags her head up and down.

Every time Mama says anything Rhonda's head rocks up and down so hard, I think it might roll off her shoulders and onto the floor if she keeps on shaking it like that. This thought makes me want to laugh, but I know it wouldn't be a good time to laugh because I know it's not nice.

I can't help it and I start to laugh, trying to keep it in with my hands over my mouth. I can't keep it in, and Mama asks me what's so funny and I say, "nothing." I hold up my menu that's covered with plastic. The pictures of food are faded and look green. I know this isn't the real color of the food, so I'm not worried.

Instead, I'm telling Mama that I want a heap of French fries when Rhonda suddenly says, "Jolene, is this your little girl that you done told me about?" She smiles at me and I want to hide behind my menu because I'm afraid that she'll shake her head at something, and I'll bust out laughing.

"Yes. This here is Isabelle. Isabelle, say 'hi' to Miss Rhonda," Mama tells me. I peek out from behind my menu and say "hi".

"Oh, my goodness! And she talks like a Northerner, don't she?" Rhonda's "i" sound is like my Aunt Gracie and Grandmama's, and I think I'll never get used to the way people talk around here, "And don't she have the greenest eyes I ever seen?" she says.

"She sure does. Ain't quite sure where she got those pure green eyes from, since mine are more gray than green and her daddy's got brown eyes so dark, they're black."

Mama's talking about the color of my eyes and it makes me squirm in my seat the way they're talking about me like I don't know what they're saying.

Some other people come in and sit at the counter and Rhonda says she better quit "chit chatting" and take our order.

I order French fries and a soda and Mama orders a grilled cheese and coffee. We sit and eat without saying a word. Mama lights another cigarette with the lighter Rhonda left on the counter and sucks a long puff from her cigarette.

She sets it in the ashtray next to her and drinks from her coffee. I watch the cigarette smoke going up from Mama's cigarette, swaying back and forth like a skinny snake dancing.

Chapter Twelve

It's Saturday morning and I'm standing in the kitchen watching Mama cook grits on top of the stove. She knows I don't really like them. I'll have to eat them anyway because it's all we have for breakfast today.

"It's all because of your sorry father!" she says. "That's why we're so poor!"

She says if he hadn't ever gone and left us like he did then we wouldn't be in this mess today, the way we're always having to scrape for food and rent.

"I got to get me a job too. Steven will just have to watch you in the summer, so I can work. That's all."

Now I don't know if Stevie will be staying home and keeping me or if he'll be going out to work because just the other day, she was saying she thinks it's high time Stevie starts making a little money around here on the weekends.

"I think he'd do us a lot of good if he'd get his nose out of his books for a little while and help out. Hell, I can't do everything," she says.

Mama stops talking to pay attention to what she's doing with the stove because she has to light the gas burner with a match. She turns it on, and I can hear the gas making hissing sounds and Mama says one day that damn stove is going to blow up the whole house the way she has to light the burner. She tells me I'm to never play with these burners because I could kill us all with the gas hissing through the lines.

"You got to time the match lighting just right, so it lights the gas," she says, leaning over and squinting just before she strikes the match and suddenly there's a ring of blue fire in the burner.

"There," she says, and puts a pot of water on the burner so she can cook the grits.

I see the food in the fridge disappearing more every day and Mama hasn't put anymore in, so it doesn't get empty in there. I wondered if she just didn't notice and I asked Stevie about it. He says it gets like that every month. The food goes low and we go a little hungry, but we always make it through somehow until the food stamps come. I ask Stevie when the food stamps come and are we close to the time for them. He says we won't get any for about two more weeks, but don't worry.

But I do worry, and I wish again that I could be back up with Mémère in her little apartment where there was always lots of food to eat. I wouldn't want to be there without Stevie, though. And then if we left Mama, I would feel sad, so I wish Mama could be with us there too, but then I remember that Mémère told me that if all three of us were there she wouldn't have enough food to feed us.

Mama finishes cooking the grits and calls Stevie out of his room. He needs to come eat because he has to go rake the grass for the old lady down the block since Mama told him he needed to make some money around here.

He comes out with the book that he's reading in his hand and Mama snaps that he can put that book down for five minutes while he eats his grits that she had to risk blowing up the house to cook.

We sit at the yellow table to eat and Stevie scoops out some for me and some for him into a bowl.

"You want any, Mama?" he asks her because a lot of times she's happy just to have her coffee and cigarette in the morning.

"No, I'll just have my coffee and cigarette," she says and looks at the ceiling and blows smoke out of her nose and mouth and makes me think of a dragon that breathes smoke.

I taste the grits and I don't like them. I ask if I can put some cheese in them to make them taste better because I know we have some cheese in the refrigerator right on the top shelf. I saw it in there, but I didn't dare touch it because it's against the rules at our house to eat anything without first asking Mama if we can have it.

"No, you can't have no cheese right now. We gotta stretch our food. That cheese can be used for a whole other meal entirely," she tells me. I try to swallow fast, so I won't have to taste the grits that much.

It doesn't take Stevie any time to eat his grits and head out the door down the street. I'm still sitting at the table with the little bit of grits to finish and Mama says I'm a slow poke with how it takes me forever to finish a little bowl of grits. She's done with her cigarette and so she takes what's left of her cup of coffee and gets up.

"I'm going to go bathe," she says, and she goes off to the bathroom where I hear the sink water running and running.

There's a knock at the back door.

"Answer the door, Isabelle!" she hollers to me, so I do.

It's a lady in a dress and a man in a suit and they smile real big smiles at me like they're so happy to see me.

"Hi, honey, is your mama or daddy home?" the lady asks me and keeps her smile even though she's talking. I wonder who she is and why she's so happy to see me that she's calling me "honey". The man isn't saying anything, but he's got his smile frozen on his face too. I can see that he's holding a Bible and some little pieces of paper that are folded in half and have pictures on them. I can't see the pictures all the way, but I can tell it's a picture of Jesus with children sitting all around him.

"I don't have a daddy, but my mama is here," I tell them, and they tell me that everybody has a heavenly father, it says so in this book the man is holding … and can they speak to my mama then?

"Who is it?" Mama calls out.

"Who are you?" I ask.

"We're from the Albany Gospel Chapel and we'd like to know if we can visit with your Mama for a few minutes," the lady tells me, and I wonder if the man can talk at all since he's still not talking but smiling all along.

"They're from the Albany Gopsel Chapel, Mama, and they got a book that tells me that Papa is in Heaven!"

"No, no it's the Albany *Gospel* Chapel, and we mean to tell you about God who is everyone's father in Heaven," the man finally unfreezes his big smile and talks.

By this time Mama is coming into the kitchen. She's got her hair back in a bun and she has on red lipstick that's so dark red it makes her false teeth look real white. Mama has false teeth that she got since last year when she had to get all her teeth pulled because they were in such bad shape. She says it's because Papa didn't take care of her enough when she was busy having babies. At night she takes out her teeth and puts them in a jar of water and stuff that fizzles up around the plastic gums. She won't let anybody see her with her teeth out, though.

The woman at the door tells Mama again who they are and what they came here for. The man stands beside her, smiling with his Bible tucked under his arm.

"Hello there, ma'am. I'm Mrs. Henrietta Savage and this here is Olan Lynch and we're from the Albany Gospel Chapel. We would like to know if we might visit with you for a few minutes to tell you the Good News of the Gospel of Jesus Christ."

I'm watching the lady talk and I think she must be older than the man because I can see she has some gray hair. His hair is all brown and combed to the side like a Ken doll's hair. I can see that the woman has some wrinkles on her face, but the man doesn't, and I know that when people get old, they start getting wrinkles. Stevie says old people get wrinkles because they worry a lot that they're probably going to die soon, and worry makes them wrinkle up. Mama told Stevie to stop telling stories about wrinkles and death because she's got some wrinkles too and she ain't about to die. I know that telling "stories" means telling lies in the South and I don't know which one is telling a story, Stevie or Mama, that she ain't going to die soon.

"Well, alright. I reckon so," Mama says.

"My name's Jolene Letourneau, by the way, and this here is my daughter, Isabelle. Y'all come on in," Mama says and puts her hand out toward the table, so they know where to sit. We all sit around the table and the man lays his Bible down and the little papers folded in half with the pictures of Jesus and the children. I'm kneeling in my chair on my knees and leaning over the table to see the pictures.

"Would you like one of these?" Mr. Lynch asks me, and I say yes, I would. I look at the picture and he points at it while he tells me that the man in the middle is Jesus and the children around him are there because he loves them and they love him and that Jesus loves all the children of the world, no matter where they are. I look at the children all smiles and all different colors of skin and different kinds of clothes. A little girl with black hair and eyes that slant is curled up on Jesus' lap and his arm is around her. She's looking up at him and her cheeks are red, and she looks so happy that even her eyes are smiling. I think it must be nice to be curled up in Jesus' lap like that with him smiling down on me.

Mrs. Savage tells Mama about how Jesus died on the cross so that we can be saved and how all we have to do is accept the Lord as our personal Lord and Savior and "We shall be saved."

I want to ask her "Saved from what?" but I don't dare because I'm not sure if that is something a little girl is allowed to ask church people who come to her house on a Saturday afternoon to tell about the Gospel. Mrs. Savage opens up the Bible to a verse and asks Mama if she would like to read.

"Well, I don't know. You can go ahead."

"Ok. John 3:16. For God so loved the world that he gave his only begotten son that who so ever believeth in him shall not perish but shall have everlasting life," she reads with a serious look on her face and looks at Mama who is nodding her head to show she understands.

I don't understand what Mrs. Savage just read and I think it's strange the way it says "believeth" and I wonder why someone would write it like that instead of just saying "believes".

Mama sighs and says she forgot all about that verse that used to be so close to her heart and I wonder what she means by that. I don't ask what she means or say anything because I have a feeling that the things they're talking about are not for children and I think if I say anything Mama might turn to me and say, "This is *not* a conversation for young'uns, so run along."

"A lot of times we forget that the Lord wants to help us, Mrs. Letourneau," Mr. Lynch says, "and all we have to do is let him back into our hearts and there he is for us whenever we need him."

"I guess I just forgot. We've been so hungry, and I didn't even think to ask the Lord," Mama cries.

"I'm sorry," she says.

"Oh well, don't you be sorry, Mrs. Letourneau," Mrs. Savage says, "the Lord understands," and she hands Mama a Kleenex from her pocket.

"Would you like us to pray with you?" she asks Mama and Mama shakes her head yes.

They hold hands and Mr. Lynch reaches out to hold my hand and they pray for the Lord to enter our hearts and to supply us with our needs as he does the sparrows and the lilies of the field.

When we're finished praying, I make a cross on myself like Mémère taught me to do at Mass but no one else does it and Mrs. Savage asks my Mama if we are Catholics.

Mama says, "No, not no more. My husband was Catholic and that's where Isabelle got that idea to make that cross, but Isabelle," she says to me, "you don't have to cross yourself no more because you ain't Catholic no more."

"Since y'all aren't members of a church already, we'd like to invite y'all to visit our church tomorrow for Sunday services," Mrs. Savage says and her big smile has returned to her face.

"Well, I reckon we could come, but I don't have no car, so I don't know how we'd get there," Mama says.

"That's where I come in," Mr. Lynch says. "I'd be happy to arrange a ride for y'all. That's part of my ministry at the church. We have folks who gladly volunteer to pick up others who can't get here on their own."

"I guess I don't have no reason we can't go then," Mama says, and they all smile at each other and I don't say anything.

After the man and the woman leave, I put the picture in a secret place between the pages of a book. Before I go to sleep, I take a peek at the picture, then close my eyes and pretend it's me sitting on Jesus' knee, since Mr. Lynch said that God is everybody's father and Jesus and God are the same person, even if I don't understand how two people can be the same person.

Sunday morning Mama wakes us up early and says we have to get dressed for church. Mr. Lynch told us to be ready by 8:00 if we want to go to the 8:30

service and that we can be sure that someone would be there to pick us up.

Stevie wants to know if he can stay home and says he isn't really in the mood for church. Mama yells at him that it's a good thing the Lord didn't say he wasn't in the mood to be crucified when it was time to be nailed to the cross to save our souls.

"From now on, we're going to church every Sunday, so get used to it. We need the Lord's help, so we have to go so he'll see that we deserve it."

Chapter Thirteen

I ask Mama if Jesus is going to be at church today because she's talking about him like he's a regular person. She doesn't give me an answer, but she laughs at my question. I wonder why grownups are always laughing at children when they ask questions about Jesus and I can't wait until I'm bigger, so I can understand more like Stevie does.

Since Stevie is going to be ten soon, he says he understands almost everything grownups do. He tells me after Mama leaves the room that Jesus will surely be at church and maybe we can get his autograph. He looks serious when he's telling me this and I ask Stevie if I might be able to sit in Jesus' lap like in that picture Mr. Lynch gave me. "Oh no," Stevie says, "he'll be way too busy with church stuff. You know, praying and stuff."

Mama yells from the other room for Stevie to stop telling stories and to go get ready and I'm to come on and get dressed too. I go, and Mama holds out to me a dress that I brought with me from Maine. It's blue and has green and yellow flowers on the front of it and it's my favorite.

Mama says it ought to still fit since I haven't grown that much in the last year and I put it on. "Well, it'll do," she says, "but it won't be long before it's too short for you. You'll have to just wear your tennis shoes with it, though. You don't got any dress up shoes that fit no more. The Lord won't mind, though. It don't matter what you wear to the Lord's house because he knows what it's like to be poor."

I never heard my mama talk about Jesus like this, so I think maybe it's true that he'll be at church because she seems very excited about going. She has on her red stretchy dress and her high-heeled shoes that make tapping sounds on the floor when she walks. She says she likes the way it fits her body and stretches with her every move and that's one good thing about going hungry is that you don't have to worry about being fat and not being able to fit in your favorite polyester dress. She laughs and looks in the bathroom mirror and pats her hair to make sure it looks just right since she slept with foam curlers in so she would wake up to a head full of bouncy curls all over.

"When you curl your hair it's important to space the curls right," she says. "So your head don't look all lopsided." She puts on her red lipstick that matches her dress and takes a little piece of toilet tissue and dabs her lips making red kiss marks on the tissue. She tucks in her lips and then untucks them making a smacking sound and then smiles at herself in the mirror.

"There," Mama says and walks to the kitchen with her heels tapping all the way down the hallway and her back held up straight. I like it when Mama dresses up like this because she doesn't bend her back over when she walks, and I think she looks like a movie star with red lip stick and perfect curls.

Mama makes the grits and pours them in our plastic bowls on the table. Stevie comes into the kitchen complaining that his pants are too short and that he looks stupid with his pants an inch above his shoes. Mama looks at his pants and tells him not to worry; that she has just the thing for that. She looks through her purse, pulls out a nail file, and bends down at Stevie's feet.

"Hold still," she says, jabbing the nail file at the bottom of the pants and pulling strings out. This makes his pants longer, but they fold at the bottom and won't stay down. Stevie says it still looks stupid.

"Like I told Isabelle here, the Lord don't care what you wear to his house. Sit down and eat your grits before Mrs. Berry comes honking for us," Mama says.

Mrs. Tallulah Berry is the lady that's giving us a ride to church. Mama knows this because she dropped by last night to let us know. She would have called but couldn't since we don't have a phone, she said. She thought it would be proper manners to come introduce herself before showing up early Sunday morning and expecting us to pile in a car with a complete stranger.

We eat our grits fast and Mama drinks coffee and smokes the last cigarette she can have until after church. She says it won't be easy to go so long without a cigarette, but she figures it's worth it if the Lord will help us when we need it since we're church goers now.

Just then Mrs. Berry doesn't honk but we hear a tapping on the front door. She's waiting there for us with a smile on her face and a lace doily on top of her head. It looks like one of those doilies Mémère used to lay out to make her kitchen table pretty. She put it right in the middle of the table as a decoration and that's how Mrs. Berry wears it on her head, right in the middle on top, except it's held on with a little black hair pin to make sure it won't fall off.

Mama grabs up her Bible off the table and hugs it close to her chest. Last night she pulled that Bible down from a shelf in the living room closet where it was tucked up in a corner in the dark where Mama said she ain't even thought about it in forever.

"It's been so long since I put it up there, I forgot it was there," she said. She blew the dust off of it and opened it real slow with her fingers hardly touching the pages.

"How come it's so yellow and ragged looking?" Stevie wanted to know.

"It's old, that's why. This Bible was my daddy's Bible and before that, it was his mama's Bible. That makes it about seventy years old," Mama told us.

"Wow, that's almost a hundred years!" Stevie said with his eyes opened wide. She turned the pages real careful and showed us where her daddy's mama had underlined verses that were important to her and then where her daddy had done the same and she could tell her daddy's lines apart from her grandmama's lines because her grandmama's underlining was always perfect and straight when her daddy's were crooked. I leaned in closer to see and I could smell the pages while Mama flipped through them. I sniffed in deep because I liked the smell of old Bible pages and almost a hundred years of underlined verses.

Mrs. Berry, at the door, is all smiles in a dark brown dress with little white polka dots on it. She told us we all looked very nice and Mama told her thank you and that she likes her little hat on top of her head, that isn't really a hat, but more like a doily.

"Well thank you. I wear it to show the Lord respect because it says in the Bible for women to cover their hair, but don't worry you're fine like you are. Not all the women wear them to church. It's okay because the Lord knows who respects him by what's in their heart," she says. That's a good thing because Mama's not wearing a doily.

At church, people smile at each other and call each other "brother" and "sister". "How are you, Brother Mike?" "Doing fine, Sister Henrietta," they say. I think they're all from one big family until Mrs. Berry explains that in their church everyone calls each other brother and sister because we are all brothers and sisters in Christ even though we are not related in blood.

We follow Mrs. Berry and slide onto a long bench right up behind the first row and I look for a place to kneel like we did at Mass. I ask Mama where we kneel, and she whispers that we don't kneel here, and she shushes me with a loud "shh!" and looks around like she's embarrassed that I would ask something like that. I look over at Stevie and he's laughing. Mama gives him a look to let him know he's not acting right. He tries to undo his smile and looks straight ahead. Mama looks at him with her eyes squinting and her jaws tight. I'm glad when the organ starts playing and a man says over the microphone to open our song books to page ten, *Shall We Gather at the River*. Everyone stands and Mrs. Berry hands Mama and Stevie a song book, but there's not enough for me, so Mama holds her book down, so I can see while she points to each word as they sing it.

While everyone sings, a man in a light blue suit walks up to the pulpit with a Bible tucked under his arm. I lean up to Mama and ask her if this is the priest and I think it's strange because he's not wearing a robe that makes me think of an angel like every other priest I ever saw at church.

Mama snaps a whisper back at me. "I told you this ain't no Catholic church. They don't got no priest."

The singing ends. We all sit down and Mrs. Berry leans over to whisper that they have a preacher instead and they call him Brother Pritchard.

"Oh," I say and sit back quiet and still because I don't like when Mama snaps whispers at me for thinking a preacher is a priest who forgot his robe that makes him look like an angel up at the pulpit.

Everyone sits quiet except for some people that can't help coughing and some babies that don't know they can't make noise at church. Brother Pritchard clears his throat and starts in by saying welcome brothers and sisters in Christ to Sunday service and do we have any visitors today?

Mrs. Berry raises her hand and motions to my Mama to raise hers. Mama raises her hand and Brother Pritchard smiles down at us.

"Brother Pritchard, I would like you to meet Mrs. Jolene Letourneau and her children Isabelle and Steven." Mrs. Berry motions for us to stand. We do, and I look over at Stevie whose face is about as red as Mama's dress. Mama is flashing her smile at every one and nodding her head at Brother Pritchard and she turns to nod at everyone sitting behind us. All the brothers and sisters in Christ are smiling back at us to show they're glad we are here.

It's then that I notice that lots of the ladies and girls are wearing doilies on their heads too just like Mrs. Berry. I wonder if Mama will get us one for our heads. I hope so because I don't like being the only little girl without a doily on my head to show respect for the Lord.

While I'm turning around, I try to look real fast at every face to see if I see Jesus in the crowd, but then I think he probably wouldn't be there, but maybe sitting up front with Brother Pritchard. I didn't see him up there, though, and I wish I could ask Stevie where Jesus would be sitting if he was here, but I can't because Stevie is sitting on the other side of Mama, so he and I can't talk to each other during church.

Brother Pritchard reads from the Bible and then talks a long time and I'm so bored I want to fall asleep, but every time I start to sleep, he bangs on the pulpit with his fist and raises his voice that sounds like thunder. He scares me awake and I open my eyes to see Mama giving me the same kind of look she gave Stevie for laughing earlier. I sit up straight and I'm glad when Brother Pritchard is finished preaching and everyone starts singing again because now, I can stay awake better.

Finally, it's time to go. Everyone stands to leave and to go over to the Hall for fellowship and doughnuts. I don't know what fellowship is, but I know what doughnuts are and I'm happy to go to fellowship if it means we can have a doughnut and so is Stevie. Everyone walks around talking and laughing and shaking hands and saying how good the Lord is and how nice Brother Pritchard's sermon was. Mrs. Berry says this is what we call "fellowship." Mr. Lynch stops by with Mrs. Savage and they say they're glad we could make it.

Another little girl comes over and starts talking to me. She looks older than me because she's plenty taller. She's wearing a nice pink dress with flowers on it and a doily on her head.

"What's your name again?" she asks me.

"Isabelle," I say.

"My mama said I should come over and invite you to have some doughnuts and milk with me," she tells me and points to her mama standing over in the corner of the room talking away with some other lady.

"My name is Lilian."

Mama nods that I can go, but I need to get a doughnut for my brother, and I go over to the table with her to get a doughnut and some milk for me and Stevie. While we're standing in line at the table, I tell Lilian that we're going to the Lord's house today and everybody in line turns and looks at me all at once. Lilian just giggles a little and looks at the floor.

"Really?"

"Yeah, my mama said we're going to the Lord's house today and it doesn't matter if I wear tennis shoes with my dress instead of dress up shoes."

I don't know why, but Lilian rushes me through the line to get the doughnuts and milk. She leads me back over to my mama and brother and says she has to be getting back over with her family and floats back across the room with her pink dress swishing back and forth when she walks.

Stevie and me stand and eat our doughnuts and drink our milk while Mama drinks a cup of coffee. Mrs. Berry is going from person to person saying hello and chatting and Mama says she hopes it won't be too much longer because she's dying for a cigarette after so long without one.

I want to know if I can have another doughnut and mama says one more and I can go get it by myself. I'm going across the room when suddenly I see a man laughing and talking to some other people across the room. He has a brown beard and hair that's down to his shoulders and his face is very kind. I freeze in my steps when I see him because he looks just like Jesus in that picture that Mr. Lynch gave me except, he's wearing a suit instead of a robe. I know he's Jesus, though because Stevie said he would be here and there he is with children around him and he's smiling at everyone.

I run toward him, "Jesus!" I yell out loud, "We're coming to your house today!" The man's smile leaves his face and he's looking at me and suddenly everyone in the room is quiet and looking right at me until a lady starts to laugh and says to Jesus, "Well, isn't that the cutest thing you ever saw? Sam, I told you better get a haircut and shave. That little girl thinks you're Jesus!" and everyone starts laughing and I wish I could shrink down small and disappear because now I know this ain't Jesus at all but only a man who looks like him.

Mama and Mrs. Berry rush over with Stevie behind them with a frown on his face. Mama grabs my hand quick and says let's go now and we leave through the side door out to Mrs. Berry's car.

Mama's sitting quiet and clacking her false teeth like she does when she's real mad. I wonder if she knows she's doing this because she never wants anybody to know she has false teeth and I'm sure Mrs. Berry hears the clacking.

"Well, it was a perfectly innocent mistake you made, Isabelle. Sam does look an awful lot like our Lord," she laughs a little shaky laugh while she's driving us home.

We pull up the back driveway and Mrs. Berry smiles and says she'll see us next Sunday at 8:00, and not to worry about that little mistake I made and that's it's actually quite funny, if you think about it. Mama just nods her head and says, "Thank you for the ride." Mrs. Berry drives away, and we walk inside the house and Mama slaps Stevie hard on the back of the head.

"It's all because you were telling Isabelle those stories! Now she done gone and made fools out of all of us! We're the laughingstock of the church and we've only been there once't!" She lights a cigarette and sits at the table, shaking her head back and forth and saying, "Disgusting. My children got to embarrass me like that. Disgusting."

Stevie goes off in his room with wet in his eyes. I don't know whether to follow him or stay with Mama in the kitchen, so I just go sit on the floor in my room instead. I don't like my room with the gray floors and no bed, so I go back out to the kitchen. Mama's still sitting at the table. I know she's mad and it's not a good idea to say anything to her, but I want to know if this means we won't be going to the Lord's house today.

"Mama?" I say.

"What?" she asks without looking at me.

"Does this mean we ain't going to the Lord's house today, so he can see my dress and not care if I got on tennis shoes with it?"

She just starts laughing. She laughs so hard she bends over in her chair and starts choking on her cigarette smoke.

"Isabelle, why you gotta believe every little thing exactly the way you hear it? The *church* is what we call the Lord's house and that *is* where we went today and ain't you smart enough to know that the Lord ain't going to be there in person, but in spirit? Stevie ought to know better than to tease you like that because you'll believe any damn thing anybody tells you."

"Oh," is all I can think of to say and that's all I can think of to say lots of times. I wonder if Mémère and the priest were telling me a joke too when they told me that the bread and wine were the body of Christ. I don't know what to think because I don't know what it means to be somewhere "in spirit" as Mama says it.

That night after Mama shows me what to say in my prayers, because she says that's something we need to start doing too, I say one that I make up myself. I ask Jesus if he can make himself appear in person sometimes to make it easier for me to understand. I ask him if he can make sure he's wearing a robe and has a cane like he does in my picture. That way, I'll be sure it's him and I won't go making fools out of Mama and Stevie and me by thinking a man named Sam is him.

Chapter Fourteen

We haven't been to church in a lot of Sundays. We went a few times since that day I mixed that man up with the Lord and embarrassed my mama so bad she doesn't want to be seen there anymore. "I know folks are still laughing at us," she says. "I feel it in my bones."

Stevie says he's okay with that because he doesn't like going to church anyhow, but he does miss the doughnuts at fellowship. Mama said she doesn't have time to go anyhow because she has to work late on Saturday night at her new job at Joe's Cellar. She found this job because the welfare lady who came to our house told Mama she needed to get a job instead of waiting for the welfare check every month.

So, Mama took this job and when her boss tells her she has to work late on Saturday night, she doesn't have a choice, or the boss will fire her. She asked him if she could try to get home before too late, because she's got young'uns alone at home. It's not his problem, he says.

Mama says she's scared that if she quits, she won't be able to pay the rent. When she started working, they cut our welfare check to nothing. The welfare lady told her she can't just quit now that she has a job. We might not get the welfare check back because it's a punishment for quitting.

I heard Aunt Gracie telling Mama one day when she was driving us home from the grocery store, that she really ought not be taking this job because she wasn't setting a decent sort of example for me. And what will people at church say? Mama said she doesn't care about church since it's not paying the bills.

"Well, we need to make sure Mama doesn't catch wind of this. She will plum die if she finds out her daughter has gone and turned into some kind of hussy, a pure floozy, I tell you!" my aunt says.

Mama doesn't say anything but sinks down in the seat where she's sitting next to Aunt Gracie, who's driving. I wish my mama would sit up tall and talk back just once.

I sit back and look out the window. In my mind, I can see my mama sitting up tall and telling my aunt to mind her own beeswax, like she said so many times she wants to tell her. I can see her tell Aunt Gracie that she ain't no hussy or floozy, whatever those things are, but I'm thinking they ain't good. I see Mama sitting up in my mind, but in real life, she's disappearing into the car seat, except I know she's there because I hear her sniffing and clacking her false teeth.

On Saturday night Mama says, "I don't got no choice," and puts on a real short skirt and stockings that look like fishing nets. She goes off to work and doesn't come back until the next morning when the sun is starting to come up. I don't like it when she's gone all night because I feel scared without her home, even if Stevie is home with me.

I tried to sleep in her bed where I usually sleep with her because I don't got a bed yet, but I woke up screaming from a bad dream. Since then, Stevie lets me sleep in his room at the foot of his bed on the nights when Mama is out.

When she comes home, I wake up to the sound of her in the bathroom at the sink washing her face and sighing out loud. I lay across the foot of Stevie's bed and listen to her talking to herself, but I can't tell what she's saying, except sometimes I can hear some swear words that I'm not supposed to say. Then, she's wearing a long night shirt when she comes into Stevie's room where it's still dark because Stevie hung an old blanket up over the window to make sure no peeping Tom can see in during the night.

She takes me by my hand and leads me into her room where the light is gray with morning to sleep on her bed. I curl up with her and she covers me with a little blanket and covers herself with a coat she bought from a second-hand store downtown. She loves this coat, because it makes her look like she's got money since it's black and made of real wool.

When I see her dressed in her fancy coat, I like to pretend she's a movie star and I'm her daughter and she's going out to work on a movie and she'll be back in some hours, but I don't got to worry because I have a lady that looks after me when Mama is out. Or maybe we got so much money, we can pay for Mémère to come and live with us and she can look after me instead.

That's what I pretend and that we live in a fine house with a swing set in the back yard and maybe a swimming pool. And in this house, I have a nice bedroom with a bed and lots of soft, fluffy pillows. Stevie has a great room too, with a stereo system because he likes music so much and a wall full of books for him to read. That's how it is in my pretend life with a movie star mama.

Mama's laying back and sleeping before I can go back to sleep. I turn toward her with my head on her. I feel the scratchy wool of the coat on my face and it reminds me of a story she told me and Stevie about her mama. She said when she was just a little thing, her mama would sew clothes before the arthritis got too painful for it. Grandma used to sew dresses galore for Mama's sister, my Aunt Gracie. She made them with soft cotton flowing and pretty flowers.

"They were the kind of dresses that could bring on springtime," Mama said. "They were sooooo pretty," Mama would say in a whispery voice.

She wanted one of those dresses so bad, but her mama wouldn't make one for her, so she figured if she asked my Aunt Gracie to ask Grandma to make one for her, then she might do it.

"Because she always did what Gracie wanted," Mama wrinkled her forehead when she explained this.

Aunt Gracie did ask for her, and her mama said she would make a dress for her. Mama was so excited. She couldn't believe she was going to have such a dress. And it would be just in time for her birthday in May.

She dreamed of wearing her pretty cotton dress on her birthday. It would be perfect, she thought to herself. It was only May but already 90 degrees in the afternoon then, Mama told us, so she imagined twirling in circles in her dress, with the skirt blowing out and making cool breezes on her legs. Oh! She couldn't wait!

Finally, about two weeks after her mama said she would make her a dress, Mama came home from school and when she was walking up onto the front porch, she could hear the sewing machine tapping away in the living room. She walked in and tried to pretend like she didn't hear anything or know that her mama was making anything because she didn't want to spoil the birthday surprise. Maybe if she did, her mama would get mad and she wouldn't give her the dress after all.

She was walking across the living room, being careful to look in the other direction, like she was looking at something out the window. That's when Grandma said, "Well, hey, there Jolene," and then in a real sing songy, sicky sweet and sugary voice, "look what I'm sewing for yoooou!"

Mama looked, even though she wasn't sure still if she should, but she couldn't resist. She wanted to see her dress, even if it wasn't finished yet.

She couldn't believe what she saw, and she had to rub her eyes to make sure she was seeing right. It was a gray, long sleeve, turtleneck dress that was made of wool.

"Well, don't just stand there with your mouth hanging open!" her mama snapped at her. "I worked hard on this for you!"

"But, Mama," she started crying. "it's going to be too hot to wear and it's going to itch me like the dickens!" is what she said to her mama.

"Well, I have never seen such ungratefulness! You know that ain't one bit Godly, Jolene! You know my hands are starting to hurt more and more from the arthritis that's settin' in, but I'm doing this for you, and you don't even 'preciate it! Well, I tell you what! You are going to wear it, missy! I'll see to that!"

And so, her mama did make her wear it in the hot summertime, especially when they went to church. She would be there dressed in her gray woolly dress with the turtleneck about to strangle her to death if the itchiness or the heat didn't kill her first. Her sister, Gracie, would be there with her dresses that not only brought on spring, but brought in the summer too, and the sweetness of a fine summer day sitting on a porch swing eating ice cream. That's how Mama tells it. Those were some powerful dresses, Gracie's dresses.

I couldn't believe my grandma could be so mean, but then Stevie said yes, she can.

"You see how she is with us, with her yard stick and all."

That made me sad to think of my mama when she was a little girl like me, wishing hard for a cotton dress and then ending up with an ugly gray woolly dress that made her feel like she was going to die when she wore it.

Now, that's how come Mama doesn't like woolly clothes, except for this coat, she says. It has a silky lining on the inside that slides over her skin and feels cool to touch when she first puts the coat on.

"That's how you know it's high class. It's for someone whose skin is worth comfort and warmth at the same time. I might be poor, but when I'm wearing this coat, it's like I'm worth something," she says, and I think I understand, but I still wonder what would make one person's skin worth comfort and warmth and one person's skin not.

I wanted to know if I got the sort of skin that's worth comfort or not, but I didn't know if that's something you can ask your Mama just after she tells you a sad story about a woolly dress that her mama made her wear.

Chapter Fifteen

It's Sunday morning and we all slept late. The sun is up, big and yellow and I'm sitting up looking around for Mama, but she's already up. I hear something in the kitchen. I think it must be her in there fixing some grits. Even if I didn't like them at first, now I love when we have hot grits on a Sunday morning, especially when we got margarine and some cheese to put in it. I'm remembering that we have a couple of slices of cheese Mama said we could have this morning. I get up and go fast as I can into the kitchen where Mama's standing at the sink with her back to me washing dishes.

She doesn't hear me come in and when I sit at the table and make a sound she near about jumps out of her skin.

"Oh! You scared me silly! Don't sneak up on a person like that, Isabelle!" she said and turned around. That's when I saw that she had a bruise on her face, on the side of her cheek.

"Mama! What happened to your cheek, Mama?! You got a bruise!" I gasp, and Mama puts her hand quick on her cheek like she forgot she had it.

"Oh, it's nothing. I just ran into a door last night, is all."

She goes quick over to the stove where the water is boiling. "I almost forgot to add the grits," she says, and pours a cup of grits in the pot. The grits boil up high and almost boil over, but she picks up the pot and holds it up away from the fire and the grits go back down.

"Whew! That was close! Grab me the cheese, will ya?"

I hop up and get the cheese. When I hand it to her, I see some marks on her arm, like bruises that look like finger marks.

"Mama! You got bruises on your arm!"

"I done told you I ran into a door last night! Let it be, Isabelle! Don't you think I'm embarrassed enough about running into a door? I don't need no one pointing it out!"

I say I'm sorry, but I want to know what kind of door makes bruises like fingers. I ain't going to ask because I know that will get Mama mad.

That's when Stevie comes out to the kitchen.

"Hey, Belly," he's started calling me Belly. I don't know if I like it or not, but I don't want to tell Stevie not to call me that, because I never told my big brother what to do.

"Would you quit calling her that? She don't like it," Mama says.

"She doesn't mind, Mama. Do you, Belly?" he asks. Of course, I don't. At least that's what I say to him.

"Well, even if she don't mind, that ain't her name," Mama says with a sigh. That's what she does when she's starting to get into a fight with Stevie over something.

"Okay, Mama," he says, and he's smiling at me sideways. He likes to get her going, but I'm glad he stopped because I don't feel like hearing them fight, because Mama gets mad and screeches. Stevie just laughs at her and it makes her madder. And I want to eat my grits without Mama screeching to the top of her lungs while I eat.

That's what I'm thinking when Stevie sees Mama's bruises right when

Mama drops a spoon on the floor and turns around to pick it up.

"What happened, Mama?" He asks, all shocked.

"Doggone it! I done explained this to Isabelle! I ran into a door last night. That's all. Now let it be."

"That bruise on your arm is from a door?" I don't think Stevie believes her.

"That's what I said, itn't it? Now leave shit be!" Mama's getting mad and I'm thinking I want to know how a door can make marks like fingers, but I want to eat my grits "in peace." That's what Mama says: "in peace."

"Can't I eat in peace?" or "Can't I smoke in peace?" She even says, "Can't I go to the bathroom in peace?" when she's in the bathroom and one of us is knocking on the door to get in.

I'm glad when Stevie leaves shit be and we all three sit around the table and eat our cheese grits. Nobody says anything. Our plastic spoons are making little plasticky taps on our glass bowls that Mama bought at the same second-hand store where she bought her wool coat. She likes them because they were only ten cents apiece even though they're worth more. I like them because they have pretty, red flowers on them.

I swirl my spoon in the puddle of melted margarine in the middle of my grits then scoop some into my spoon and let the grits sit on my tongue all warm and cheesy before I swallow them.

Mama's finished hers and she's sipping her hot coffee from an old mayonnaise jar she said is perfect for her coffee cup. Stevie's eating his grits slow while he's reading to himself. Mama lets him read at the table, but only on Sunday mornings.

Mama lights her breakfast cigarette and breathes the smoke in and out. The smoke swirls up and then hangs in the air above our table. She puts the cigarette to her mouth again and I'm looking half at my grits while I put more on my spoon and half at her finger-shaped door bruise that's on her arm.

Chapter Sixteen

Mama's got money to take us to the zoo because she got some good tips on Friday night since on Friday night men drink a lot. So, they don't have their mind about them. She's telling us on our walk to the zoo, "They give more tips that way. One man gave me five whole dollars!" she said the first night she got back from working on a Friday night. "Of course, he was so drunk, he fell asleep right at the bar and my boss had to call the police to come get him. Oh well, at least I got my tip before he passed out," Mama laughed.

She's been working at Joe's Cellar for two months. She said she's getting used to it and at least she has some friends she met there. She tells us about a friend named Gigi who's a dancer.

"You mean she's a ballet dancer?" I ask.

"No. Not ballet ...," she says, "just a dancer, is all."

"Does she dance like on the dance show?" I want to know because I think maybe one day her friend, Gigi will be famous on a dance show or something and I never met someone famous before.

"American Bandstand," Stevie says because he knows all about what shows are on TV. He learned this from the TV Guide. Mrs. Parker always lets him take their old TV Guide when they're done with it when he goes over and cuts their grass.

Mrs. Parker is the school librarian and she took a liking to Stevie on account of he loves books more than any child she ever knew. "She talks so much, she'll talk your ear off if you let her," Mama says. Stevie doesn't mind how much she talks because she gives him a chance to make a little money every other weekend when he goes to cut her grass and he gets to stuff his face with Burger King food and cookies.

"No, not disco," Mama says about her friend, Gigi. "Never mind what kind of dancing she does, Isabelle. You ask too many questions."

I only asked two questions, but I'm in the middle of guessing that's the limit when my thoughts are broken up because Stevie is kicking a soda can down the sidewalk. Mama barks at him that he's kicking money around because that's worth a whole nickel. He stops kicking it and tucks it behind a shrubbery bush to hide it so he can pick it up on the way home.

At the gate to the zoo, it takes $3.00, but Mama said I could say I'm four since even if I'm five and a half since I'm little for my age. Kids under five get in for free today. I'm afraid I'll go to Hell for lying, but Mama said it's a white lie so it's okay. I want to know if a white lie is a lie told by a white person, but I forget to ask because I'm carried off in my thoughts about lying and if it might get me to Hell or not.

"It's the hurtin' folks the Lord don't like," Mama says, "and we ain't hurtin' nobody by saving us 75 cents."

In my Sunday school class where I go sometimes before church, the teacher said lying is wrong, no matter what kind. And when someone is lying or being bad, the branch from the tree outside the window will scratch the window. So, in class when the tree branch scratches the window, I wonder who is being bad in the classroom. Or maybe it does it every time anybody is bad anywhere. I asked Mama and she said I wasn't making sense and to quit asking so many questions.

Mama says it depends on what kind of lie you tell if it will land you in Hell. If it's a lie that doesn't hurt anybody, then it's okay. I know I couldn't stand to hurt anybody anyhow. Even if it wasn't a sin, I couldn't do it. I feel like when I see something hurting, it's me hurting.

Aunt Gracie always says I have too thin skin. I don't know what that means, and I wonder why grownups are always talking about skin, whether it's thin or worth comfort or Black or white. Anyway, I think it might mean I need thick skin like an alligator. Sometimes I look in the mirror and try to imagine my skin thicker, but I don't want to look like an alligator, so I leave that thought be.

It's hard to know what will get you sent to Hell really. Stevie told me once it was it was a sin to burp and an even bigger sin to fart. Mama told him to stop making up stories to tell me again.

We're at the gate and the man in the booth is looking out to us and asking my and Stevie's ages. Mama tells the truth about Stevie but tells him I'm only four. He leans over to look at me like he's trying to decide if it's true. I look up and I see his face real clear. He's got thick brown hair and a moustache. His cheeks are red, and he has sweat on his forehead because it must be hot in that wooden box he has to sit in all day to take people's money to get in the zoo. I'm looking at him and I think that his eyebrows look like furry brown caterpillars. I think in my head what if they grew into butterflies and this makes me want to laugh. I'm glad I don't, though, because, just then, he believes I'm four and lets us in.

"Wheew! I thought he was fixin' to not let us in for a second!" Mama said when we got far enough away that he couldn't hear us.

"He had caterpillars for eyebrows," I said, and Mama and Stevie laughed out loud and I think it's great when you get into the zoo for free, and you won't go to Hell for lying, and then you make your mama and big brother laugh out loud.

"Welcome to Tift Zoological Park," Stevie reads the signs. I never heard the word "zoological" before and Mama says it just means "zoo."

"Why don't they just say, "Tift Zoo","" Stevie wants to know.

"Because 'zoological' is more fancy, and people will pay more for fancy," Mama says, but then Stevie wants to know what's so fancy about a chimp in a cage because that's the first animal we're going to look at.

"Joe, the Chimp," Stevie reads the sign and points to the words to show how the letters make the sounds.

Joe, the Chimp is peeing in his cage. The kids crowded around all laugh at him and he screeches at them in chimpanzee screeches. He calms down and puts his furry arm out and begs for peanuts. I'm looking at his hand and I think it looks like a person. I stare at his face and his eyes that are orangey brown and look right into mine. I can't look away because I think I see sad in them and think maybe he's hungry.

"Can we give him some peanuts?" I ask Mama.

"No, we don't have money for that," she says.

"But he's hungry," I make a whining voice.

"He's okay. Zookeepers will feed him," Mama says.

"He just wants extra snacks," Stevie says.

Just then a boy standing on the other side of the cage throws a rock through the bars and hits Joe in the backside. Joe turns quick and spits a fountain of chimp spit in the boy's face. The boy cries out loud and the other kids laugh at the boy the way they were laughing at Joe before.

Mama says it's perfect justice and even though she knows she shouldn't laugh at a young'un, she can't help it. Stevie says that boy had it coming. I'm glad he got spit in the face and I think Mama and Stevie are right because I feel bad for Joe for having to go pee in a corner of his cage with no privacy at all with kids laughing and throwing rocks at him.

The next animal we look at is an elephant whose name is Laska. Laska is holding a rock with her trunk like it's a hand and scraping it on the iron bars that wrap around her cage. The ground around her is dirt and concrete and almost the same kind of gray as she is. I have this trick I like to do sometimes when I look at streetlights or Christmas lights where I strain my eyes to make everything blurry. If I do this while I'm looking at Laska, it's like her gray is mixed in with the gray of the dirt and concrete and she disappears into them. I tell Stevie and Mama that I'm making the elephant disappear with my eyes. Mama says I'm touched in the head with a thought like that.

Just then I see Laska's elephant eye looking at me. I'm thinking she heard me say I could make her disappear and I tell her I can't really do it and not to worry. Mama says I'm not just touched in the head. I'm plum crazy with the way I'm talking to the animals, but I think she doesn't really mean that because she's smiling while she's saying it.

I hang on the fence that's on the outside of the iron bars where Laska is still scraping her rock. Mama says the doubled-up fence is there to protect people from the elephant, who's a "mighty creature indeed." I don't think she looks that mighty with the way she's like a prisoner behind not one, but two, cages.

I'm pressing my face against the outside fence and looking at her feet that are giant and wrinkly and kicking up dust every time she picks up her foot and puts it down hard. The dry dirt goes up and out through the two fences with the wind carrying if off away from us.

I don't think I like the zoo.

We move along and look at the tigers in a concrete double cage. They walk back and forth, and Stevie says they must be bored to death in those little cages with the way they have them packed in three to a cage no bigger than his bedroom. There are little shelters in the corner for shade, but no other place for them to go to get out of the sun that's burning down on everything.

The lions nearby are making a loud roaring sound, so we go over to see what it's all about.

"What's all the commotion?" Stevie is teasing with them through the double cage.

"Now I got two young'uns talking to animals!" Mama laughs.

The lions calm down but walk back and forth panting to themselves because their cage is little too and Stevie tells Mama, "See? I have powers." I think maybe he does have powers when he tells the lion he better go ahead and drink some water so he doesn't get sick from heat and the lion closest to us goes over to this big, long water bowl and starts drinking, just like that.

"Wow. A regular Doctor Dolittle here!" Mama says, since Stevie can talk to the animals and so can Doctor Dolittle, who's an animal doctor in a story we read one time. I like that my brother can talk to animals, but I don't like that Mama's talking to him like she likes him best.

We look at a black bear and the sign next to it says, "Coco, the Dancing Bear."

Coco is rocking back and forth on her feet.

Stevie says, "I don't think she's dancing. She doesn't have anything else to do."

"Maybe if we sing to her, she can really dance," I say, but Stevie doesn't want to sing, so that means I have to sing by myself. My favorite song is one that I heard on Stevie's little radio he got for his last birthday. It's called "Ooh-wakka-doo-wakka-day" and every time it comes on the radio Stevie has to call me in to hear it. So, I start, and I dance from side to side like Coco.

Mama and Stevie laugh and so do the people around us, an old man and a woman holding hands and a mama with two young'uns in a wagon to pull them around in. The young'uns are smaller than me and they clap too for the dancing bear. Now, it's okay that Mama said Stevie is Doctor Dolittle because I know since I made her laugh, she won't think he's the best because what's better than laughing?

We move on to see the peacock with their feathers out and a bunch of other birds looking at us with their beady eyes rolling sideways to see us. I think they're wondering why we're all standing around staring at them doing nothing.

We go through the rest of the zoo and it's starting to get boring looking at all these animals all packed in together in little cages. We see sea cows squeezed into a water tank with no room to swim. There's green stuff Stevie says is called algae growing all on the side of the tank and we're all holding our noses.

"Smells like feet!" Stevie says.

The alligators' cage has the same feet smell with alligators piled on top of each other in the heat. They're all trying to get to the water that makes a circle around a cement stage in the middle.

"What's the stage for?" Stevie asks Mama, but she says she has no idea.

Just then, an alligator snaps its tail fast and hits another alligator who gets mad and growls out loud. Mama didn't know alligators growl, she says, and that she'd growl too if she had to be stuck in a cage with that many other alligators. Just then Stevie sees one on the bottom pressed hard against the side of the glass with other alligators on top of it. Its head is twisted in a weird way and Stevie says he thinks it might be dead.

"Well, I'll be," Mama says. "I reckon you could be right about that. I don't reckon nobody working at the zoo even notices. The next zoo person we see we'll tell him."

I didn't know I could feel sorry for an alligator since it isn't pretty or fluffy. But I do, especially when I think in my mind what it's like to be one of these here alligators. The sun is burning my skin so bad it cracks and there's nowhere to hide from it. And if I'm stuck under others, I could die, and no zoo person would even know.

We're tired of watching animals suffer, so we go to a part of the park where there are great big magnolia trees. Stevie and me run up to one big tree and hug it around the trunk like you hug a daddy if you got one. I'm looking up and the tree is covered with big white flowers. It has strong branches like giants' arms.

Mama's sitting at a picnic table close by.

"Mama, can we climb it?" Stevie wants to know.

"Yeah, but don't go too high," she's answering and before she finishes, we're already headed up.

I copy what Stevie is doing when he climbs up on the lower branches and then we keep going higher and higher. He reaches down and pulls me up when I get scared or have problems. It's like we're playing follow the leader, in a tree.

"You climb as good as any boy I know," Stevie says, and I feel all puffy with a proud feeling.

We keep climbing. Mama yells at us that we are going too high in the tree.

"Y'all are going too high, I said!" she's making a shriek.

Before we could climb down fast enough, Mama gets sick and throws up on the grass beside the picnic table. We climb down as fast as we can because we didn't know that would make Mama sick to see us climb too high.

"We're sorry, Mama," Stevie says, and we rush over to her side.

"Yeah, Mama, we didn't mean to make you throw up," I say, and I feel bad because I know that throwing up is the worst thing that can happen because all your insides come out and it's terrible.

Mama says, "No...y'all didn't. I just don't feel good, is all," and she throws up some more while Stevie and me stand behind her with our hands on her back.

"I'm sorry," she says, but I don't know what she's sorry for because I never felt sorry when I threw up since I didn't know it was something to be sorry about. Mama says she's okay, so we can walk home after she washes her face in the water fountain with the water that tastes like metal. On the way back, Stevie looks for the can he hid in the bushes, but it's gone.

Back at home Stevie is in his room reading to himself and he doesn't feel like reading to me right now. Mama went to lay down.

I'm going on my own little adventure by myself, even though I'm pretty sure I'm not supposed to go off alone. I go across the field where there is an empty apartment Stevie said no one lived in for a long time now. The door isn't locked. I think I'll go in and look around. I like to climb, especially now since Stevie told me I'm a good climber. I climb up on a bureau that someone left and lean over to see if anything is in the closet or on the shelf. I'm a treasure hunter. I see an old box all covered in dust and lean over as far as I can without falling to look at it. I want to pull it down, but I can't reach so I need to find something to pull at it.

I don't see anything here, but I got an idea I can take a drawer out and put it on top of the bureau and stand on it to make me taller. Now, since I can reach the box, I pull it down and have me a look inside.

"Oh look!" I tell my pretend treasure hunting partner that's with me because treasure hunters always have a partner.

"I found a box of jewels and a diamond necklace!" I say loud and all excited when I see an old rusty dog chain in the box with a dog collar.

We're standing on the bureau that's now a mountain and we're two treasure hunters looking around in a castle that's empty and no one knows where the king and queen or the prince and princess went who lived there.

I put the chain around my neck and the dog collar on my wrist like a bracelet.

"Oh, what a find!" my partner says. "Don't forget to share with me!"

"Oh, I won't forget. Here, do you want the necklace or the bracelet?"

She wants the necklace, so I move the diamond necklace off my neck. She can have it.

I'm here looking at my bracelet with a magic red jewel in it and my partner says she has a secret to tell me. She tells me that she's really a bird and just changed herself to a person, so she can have a person friend, but she has to change back to a bird now and she can fly.

"I can fly too," I tell her. She tells me I can't fly, but she can once she turns back to a bird, but only if her person friend lets her go from her hand.

I want my treasure hunter partner to stay and not be a bird, but she begs me. I say okay and tell her I'll let her fly off the side of our mountain from my hand, but I have to wait here for a little while because there are alligators swimming below and they're mad about the sun shining on them all day.

The alligators are gone and so is she. I jump down and I'm walking through the kitchen alone. I climb on the counter to look in the cabinets to see if there are treasures there. When I'm standing there on the counter, I can see down into the old wringer washer that's there. There's gray/brown water left inside and there are flies buzzing around in the tub and bumping into the sides.

That's when I see a little mouse in the water trying to swim. His little head keeps coming up and going back under. He can't swim. I need to help him. There's an old rickety stool over by the window. I push it up to the washer and climb up. I'm leaning over with the top part of my body in the washer, stretching my hand to try to scoop the mouse and save him.

I can't reach him though and I almost fall headfirst into the dark gray water with the flies buzzing about. The little mouse is sinking into the water, so I can't see him anymore.

"Oh no!" I cry out and climb off the rickety bench and run out of the apartment and back across the field as fast as I can. I get to my front porch and sit on the stairs and cry for the little mouse.

I think this is a time when Aunt Gracie would tell me my skin is too thin and that I hurt too much, even when it isn't my hurt to feel.

Maybe I need to be more like the alligator. They don't cry when they're upset, but they *do* growl.

Chapter Seventeen

I think Mama forgot my birthday. I turned six a week ago, but she didn't say anything to me about it. She didn't get me a crème twirl like she usually does, so I couldn't eat it all since I don't ever have to share my birthday crème twirl with anyone.

Stevie gave me a surprise, though, when he let me come into his room and reach my hand into his grab bag of cereal box toys and choose three things for my birthday. I reached in and felt around for the things I wanted. I knew what was in there since I helped him put all the toys in there one day when we were playing "clean up" in his room.

I felt around until I felt the parachute man, the Match Box car with the doors that open and close, and the little blue bird that has wings that move up and down when you pretend fly him in the air. Stevie said it was cheating to feel around before choosing something, but that he would let me get away with it this time since it was my birthday and all.

"Mama forgot my birthday," I said to Stevie. We sat on the edge of his bed and he didn't say anything for a long minute, because what do you say when your little sister is turning six and your mama forgets?

"Hey, you wanna play store?" he asked, and I said I do. Stevie made some pretend money out of paper and he gave me ten pretend dollars to spend in the store.

"You gotta go out for a few minutes so I can set things up for you to buy, okay?"

I went out into the kitchen where Mama was sitting by the kitchen window feeding the new baby she named Joseph, with a bottle. She feeds the baby special baby milk made of powdery stuff and I don't think he likes it with the way he keeps trying to turn his head away and crying.

"Come on, now!" Mama says and wrinkles up her forehead.

"He just don't wanna eat. What am I supposed to do?" she's asking, but I don't think she's asking me because I don't know anything about feeding babies special baby milk in a bottle when they don't want to eat.

I'm just sitting here at the yellow table playing with my pretend money, Match Box car, parachute man, and blue bird.

"Look, Mama," I say and hold up the little blue bird, because I know she likes birds a lot, but she doesn't even look at me while she's trying to get the new baby to drink from his bottle of powder milk.

"Oh, forget it! Doggone it! I'm too tired for this," she finally says and, "hand me my smokes, will ya? They're on the stove over there." She's pointing and sitting slumped over like she's wrapped around the baby.

I hop up and get her cigarettes for her and she lights one up and sucks in on it for a long time and lets the smoke come out of her mouth and nose, so it looks like her insides are on fire. Smoke is hanging in the air just above the baby's head and it falls onto his face while he's falling asleep.

Mama said Joseph was a Christmas baby since he was born just before Christmas. That Christmas we didn't have a tree or anything, but some people came and brought us some groceries in paper sacks and Stevie did the best he could to make us all a Christmas dinner from the stuff that was there. We had corn, and peas, and instant potatoes and some cookies for dessert. Mama said she was right proud of Stevie for being the man of the house at ten years old, when she was too worn out to cook or even celebrate. Santa didn't come by neither because he had a bad cold, Mama said.

On Christmas day, just before it was getting dark, Stevie and me ate our dinner without Mama because she just went to bed and slept with the baby next to her most of the day. She wasn't sleeping the whole time, though, because we heard her crying in the night after we had washed up from dinner.

We were in Stevie's room and he was reading me the story about Ebenezer Scrooge for the second time that Christmas when we heard her.

"Can we go tell her don't cry?" I asked Stevie.

"No. We should let her be," he said and so we did, until late that night when I went in and curled up next to her with me on one side and the baby on the other. She was sleeping and so was the baby. I looked at them there with the moon light across them and wondered how she got the baby in the first place.

I didn't figure that out since Papa was gone a long time ago. I think that to make a baby you need a mama *and* a daddy. I just noticed Mama was getting big in her belly, but at first, I didn't know that meant she was having a baby. Then, one night she woke me and Stevie to tell us she was going to the hospital to have the baby and she would be back in a few days. There was some food in the refrigerator and some canned goods in the cupboard. She said that Mrs. Harris next door would peek in on us and see to it we were getting fed and we were to behave ourselves like we knew how. Then she went out the door and hopped in a taxi.

I asked Stevie how Mama got a baby in her belly since we don't got a daddy. He told me it was a miracle and to go back to sleep. I went back to sleep thinking maybe Mama was bringing home a baby Jesus when she got back.

A few days later Mama came home with the baby. I just couldn't wait to see what a miracle baby must be like. I thought maybe he'd have a halo or something. He was cute, but he didn't look like me or Stevie. This new young'un had thick wavy black hair and some of the biggest, brownest eyes and longest eye lashes you ever did see. He didn't have a halo, though, and he cried almost all the time and Mama didn't have much patience with him. She even cussed him when she's mad. And she seemed to be always mad at him. Like maybe she wasn't even happy he was born.

Right now, I'm sitting here playing with my birthday toys that Stevie gave me since Mama didn't get me a crème twirl, and Mama's smoking her cigarette while baby Joseph is sleeping because he doesn't want his bottle. My parachute man is jumping from the table. My Matchbox car is going in circles, and my little blue bird is flapping his wings.

Mama looked over at me quick, but it was like she was looking through me to the other side of me, like she doesn't really see me. I know she saw me since she asked me to get her cigarettes, though.

Stevie comes into the kitchen. "I've got the store ready," he says.

He looks at me, then he looks at Mama, then back at me. He shrugs his shoulders up and waves for me to come with him. Mama is staring out the window like she doesn't hear a thing. At least the baby isn't crying.

I slide down from the chair and scoop up my toys and my pretend money and go back to Stevie's room where everything is laid out like it's a real store with price tags on things. Stevie says anything with a price tag on it is for sale and I can have it for my own once I pay for it with my pretend money. I'm so excited.

I see so many things I want: story books, race cars, a bear that I still like even though he doesn't got much bear fur left on him, a Mr. Potato Head who is only missing one eye, a fire truck with lights that Stevie said still works, but we gotta get batteries for it, a train that's missing a wheel but can still go on the track that comes with it even though the track itself is also missing a piece, some yellow drinking cups with smiley faces on them, and a whole box of lots of other toys that I can pick from. I want everything, but Stevie reminds me that I have only $10.00, so I'll have to add up all the prices and he'll help me since I can't do too much math yet.

With my money I buy some race cars, the fire truck, the train with the missing wheel, and the track with the missing piece.

I wanted a train for a long time. Once I saw a train in the window of Kresses. It was going around and around a Christmas tree in the window. Mama and me were standing on the corner waiting for the bus and I went over and pressed my nose on the window to look at it.

"Isabelle! What on earth are you doing?" my mama came and pulled on my hand.

"I want a train, Mama. Can I have a train for my birthday?" I tried to pull away from her, so I could watch the train some more.

"Girls don't play with trains," Mama said. Then the bus came up to the corner. Mama didn't hear me when I asked her why, because the bus was too loud, and she was afraid we were going to miss it. She pulled my hand until we climbed up onto the bus.

So, even though the train in Stevie's room is missing a wheel, I want it and I'm going to find a way to make it go.

"You can get one more thing," Stevie says after he counts my money that's left. "You got a dollar left."

I'm looking all over when I see at the bottom of a box of books a story book that I always loved for Stevie to read to me. It's called *The Boxcar Children*. It's about some children whose mama and papa died, and they live alone in a box car. It's sad that their mama and papa are dead, but at least they get to have adventures together.

I ask Stevie to read it to me, and he says he will, but that I can read some of the words in it too by now since I'm six and isn't it fun to almost be a big kid, so I don't need Mama much since she has a baby that she has to care for now?

I say, "yeah," but I think I might be telling a lie, because I wish Mama didn't forget my birthday and I wish she got me a crème twirl that I could have to myself, even though I would think that I should share it since that's what the Sunday school teacher said Jesus would do. Then Mama would smile at me and take some of the crème from inside the crème twirl with her finger and put it on my nose and kiss it off. Then she would say, "There, you shared it. Now eat the rest because it's a sin to waste."

Chapter Eighteen

Mama had to quit her job at Joe's Cellar when she was pregnant with Joseph, because the boss man said she was too fat from a baby in her belly. I knew Mama was a waitress because that's what she said, and I know I saw some fat waitresses before. I even saw a waitress once with so much baby in her belly she looked like she might pop open on the restaurant floor. So, I didn't know why Mama couldn't still be a waitress at Joe's Cellar.

After she had the baby, she tried to get her old job back, but they weren't hiring then. They'll let her know when they are, they said. Mama said they're lying, though, and she doesn't believe them for anything.

"They don't want someone who's been all fat and pregnant and now got a little baby to care for on top of that," she said.

Mama went to work at a place called Hasty House, where they serve a lot of breakfast stuff like eggs and bacon. She's a waitress there too, so Stevie and me really don't see why she could be a waitress at Hasty House, but not Joe's Cellar.

The tips were better at Joe's Cellar. Sometimes Mama would come home from work with as much as $10.00 in tips. Then, she would give the money to Stevie to take us to the Pac-a-Sac to buy some food while she was at work or at home resting up, so she could go back to work. With $10.00 we could buy some macaroni and cheese, three boxes for a dollar, some milk, and a couple of loaves of bread and some margarine. We could even get some Vienna sausages to go with the macaroni and cheese. The best thing was that after we bought all that and Mama's pack of cigarettes, we could get us a bottle of Coca Cola if they were on sale and maybe a pack of Now and Later candies.

At the Hasty House, Mama hardly brings home enough tips for anything. When the food stamps run out Mama takes us to the Pac-A-Sac and we wait while she talks to the man named Allen that's the cashier man and she asks him if we can have some credit. She'll pay him back in whatever way she can, she says to him and winks.

He says maybe they can work something out and tells us we can have $5.00 in store credit. He says we can go ahead and pick some things that we want. Mama hands Joseph off to Stevie and tells us that we can't get the Vienna Sausages we were hoping to get because they're too expensive since she needs her smokes, so she won't get cranky from quitting cold turkey.

Then Mama and the Pac-A-Sac man went into the little room. I asked Stevie why they had to go back there to talk and why couldn't they just talk out here with us. He said he didn't know why either.

He's got Joseph laying across his shoulder like he's a daddy and he says, "Let's just get what we need and be happy for it." We get some mac and cheese, margarine, milk, and bread and Coca Cola since it's on sale.

I'm glad we get to pick stuff out, but there's something that makes my stomach feel all upside down with the way Mama winked at the Pac-A-Sac man.

Mama's at her job at Hasty House and Stevie is making us dinner like he always does when Mama's at work while I tend to Joseph on a blanket on the kitchen floor, so Stevie can keep an eye on us both. He boiled the macaroni and he's draining the water out it by holding the top of the pot on it tight with potholders and turning it upside down over the sink. He has to hold the top on it so it's opened a little where the water can drain out.

He's shaking it to get all the water out and steam from the boiling water is rising up like smoke in his face. Just then, his hand slips and the top of the pot crashes loud into the sink, spilling all the macaroni into the sink.

"Damn it!" he swears like a grown up and this makes Joseph start to cry.

"What we going to eat now?" I ask and shush the baby at the same time.

"I'm going to scoop it up. That's all I can do," he says, and he scoops it up with his hands and splats it back in the pot like he's mad.

"You mad, Stevie?" I ask, hoping he isn't mad at me for some reason. Even though I don't know why he would be since I was clear on the other side of the kitchen when the macaroni went falling out into the sink.

"No, I'm not mad. That was just disgusting. Let's just try to forget it fell in the sink," he says.

Now that the macaroni is back in the pot, he lets me put the cheese powder and a spoon of margarine. He puts a tiny bit of milk Mama said we could use. He won't let me pour it because I might pour too much and waste.

"Go easy on the milk!" Mama said before she left because she needs it for Joseph to help him sleep.

I get to stir everything together, but Stevie says to stir it gentle because every time the spoon touches the pot when I'm stirring, little black bits of metal come off the inside of it and mix up with the macaroni and cheese.

It doesn't matter how gentle I am though, the little bits of metal come off anyway. Stevie serves us each a helping in bowls, and we start off trying to pick out the metal bits before we eat, but before too long, Stevie says it won't hurt us, so we just eat and try not to think about it.

It's hard not to think about though, because they make little crunching sounds in my head when I bite down on them.

Joseph won't eat it because he can't yet with only two little teeth in his head, so he eats some bread and margarine soaked in warm water. He sits on Stevie's lap cooing and patting the soggy bread with his pudgy little hands. He splashes the bread in little pieces across the table.

"No, Joey. Eat. Don't splash," Stevie tells him, because Mama told us we need to keep him from wasting because she can't have him crying from hunger in the middle of the night.

Stevie and me eat what Joseph can't.

"Oh well, they say iron is good for you. I reckon we're getting our iron," he says and tries to make it funny.

I say, "Yeah. I reckon so," but I worry that the metal is going to cut up the insides of my stomach.

Chapter Nineteen

I'm seven going on eight because it's been six months since my last birthday and that's when you can say you're "going on" the next year, once you are half-way there.

Ricky Adair across the driveway *likes me*, likes me, and he wants me to be his girlfriend. He used to play ball with Stevie a lot but not since he started acting like he wanted to talk to me more. I know this because he gave me a Valentine that said, "Will you be mine?" on it last Valentine's Day and now he doesn't ever want to play outside with Stevie like he used to because he always wants to hang around me on the porch instead. After school under the big oak tree in the schoolyard, he gave me the Valentine card. He almost got into a fight with another boy who gave me a Valentine that day.

That boy, whose name is Willard, lives across the front field and down the sidewalk from our place, so he isn't right near where I can see his apartment and he can see mine. It's a good thing, because I don't like that boy one little bit and the Valentine he gave me had blood on it. I don't know if he put it there on purpose or what. Stevie said he must have put it there to show his true love.

I told Stevie to stop and whined out loud, so Mama would make him. She screamed at him to stop that shit and he did, but he laughed at Mama with her face all red in the doorway of his room screeching to the top of her lungs.

Anyway, I was sitting under the tree with Ricky and he was giving me the Valentine and I was blushing and thinking maybe I could *like him*, like him, when Willard came up from nowhere and told Ricky I was *his* girlfriend.

"No, she ain't. Are you, Isabelle?" Ricky said.

I shook my head "no."

"She said she ain't." Ricky stood up with his limp like he was near about ready to fight.

"Well..." Willard didn't know what to say, I guess.

"Well, nothin! She ain't your girlfriend. That's all!" Ricky's cheeks were getting red like they do in the summer when he's riding his bike up and down the driveway, jumping ramps to show off. That's what Mama said he's doing anyway, showing off.

"Well, I don't care, no how! I got me another girl!" I'm sure Willard was telling a lie, but that was okay because he was backing away and fixing to leave us be. It's a good thing, because I don't think Ricky was supposed to get in a fight, seeing as his family is all God-fearing Christians.

They're so religious, everything they do is about the Lord. They go to church three times a week. When Ricky told me that, I was thinking how glad I am that we don't go to church anymore and wouldn't it be really boring to have to go three times a week. I'd go crazy is what I was thinking.

Anyway, they're so religious they have a country music band that sings only Christian music because they believe other music is a sin. Ricky's mama doesn't sing in the band though. She makes money for the family making Christian wall plaques out of plaster and she sells them around the neighborhood. In the summer, the Adair's back yard is covered with plaster plaques of every religious shape you can think of; crosses, the Lord's head looking upward in prayer, praying hands, the Lord with children around him, a church steeple, Mary and Joseph head plaques for hanging side by side at Christmastime, a Bible opened up to verse John 3:16, all poured into their molds like cake mix and drying in the sun.

After they dry, Mrs. Adair paints them. One time she let me help her because she said I have a steady painting hand.

"They're just like paint by numbers," she said and showed me the colored pictures of the plaques to show me what they're supposed to look like. I painted a cross, but it was easy because it was all brown.

After that, though, Mrs. Adair surprised me and said I could paint the Mary head plaque. I painted it like the picture she had of Mary, with yellow hair and blue head scarf on with her eyes looking downward and her mouth in a frown.

I thought for a second that I wanted to paint Mary looking happy and smiling, but then I thought I better not go against the coloring rules. Besides, her mouth was in such a sad frown, if I painted the pink of lips going upward, it would look like Mary was putting lipstick on and missed her lips entirely.

When I was done painting, Mrs. Adair gave me an even bigger surprise when she said I could take the plaque of Mary home to my mama. I did, but Mama didn't get so excited about it like I thought she might, being as she isn't Catholic anymore and Catholics are the ones that are all crazy for Mary, Mama said.

I figured I'd keep it and maybe one day, I'd give it to Mémère, since I figured she's still a Catholic, even though I haven't seen or heard from Mémère in going on three years. I had to forget about that idea anyway when one day Joseph climbed up to the shelf in my room and pulled it down from where it was. Just as I was turning to tell him to get down from there, he dropped it and Mary's head broke into a dozen pieces on the floor.

I was little sad about it, but then we noticed that the plaster could work like chalk on the sidewalk outside, so Mary's head became sidewalk chalk. That was okay, as long as I didn't let Mrs. Adair know about it. I thought maybe she would get mad at us for using poor Mary's head for chalk, but then I remembered that since the Adairs aren't Catholic, they probably wouldn't care too much anyhow. Still, I figured it's just as well that Mrs. Adair didn't find out, just in case.

Two days after Mary's head became sidewalk chalk, Ricky is over on our porch playing his guitar for me. He's playing and singing "You are My Sunshine" even though it's not a Christian song and his mama would get mad at him for singing it. He told me that he can be my boyfriend since he's ten going on 11 and he's old enough and I can be his official girlfriend. He said it's okay if I'm only seven because it's normal for the girl to be younger, plus I'll be eight before too long anyway.

I said, "okay," even though I didn't know exactly what the job of being a girlfriend is. I'm leaning on the railing and Ricky is playing his guitar and I think it might be alright to be his girlfriend. Then he finishes the song and hops down from the railing. Next thing I know, he puts down his guitar and he's pressing himself against me with his body, so he's pinning me to the railings with the railing pressing against my back. I'm trying to squirm lose, but then he puts his mouth on mine and kisses me with a kiss that's all wet and warm and smelling like bologna sandwich. Suddenly I feel a burst of strength and squirm hard away from him.

"Aaagh!!" I yell and pull open the screen door to my kitchen. I'm quick on the other side of the door and I yell at him to go away because I didn't like that one bit and if he doesn't go, I'm going to tell his mama he's singing a song that's not even about Jesus. She will surely tell his daddy, who I'm sure won't spare the rod, as they say in the Bible.

That's the end of that boyfriend and girlfriend plan. I steer clear of Ricky, though I haven't told anyone about that nasty bologna kiss because I don't want Stevie to tease me about it.

It doesn't matter, though. Because two weeks later, I see a moving truck out in front of the Adair's apartment and by sundown they're gone.

It's like it never happened, the Adairs and their Christian band, the plaster plaques, Ricky and his guitar, and his wet bologna kiss. I threw away the Valentine he gave me after that day on the porch. It's like it never happened, except, it's still in my brain. And we still have some pieces of Mary's head that makes good sidewalk chalk.

There's a Black family moving in where Ricky's family moved out. I don't care what color they are. I just want to see if there are any girls my age and what kind of toys she might have. I don't think there's a girl. I do see a couple of teenage boys that are bigger than Stevie.

I asked Mama if we're going to bring them something, like cookies, like we do sometimes if we can when someone new moves in. "It's a good thing to be a good neighbor," Mama said, and "You never know when you might need a neighbor, so you should be friendly when they move in nearby."

She doesn't think we should bring this new family any cookies or anything though, especially when we hardly have anything of our own in the first place. Mama's peeking out the curtain in the kitchen and shaking her head back and forth as if to say, "for shame" like she does sometimes when she doesn't approve of something.

"What's wrong, Mama?" I ask.

"Well, ain't nothing really. Just... I hope they're the onliest Blacks that move in here. I just don't want the neighborhood to get bad."

I'm confused. Because it was just last summer Mama told me I can't walk anywhere by myself since there's lots of pervert men that drink whiskey and smoke funny cigarettes. I thought that meant it was already bad.

I want to ask Mama, but she's wrinkling up her forehead while she's looking out the kitchen window and I don't know if she'll get mad if I tell her I thought the neighborhood was already bad. Just like it's hard to know what things will get you sent straight to Hell, it's hard to tell which things will send Mama into a fit. I just keep my thoughts to myself about this.

Over the next year, Mama's fear comes true. Each time a white family moved out, a Black family filled the space and Mama would peek out from behind the curtains in the living room and wrinkle her forehead and make hissing "for shame" sounds through her false teeth.

With all the changes in the neighborhood, Mama won't let us go out and play because she's afraid of what will become of us. She says we would move too if we weren't so piss poor.

"We're stuck," she says. "Plain stuck."

Even if she doesn't want us to go out, Mama can't keep us in for too long because we bug her and bug her to let us go out and play. We've been kept inside so long it feels like we're walking out of a cave, or onto some new planet from a spaceship where we've been for days.

I'm stepping out onto the back porch with Joseph and I'm showing him how to climb the mimosa tree. I had plans to show him how to get on the roof, but Mama said I better not.

Folks are staring at us like they don't know what we are. The new family next door has two girls that look the same age as me and a little sister who's small like Joseph. They're sitting out on their back porch too and coloring in some color books.

The little one keeps trying to eat the crayons and her sisters keep telling her "Bookie, put that down! Quit eating that!" and "Mama's gonna whip you if she sees you eat that!"

One of the girls waves at me. I wave back. I keep shimmying up the tree with Joseph. I'm careful to hold on tight and watch Joseph too, but I'm wondering if Mama would let me play with them if they want to play.

Every once in a while, I look over at them to see if they're looking at us. The bigger one notices and asks me what my name is.

"Isabelle, and this here is Joseph," I answer and put my hand on Joseph's shoulder while he's sitting on the branch next to me with our legs hanging down off the branch side by side.

"My name is Sephina," the tall one says, "and this is Bretta." She's pointing to her little sister, but not the one who was trying to eat the crayons. I figured out the youngest one's name is Bookie since her sisters were yelling at her not to eat the crayon.

"Who do you live with?" the sisters want to know.

"My brother here, my mama and my big brother who's named Stevie."

"Y'all don't got a daddy?" they want to know.

"No. I ain't. We ain't." Because it just came to my mind that Joseph's got a different daddy than me, but I don't know who it is.

"We ain't got a daddy, neither," one of them says, and then, "y'all want to color with us?"

I do. I'm worried that Mama's going to get mad if we go over to their porch, but Sephina is holding out a big thick coloring book and they got a giant pack of crayons with the built-in sharpener in the side of the box. I think it might not be polite if I say no thank you. Besides, Joseph is already on his way over because he wouldn't miss a chance to color for anything.

We go over and they let us choose what page to color. It's okay if they tear it out because their mama said they could. I got a picture of a little girl with a big flower in her hand. Joseph got a picture of a puppy dog with a ball. Bretta and Sephina both have Disney princesses to color.

We're coloring and talking about whose class we're in at school and we find out that me and Sephina are in the same grade but she's still seven and I'm eight. I ask her if she skipped a grade and she says, she just doesn't get her birthday until late in the year. That's when I notice that maybe Bookie ain't right in the head, because she mostly makes grunting sounds and scribbles like a baby even though she's older than Joseph. They said she doesn't go to school yet because their mama didn't want her in the special class like they told her she needed to be in at the school if she goes.

I'm coloring my little girl in my picture with brown hair like me and pink skin. I notice that Bretta and Sephina are coloring their pictures of Disney princesses with brown skin and black hair even though everybody knows that Disney princesses have pink skin and yellow hair. I don't say anything though, because I figure it's none of my business if they color it wrong.

I'm finishing up my coloring and so is Joseph just about the time that Mama is calling to us to come in. I think at first that we'll leave the pictures we colored because I don't know if Mama will get mad that we were over here in the first place. But Joseph is fixing to pitch a fit if we leave our pictures here.

"Y'all should take 'em and give 'em to y'all's mama," Bretta says.

"I reckon we will," I say and then I say, "thank you" because that's having some manners.

I'm not sure what to make of the neighbors next door, though. One day they're friends with us, like they were on the first day that we met and then suddenly for no reason that I know, they're ready to kill us by throwing rocks at our heads the second we step outside.

Today, they want to kill us because they threw a rock and it hit me in the leg. I started crying when it hit me and ran inside to tell Mama.

I'm screaming out loud and trying to tell Mama what happened, but I'm not making sense with the way my words are all mixed in with crying.

"They ... threw ... aaaah ... ahhhh ... rrrock!"

Joseph is standing next to me with his fingers in his mouth. He's starting to cry too.

"Did you get hit too?" Mama's asking him while she's putting some ice cubes in a dish cloth and putting it against my leg.

Joseph shakes his head "no," but he's still crying with his fingers in his mouth and playing with his hair with his other hand.

"If you didn't get hit, you don't need to cry. I can't take care of two crying young'uns at once't, doggone it! Stevie! Get out here and help me with this! Can't you hear all this racket going on?!" Mama's yelling at Stevie.

Stevie comes out all wide eyed. I stopped crying since Mama put the ice on my leg.

"What happened?" he's asking.

"That Black next door done threw a rock. I told y'all to stay in, now, didn't I? You can't trust no Black." Mama's going on and on and at first, I didn't know what she was talking about with "that Black." I thought she was going to say black and name something, but then I understood that she was talking about the Black *girl*. I think it's strange that Mama just says "a Black", since black is a describing word, but then she leaves it hanging with nothing to describe.

Mama says we have to stay in from now on. We whine that we can't. We want to go out and play. She won't let us, though. So, we spend a lot of time inside playing games.

Chapter Twenty

We got a closet in the living room with a bunch of games some church people gave us when we used to go to church before. We have Candy Land, Mouse Trap, The Game of Life, Monopoly and checkers. Joseph and me like to play Candy Land, because it's about candy.

Stevie says that's a baby game and tries to teach us the other games, but we don't want to play those. Mama tells Stevie not to be selfish and to play what we want to play. Stevie doesn't have a choice but to play games with us because they're kept locked up in the closet and he's in charge of the key to the door. We aren't allowed to play without him. We *have* to play so we're doing something, so we don't drive Mama crazy, she says, and they'll have to send her off to Milledgeville, which is a crazy house.

Before too long she says we're going to send her off to Milledgeville anyway, games or no games. We're driving her crazy, so to save herself, she lets us go outside. She tells Stevie to go with us to keep us safe from the Blacks throwing rocks.

"Mamaaaah!" Stevie's not happy about that. "What do you want me to do about it if someone throws a rock? I can't jump in the way of it."

"Just go so they might not throw a rock with their big brother out there. Git!" Mama's shooing us like you shoo flies.

We get out on the porch and look around first before we sit on the steps. Stevie is sitting on the step with a book in his hand reading and Joseph is hanging on to my shirt like he's scared.

"It's okay. Nothing's going to happen with Stevie out here," I tell him and get him interested in climbing the mimosa.

We shimmy up the branches and sit with our legs hanging over.

Just about that time Bretta and Sephina came out onto their porch. Joseph holds on to my shirt again and starts to whine.

"What's wrong with your brother?" Bretta asks like she doesn't remember at all that one of them threw a rock and hit me with it.

I look at Stevie and he shakes his head "no" because he's telling me not to answer her.

"Y'all wanna color?" Sephina asks.

I shrug my shoulders to say I don't know. Joseph does want to color. That's about his most favorite thing in the world to do.

"We can coyor, Stevie?" he's already asking Stevie. Before we can say anything, he's sliding down the tree branch on his stomach.

I get down after him and he's headed over to the neighbor's porch.

"Joseph, no. Mama ain't going to let us," I say and try to grab hold of his hand. He pulls away and starts to pitch a fit, so I let him go.

We don't know what to do, Stevie and me. If we tell Mama she's going to get mad and Joseph will maybe get a whipping for going over there. And we might get whippings too for not stopping him.

If we tell Mama, she'll make us march down to the alley and get switches for our own whippings. That's what she started doing when we're in trouble. And when we're going off to get our switch, she'll yell behind us, "Make sure you get one that will wrap around your legs!"

"It hurts me worse than it hurts you," and "my mama did it to me and I turned out alright," she says later, after the whipping is done and over with. Then she tells us the story about how her own mama used to whip up on her legs with a switch and put welt marks all across the backs of them. The kids at school used to laugh at her legs all striped with welt marks.

She says she turned out fine, but I don't believe her because her eyes still get wet in them when she tells this story.

Then, since Stevie is growing into a smart aleck, as Mama calls him, he sasses, "If you're fine, why are you still crying about it?"

Mama tells him to stop back talking or he's going to get a smack on the mouth because he ain't got no respect no more, she says to him.

Instead of telling Mama, we have to go over there with Joseph. Because you can't sit over on your own porch away from the girl who near about killed you with a rock, while your little brother is over there acting like they're the best friends in the world since they got coloring books.

Stevie is sitting on the bottom step of their porch while Joseph and me are sitting on the porch with Bretta and Sephina, coloring away. Bookie comes out and wants to color. Bretta and Sephina have to keep her from eating the crayons. It's almost exactly like it was the first day that we went over and I'm starting to think they really don't remember hitting me with the rock.

I started to wonder if maybe I just dreamed up the whole thing, but then I see when I unfold my leg out from under me, the yellowish-brown bruise that's going away, but it's still there on my leg.

That's the way it goes from then on. We don't know if we're friends until we step out on to the porch when they're on their porch. If we step out and one of them throws a rock or yells something like "old shitty girl!" then we know we're at war. We've taken to fighting them back sometimes because you get fed up sometimes.

I never hit one of them, but I did throw a rock once, but my aim was way off, and it landed clear on the other side of the yard. They laughed at me.

We did notice after a while that every time their cousin, Gail, is around, they fight with us. Gail is the same age as Stevie, but she's taller.

She comes out on the porch and says "What y'all lookin' at? Y'all wanna fight me? I'll kick all y'all's asses." Gail says swear words all out loud and she doesn't even get in trouble. It's like even Bretta and Sephina's mama is scared of her because she doesn't even tell her not to cuss like I've heard her say to them.

I'm scared of her and Stevie says we just have to steer clear of her. So now we know when we see her daddy's big blue Buick pulling up in the driveway, we're fixing to be at war with the neighbors.

Stevie comes in with a full report. "Gail is here. I saw her and her daddy when I was coming across the yard after school. She looked at me and made a fist pound in her hand and pointed at me."

Stevie said she gives a new meaning to "gale force winds." I ask what that means, and he says, "Never mind. It's just a pun."

I ask, "What's a pun?" and he says never mind again and gets the key for the game closet out so we can stay in and play Candy Land and Mouse Trap, and maybe checkers, until Gail leaves and the neighbors are nice again.

Chapter Twenty-One

When Black families moved in, all the white families moved out by the bunches except for my family and "bloody Valentine" Willard's family.

I don't know what to do because I don't have anything against the kids around me, but they sure are mad at me lots of times. I wish that I had some friends to play with that wouldn't turn on me for no reason that I can think of. I always have to watch my back since I never know what's going to happen around the next shrubbery bush or the next corner.

Then, I'm sitting in the living room one night and I figure something out. I'm watching a show called *Roots* on the TV Aunt Gracie gave us out of the kindness of her heart and it works just fine to get channel ten and two with the clothes hanger on there just right. Mama says it's good as long as she gets to watch her story called *Days of Our Lives* when she finally gets a day off.

So, I'm watching *Roots* about a slave named Kunta Kinte who was brought over here on a ship. They want him to say his name is something they made up and not his African name. He just won't do it and they whip him bad with a whip. This made me so sad and angry at the same time and that's when I realize that the kids in the neighborhood were mad at me because they think I'm like those white slave owners that beat Kunta Kinte.

They don't know I'm sitting here with my jaws tight because it makes me so mad while I'm watching this. They don't know that I'm fighting back tears, while my mama is asking me what I'm crying about when it's only a TV show.

I know it isn't only a TV show, because Stevie told me so. My teacher told us so too. So, when Mama asks me what I'm crying about I just tell her I got something in my eye. Then late at night when I think no one can hear, I cry about Kunta Kinte getting whipped for not saying his name is something else. I don't understand why folks got to be so mean and I'm starting to think the world is a really ugly place and it's been like this for a long time, though when you're a little baby, you don't know it yet.

Mama says we aren't to walk alone, but sometimes I do anyway, because I just want to. I'm in the third grade now and it's normal for me to walk about without my mama or my brother to keep me safe. We know that after an episode of *Roots* is on, that's when folks are the most mad. They come up behind Stevie and me when we're walking home from school and push us on our shoulders and backs.

I'm trying hard to fit in a place that doesn't want me. I feel like a puzzle piece that got lost from the right puzzle box and there ain't a single soul around like me in this place except Stevie and Joseph, until I met Evelyn, that is.

It happened one day when I was walking home from school alone. Two girls decided they were going to follow me home and they were picking on me about my mama, saying she doo-dooed on the toilet stool at school. I had no idea what they were talking about, but they kept saying, "Your mama doo-dooed on the toilet stool!"

Then they said Joseph was 'flicted in the head and that he looks like an

Arab, no ways, with his hair looking all wild or maybe he's a high yellow, they said. I tried to tell them he isn't neither, even though I didn't know what a high yellow was. They weren't listening though and one of them grabbed my book bag and threw it to the ground.

That's when we heard a voice come up from behind us.

"Hey! Why y'all want to mess with that girl? Why don't y'all go on and leave this girl alone? She ain't doing anything to y'all!" A Black girl who was just a little bigger than me caught up to us and was yelling to those girls.

"Why are you taking up for that white girl?" one of them asked.

"She must think she's white," the other chimed up.

"No ...I know what it is ...it's because she must got white folks in her family."

They laughed all loud and then my new friend said, "Well y'all need to just go on and leave us alone ... because we're walking together now."

"Why do you think we should leave y'all alone just because you're with her? You ain't so bad," the tallest one said. I was just watching this exchange like when you watch a tennis game. The words were going back and forth kind of fast.

Then my new friend said, "Well ... I ain't so bad ... No ... but I got a brother who is bigger than both of y'all put together ... and he's mean as hell. As a matter of fact, he just come home from prison today because he was in for killing somebody for saying bad things to my mama. He's real crazy and he's got real bad temper. I think I might just tell him about y'all." And at that, those girls took off running.

My new friend turned to me and asked, "What's your name? My name's Evelyn. I just moved in across the driveway from you. What's your big brother's name? I saw him in the front yard. He sure is cute looking. You ain't got no daddy, do you? At least I ain't seen any. That's ok... because I don't got a daddy neither. Mama says we didn't need him anyway."

Finally, I squeezed a word in between hers.

"Isabelle" I said.

"Isabelle? What about it? What's that?" she looked at me all puzzled.

"That's my name," I said.

"What kind of name is that?"

"It's a French name. My daddy gave it to me just before he run off one day.

"Y'all speak French?" Evelyn wanted to know.

Then she got a look on her face like she just remembered something.

"Hey, I got a china tea set. You ever had one of those?"

"No, I guess I ain't never had one really. I ain't never thought of it neither. What's so special about a tea set from China?"

"No, girl, it ain't a tea set made *in* China. It's made *of* china. I mean it's made of a special glass. You know, real delicate and fancy. My Auntie Catherine gave it to me for my birthday. You wanna see it?"

"Yeah, but I don't know about your brother who just got out of prison," I said.

"Oh, girl, I don't have a crazy brother! I don't even got a brother! I was just telling a story so they would get scared. Now they aren't messing with us anymore, see?"

"Oh," I smiled.

I didn't see the china tea set that day though because something distracted us. Once we got home Evelyn and me got carried away with talking on the back porch about near 'bout everything from boys we think are cute to ice cream flavors to what scars we got on us and how we got 'em. When it started to get dark, her mama called her in for supper.

Chapter Twenty-Two

Ducy Jones, who lives across the way at the end of the driveway, walks on his tip toes so everybody says he's part dog. In The Projects they like to say you're part animal if you got some kind of affliction that makes you look different from everybody else. Ducy's mama is part rhinoceros because she's so big. Somebody once said she was part elephant, but then it was agreed that she must be more part rhino because elephants are gentle, and rhinos are mean and so was she. If you have a bald head like Marcus Pace you're part orangutan since an orangutan's got hair on every part of his body *except* his head, and if you got really long arms like Regina Tate you're part orangutan too, you just got the long arm trait instead of the bald head trait. If you had big ol' teeth in your head hanging over the bottom ones, you're said to be part horse. Old Man Percy down the alley is said to have been born with a goat leg since he walks with such a bad limp. Nobody ever really saw his goat leg because he's always wearing long pants and a special big ol' black boot to cover it up.

Ducy claimed to see it once, but I think he was just trying to get somebody to like him because he's seen something nobody else had. Nobody believed him, though, and those boys he was telling that story to, told him to quit that lying or they'd have to whip his ass again for it. Ducy closed his lips tight and tip toed off down the sidewalk going nowhere.

We *all* walk around this place like we're going nowhere. Every block in this neighborhood looks the same as the last and the same as the next. We could walk around this place all day and get the feeling we're passing the same apartment row over and over.

My friend Evelyn and me lots of times in the summer sit on the back porch and watch and listen to everything around us late into the evening. It's always like we're watching a movie. Tonight, while we watch, one of the boys in the apartment next to Evelyn throws something across the kitchen while their mama's yelling at them to stop. Evelyn's baby cousin over from Macon is making a big fuss over something at Evelyn's house. Bretta and Sephina are getting ready to fire up some sparklers from the side yard, near the other end of the driveway. We can hear Ducy's mama all the way from inside their place, screaming at him to bring her some lemonade and does she have to be dying of thirst before the boy cares to bring her something because Goddammit! Her legs are tired!

Evelyn and me tell each other how we feel sorry for Ducy Jones, not only for his dog feet and mean mama, but also because since he's so light skinned, no one wants nothing to do with him since he doesn't look quite Black, but not quite white neither. We wonder a lot how he's going to make it in this neighborhood where if you're all Black, like Evelyn, you can play with just about anybody. If you're white, like me, you might get whipped on sometimes by the other kids for being about the only white kid around, but at least you're let to play sometimes until someone gets mad at you for striking out or kicking the ball all 'flicted like. In The Projects you can be part dog, part horse, part elephant, goat, pig or whatever and the other young'uns might tease you, but they at least will play with you some of the time, but the worse you can be in this place is half-n-half because that meant someone in your family was a traitor and had turned his back on his African brothers and got with the enemy. If you turned out "high yellow," you were marked.

Ducy is near 'bout the most marked boy ever to roam the walkways of this here neighborhood since even his hair was right in the middle of being the hair of a white person and hair of a Black person. It isn't quite straight, but it isn't quite curly as a Black boy's hair neither and it sticks out every which a way like a blackish brown explosion of tangled waves from off his head. Sometimes his mama makes him get a crew cut right down to his scalp and everyone can see the line where his hair was because his scalp under where the hair was looked a lighter shade of grayish yellow.

Then on both sides of his head just around his ears there are big dark splotches under his skin. Mama said one day after seeing Ducy with a fresh crew cut, "That is the most unfortunate placement of birthmarks I have ever seen on a person. And to be matching on both sides and all. It just ain't right." She shook her head like she was talking about something shameful and covered her mouth to hide a little smile behind her hand. Because to be a grown up caught laughing at a most unfortunate placement of a birthmark on a little yellow skinned boy would be a shameful thing itself.

The kids in the neighborhood just said the marks on both sides of his head right around the ears proved that Ducy is indeed part dog and that's where his dog ears would have grown instead of people ears...if they had sprouted out right.

As if all this wasn't enough, Ducy is skinny as a whippet dog and even though he's eight years old going on nine, he's no bigger than Joseph, who's only five going on six.

So, on the playground at recess all the kids his age tell him to play with the first graders since he's more their size. He always just goes to swing on the swings by himself instead and I can't help but watch him out of the corner of my eye. There are lots of times I catch myself just staring at him from a distance.

Late in the school year in Georgia, when it's already almost 100 degrees in the shade, he takes off his shirt and ties it around the metal leg of the swing set and swings just as high and free as a bird with the chain of the swing pulling straight out on the upswing and then snapping quick and hard on the downswing. Everybody knows that at school even boys aren't supposed to take off their shirts and run around half naked and half decent, but Ducy doesn't seem to care at all about this rule anyway since none of the teachers said anything to him about it.

I watch him in a way that no one notices and I feel like I'm studying him to learn how he survives with all his troubles. I want to know how it is that no matter how bad things are, he can climb up on a swing with his shirt all off, not caring about any rule, with his ribs showing so you can see them moving under his skin each time he moves backwards or forwards, his chest moving up and down with a hollow looking hole where it's all sunk in between his sliding ribs. I wonder how, since he's so skinny, so small, so tormented, so lonely, so unfortunate, and so sad, how can he climb up on that swing, pull himself to a high point nearly touching the branches of a nearby pecan tree, and sing? He sings. He sings like he's doesn't have a trouble in the world then and I want to know what it is he singing. I strain my ears to hear him over the girls' jump rope songs right next to me. I can never make out the words, but I can tell it's always the same tune and when he sings it, he's not quite on earth anymore. He acts like as long as he's swinging, with the song floating out of his lungs, he doesn't hear a thing around him, except when the teacher blows the whistle, sharp and ripping through the hot air like a scream, saying it's time to come in from recess.

Then he jumps from the swing on the way forward and sails through the air, landing hard on the red clay ground, unties his shirt from the post, throws it on with the collar of the shirt hanging loose off one shoulder, and then hangs back in silence to be the last one in line of his class to go inside.

So, I keep my eye on Ducy, feeling sorry for him, but not knowing what I can do to help him, all the while worrying that if he didn't have the will anymore to sing, that we all would be doomed too. It didn't make any sense, really, to worry about the rest of us being doomed when it was plain to see that Ducy Jones is the one to be suffering the most anyhow. The most anybody could do in a case like his is to try to pick him up after he got beat up, like cleaning up a mess or something.

I had a dream one night that Evelyn and me picked him up dead off the school ground. We set him in the swing and said, "Sing, Ducy, sing! Move your legs, Ducy, and sing that song!"

It was the strangest thing that I had forgotten about this dream of mine until one time a bunch of boys followed behind him and demanded to know how in the world his mama could fit in the narrow door to the bathroom since she was part rhino. Evelyn and me were walking on the other side of the road and we witnessed the whole next thing that happened. Those boys were shoving him and calling him Old Yeller, like the dog in the movie. They said they were going to have to shoot him like an old dog. One boy grabbed his shirt and tore a hole in it and jerked him around like he was a rag doll. He started crying.

"Tell me how your mama fit through that door!" that boy yelled.

"Why you wanna know that? Stop! You ... you tore my Sunday shirt!" Ducy said, trying to be brave.

"I'm just curious," that boy said, "and you better tell me, or I'll kick your ass!"

I was curious about this too because the bathroom doors in these apartments weren't but about twenty inches across so anyone the size of Mrs.

Jones couldn't even fit in there sideways and greased up if she tried with all her might. But I wouldn't ever beat up on a person over a curiosity.

Evelyn and me looked at each other from the other side of the road and wanted to do something to help him, but we were too scared. I looked to her for answers being as she was older than me, but I don't think she knew what to do in this situation on that day. Folks found out by now that Evelyn doesn't have a convict brother, so nobody's scared of her anymore.

"We ain't studying that story of yours. We know you ain't got no bad brother. We can kick your ass now easy as shit," they told her. So even though we wanted to do something to help poor lil' Ducy, there wasn't much we could do aside of be a witness to his torment.

Then that boy that had hold of Ducy's Sunday shirt dropped him hard on the hot pavement busting open the skin around both his knees and blood was trickling in little rivers down his shins and on to his white socks when he tried to get up. Instead of getting up, though, Ducy fell backwards on the ground and then curled up in a tight ball.

"Tell me or I'll kick you!" that boy screamed in Ducy's face, with his foot held back and ready to kick.

Ducy cried and told those boys that his mama had a bucket that she used in her bedroom and that he had to empty that bucket into the commode. They almost fell over laughing at poor Ducy.

"Oh my God! You ain't serious! Oh my God!" they laughed out loud. Finally, they left him there crying and they walked off singing and chanting,

"Ducy's mama shit in a bucket in her room! Ducy gotta empty it!" Now everyone in The Projects no longer has to secretly wonder how in the world Mrs. Jones goes to the bathroom.

We rushed over, Evelyn and me, and scooped up Ducy off the sidewalk. We were trying to comfort him but there wasn't any comfort for him. That's when that dream of mine came to my head at this very strange time and I thought to myself, "Sing, Ducy, sing" when we were picking him up. He kept right on crying with tears and snot running down his yellow face and onto his Sunday shirt that was no longer going to be a Sunday shirt on account of it was torn up now.

"My mama's going to kill me!" he kept saying over and over again.

We were holding him up and his legs were limp like someone bereaved at a funeral so bad they can't stand up. We didn't know what to say, since we knew it was true. Mrs. Jones was always stomping around mad at everyone. And everyone, even the baddest boys in the neighborhood, didn't mess with her when she came thundering down the sidewalk in her bright pink house dress with her leather belt strap in her hand.

One time she was coming down the hill toward a group of us gathered on the sidewalk, writing on the cement with some pieces of chalk. I don't think it was my imagination that I could feel the ground shake a little underneath, the closer she came. We scattered from off the sidewalk in such a hurry that we left some of our chalk on the ground. The next thing we knew Mrs. Jones must have slipped on a piece of chalk or stubbed her foot on the uneven sidewalk because she was falling over headfirst like a dive onto the concrete and then rolling with her fat legs flying up over her head, so she was totally upside down.

Even her slipper shoes came off when she hit the ground and with her dress up over her head, the whole world could see her giant underwear glaring at us like a light with the way the midday sun beat down on them making them seem all lit up with whiteness.

We couldn't believe what we saw, all of us standing there when we should have been running for our lives. For a second, we must have been frozen until suddenly three of the boys that were with us started laughing so hard, they were near about falling over themselves while they tried to laugh and run at the same time.

Ducy's mama got up as quick she could and was yelling and screaming at us for staring and laughing.

"Y'all stupid ass Goddamn sons of bitches! Laughing at me! I'll whip all y'all's little asses!" and she came running at us bare footed like some great bull in pink, ready to kill, and swinging her leather strap around in every direction.

We all ran and she ran off down the sidewalk screaming for Ducy to make himself found and that she was going to whip his ass when she finds him. I hoped she wouldn't find him while she was still mad like that. I hoped she wouldn't find him ever. I hoped he had run away and that she'd have no one to beat up for being laughed at when she fell on her face on the sidewalk with her under wear shining on everybody.

Later that evening, when the day light was turning gray, and I sat on the back porch with Joseph, we saw Ducy tiptoeing down the sidewalk to pick up his mama's shoes. He could only find one and so he threw himself down in the grass and cried and didn't care who saw him. Mama said I could go see if I can help him and I brought Joseph with me.

"Why you caiy?" Joseph asked him and looked up at me for answers.

"He can't find his mama's shoe," I answered. I was sure that must be the reason.

"Is that why you're crying?" I asked Ducy.

"Yeah. It ain't here. I found one, but not the other," he sobbed and sniffed in deep after every two words or so.

"She have my mama soos," said Joseph.

I shook my head 'no' at him because I knew that there wasn't any way Mama's little size six shoes would fit Ducy's mama's giant feet.

"No, that won't do," Ducy said and kept on crying with his face buried in his hands while he kept right on laying in the grass.

"Yook dat!" my brother suddenly yelled pointing to a drain grate in the driveway just under the light post with the pale orange light that blinked off and on like it was about to go off for good. "Dat stick up dhere!" Ducy looked up and finally got up off the ground.

All three of us rushed over to the drain grate and that's when we saw his Mrs. Jones' other shoe halfway stuck in the grate like somebody tried to shove it all the way in. Ducy bent down to pull it out and the orange flicker of the light above flashed across his face so we could see he had a bruise on his cheek.

"What happen?" my brother asked quick before I had a chance to say anything.

"It ain't nothing," he said and wiped the back of his hand across his eyes and under his nose. That wasn't enough to clean his face, so then he stretched his t-shirt up over his face to wipe it dry from the tears and snot left on there. Then, "thanks," was all he said before he went off toward his apartment with his mama's shoes tucked up under his arm.

So, we knew it to be true what Ducy said about his shirt that those boys tore up that day. His mama was going to whip him. Every time Ducy comes home with a new black eye or busted lip, his mama whips him for letting himself get whipped by someone else, as if he could help it.

After we picked him up, we brought him home to Evelyn's house to clean up his wounds. I wanted to keep him there, hidden, if I could, but Evelyn's mama said we can't hide him from his mama because she'll surely worry for him. Evelyn told her she's not going to worry for him, she's going to beat him again. Her mama just sighed a heavy sigh and went about folding her laundry, since that was what she was doing before we showed up with Ducy bleeding all over the place.

Not too long after that we heard Mrs. Jones calling out, "Ducy! Ducy Jones! You better get your ass home!"

Ducy looked at us and tip toed over across the yard, across the driveway, and down the sidewalk a little ways to his apartment. Before he went inside, he looked back at us one more time.

Evelyn's mama told me I should go home now and say a prayer for him and that she and Evelyn would do the same. I hadn't even crossed the driveway before it started.

I could hear Ducy's mama screaming at him, "What the hell you doing telling folks I piss in a bucket!"

And I could hear the swing of the leather strap she uses to beat him, and I could hear it land on his yellow skin. I heard him scream and cry, "Please, Mama, please!"

But she kept on beating him and yelling out her reason for it. First, she beat him because he told the secret about the bucket, then she beat him because he let those boys beat him. Then she beat him because he wore his Sunday shirt when, "Goddamn it! It ain't even Sunday!" Then she beat him because he let her beat him, and because he walks on his toes when she told him to stop that shit, and then while she's at it, she beat him because somewhere in his father's background someone got with the enemy and made him come out all light skinned.

I went to my room, closed my door and put my fingers in my ears to block it all out. My room was getting dark from the evening coming. It was the kind of light that always makes me think of gray clouds hanging thick, taking up the air around me, making it hard to breathe. I tried to pray, but I just kept hearing the leather strap and the screams and I couldn't understand why I had to ask God to stop that from happening. Couldn't He see it from where He's sitting in Heaven? And didn't it make sense to Him to help without being asked in the first place? I started to cry and wished I could take Ducy Jones away from his rhinoceros Mama and hide him away somewhere and treat him kind, with nothing but sweet words and quiet, starry nights where no one would hit him for being born with dog feet and yellow skin.

Chapter Twenty-Three

It's 1:00 in the afternoon on a very muggy day in August. I'm sitting on the floor in the living room playing with the fan with Joseph, like we'd been warned a thousand times not to do. To hear Mama tell it, anyone that'd be so foolish as to play with a running fan doesn't have a real appreciation for what it means to have all his fingers intact and if we were to accidentally cut ourselves, don't come running to her expecting all kinds of pity, because she's done warned us… "a thousand times," she always adds. She can never leave that warning without adding at the end, "a thousand times."

The thing Joseph likes to do most with the fan is talk into it and listen how the fan blades cut our voices up when it goes around. I'm sitting here and making "maaaaaaaaah" sounds into the fan and he's giggling and covering his mouth so Mama, in the other room, won't peek in to see what's so hilarious happening with us and give us the warning about the chopped off fingers.

The Carpenters are belting a song about rainy days and Mondays from Stevie's FM radio. I figure I'll amuse Joseph by joining in on the song, into the fan, of course. "Aaaaaaalways get me dowwnn," I stretch out the words, so the fan blade has more to chop. I was just in the middle of "aaaaaaalways" when the fan suddenly stops. And so do the Carpenters. And out goes the overhead light in the kitchen. And off goes the refrigerator with a rattle and a thump in the back of it.

We expected it would happen since we got the red tag and a note on the door warning us to pay the electric bill at once or else "services will be interrupted", with the "services will be interrupted" part in bold letters to call our attention to it and to let us know that they meant business down at the City Utilities Company. Mama's job at the Hasty House just doesn't pay enough. She just got paid and by the time she buys some food and soap powders and stuff for the house it's all gone. She won't be getting a paycheck for a week. That means at least a week in the dark, maybe longer because once you get the lights off, you have to pay a reconnect fee, which, as Mama tells it, really adds up. Sometimes we have the money for the bill to get them turned back on, but no reconnect fee money. Then we have to wait again until we have the reconnect fee somehow.

The City Utility Company turns off the utilities in phases. I haven't figured out if it's out of kindness they do it that way or if it's a punishment. After your lights are cut, you have a couple days to pay before they cut off the water. A couple days from that, if no bill is paid, then off goes the gas. In a way, in seems kind not to have it all go at once because once the lights go out, we know we have time to gather up some water in milk jugs to use in the coming days after the water is cut too. And if that saved up water went gone – and it usually does – we have to march across the way to the neighbors', with our milk jugs to borrow water. Mama says there ain't nothing that can bring a person much lower than when he has to borrow his water for drinking because he can't afford to have some of his own.

Everything has gone silent and still. The air is hanging thick in our faces without the fan to blow it around. Mama is sitting in the dark kitchen as quiet as a mouse and Stevie, who just turned 16 and knows everything now, comes out into the living room with a book called *Papillon* in his hand.

"You wanna come listen to me read for a while?" he asks, wiping the sweat off his forehead with the back of his forearm and getting sweat on the edges of the pages.

"I reckon so," I say and take Joseph by the hand and into Stevie's room where the Carpenters aren't singing anymore. Joseph stretches out on the bed next to Stevie and falls asleep before the reading gets going. I sit up and listen while Stevie reads, making special voices for each character. I like to watch his face change with each scene and sometimes his hands fly up in the air like he's acting out each part all by himself. Lots of times he stops and pauses. Turning pages, he doesn't look up at all. I know what he's doing because once I snuck in his room and took me a peek in the story of *Papillon* to see if I could figure out why he was skipping parts. What I found was cuss words. Lots of them. And scenes that had violence in them that young'uns like me or Joseph weren't supposed to know about yet.

I always felt lucky to have a brother like Stevie because when all the other eleven-year-olds in school are reading chapter books about a pig named Wilber with a spider friend named Charlotte, I'm here listening to stories about *Papillon* who is in prison facing all kinds of hardship and wishing to the Lord one day he could be like some sort of butterfly and fly up away from that place. Seemed like the story of *Papillon* would be more valuable to me seeing as I have near about the same kind of wish for myself and maybe somehow, if he learned how to escape from all his sufferings, then maybe so could I. And if I could figure that out on account of this story book, I'd be so proud, I'd bring the book to school and show it to my teacher, who would be so happy to see a child my age interested in grown up stories that she'd tell me how incredible it is that I could be so wise and yet so young.

That's not what happened, though. Once I told my teacher that my brother was reading the story of *Papillon* to me, she said, "Oh dear! With such profanities and all?!", and she sent a note home to my mama, which I threw away instead of giving it to her because if I gave it to her, she'd make Stevie throw out his book and then I may well never learn how to fly away like a butterfly from some place terrible.

Anyway, Stevie reads like that for at least an hour before the heat of the day is about to put both of us to sleep, so he decides he'd best give in to it and stretches out next to Joseph and falls asleep. Stevie says the best thing to do when our electricity is off is just go on to sleep, even if it's the middle of the day. That way, you don't even feel how the day crawls by as slow as molasses.

When night comes, we sit huddled on the living room floor with a lit candle stick in the middle of us. The light flickers orangey yellow on our faces while we squint to play Go Fish until the candle burns down and then we feel our way to the couch for the night where we lay clumped up like the alligators in the zoo because none of us like to be alone in the cinder block bedrooms where the darkness is weighty and smothering. I'm always the last young'un awake, and I lay there for the longest time watching the red tip from Mama's cigarette getting bright and then dim with each time she takes a puff. In between puffs, she sighs heavy and makes clacking sounds with her false teeth.

Right now, while my brothers are sleeping away the slow-moving afternoon, I'm laying down at the foot of Stevie's bed and watching the dust floating in the sun rays pouring in through the window. I blow at pieces of dust and wave them around with my hand, watching them swirl around and then drift on downward. I wonder if I try to count the dust specks if it'll help me fall asleep.

I can't sleep, though. I decide to go back out into the living room to go see what Mama is doing. I wonder if I'm the only one awake. I walk tip toe down the hall, running my fingernails across the grime on the cinder block wall and take a pause to look at where I was showing Joseph how to write his name by scraping in the grime with a little stick before Mama screamed at us that we were like pigs playing in the filth. So, we left it there, in the middle of Joseph's name with a backward "s" hanging at the end sideways.

When I turn the corner into the living room, I know Mama's not asleep. I can hear her, still in the kitchen, whispering something to Jesus. I climb up on the back of the green couch that's under the living room windows and lay on my stomach. I rest my head so I can see through the kitchen door. Mama's sitting at the kitchen window, a sort of gray silhouette, there with her cigarette and whispered prayers.

When the utilities are cut or the food is low, she sits at that window like this a lot. She always seems like she's waiting for someone there. She's just watching and smoking out the window, with the smoke from the cigarette flowing from her nose and mouth, dancing twirls around the green leaves of the avocado plant floating in water filling the jar that's on the sill. Then the smoke wanders upward and out the window through the screen, leaving the plant all alone.

I know what Mama is waiting for sitting there by that window. She's waiting for Jesus to come, that's what. I figured as much because once she said to me just out of the blue, "One day Jesus is going to come and there'll be no more waiting. We won't suffer no more. There won't be no pain and we won't be hungry no more. There'll be milk and honey flowing, and that's what we'll eat. We'll be able to eat all we want." And she went and perched herself by the window, smoking and waiting for that glorious day.

I remember thinking to myself how fine that would be that there would be no more pain and suffering and hunger, but I couldn't understand why a person would want to get full on milk and honey, if they're in Heaven, and certainly there must be other choices of what to eat in Heaven.

Anyway, while I lay here watching my mama wait for the second coming of Christ, I have a feeling that glorious day isn't going to be today because I remember the Sunday school teacher said that Jesus left about 2000 years ago and said he was coming back "in the twinkling of an eye," but no one's seen nor heard from him since. Now, I'm not that smart of a young'un, but the Sunday school teacher also told us that children lots of times got some kind of "infantile wisdom" that tells them truth because their young hearts are open to it. Me and my "infantile wisdom" keeps thinking that if it's been 2000 years, that's a lot of days Jesus hasn't showed hide nor hair of himself. Something inside me tells me there's nothing special about this day that would make the Lord want to pick it to re-appear on.

I think about telling my mama what I'm thinking, but about the worst thing you can tell a person on a hot summer day when the fan went dead, the lights went out, and the refrigerator went silent with a gurgle, rattle, and a thump in the back of it, is that the one she's sitting by the window and waiting for, probably isn't going to pick this day apart from all the days of 2000 years of days to come again in glory.

So, I just lay there on the back of that couch, under the window and listen to Mama whisper. Right about that time, God blesses me with a little breeze that makes the raggedy edges of the curtain behind the couch rise up and brush across my face. I fall asleep then and dream that angels are touching my cheek with their feathery fingertips.

Chapter Twenty-Four

Well, me and my infantile wisdom were right, and the Lord Jesus didn't come back that day and rescue us all from our suffering. Two days after the lights were turned off, the water was shut off in the middle of the day. We had saved up jugs and bottles of water for a couple of days ahead, but that was never enough. We knew we'd end up having to borrow water from the neighbors.

Mrs. Williams, who is Evelyn's mama, and Miss Wallace, who lives across the front field, both said we could get water from their outside spigots any time we wanted to without asking each time so we could save a little bit of pride. We always get it from Evelyn's mama first even though I'm embarrassed for Evelyn to know that our water is off. She said I don't need to feel bad because they had theirs off before too, but there was no way of saving pride when my brothers and me had to carry the pails and jugs across the field or driveway and back. Mama needs us to go get the water anyway on account of her back muscle is pulled something terrible, she tells us.

So, all the other kids around are laughing at us white folks who have to borrow water from Black folks and "ain't that some shit?" they say out loud to each other.

We're coming back from Miss Wallace's house with our jugs and pails full to the top and Joseph trips and wastes his pail all over and he starts to cry.

"That's okay," Stevie and me try to tell him, but he keeps on crying and when we get back to our place, Mama wants to know why his bucket is empty and can't he do anything right?

Stevie says, "Mama, he's only five and that bucket is heavy when it's full of water."

"Well, he needs to go back and get some more then. We need all the water we can get because it's hot as Hell today and we need a lot of drinking water."

"I'll go get it, then," Stevie says.

"Well go ahead, then. Spoil him! Y'all ain't doing nothing but making a pure sissy out of that boy."

Stevie heads out back across the field with his pail. I grab a jug and Joseph's hand and follow behind him. We fill the pail and the jug and set out back across the field with our heads hanging low and our hands clutching tight at the buckets and jug for fear we'd drop them. Just then somebody calls out in a teasing way, "The white man cut your water off! Hahahaha! The white man cut your water off!"

Stevie has his jaws shut tight and hard while he's walking and staring at the ground.

"Just keep walking," he says. "Act like you didn't hear them."

That's the way it is around here. We're always having to act like we didn't hear something, like the men in the alley who say to little girls, "gimme some" or when somebody's following us home making fun of us and our mama, or when Ducy Jones is getting a whipping again, or when Mrs. Jackson's husband is slamming her on the sidewalk down the block. We have to act like we don't hear or see anything and maybe that way we won't get sucked into it and swallowed up alive by all the ugliness that's closing in.

No matter how many times I have to act like I don't hear something, it doesn't seem to get any easier, because every time I do, I get a feeling like I'm going to boil up on the inside and it comes out in hot tears down my face.

Joseph sees me crying and says, "Okay, Izzee. I not drop the bucket now." He doesn't know that I'm not crying about his spilt bucket of water, but I'm crying about always having to act like I don't hear something I know good and well I hear. These things fall into my ears and sink low into my chest and sit there heavy, making my heart hurt.

Mama says to go easy on the water that we borrowed from the neighbors and it's not to be used for flushing the toilet but once every other day. She gets mad at us if we go number two in the toilet if it hasn't been a day since it was flushed with a bucket of water.

There is to be no cleaning of anything during these days. No washing of clothes or bodies. No scrubbing of the floors, which get so black with dirt, we can write our names or play tic-tack-toe in it by scraping with a stick. And by the way, "don't be inviting anyone to come over to see how filthy our house is." Mama's got her pride, she does. And she shoos us away when she catches us playing in the dirt on the floor.

"What the hell are y'all? A bunch of pigs?" she screeches and sits in the chair and cries with her tears dripping on the floor, making little spots where they land on the dirt.

I run outside with Joseph tailing behind me. Maybe we *are* just a bunch of pigs. I want to hide my face from the world. I want to hide my clothes that haven't been washed in so many days. I want to hide behind a thick green shrubbery bush where no one can see me, but Joseph wants me to climb the mimosa tree with him.

So, I do. I show him how I slide over on a limb and step down onto the roof where I can go and crouch low under a thick branch that's heavy with puffy pink mimosa flowers. He follows. I'm surprised that he's not scared at all, high up here.

"The only thing you really gotta worry about up here," I say, "is the bees. They love this smell as much as we do. Maybe even more."

I look at him and he doesn't seem to mind sharing the flowers with the bees, in the way that he doesn't pay them any mind at all.

"In Garden of Eat-in, yike Adam and Eve. These flowers? These flowers, Izzee?" he says.

A lot of people don't understand Joseph when he talks, but I do and so does Stevie and even Mama. Except Mama gets a little bit mad because no one knows why he can't talk right yet when he's five, going on six years old.

Right now, he wants to know if they had these kinds of flowers in the Garden of Eden.

"Well, I think they did," I answer.

"Now need an'mals, we name," he says.

Then, at just the right moment a squirrel pops his head from around a tree branch. "Yook!" Joseph whispers all excited.

"We gotta name it, Adam." I say.

"Call him 'quirrel, 'kay?"

"We call you, squirrel, squirrel!" I say it like I'm God in a big voice and we laugh.

"Oh, look, a bird!" I say in a loud whisper and point to a bird that perched itself on the edge of the roof.

"Call you bird, bird!" Joseph says in a big voice too.

"No, Adam," I say, "that there bird is called a sparrow. I saw it in that bird book at the library."

"Ok, bird, you 'parrow!"

We laugh again and the sparrow is afraid of our voices and flies away.

Chapter Twenty-Five

It's raining hard and Mama is delighted because this means we can take our buckets out to collect the water in them. She says, "Put the buckets out until they're full then bring them in and empty them in the tub, make sure the plug is in because if you don't, you'll waste water. While the buckets are filling, run and hang your clothes on the line. Hurry! Let's scrub them with some soap. Let the rain rinse them off. The sun will dry them after. Never mind if there is lightening! We ain't got no choice. Let's hurry up before the rain stops."

It's great to have a tub full of water that God saw fit to give you on a hot summer day when before you hardly had any water at all. Now you can flush the toilet twice a day for a couple of days and your mama won't get mad at you for going to the bathroom in it. You don't have to use it to wash clothes because it's like God himself already washed them, rinsed them, and dried them for you outside on the clothesline. It's great because you and your brothers can take old rags and scrub the kitchen floor with them and get up all the dirt, so your mama won't have to sit in a chair and cry over it making tan spots where her tears land. You'll still have to borrow some water from the neighbors, but at least you won't have to go as many times because even with the tub full of water, it's only fit for washing things or flushing toilets. You still need water for drinking on summer days, as long and hot as they are.

A few days after the water was turned off, the gas is turned off too since Mama hasn't been able to pay the utility bill yet. We eat cold canned green beans and some potted meat on the side by candlelight.

Mama says, "Oh ain't this a fancy dinner by candlelight?" She laughs, but her laugh is sad sounding even if it is a laugh. Stevie calls this Mama's cry disguise because it's a laugh to try to cover up how sad she feels and when she does it, there's no sparkle at all in her eyes, but a flat look like something that's running out of life. It's like that bird I found with a BB pellet in its head down the alley. The bird died in my hand. I know because I felt its heart like a little rumble against his chest until it just stopped. I wrapped it in leaves and let it rest on a patch of green moss under a shade tree on the side of the house.

I asked Stevie if that flat look in Mama's eyes meant she would die soon like that bird and he said, "Oh, God, no, she'll just go ahead and cry later, when she thinks we're all sleeping. That's all." I knew Mama cried at night a lot in the living room because I heard her when I was laying in bed and whispering to God and staring at the moon that would stare back down at me through the window.

It's nighttime and Stevie is reading to Joseph and me by candlelight a story called *Of Mice and Men* about a big, retarded man named Lennie who has a friend named George. He's making the voices of the characters like he always does.

I love when Stevie reads to me because for the time being it's easy to forget about everything else around us. I love this story about Lennie and George because it seems like they have to struggle for everything, even a drink of water, just like us. Somehow there's comfort in that and before too long I'm off to sleep with the smell of books from Stevie's room and the candlelight glowing on his face and the pages of the book.

I dream I'm in the story and that I fried up a big ole mess of fish that Lennie and George eat, thank me for and declare ain't I the sweetest thing they ever knew under the sun to cook for them? The next thing I know I'm in a different world and surrounded by a big flock of birds. It's like I'm one of them because I'm sitting perched up next to them on a roof and I hear a voice from inside the house. There's a toilet flushing over and over again inside the house we're sitting on and that voice is saying, "Thank you, God, for the water," and "Look, there's a sparrow!" And me and the other birds are afraid, and we fly away.

When Mama's welfare check comes, she says it's a good thing we still get a little check to help out, even though she has her job at the Hasty House. We go down to the Urban League to see if they might help us with the reconnect fee on account of Mama has the money for the bill itself she scraped up from tips, but not the reconnect fee. We sit in the waiting room for our name to be called and the rows of chairs are all full of folks needing help of some sort or another. We are the only white folks here and I feel like everybody is looking at us and thinking, "Now ain't that some shit," like the folks in the neighborhood when we have to borrow water.

The lady calls us in and starts to explain that their funds are low and it's hard to help everyone that comes through here and did we go to the welfare office first to see if they could help? Mama says, "Yes, but I couldn't get no emergency aid since my check just came and my lights have been off a long time now."

"Well, wait right here. We'll see what we can do," the lady says and stands up to leave the room. Then I can't believe the words that come from my mouth. It's like I'm thinking out loud something I didn't mean to say, but to only think.

"Do y'all help white folks?" I ask and Mama turns and looks at me all shocked and the lady isn't sure what to say either.

"Well, yes, we help all we can. This *is* the Urban League, that's right, and we do serve mostly Black urban folks, but we might be able to help y'all." She goes out and Mama gives me a pinch like she does if we're in public and she wants to punish me in secret.

"Just keep your smart mouth shut! It's hard enough to come down here begging without you asking stupid questions that might well make someone mad enough not to help us!"

I shut up with wet in my eyes and the lady comes back in and says they'll help us this time. With their help, our utilities are turned back on and that night, we cook on the stove and sit around the table eating with the fans blowing the warm air that smells like mimosa into our kitchen.

We all take long baths until Mama tells us we have to get out of the water, or we'll turn into prunes and she'll have a bunch of prunes for young'uns and wouldn't that be a terrible thing because with the shortage of food in our house we're liable to be eaten by her the next time food is low.

She laughs at this and we do too even though I think it's a strange kind of thing for a mama to say to her young'uns and I hope it doesn't give me nightmares tonight about being eaten alive by my mama or some kind of animal.

Chapter Twenty-Six

I'm getting way too big to sleep with Mama, but we still haven't got me a bed to sleep on. Besides that, the bed is crowded since Joseph was born because most nights he sleeps in here too, except on some nights when he falls asleep in Stevie's room when we're all three in there. Stevie lets us just come in while he plays his record player while he's reading. Joseph and me sit and color until Joseph falls asleep with a crayon in his hand.

I thought I could maybe sleep in the living room on the couch, but then there was a scratchy sound in the closet that chased me out of there right quick. Mama promised it was only a mouse, but that wasn't enough to keep my imagination from running wild about what it actually was; a giant spider like that one I saw in *Night Gallery* once, or a devil with fangs and claws.

Mama said we just can't afford another bed since we can't even afford food and electricity half the time. She's sorry, she says. And I know she is because when I mention that I want to sleep in my own room since I'm getting older, she gets wrinkles on her forehead and tucks my hair back behind my ear like I do my doll's hair.

Then sometimes I pretend my doll is one of those babies that just likes to take her clothes off and run naked, like Joseph liked to do when he was a baby. I pretend that so I can feel like it's normal that I don't got any clothes for her. That way, I can just laugh about it.

I wish I could tell Mama that she can pretend it's normal for me not to have a bed. But you can't just pretend that sort of thing is normal. And I can tell it makes her sad, so I try to keep it just in my head most times when I think of it and make myself a bed from the old cloths and rags in the closet and sleep there.

Today though, I got an idea that I'll do when I can get Stevie to help me with it. That door of "the back room" came off its hinges since the other day when we were playing "climb up" where you climb up on the door and stand with your feet on the doorknobs and swing the door back and forth like it's a carnival ride.

Mama said we weren't supposed to be up on the door like that, but one day when me and Joseph were home alone, I got the idea that we could do it and no one would know about it. And no one would have known, except somehow, we pulled that door off the hinges.

Stevie found out about it before Mama. He said she was going to be so mad that she might start pounding her head with her palm again like she does when she gets upset because she "can't have nothing nice."

"Even though, that door wasn't that nice to begin with," he said.

That door had holes in it that we put there with a metal stick, by accident of course. Mama said we didn't need that metal stick and where did we get it anyway? We pulled it down from the closet wall. It was a thing to hang hangers on. We figured since we didn't have any hangers, we didn't need it up there anyway. Stevie can't believe how we tear stuff up, me and Joseph, and he tells me not to ever go in his room without him and touch things.

Of course, that makes me want to do just that, so I get me a hair pin and pick the little lock he bought from the Woolworth Store and I go in and touch things. I'm careful and I don't let Joseph in with me because he'll break stuff for sure.

So, I figure I'll go in without Joseph and borrow his little record player that's portable and has its own box attached and you can close it up and carry it like a suitcase. And since I'm borrowing the record player, I need some music to listen to, so I borrow some record albums too.

I borrow Beethoven's Fifth and Ninth Symphonies that Mrs. Parker gave him one time for cutting her grass. He listens to them when he's doing his homework or sometimes when he's going to sleep because he said it's good for the brain to listen to classical music while you sleep or study.

"It makes you smarter," he said.

I want to be smarter too, so I go for the Beethoven music. I want to show it to Evelyn. So, I got the little record player and the Beethoven albums, and I bring them over to Evelyn's to show her.

"Wow. Your brother is smart, girl," she says, closing her eyes to listen to the music that she says makes her think of something powerful like flying up high as the clouds, "especially the Ninth Symphony," she says.

"You feel that?" she wants to know.

"I don't know," I say because I didn't know the music was supposed to make you feel like flying, but that it was supposed to make you smart, like Evelyn says Stevie is.

"Close your eyes," Evelyn tells me, "and put your arms out like you're going to fly up."

I do, and I guess I get it, but not exactly like she does.

"Hey, that thing works with batteries too, doesn't it?" Evelyn asks.

"Yeah, but I don't got any," I say.

"I got some. I think they might just fit." She goes and gets some batteries out of a talking doll that she says she doesn't really play with anymore anyway. Then she needs one more, so she gets it from a kitchen drawer that's got all sorts of stuff in it like old batteries, strings, a hammer and pliers and emergency candles for when the lights go out during tornado season.

"Let's go to the Limesink Park and sit in the sun on a blanket and listen to Beethoven!" she says, all excited.

I say okay, but I have to get that record player and records back in Stevie's room before he gets back.

"I borrowed them," I say.

"If you borrowed them, why you gotta bring them back before he gets home?"

"Well..." I don't really want to tell her I snuck them out. She knows about the hair pin trick I got, but this is the first time I took something out like that, so I'm not sure if it's a big sin I should be ashamed of or not.

"Well? Girrrl, you ain't borrowed this stuff! You stole it!" Evelyn said, but I don't think she thinks it's a big sin that will get me thrown into Hell, because she's smiling, and she wouldn't smile if her best friend was fixing to be thrown into Hell.

"No, I borrowed it because I'm going to put it back," I set her straight about the stealing thing.

"Mama says, if you ain't asked permission to use something, you're stealing if you use it, even if you got plans to put it back," she said, and I thought she changed her mind about going to the Limesink Park since she might think now that I'm going to Hell and she doesn't want to end up there too for being an accomplice to my sin. But just when I'm having that thought, she's pulling an old blanket down from the closet and stuffing it into a pillowcase to bring with us.

"Let's go," she says and grabs the record albums while I grab the record player and we head off out the door.

The walk to the park seems long because the record player is swinging back and forth with each step and scraping my knuckle on the plastic latch that keeps it closed. By the time we get to the park my knuckle is busted open like I punched something hard with it.

"Damn! That looks bad!" Evelyn says, "You need a Band Aid on it."

She spreads the blanket out on the ground on top of a mess of yellow and orange leaves that fell to the ground since cooler weather has started coming in. She starts digging through her pillowcase sack for what I thought was a Band Aid.

"I don't got a Band Aid, but I got this handkerchief. Mama made me carry when I had a cold last winter, even though, I never used it. I don't know how folks use cloth handkerchiefs anyhow. What you going to do with a dirty old thing like that after you blowed your nose on it?" she's asking me, but I don't think she really wants an answer from me about that because I don't know anything about dirty handkerchiefs and what you're supposed to do with them when you're done using them.

She's wrapping the handkerchief around my hand and tucking it up under itself.

"Now, at least that'll keep dirt from getting in it, but you need to wash that when you get home, so it won't get infected," she said.

After Evelyn bandages up my knuckle with her handkerchief that's never been used, we put the music on and lay out in the sun and watch clouds passing by overhead.

"You think we'll go to Hell for this?" I ask.

"What you mean, 'we'? You're the one who stole the stuff, not me," she has her eyes closed and she's smiling.

"You're my accomplice now, though, since we're here together with the stolen stuff."

"No. We ain't going to Hell," Evelyn said, and we lay there in the warm sun listening to Beethoven's Ninth Symphony with cool breezes brushing over us until I start worrying that I should get the records and record player back before Stevie gets home.

Chapter Twenty-Seven

On the way home Evelyn is carrying the record player on account of my injury from carrying it before. When I get back home, I go quick to put the record player back, I put the record albums on top of the space heater in the living room. With the record player back in place, Stevie would never know I had it. I even remembered to take the batteries out.

I go wash my knuckle wound with soap and water, so it won't get infected.

"That ought to do it," I say to myself and look out the living room window and wonder when Mama and Joseph will be back. Mama took him to go swing on the swings at the school yard, so I figured it would be any time now since it's getting near about supper time and Mama said she was going to make corn bread and butter beans tonight for dinner.

I'm standing in the kitchen wondering if I should start cooking the butter beans since they take so long to cook, but I figure I probably shouldn't because the gas burners always scare me with the way they hiss gas out and you have to light it with a match to cook. I'm afraid it will explode and blow up the whole house.

Then, I hear the ping pinging of the space heater in the living room like it does when it comes on by itself to take the chill out of the air in the living room. It's also about that time that I remember that I put the record albums on top of the heater before I went to wash my sore knuckle.

I rush into the living room to grab the records off the heater. It's too late for Beethoven's Fifth, though, since it was on the bottom and right on the heater. When I slide the record out of the cover, I see it's already warped around the edges making "s" shaped frills all the way around.

"Oh, no!" I cry out.

I can't think of what to do, except cry and put the record back in the sleeve it came from and put the records back in place in Stevie's room, even though I know there's no way he won't notice it.

After supper, I'm in my room and whispering to Evelyn on my half of her set of Walkie-talkies about what happened to the records.

Not long after we met, we started talking over these Walkie-talkies when Evelyn got them for her birthday. She brought them over all excited and said I could keep one half and she could have the other. That way we can communicate from across the driveway.

"Now we gotta think up some nicknames to use as our handles," she said.

"Huh?" I had no idea what she meant by that.

"Handles, you know, like the police use or the CB folks when they talk over their CB radio. The nickname is called a handle," she explained.

"Ok," I said, still thinking it didn't make sense to call a name a handle.

"So, what's your s gonna be?" Evelyn asked.

"I don't know. Hmmm. Let me think on it for a minute," I said.

"Well, I already sort of know what mine's gonna be. I was thinking about some name of a bird, but I don't know what kind yet," Evelyn said.

"Okay. I like that idea. I know some bird kinds since I read about them from a bird book I got from the school library. What about Sparrow for a name? They're cute and they're also tough," I said.

"That's a good name," Evelyn said, "but we can't both be called Sparrow."

"Could we be Sparrow One and Sparrow Two?" I asked.

"Nah, we should have two different names. What other birds you know about?

"Well, that one called a Black-capped Chickadee is cute and it looks like it's wearing a little black hat. It's got a real nice song when it calls out. It sounds like it's calling somebody's name. You heard 'em before. They go like, Eeeev-lyyyn!" I did my best imitation like it was calling Evelyn's name all sweet, but kind of sad.

"I like it and we could call me Chickadee for short. I don't know, though. What other kind you know about?" Evelyn asked with her hand on her chin like she was thinking hard.

"I know! How about Eagle? Eagles are fierce and strong and it's even against the law to kill 'em here. For real, 'cause it's a symbol if somebody kills one, he can go to prison," I said.

"Dang. Really? I ain't even know that. Maybe I'll be Eagle. That sounds cool. I do like Sparrow though," Evelyn said.

"Well, you want that name, then?" I asked.

"Nah. You keep it. You thought of it first. Mama says we're *all* sparrows."

I looked at her puzzled because I didn't know what in the world that meant.

"We're *all* sparrows. Like in the Bible," she explained.

I still didn't understand, but just said, "Oh, yeah," as if I did and let that subject go.

So, we're talking on the Walkie-talkies about the record that I ruined.

"Oooh...wooo...girl! You gonna get a whipping? What you gonna do?" she's asking.

"I don't know." I really don't know what I'm going to do.

"You could fess up. Maybe you won't get in trouble since you're being honest," Evelyn suggests.

Right about that time, I hear a deep hollering sound from Stevie's room.

"Hey!! What the hell??!! Mama! Do you know what happened to my album?" he's hollering out to Mama.

Mama came quick and then just as quick is calling me and Joseph to come fess up to who did this to Stevie's records. Joseph right away is saying, "I di'n't do it. I di'n't do it. Izzee do it."

We're standing in the hall and Stevie right away believes Joseph because he knows that Joseph can't get in his room because of the lock and when would he have gotten his hands on his album and why would a five-year-old want to fool with boring classical music anyhow?

"I did it," I have no choice but to confess. "I picked the lock on your door and borrowed your albums," I say. "I thought if I listened to them, they would make me smart!" I add all dramatic and already in a full wail hoping my tears would make Stevie feel sorry for me.

"You picked my lock?! What?! What happened to my album?!" I never saw Stevie this mad, especially at me.

"I forgot it on the heater. I didn't mean to. I'm sorry," I cry because I really am sorry.

"Mama, are you going to do something about this?" Stevie is asking Mama and he throws the record album on the floor, breaking Beethoven's Fifth into pieces.

"*Now* look what you done!" Mama says.

"Look what *I* did? It's what *she* did that's the problem! Anyway, it's '*did*',

Mama! Why can't you speak right? How come I can? I'm tired of this family! Everybody acts like thieving, white trash!"

Mama doesn't know what to say. She's just shocked that he's saying such things. Finally, she says she thinks somebody brainwashed Stevie to hate his family and think he's better than them. She stomps off and leaves me standing there and leaves Stevie to deal with me, the thieving white trash.

I don't know what to do, so I just walk away and go into my room. I sit on the floor that's like metal with the way it's made of concrete and all polished up smooth.

I can't help but cry because I never meant to upset Stevie like that. I'm tired of sitting on the cold floor, so I dig in a big old bag of raggedy clothes that's in the closet on the floor. I spread the clothes out and lay myself down and cry.

Suddenly, I hear a commotion and Stevie's coming down the hallway yelling at me some more.

"Isabelle! Now, you're going to know what it feels like to have your stuff destroyed!" he's yelling.

I don't know what he's talking about and just as I'm wondering that, he pounds on my door. I say, come in, because I really want to know. He opens the door and when he does, he's standing there with my old, winking eye doll in one hand and a pair of scissors in the other. He's holding her by her curly lock that she has on the front of her head. Just then, he takes the scissors and snips the curl. My doll falls to the floor with a thud on the slick concrete. I scream as if Stevie cut a real baby and rush over to scoop her off the floor.

I think Mama might come running and he'd get in trouble for what he just did, but she doesn't. I can hear the TV in the living room on. The News is coming on and telling us something about Elvis, who was Mama's favorite rock-n-roll singer, who died a couple of summers ago 'cause he fell out in his bathroom.

161

"I still can't believe it!" Mama's saying out loud to the TV.

Stevie went off into his room and I just go back to my pile of old clothes on the floor to lay down with my doll with the hair chopped off. I take an old shirt that must have been Joseph's when he was a baby and put it on my doll like it's a dress.

Since I wanted to stop sleeping in the bed in Mama's room, I start sleeping on the floor in my room. My back hurts like an old lady when I wake up in the mornings and I'm freezing on the floor. That's when I got the idea about the door that came off the hinges and how I can make a bed with it when I can get some help to do it. I have some plastic milk crates I could put on the corners and lay the door on top of it.

Two days after the whole nightmare with Stevie's record and my doll, Stevie says he's sorry about what he did with her hair. I say I'm sorry again about the record and sneaking in his room. I promise him that I will never pick the lock again. We make peace with each other and he lets me come in his room to listen to him read again.

I tell him about my idea about the door, but that I need help to carry the door into my room and set it up on the crates. He says he'll help me. We drag the door into my room and prop it up like a bed on the four crates.

"Now it just needs some covers," I say.

We look in the hall closet and find an old sheet. It has holes in it, but we figure we could make it work. I cover the door.

"You need some pillows and a blanket," Stevie says and goes into his room and grabs the pillow off his bed and an old army green sleeping bag that was stuffed at the back of his closet.

"It's kind of dusty, but it'll do for a blanket, if you want it," Stevie says, so we spread it on the door to cover it and fluff the pillow up at the head my "bed".

"If you stand back and look, it looks like a real bed," Stevie says.

Just then Joseph comes bounding in asking if he can jump on it.

"No, no! It's not a real bed, Joseph. See?" I knock on it like when you knock on a door.

"Oh, oh-tay," was all he said, because what else is there to say when your big sister makes a bed out of a door because she's tired of sleeping on a floor that might as well be metal.

Joseph and Stevie leave me to my room, and I sit on the edge of my door-bed. I swing my feet and pretend like it's a real bed. I hop up and stand off to the other side of the room and look at it with the sleeping bag blanket covering it, making it look fluffy and the pillow at the head.

I stand there for a while, just staring and pretending. I like how it feels to stand across the room and look at my bed, even if it isn't real. Even when I'm sitting cross legged on the floor, I keep looking out of the corner of my eye at it. It's like I'm a girl who lives in a house with her mama and brothers and we have plenty of food and electricity all the time, and a bed to sleep on in my own room because I'm plenty old enough. I can look and pretend I'm normal, almost.

Chapter Twenty-Eight

Winter came rolling in in stops and starts where the day is like a snap of cold, then a wave of warm. On the warm days, yellow jackets appear from out of nowhere and stagger around when they crawl looking for one last chance to sting someone.

Last year, one found my foot when I was sitting on the living room floor minding my own business watching *Little House on the Prairie*. The pain was like someone put a hot needle right into the bottom of my foot. Mama took a penny and pressed it against where the sting was because that was supposed to draw out the poison, she said. The next day, my foot puffed up like a balloon and that's when Mama said she needed to take it to another level, so she put a mix of dirt and water on it to take the swelling out. When that didn't work, she dug out some old cigarette butts from her can of used up cigarettes and she mixed the bits of tobacco with water and slathered that on my foot, same as the dirt. Finally, some days later, the swelling was gone so Mama said it's a good thing she's a smoker since it was the tobacco that cured my foot when nothing else would.

Now when the winter is coming in slow like a seesaw of warm and cold days, I watch out for yellow jackets, so I don't get bit again.

The slow rolling winter coming in brought us the Christmas season. Folks, especially kids, get all excited for the celebration to come. Mama reminds us that we need to guard against getting too excited because we can't count on having a reason for all that merriment folks were having around us. On account of that, Joseph, Stevie and me were excused from dreams about Santa and toys and such. She thought it would be better for her to be honest just so we don't get our hopes up every year only to find out we got nothing from Santa. But Mama also told us that we weren't to tell other kids. Just because we had no dreams of Santa didn't mean we ought to be going around spoiling the hopes of all the other young'uns we knew.

When Evelyn invited Joseph, Stevie, and me over to help decorate their tree, Mama said we could go. Evelyn felt bad for us that we weren't going to have one. Even though Mama tried to guard herself from the Christmas season sad feelings, she was broken hearted over it and said it didn't seem like Christmas at all without a tree to decorate. She does a lot of sighing and not looking straight at us. She tucks herself away in her room for a long time without making a sound.

"I can't imagine a Christmas without a Christmas tree," Evelyn said. She let Stevie put the lights on just the way he wanted, with one set of blinking ones, one set of twinkling ones and last, some stay-on ones. Stevie's letting the rest of us put on the ornaments, as long as he gets to oversee where they go.

Evelyn's got a box of origami birds she wants to hang on the tree. She made the whole box of them when we were spending all day in her room under a sheet tent we made on her bed. She had a whole note pad of paper with light tan and white colors with one odd sheet of red. Her mama bought it for her from the bargain bin at Woolworth's.

"They said the red paper made it defective because it wasn't supposed to

165

be in there. Folks don't want it because it ain't perfect," Evelyn explained. "I think it *is* perfect, though. I'm gonna make a bunch of tan and white ones and one beautiful red one. You want to make some? I can show you how," she offered.

I really like it when she shows me how to do stuff she learns in art class, so she showed me and I tried to make a bird like hers. Mine was kind of 'flicted looking though, so we got a good laugh out of it.

"You don't have to make any more if you don't want to. You can have some paper though, to draw on it if you want," Evelyn said, still laughing at my lopsided bird.

We spent a long time under the tent, her making birds galore and me drawing all kinds of things from a birds' eye view. I used up every piece of paper she gave me drawing things like our neighborhood how a bird would see it, the school yard and how it was laid out and even inside our apartments how they would look to a bird if he got in and flew around.

We're putting little hooks on the paper birds and hanging them all around with the red one right in front all Christmas-y looking. Evelyn's little sister, Barbara, is going on and on about what she's hoping Santa will bring her for Christmas when Joseph starts blurting out, "Dhere no S- ..." I catch him on the 'S' part of Santa, and I cover his mouth to hush him up. He just sits quiet for that moment with my hand held over his mouth until it's safe to uncover his mouth without words flying out. We get back to what we were doing before Joseph almost killed Barbara's hopes in one single sentence.

There's some wonderful smell coming from the kitchen where Evelyn's mama is cooking and singing a song about telling on a mountain that the Lord is born. I'm listening to the words of that song, especially a part that said something about sinning both night and day. I wonder how someone can sin at night while they're fast asleep. I asked Mrs. Williams if that meant that folks had improper dreams. She told me I needed to just quit thinking too hard about every little old thing and just let a song be.

I did let that song be when she came out into the living room with a plate full of warm sugar cookies and five tall cups of milk for us to drink. We all lined up in a row on the couch with Evelyn in the middle of me and Stevie. She huddled up next to him. Then, quick as anybody could guess what she was going to do, she stuck her hand up above their heads holding a twig of mistletoe and she gave my brother a big kiss right on the side of his face. He stood up fast and dropped his cookies on the floor.

Evelyn and me are busting laughing, but Stevie's mad and he says he's leaving.

"Ok...Ok...I won't do that again," Evelyn promises. "I'm sorry. Really. I couldn't help it, though. You're just so cute!" she says right out loud. I can't believe she's saying this all out loud like that. That's one thing I like about Evelyn. Things everybody else would be afraid to do, she steps right up and does it.

"Cut it out!" Stevie hollers all red-faced. Then Evelyn's mama comes in and tells us to stop that bickering because that's not in the Christmas spirit.

Anyway, we all get up from the couch and Stevie has plans to go home. Evelyn and me are going to hunt for pecans so we can sell them door to door and maybe buy our mamas something for Christmas. Evelyn tries to talk Stevie into coming, but he wants no part of it.

We get an old, stained pillowcase to collect the pecans in from the closet in the hall. We put on our sweaters and laugh when the static in mine makes my straight hair stand up. Then when we smooth our sweaters down, they make those little popping sounds of electricity, giving us little shocks up and down our arms and stomachs.

We set our sights on a bunch of pecan trees over by the Jr. High School. We know that if there were any pecan trees that would still have plenty of pecans left, it would be there. The trees are near one of the nicer neighborhoods, where folks wouldn't be caught picking up pecans to sell or eat because it just isn't something you do if you got the money to go buy them in the store.

Chapter Twenty-Nine

When we get to the good pecan trees we grab us a hand full of pecans and sit on a big rock just under one of the trees. These pecans are nice and big and fat. They crack loud in our hands when we take two in our palms and press them hard against each other. We eat a few of them, put the rest in the pillowcase, and get up and rake pecans from the ground with our hands into the case. There's hardly a spot we can stand without cracking pecans under our feet. I don't believe I've seen so many in one place before. In no time at all we fill the case halfway and decide that it's enough.

We start back home, taking turns carrying the sack of pecans over our backs. We decide to cut through the backyard of the Jr. High School. Turning the corner around the side of the building, we stop cold in our tracks catching our breath, both staring at what we see. Setting up all tall as ever right by the Dixie Dumpster was the school Christmas tree. Since school is out until after the New Year and no one had any use for it, it got tossed out.

"Isabelle!" Evelyn says, all excited, "Are you thinking what I'm thinking?"

"I reckon so," I say, but I'm not sure.

"Let's drag that tree home to your mama!" she says.

"That's what I was thinking," I say, in kind of a lie, "but how are we going to do that?"

"We're just going to drag it. That's how. You take one end and I'll take the other, and we'll drag it."

"I guess we can do it," I halfway agree.

"Grab that end," she says, after knocking it over and pointing to the top half of it.

"What about the pecans?" I ask.

"Girl, you worry too much. Now come on, grab that end. I'll hold on to the pecans with one hand and the tree with the other."

So, we drag that tree all five blocks home. On the way, Evelyn tripped and fell in a puddle and I accidentally stepped in that same puddle. Our shoes were all wet and we walked at a steady pace making a rhythm, with first our shoes squeaking, then the clunk of the pecan sack hitting the end of the tree trunk and the brush of the branches on the sidewalk. Squeak, squeak, squeak, squeak, clunk, clunk, sweep, sweep. We laughed so hard at one time that we fell out right there on the sidewalk, still clinging to the tree. I fell straight on my back with my feet in the air and Evelyn said I looked like a big bug with my arms and legs waving away.

When we finally got going again, we decided not to pay attention to the rhythm we were making because we might never get home if we kept falling laughing. The branches of the tree were scratching my face and making me itch, but I didn't care. We walked in silence for two more blocks with the smell of pine hanging in our faces.

We get home all itchy and wet, with pine needles all stuck in our sweaters. My brothers are outside, making dirt castles and mud pies next to the porch.

Joseph runs up to us screaming and clapping.

"Tee! Tee! We got teeee!"

"Where did you get that?" Stevie was smiling.

"It was by the school. Evelyn and me dragged it home. It was Evelyn's idea," I said, "Somebody threw it out. Where's Mama?"

"She's inside," he answers, "I'll go get her." And he's off into the house.

Mama comes to the door and acts like she's afraid to open it to see why everybody was so excited. She's looking at Stevie like she's not sure what to think.

"We ... I mean Evelyn and Isabelle got something for you, Mama. Come on."

She steps out and sees us standing there all dirty and smiling, each one of us on one side of the tree, holding it up. Mama sucked in air and held it in for a moment. Then she rushes over crying and hugs me and Evelyn both, dripping happy tears on our heads.

"Where did you get it?" She asks us. We tell her how we rescued it from the side of the Dixie Dumpster in the schoolyard. She cries some more and rubs her hands up the branches of the tree.

My brothers come over and Joseph puts his muddy arms around Mama's legs. I think maybe she'll scream at him for getting her dirty, but she surprises me and just reaches down and touches his head.

We all stand, Mama, Stevie, Joseph, me, and Evelyn, around the tree like we're hugging it and Joseph wants to decorate it, so then Santa is sure to come to our house.

"Santa come now?" he jumps around in his excitement.

Stevie starts to remind him that Santa is made up, but Mama gives him a look and put her finger to her lips.

"Sure, he will, Joseph, he will," Mama says, but she's wrinkling her forehead when she says it.

Stevie drags the tree in and after we push the couch over to the other side of the room, we set the tree up in front of the living room window in a stand that we had tucked away in the closet. We pull out our old Christmas tree decorations that we've had for years, for when we were able to have a tree. Only Stevie can touch them. He lays them out on the floor and blows the dust off them. The lights are a mess of tangled black and red cords with a few of the light bulbs missing.

I'm worried they won't work, but Evelyn says not to worry, she thinks they still have a string that they didn't use for their tree and she'll go get it if we want.

"Thanks, Evelyn. That'd be nice," Mama says with a smile she can't get off her face. So, Evelyn goes over to get the lights and comes back with Barbara to help and Joseph is jumping around and up and down off the couch. It's great because Mama is so happy, she doesn't screech at him like she normally would when he does this sort of thing. I think for a moment how it would be great if Mama could be this happy all the time because I believe her happy self is her true self.

Stevie plugged in all the lights and Joseph and Barbara clapped and screamed, "Lights! Lights!" They settled down and stared into them, with the deep reds and greens of the lights reflecting off their dark brown eyes.

"But, Stevie, I don't know about those ones that don't got no bulbs." Mama says, "I'm scared somebody can get shocked on those."

"I don't think so, Mama. If they don't touch them." Stevie is sure.

"Well, alright then. I reckon. Y'all don't go touching those lights without no bulb," she warned. We all shake our heads to say okay and watch while Stevie strings them around the tree. We watch like it's a ceremony. Mama's leaning against the wall and puffing on her Winston, with the lights dancing across her.

With the lights on, the rest of us hang the ornaments. Many of them are so old, the red paint on them has gone and turned orange pinkish and a lot of paint is all worn off.

"Well, go ahead and hang them," Mama said," It's the lights shining in them that makes them look pretty anyway."

After we finish decorating, we all rush outside to stand on the sidewalk in the dark gray evening and look at the tree from outside. The six of us lean into each other to keep warm and stare all quiet and it starts to rain a soft slow rain that turns to snowflakes.

Barbara puts her hand out and a perfect snowflake lands on her palm. "Look! It's snowing!"

And with that the sky lets loose a whole bunch of perfect flakes. Mama gasps. Stevie raises his face to the sky. Joseph and Barbara grab hands and spin around hollering, "Snow! Snow! Snow!" Evelyn and me, we stand with our shoulders touching and smile at each other and nod our heads, "yeah."

It's at this storybook sort of moment that some ladies and a couple of teenage boys are coming up the sidewalk with some grocery bags in their arms. When they get closer, I recognize one lady who I'd seen before at church, but whose name I can't remember. They get closer and smile at us all.

"Mrs. Letourneau?" One lady I've never seen before speaks up. She's flashing her smile all around at everybody. The lamplight outside is shining across her face and I can see her lipstick is thick and red and shiny, the color of candy apples.

"Yes?" Mama looks puzzled.

"We're from the Albany Gospel Chapel. We know y'all don't attend anymore, but we thought y'all might could use some help around Christmas time."

They're all beaming at us and Mama shakes her head, "yes."

One of the boys hands a bag out to Mama and she moves quick to drop her cigarette she was smoking and stomps it out, so she can take hold of the bag. And the other boy just a little taller than Stevie is standing quiet and holding on to two other bags.

"Well, come on in," Mama says, looking down at the pavement. She leads the way up the steps going inside, with everyone following behind her.

"How y'all like the snow? It's *some* surprise, itn't it?" one lady asks Barbara and Joseph.

"Good! It's fun!" Barbara says.

"Oh, it sure *is*!" she says.

"We catched yike dis!" Joseph says and shows the ladies how they were catching snowflakes on their tongues. The ladies and the boys laugh, and Joseph blinks his long eyelashes at them and the lady with the candy apple lipstick says he looks like a doll with those long eye lashes.

She set her bag on the kitchen table and the two boys set theirs on the table too.

"What in? What in, Mama!?" Joseph climbed up on the chair to get a look inside the bags.

"Why, it's some groceries for your Christmas dinner, honey," the other church lady says.

Just then, Mrs. Williams was calling Evelyn and Barbara home. They left and then the church folks said they had to go too. They say a prayer over us, wish us a Merry Christmas, God bless us, and they hope to see us at church sometimes.

Now, with just me and my family around the table, Mama is taking things out of the bags one-by-one thanking God for each item.

"Thank you, God, for the turkey. Thank you, God, for the instant potatoes. Thank you, God, for the canned peas. Thank you, God ... Thank you, God ... Thank you, God."

I'm right thankful too, but I'm wondering if maybe we could make it shorter by just saying something like, "Thank you, God, for all this food."

We sit through it quiet, though, and get excited whenever she pulls out a sweet to thank the Lord for.

"Thank you, Lord, for the cinnamon buns. We'll each have us one of them when we're all done here," she turned from her prayer and told us.

Joseph and me make a line of food on the table and Stevie is taking them from the table and putting them where they go in the refrigerator or the cupboard.

When Mama is all done thanking God for the food, she also thanks him that our utilities are on, because a lot of good this food would do us with no utilities.

Stevie tears open the cinnamon buns and gives us each one and Mama mixes some powdered milk with some water and gives us each some.

"Can we go in the living room and eat by the tree?" I ask Mama.

"Sure," she answers.

Mama's in a good mood.

We sit on the floor right next to the tree, all four of us and eat and talk. I lick the frosting off my fingers and Joseph does the same with his.

"It looks so nice," Mama says about the tree.

"I can't get over how pretty it is," she says all dreamy and lights up another cigarette and just stares quiet at the tree for a good long while.

"Now Santa put toys," Joseph says.

Mama just says in almost a whisper, "yeah, I reckon he can," and didn't look at us while she was saying this.

After a while Mama gets up and goes into the kitchen. She's clinking things around running the water, tapping a spoon on the side of a coffee cup. She starts whistling Silent Night as lovely and clear as any bird I'd ever heard.

"Mama whistle," Joseph whispers. He knows that usually means something good.

Chapter Thirty

There are only a few days left before Christmas, so Evelyn and me decide we better get a move on the pecan selling if we plan to buy something from our earnings before Christmas. Barbara and Joseph beg to come with us.

"Y'all are just going to slow us down," I tell them.

"We won't!" Barbara cries.

Joseph starts crying and then goes into a fit on the ground screaming that he's going to tear up my things while I'm gone if I don't bring him and Barbara along.

"You ain't! I got nothing you can tear and besides that, Mama will switch you for it." As soon as those words come out of my mouth, I felt terrible guilty, because I knew my mama *would* switch him for it, worse than she switches any of us for anything. It's like Mama's got a permanent mad feeling toward Joseph that's just underneath her skin. Sometimes it comes out in screeches and pops or maybe even a switching if what he did was bad enough. When I think of this, I get a change of heart.

"Alright, come on, then. But it's not because you had a fit that I'm letting you go. It's because I just changed my mind. We gotta make sure Evelyn doesn't mind though."

Evelyn doesn't mind. Not one little bit. That's another thing about her that I wish I could be like. She walks around not minding one bit about things that make me all upset.

The four of us head out for the other side of town, where folks don't pick up pecans off the ground to eat or sell, but they might buy them from four kids from The Projects a few days before Christmas.

Things are going good, and after we sell about seven medium sized bags of pecans at one dollar apiece, we decide we can take a little break. We're right around the Midtown Mall so we go into Woolworth to see if we can find anything for our mamas for Christmas. The cashier lady looks at us and smiles and thinks we're all so cute with our bags of pecans that we're selling.

Joseph starts complaining that he's hungry, and can he have some candy. He can. I give in quick and bought some since I didn't want him to have one of his tantrums in the store with Barbara all good mannered, Evelyn all patient, and all of us standing there with bags of pecans, no longer thought to be so cute by the cashier lady with Joseph screaming and wailing on the floor for candy.

After we bought the candy for Joseph and Barbara, that left us with six dollars between Evelyn and me. Three apiece. Evelyn bought her mama some salt and pepper shakers and a powder puff box with sweet smelling powder inside. I couldn't find anything my mama would like, being as no matter what I got she'd probably chime up and say she wished I got her something else. That's what she always says when someone gives her something.

"I wish they'd just give me the money for it. Then I could buy me what I want ... something useful like a pack of cigarettes when I'm out," she'd say.

I thought I'd just wrap up the three dollars in an envelope that I'd make from construction paper and give it to her.

"That's what you're giving your mama?" Evelyn wrinkles her nose up and asks.

"Yeah. That's what she would want. That's how she is," I say.

"That just ain't right." There goes Evelyn saying things right out like she thinks them.

I want to defend my mama even if Evelyn is right, but the only thing I can think of to say is, "I know."

Chapter Thirty-One

We leave Woolworth's and sit on the bench by JC Penney's. Joseph and Barbara eat candy while Evelyn and me eat pecans. We have a contest to see who could eat the most. I'm pretty good at cracking them in my hands, so I eat more than she does, and we leave a mess of shells on the concrete under the bench.

"Oh, look at that!" Barbara says out loud and excited. She's pointing at the window of JC Penney's with all the Christmas decorations inside on display for folks to come and buy. The decorations are so pretty it's like we're all pulled inside to take a closer look.

We go in and stand staring at the twinkling lights, the fat Santa statues, complete with Mrs. Claus and reindeer, and the statues of Jesus and Mary and Joseph with bright yellow hair.

"Stevie said Jesus didn't have yellow hair," I tell Evelyn, "since he was from part of the world where all the folks have black hair, he probably had black hair. Stevie read that."

"That's probably about right," Evelyn says agreeing with me, but I wonder if she's really listening since she's got her eyes fixed on a row of angel dolls standing on the shelf.

"Look at them! Look at that one in the middle with the great big golden wings!" she says. I'm looking at those wings and thinking how fine it would be to have wings like that and fly around all over Heaven with a golden harp and when I get tired, I could take a nap on a soft cloud.

"They sure are pretty with all that blond shiny hair and white skin, but it sure would be nice to see a Black angel with curly black hair sometimes," Evelyn says.

"There's no such thing as a Black angel," Barbara declares.

"Of course, there is," Evelyn answers back. "Who told you that?"

"Nobody told me. I just never saw pictures of Black angels," Barbara shrugs her shoulders.

"Well, there *are* Black angels for real. These here are just dolls, but in real life there's got to be Black angels because there's Black people, aren't there?" Evelyn explains.

"That's right," I added. I think there might be Black angels, but I do wonder why we never see any pictures or statues of angels that are Black skinned. I never really thought of that before. They're always yellow haired like the Jesus, Mary, and Joseph statues that Stevie says are all wrong anyway. So, I figure maybe folks got the angel thing all wrong too, with them always yellow-haired, with skin that's bone white, and eyes that are almost always blue.

Barbara is happy with Evelyn's answer and Joseph wants to ride on the escalator, so off we go up the escalator. Joseph thinks the stairs are magic the way they move, and he giggles while we're moving up. We go up, then down, then Joseph wants to go up again. We do, but the store people are starting to look at us all nervous because we aren't supposed to be playing on the escalator.

Evelyn and me clutch our left-over bags of pecans tight in one hand and each one of us also has to hold onto the hand of Barbara and Joseph. We're about halfway up when Evelyn's foot slips. She cuts her knee open on the edge of the moving step and drops her bag of pecans which went by the dozens rolling down the up escalator and onto the people standing below us.

A string of strong swear words fly out of her mouth and the people behind us don't know what to do. It looks like they don't know if they should turn around and try to walk back down the up escalator or just keep going and try to pretend like nothing happened.

All this scared Joseph and Barbara who started squawking out loud and people all over the store stopped in their tracks to look. The folks working there went on full alert and a manager rushed to meet us at the top of the escalator.

"Y'all are going to have to leave!" Her face is splotched with red and she's breathing hard.

"Y'all are not supposed to be roaming the store, playing around anyway. This is not a playground. Where is your mama? Your mamas? Y'all certainly can't be all from one mama … or can y'all?" She went on.

"No, we aren't … can I …," Evelyn starts to ask something, but before she could get her question out, a lady we don't know walks up and says, "Oh, I know these children! Whatever are you doing here without your mamas? And, oh my goodness, what happened to your leg?"

Evelyn is bleeding through her britches leg which has a bad tear.

We're standing there speechless, on account of we have no idea who this lady is. Joseph and Barbara stop crying and are taking turns taking quick deep breaths. They're standing there clinging to me and Evelyn, quivering and breathing, breathing and quivering.

"Well, sorry about this," the lady we don't know says to the store manager. "I'll take care of it from here and see to it that these kids get on home."

This satisfies the store manager, and she rushes off probably to see to it that the pecans and blood is cleaned off the escalator.

The lady we don't know says her name is Mrs. Wingate and she's a social worker at the Department of Human Services. She's dressed nice in a dark blue suit coat and skirt. Her brown hair is combed to the side and held down with a gold-colored barrette. She smiles a lot and says she hated to tell a lie that she knew us, but it looked like we were about to get in big trouble unless somebody stepped in. She comes with us to the bathroom where Evelyn is washing her knee and when she gets soap and water in it, a similar string of swear words like the ones on the escalator come flying out of her mouth again.

"Now, that's no kind of language to use around your little sibling," Mrs. Wingate scolds Evelyn.

Evelyn and I look at each other. I shrug my shoulders.

"What's a sibling?" Evelyn asks.

"Oh...I mean your little sister."

I wonder why she couldn't say "little sister" like anyone else instead of "sibling".

She offers us a ride home and we decide to go with her, even if we know we aren't supposed to go with a stranger. It's already after 2:00 and we're all tired out from our day of adventure.

"Besides, she seems safe," Evelyn says, when we step aside for a second.

"Since she's a welfare lady, she probably isn't out for harming anyone and social workers aren't especially known for kidnapping and harming young'uns," she says. I'm convinced, so we follow Mrs. Wingate out to the parking lot.

"Now, where did I park my vehicle?" she says and scratches at her head. I notice that she said "vehicle" instead of car.

"Oh, there it is!" she says, laughing a little at herself. "I'm always forgetting where I park."

We go with her and pile into a funny looking orange car that looks like a cross between a Rolls Royce and a Volkswagen beetle.

"Looks like Herbie the Love Bug got with a Rolls Royce," Evelyn jokes. I give Evelyn a look, hoping she would take it as a hint that maybe she shouldn't insult this lady about her car since we want a ride.

Mrs. Wingate leans out and smiles a kind of a half-smile and says, like she was getting a first look at the shape of her car, "Why, is does, doesn't it?"

While we're riding, Joseph pulls some of his leftover candy from his pocket, "I got yunch canny," he said.

"What you got there?" Mrs. Wingate wants to know and looks in her rear-view mirror to catch a glimpse.

"Don't worry. It ain't messy," I say, "It's just a piece of chocolate. Pop it in your mouth, Joseph, so you don't mess up the seats."

"Oh my! That's what you had for lunch? Why, that's not proper nourishment! Growing children need proper nourishment. Like, you should have fruits, vegetables, and bread."

I noticed that she said "nourishment" instead of food and I wondered if Evelyn was noticing that Mrs. Wingate keeps using big words when she could just as well say the same thing with more simple words that we could understand better.

Anyway, after we got the lesson about what kind of "nourishment" we should have, we all sit quiet in the back seat of Mrs. Wingate's car. It's beginning to rain, tapping hard on the windshield. I'm thinking about the day and how funny it is when you can start off with simple plans of selling pecans to get a gift for your mama and you can end up spilling them by the dozens down a moving escalator, sending the store clerks into a tizzy, and the folks behind you confused and scrambling in circles, with your friend who cuts her knee and tears her britches. Then, just when you're about to be in a mess of trouble with the store manager, you meet up with a welfare lady who says she knows you when you never saw her in your life. That same lady offers you a ride that you know you're not supposed to take, but you take anyway, and on the way, she gives you a lesson about the "nourishment" you need to fill your empty stomach.

I know about what kind of food we're supposed to eat because we learned about it in health class at school. I know what we're supposed to eat, but when my brother is crying for candy, and it's only a few days before Christmas, and he's gone and found a new belief in Santa, which I know is only going to disappoint him on Christmas morning, I just want to get him candy. That way, I get to see his eyes excited when he opens the candy and pops a piece in his mouth. I just want to see that and even if he wasn't about to pitch a fit, I would get it for him anyway.

Mrs. Wingate drops us off about a block from home when we lie and tell her this is where we live. We don't want our mamas to know we took a ride from somebody we don't know.

"Okay. You all take care now," she says.

We hop out quick before Barbara or Joseph pipes up and says this isn't exactly where we live.

"Thank you, ma'am," Evelyn says.

I thank her too and we're off down the sidewalk with rain beating us from all sides. We get soaked to the bone and what pecans we have left bust out of the wet paper bags and make a long trail down the sidewalk.

"Hey, I know!" Barbara says, "maybe that lady was an angel! Mama says angels are all around us and we just can't see them always."

"Hmm…," I say, thinking if it was possible. Evelyn thinks so.

Joseph doesn't care one way or another. He's running ahead and splashing water all over and holding his face to the sky with his tongue hanging out to catch the rain.

Chapter Thirty-Two

On the 23rd of December two men come knocking on the door. They're loud and happy. One is round and peachy red with great big hands that look like hams that he waves around in the air when he talks. The other man is skinny and white as school glue and has hair that's dark and shiny and combed flat to one side, greased that way with Pomade. It seems like everything they say, they say it with a laugh attached at the end of it. They're from the Jaycees and they have a special delivery for us. My mama lets them in. The happy men drag in a huge cardboard box that's taller and wider than either of them.

"We'll, we've got a little something here for y'all!" the ham-handed one says in a voice that's like a boom. Joseph is climbing on the couch and jumping up and down and yelling.

"Wanna see! Wanna see! Pick up, Stevie!"

"No, Joe. You can't see yet. Isabelle, you take him back to your room and y'all stay in there until I say come out," Mama says.

"Mama, I don't want to be cooped up in the back of the house with him!"

"Get on in there now, Isabelle. I ain't kiddin' with you."

"But…"

"But nothin'. Don't you be sassin' me in front of these folks from the Jaycees."

I noticed her nostrils flaring and I know that's kind of like a signal that somebody's about to get popped. I figure it might be best if I don't argue right now and I take Joseph by the hand and drag him into my room, kicking and screaming all the way.

"Wanna see! Wanna see!" he's screaming and scratching at me like some kind of wild animal.

"Quit scratching at me!" I yell back at him and close the door to my room behind me when we get inside.

After we wait in my room a while, Mama calls us out.

"Where's the big box?" I ask, 'because I don't see it anywhere.

"It's put away in 'the back room," Mama says. "Now don't ask me anymore until later, after Joe is asleep. I got something for y'all, though, in the meantime just to keep him from fussing."

She hands Joseph a toy truck that has batteries and lights and a little motor inside. He flips a little switch to turn it on and puts it on the floor and shrieks with excitement when it goes in circles. She gives me a special book that has flowers on the cover. It has a key and the words "My First Diary" on the front of it. I asked Mama, "Why do they call it a dairy?"

"What? It don't say dairy! It says diary! D-I-A-R-Y. Don't you know what a diary is?"

"No Mama, I don't reckon I do since I ain't never heard of one before."

"Well, it's a special book that you can write all your thoughts in and it has a key to keep them secret."

I'm happy with my diary and right away plan to write in it every day from now on.

Stevie gets a new book and he's already off in his room reading it.

"That boy reads more than anyone I know," Mama says. "Something just ain't right about how much time he spends in his room alone with his nose stuck in a book."

She looks at me as if she was expecting me to say that I think so too, but I don't. I want to tell her that I think she ought to be proud that Stevie is so smart and reads so much and that he probably spends all his time in his room to hide away from the hunger that hangs over our house like a cloud. Maybe he's hiding from her always pacing the floor whispering swear words or smacking her head with the palm of her hand. Once I think of this, a parade of things I'd like to say pours into my head because it's like I got angry feelings for my mama stored up in my chest so full I feel like I might explode. I want to sass her when she talks about Stevie like that, but I don't because it's Christmas.

Instead, I write all these feelings in my new diary and carry the key around with me, so that no one can read it except me. It feels good to write secrets like that because it's almost like telling someone.

Later that night when Joseph is fast asleep, Stevie tells me that there were lots more surprises in that big box that the happy men from the Jaycees brought.

I rushed over in the morning to tell Evelyn about the box of surprises, but she was over at her cousin's house. I went around all day Christmas Eve so full of excitement I didn't know what to do with such feelings with no one to tell it to, so I just started cleaning the house to get rid of some energy.

I washed the kitchen counters and cleaned the kitchen floor with a rag and soapy water. I swept the old green carpet in the living room. I washed our plasticware that was in the sink and I washed out the tin pie pans that we use to cook in the oven.

"I don't know what's got into Isabelle. She don't never like to help clean. Now I can't make her stop," Mama says to Miss Mattie, the grandma from next door. They're leaning outside on the wall on the porch and smoking.

"Maybe she's getting her period," I hear the grandma say.

"She's still a little young yet, but that might well be it. I remember when I was getting my period, I went through something like this myself. I ain't thought of that. Well, I hope that ain't it. The pain from it can be so terrible sometimes it'll make you wish you was born a boy," Mama says. They start laughing and I sneak away from the window where I was listening, so they wouldn't know I heard.

I'm wondering what they were talking about. I don't know what a "period" is, but I don't like the sound of it if it's going to give me pain and make me wish I was a boy. I don't know why they were laughing at this because it doesn't sound to me like something that would be a laughing matter.

I stop cleaning right away in hopes of keeping away my "period" ... whatever that is. I wished I could go ask Evelyn because I'm sure she would know. I don't know how, but she knows near about everything that grownups keep in secret.

I guess I didn't get my "period" since nothing strange happened being as I stopped cleaning right away and I felt relieved that maybe Mama was wrong. I forgot about worrying about it when the sun went down, and our tree lights went on and we all sat around it and watched the lights blinking.

We drank hot cocoa and Stevie read the rest of *A Christmas Carol* to us since he had started reading it to us a couple of days ago. He finally finished and for the rest of the evening Joseph kept saying "Gah bleth uth evyone," like tiny Tim in the story until Mama said, "Enough, Joe, enough."

Tonight, Joseph and me have to go to bed so Mama and Stevie can stay up in case Santa comes. That's what they tell us, so Joseph doesn't have a fit. Joseph says he wants to lay with me in my room since he doesn't want to be in a bedroom by himself.

Mama said it was okay since I have a mattress instead of a door for a bed now. We got it when the neighbor out front was fixing to throw it out when she got a new one.

"Ain't nothing wrong with it, except it's lumpy," she told Mama that day when she saw her dragging it down to the curbside. "Y'all want it?" she asked.

Mama said, "Well, I'm sure my daughter could use it since she's been sleeping on a door." The lady looked mixed up by that and Mama explained about my door-bed and they got a big laugh about that story before Mama called Stevie to come help us drag it to our place.

Anyway, it's warmer on the mattress with two of us there once we cover ourselves with the sheet and Mama came along and put her blanket over us. When Mama put her blanket on me and Joseph, I felt bad about those things I wrote in my diary about how much I don't like her.

That must be about the time I went off to sleep because the next thing I know, Joseph is shaking me awake and it's very early in the morning before the sun had a chance to come up.

"Wake up, Izzee. Wake up. Wanna go yiving room."

"It's not time yet, Joe. Go back to sleep." It's so quiet in the house I think no one else is up and Mama is sure to get mad if we get up without her if there are surprises in the living room.

"No, wanna go see!" He's getting louder.

Then Stevie comes and opens the door. "Shh! You'll wake Mama," he says with his finger to his lips. We can barely see him in the dim light coming through the window. Just then Mama calls from her room for us to come here.

We go, thinking we must be in trouble now for waking her, but she doesn't seem mad when we get there. Instead, she tells us to come sit beside her on her bed. She's sitting up against the wall all huddled up with her coat over her to keep warm. I remember how she gave me her blanket last night and feel bad again for saying how I don't like her to my diary. I tell myself I'll scribble through it and say something nice about her today to my diary instead.

189

Joseph and me crawl up next to her and then we all three huddle with the blanket Joseph dragged out with him from my room. Stevie is sitting at the edge of the bed looking toward us and I think he's smiling though I can't really tell since it's still so dark. I can just feel it. I feel wonderful for that moment there crowded up with Mama and Joseph and Stevie smiling at us in the dark.

"Santa come, Mama?" Joseph wants to know.

"Well, I don't know, Joe, I reckon we'll have to go see, won't we?" she says.

Stevie gets up then and goes out into the living room.

"I'll call y'all when it's time to come out, okay?" he says on his way out.

Mama walks ahead of us down the hall and we can see the tree lights bouncing red and green and white on the wall. It's the only light in the whole house and I think it's beautiful. We get to the end of the hall and Mama sticks her head around the corner into the living room and sucks in a big gulp of air with her mouth open. Then we go around the corner and I can't believe what I see.

Joseph starts jumping up and down and shrieking because there are presents piled up from just under the tree to all the way across the room, with hardly any room left to walk. Some of the presents are wrapped and some of them aren't. The ones that aren't are from Santa and they have little handwritten tags on them that say, *"From Santa"*.

Joseph is so excited he runs from one gift to another and holds it up for a split second puts it down and moves on to the next.

"Yook I got!" He says holding up a toy police car with lights and a siren sound.

He puts down the police car and moves on to the next toy.

"Yook!" he says again this time showing us a fluffy green teddy bear.

I'm still rubbing my eyes in disbelief, looking at the things that are mine. A transistor radio, a party doll that blows bubbles and a party horn, a great big tea set in a bright pink box, a Barbie doll and a thick pad of paper and some pencils. Then there are the things that are wrapped that we have to open. I keep thinking that those happy men who brought that big box must have made a mistake and left all those things here when they meant to pass some of them around to other kids around town too.

I keep this thought to myself, though, for fear that if I mention what I'm thinking Mama might say, "You know what? That's right! We better get in touch with those men and tell them they made a big mistake by leaving all these things here."

So, I keep my mouth shut on that point. That thought keeps creeping into my head, but each time I just push it right away.

We all sit around the tree for a long time, opening presents one-by-one while Stevie hands them out and it's the best morning ever when we're all there with the only light in the house bouncing colors from the Christmas tree. The space heater is on, making pinging noises while it heats the room. There are Christmas songs playing down low on my new transistor radio and Joseph is saying, "Santa real! I happy. Santa real!"

Chapter Thirty-Three

It's April and we don't have but two full months of school left before summer. There's a new girl in our class named Katrina Arnold. She's white so that makes the number of white kids in our class six, Black kids 20. None of the white kids want anything to do with her because she's tall and skinny, her knees look like knobs and she has a large nose that's always runny and looks like a beak. The Black kids don't want anything to do with her because, first of all, she's white. Second, she's tall and skinny, has knees that look like knobs and she has a nose like a beak. She's very quiet and she doesn't say anything to anyone except for our teacher, Mrs. Phillips, who's real nice to her on account of all her "unattractive qualities" as Mrs. Williams would say about someone who isn't all that pretty.

I'm thinking I might try to make friends with her in spite of those things about her just to be nice. At recess, I sit in the swing beside her where she was swinging alone and kicking the dirt up each time she goes forward or backward. I'm waiting for her to say something, like hi, but she's just looking up at the sky while she's swinging and kicking up a cloud of dry dirt all around us. I decide I'll say something first.

"Hi," I say.

"Hi," she says back, still looking at the sky.

"What's your name?" I know her name, but I'm not sure what else to say to get her to start talking.

"Katrina. Katrina Arnold," she says and finally glances over at me.

"Did you just move here from somewhere?"

"Yeah," she answers.

I'm thinking she's going to tell me from where, but she doesn't, so then I have to ask. I can tell this won't be easy and I wonder if she ain't a little touched in the head the way she doesn't say much to anybody even when it's plain to see you're trying to get her to talk.

She says she's from Alabama, she's got a dead mama, and lives in a house with her daddy and her uncle, who drinks whiskey and comes home late at night and fights with her daddy, who is his brother. And she's got a brother, but he ain't right in the head at all and don't do anything all day except hang around in his room and play with his private parts.

Now I'm thinking, "First she says nothing, now she won't shut up when she's telling me stuff I don't want to know about."

I try to change the subject. "I don't have much friends at school, myself, except for one good friend named Evelyn who's a grade ahead of me. She walks home with me every day and I don't think she'd mind if you walk home with us, even though you probably don't live where we live. Where do you live?"

She tells me she lives on Third Avenue on the east side of Slappey, which I know is a white section with mostly houses that look all run down and in need of paint or shingles on the rooftops and the grass in every yard is tall with weeds and not cut neat and trim like the white neighborhoods on the west side of Slappey. A lot of the houses have cars in the driveway, but whether the cars run or not is another story. Half the time they're up on cinder blocks. Stevie says the cars in the driveways are more for show than anything.

I asked what he means, and he said, "It's just to make it look like they have something they don't, like lots of money, so they can afford a car."

I think it's a lot like my mama the last time she got a new mop and broom and she hung it outside on the porch. Then, the whole neighborhood could see that she had something new. But after it was hung outside for two days, somebody noticed it and decided to take it for themselves and Mama was upset for days walking around saying, "I can't have nothin'. I can't have nothin'."

Some two weeks later she comes home from the store and declared she knew who stole her mop and broom. "It was that old bucktoothed bitch down the block. That one that walks around half-naked and got men coming and going all the time. She's got seven young'uns, each one with a different daddy that ain't nowhere to be seen. I know it's her, because I done seen it hanging on her porch, plain as ever. She ain't even got no shame in stealing it. It just goes to show you, we can't trust no Black." And when she says this, she's wagging her head and I know she's including me in the "we" she just talked about. It's strange, because I don't feel right to be clumped in this "we" because I know that Evelyn would never steal no mop or broom.

After school one day I tell Katrina if she'll hang on a minute, we can meet up with Evelyn and we'll walk her home, so she won't be alone. She says "okay" and we sit on the front steps of the school for Evelyn to come out like she always does.

Katrina doesn't say a word while we're waiting. I'm kind of glad about that because I'm afraid that once she gets started, she won't know when to quit. We sit and say nothing, and I find myself noticing how her nose looks like a beak of a hawk. I think it must be terrible to walk around with a nose like that that's not only big but runny too.

Just then Evelyn comes out and I tell her all about who my new friend is, and would she mind if we walk her home since she doesn't live at all that far from us. Of course Evelyn doesn't mind, but Katrina has a funny look on her face and I'm not quite sure what it means, but she's looking at Evelyn in a way like she's surprised or like something about Evelyn isn't quite what she expected.

"What you looking at me like that for?" Evelyn asks her.

"Oh nothing. I just...I just...like your hair bows. That's all," she says and looks at me like she's expecting some kind of help with what to say next, but I'm not sure exactly what kind of helping she needs, so I just break into the uncomfortable moment by saying, "Well, let's go."

We walk, and every time Evelyn happens to end up next to Katrina, she always hops over on the other side of me, so I am in between them.

"Why do you keep hopping over there every time I get along side of you?" Evelyn wants to know and she's starting to think, just like me, that Katrina might not like her for some reason.

"I ain't. I just happen to get over here," she answers.

"I don't know about that," Evelyn says and hops over to the other side of Katrina, putting her in the middle of us. We hardly took ten steps before she's hopping back over to the other side of me.

"Okay, that's enough! You're doing that on purpose! Why you keep doing that?"

We all stop in our tracks and we're just standing there looking at each other like we're waiting for the other to say something.

"Isabelle. What's wrong with your new friend? Why's she acting like that?"

"I don't know," I shrug my shoulders like I have no idea, but I'm thinking I might have some idea that it has something to do with Evelyn's Blackness and Katrina's whiteness. I think we're all thinking this, but nobody wants to say.

I'm wondering why Evelyn isn't coming right out and saying what she thinks like she usually does. I'm beginning to think it wasn't such a good idea after all to try to be a friend with this girl when I thought she was strange in the first place. Now I'm feeling like I'm stuck right in the middle of something uncomfortable, like a field of sandspurs where it doesn't matter which way we step, somebody's going to get picked.

We start walking again, leaving the question of what's wrong with Katrina hanging in the air with no answer. Evelyn gave up trying to get her to walk beside her.

Finally, Katrina says, "Oh, I'll be alright from here. My house ain't but a block away. I can see it from here. Y'all can go on now."

"You don't want us to walk you all the way?" I ask.

"No, that's okay." Katrina looks down the road toward her house and wrinkles her forehead.

"Why not?" I ask thinking I might press her to say, but Evelyn pipes up with, "Never mind that, Isabelle. She just doesn't want us to. We need to go home now anyway."

Now I'm puzzled. This is the first time I have ever seen Evelyn back down and not say just what she thinks. I'm wondering why, and I wonder if I should be the one to speak up now, but I decide not to.

Katrina tells us she'll see us later, turns and near about cuts out running up the block toward her house. She doesn't look back at us while she's leaving. Evelyn and me both agree that something's not right with that girl.

We head off toward home and then we start cutting up, talking and playing around just like we always do on the way home.

"You know that boy name Isaiah in your class? He sent me a note today that said he likes me. He wants to be my boyfriend," Evelyn says.

"What you going to do? You like him too?" I ask.

"No. I'm going to tell him he isn't old enough for me. You can have him if you want him. You want him? I'll tell him he's got to go with you because I'm already taken," she says, and "No, I'm just messing with you, girl. I ain't got no boyfriend. I don't want one right now."

"I don't know," I say. "Maybe I don't want a boyfriend neither, then. I reckon he's cute and all, but what do I do with him if I go with him and where do I have to go with him?"

"Girl, don't you know anything?" Evelyn taps my shoulder.

"To 'go with him' doesn't mean go with him anywhere it means you just be his girlfriend, so he can give you flowers sometimes and maybe a Valentine card or a piece of candy on Valentine's Day."

"I'll think about it," I say, but I don't really have a mind to, because if Evelyn doesn't want a boyfriend, I don't either.

While we walk, we move from one subject to the next without a mention of how weird Katrina was acting, but I'm thinking about it in between our bursts of conversation. I wonder if Evelyn is thinking about it too. For the first time since I met Evelyn it feels like there is something invisible dividing us.

Chapter Thirty-Four

At recess Katrina and me sit on the swings and I decide I'm going to ask her about yesterday, why she wouldn't let Evelyn walk next to her.

"I ain't supposed to be walking with no nigger," she says and that word at the end of her sentence makes me think of a dagger. I wonder if I'm crazy to think of a dagger at a time like this, but I let that thought pass because I need to let Katrina know that Evelyn ain't that word that starts with "n", and that's she's my friend.

"You ain't supposed to use that word because that's a bad thing to call someone. And Evelyn isn't one anyway."

"Okay, I ain't supposed to walk with no Black," she says, like I'll be okay with that since she didn't use the "n" word this time.

"Well, I reckon you'll have to walk by yourself from now on," I say, and I feel proud for declaring that I'm not going to side with her just because we're both white.

"Can't you just walk with me? I'm afraid to walk by myself. It ain't me that don't like your Black friend, but my daddy will whip me if he sees me walking with her. He says it's bad enough I got to sit with them in class all day, but that don't mean I got to go hanging around Blacks when I ain't in school and if he ever catches me with one, he's going to tan my hide," Katrina says to me in full on bawling. She's looking at me and her hawk nose is running, so she pulls out a tissue and wipes it.

Now I feel like I'm slipping into some kind of hole where there's no easy exit with this situation working up. Now I feel sad for Katrina walking alone and scared with no friend in the whole world. But I can't go and turn my back on Evelyn, who's been my best friend since the day we met.

"Please walk with me instead. Evelyn don't need you as much as I do because she can walk with any Black person and be fine, but there ain't no other white kids who'll even talk to me," she adds.

Now I wonder how I'm going to do this without getting Evelyn mad at me, so at the end of the school day Katrina and me don't bother to wait for Evelyn, but we head out straight for her house right after.

Since Evelyn isn't with us, she lets me come all the way to her house and even invites me in. "Well, I guess, for a little while," I say, getting that feeling again like I'm crawling into some deep hole with no easy exit. We go in and her daddy isn't home, but her uncle is sitting on the couch watching TV and cussing out loud that the TV ain't nothin' but a Goddamned piece of junk the way it cuts off when it wants to. He gets up and gives it a good whack on the side but walks past it out the back door and on to the porch where he sits and smokes one of those cigarettes that just look like paper rolled up and it has a funny smell I don't like. It's the same smell that I smelled before when I was walking down the alley with Evelyn and there was a group of men on a back porch smoking one of these cigarettes, passing it around. They looked at us all red eyed and one of them said, "hey girl, gimmee some."

Evelyn told me not to look at them but to keep on walking like we don't see nor hear them. So, we did. When we got up the alley a bit away from them,

I asked her what was that that they wanted some of because we didn't have anything in our hands or anything that they might want.

"They want some sex with us," she said with a flat voice.

"Huh?" I didn't understand.

"Yep, that's what they want. Once I was walking with my cousin, Sheila, past some men and they said that to us. I had some Now n' Laters in my hand that I just bought from the corner store and I thought they wanted some of my candy when they said that, so I was going to walk over and give them each one. My cousin slapped me hard on the back of the head, grabbed me by the arm and told me to keep on walking. She said when men look at you that way and say, "gimmee some" you gotta keep on walking because if you don't, they might well rape you," Evelyn cleared that right up for me.

"Oh," I answered, which is what I say when I can't find any other words that are right to fill the moment with.

Now, I'm here at Katrina's house thinking about how Evelyn must be wondering where I am and I'm smelling Katrina's uncle's homemade cigarette and worrying that after he smokes it, he's going to come and try to rape us if his eyes are all red and cloudy looking.

Katrina doesn't seem to be worried about her uncle and his funny cigarette and she offers me a Twinky cake. I take it, but I don't open it right away because I know it isn't right for me to be eating anything at someone's house when my brothers are sitting at home with no Twinky or anything else of their own to eat.

"Well, ain't you going to eat it?" Katrina pressures me.

I think maybe I'll eat it and they'll never know anyway so why not. Then she offers to cook some hamburger and asks can I stay for supper. She doesn't wait for my answer before she grabs a pack of ground beef from the fridge, starts patting the pink meat in her hands and throws it sizzling into a frypan. The smell of the meat cooking makes my mouth water and even though I'm still worrying about Evelyn, who's probably worrying about me, and Katrina's uncle with the homemade cigarette and my brothers sitting home with maybe only bread and mayonnaise to eat, I say, "Yes, I'll have a burger," and, "Oh, yes, I would love cheese on it."

The smell of the burger brings Katrina's brother, who she says isn't at all right in the head, Patrick, from his room. I can see what she means right away because he comes into the kitchen and starts walking in circles and mumbling something I can't tell what he's saying. Her uncle comes in from the porch and yells at him to stop walking in Goddamn circles because he's making him dizzy. Then her uncle says he's got the munchies and tells Katrina, "Fix a burger for me and your Goddamn brother." Katrina does, and I wonder what I'm supposed to do sitting here with my burger right in front of me. Should I eat it now or wait for her to finish cooking and sit with me? If I don't eat it now, I might not get a chance to eat it before I have to cut out of this place because things are going kind of strange around here and I'm not sure I want to stick around much longer.

Patrick is still walking in circles and Katrina's uncle yells at him. "Patrick! Stop that walking in Goddamn circles and sit your Goddamn ass down before I hit you with a Goddamn frypan!" and he grabs him by the arm, forcing him to sit in the chair across on the other side of the table.

Patrick sits and repeats over and over, "G'damn fy pan. G'damn fy pan." Then he starts licking his hands and I wonder how anyone can eat around this place with all this happening anyway. Katrina's uncle declares that the boy don't know his ass from a hole in the ground and I think that must be a terrible kind of ignorance when a person can't tell the difference between those two things. I decide to wait for Katrina to sit with me before I start to eat.

Finally, she's finished cooking and she takes a seat across from me and next to Patrick, leaving the seat next to me open for her uncle who sits down and pours himself a shot of whiskey to wash down the burger.

I take a bite out of my burger and the juice drips down my chin. I know now that I have to finish eating it because to waste it would be a big sin, even a worse sin than eating when my brothers are hungry with hardly any food at home.

It tastes so good I close my eyes for a moment and try to pretend I'm somewhere else, but I'm not able to keep up my fantasy because her uncle suddenly acts like he just notices me here and he says to Katrina, "Who's your cute little friend here? Ain't you going to introduce us?" I open my eyes and I'm looking at Katrina and then at him with his red eyes squinting at me with a smile that makes my stomach feel upside down.

"Oh, this here is Isabelle, Uncle Mike."

"Well, ain't that a right fancy name?" he says. I don't like how he's looking at me and I set my burger down and something inside me tells me to get up and get out of there, never mind the juicy burger with cheese, that I know would be a sin to waste. Just as this thought to leave was entering my mind Katrina's Uncle Mike reaches over and grabs me around the waist and makes me sit on his knee.

My heart is beating fast because I'm scared, and I remember what Evelyn told me about men when they give you that look, and I want to cry. He squeezes me hard and scrapes his whiskers across my face and it feels like a hairbrush against my cheek, and he breathes whiskey and funny cigarette smell in my face. I whimper and start to cry and try to wriggle away from him.

"Let me go!"

"Just give me one kiss," he says, and his whiskers scrape me some more and I squirm loose from his arms and back away from him, crying.

"Hey, I ain't gonna hurt you. What's wrong with your little friend, Katrina? She don't like hugs and kisses?"

"I guess not, Uncle Mike," Katrina answers with her eyes fixed hard on the table.

"Not like you at all, is she?" her Uncle Mike says to her and smiles at her, and I notice how his teeth are gray and crooked and set wide apart in his mouth like tiny tombstones in a graveyard.

"I guess not Uncle Mike," she says again and stares down at her burger that's getting cold.

"I gotta go," I say, wiping my face with my sleeve while I go for the door.

"Don't forget your books," Katrina's uncle says. I walk fast over across the room to get them keeping my eye on him in case he was to get up and I'd have to make a run for the door. I scoop up my books and go for the door. I go to turn the knob and it's playing some trick on me and won't turn. I look at Katrina for help and she tells me, "You gotta turn it hard."

I do, it opens, and I look back for one brief moment at Katrina and her not-right-in-the-head brother who doesn't even know there's anything strange happening at all. He's sitting there with his face to his plate chewing with his mouth open, with mayonnaise and mustard all over his face. I don't dare even glance at her uncle.

Once I'm out the door I start running toward home. While I'm running, I'm thinking how terrible it must be for Katrina, to live in that house as it is with everything damned by God.

I get about two blocks away and I figure I can stop running now. That's when I realize I got my Twinkie cake held tight in my fist, kind of smashed up. I don't even remember picking it up. Anyway, I reckon I might as well eat it down since it's hardly in any shape to share with anybody. I eat it quick and stuff the wrapper in my pocket and tell myself not to forget to throw it away so no one at home sees I had it and Mama won't get mad at me because I'm out here eating like a queen when everybody else is at home starving.

When I explain everything to Evelyn about why I left her yesterday, she didn't stay mad at me for long. I tell her I'll never do that again and that I'll walk with her from now on. I'm sorry that Katrina's alone, but I can't be friends with her if she can't be friends with Evelyn too.

Evelyn says she knew that Katrina was doing that that day because she didn't want to play with a Black girl. She says she didn't say anything that day because she just didn't feel like it. She figured it wasn't going to change anything and what's the use of saying something if it won't change anything.

After school Evelyn and me walked home together without even a mention of Katrina. Some weeks later Katrina just moved away, right out of the blue.

I didn't want to tell Evelyn how sorry I felt for Katrina because I was afraid she would get mad at me for feeling sorry for a white girl who used the "n" word.

So, I tell it to my diary.

"Dear Diary,

I feel sorry for Katrina because her mama is dead and she's got stringy hair, and a nose like a beak, and bony knees like knobs. Her older brother doesn't know his ass from a hole in the ground. And isn't that sad? She lives with her uncle and daddy. I didn't see her daddy, but her Uncle Mike drinks whiskey, smokes those funny smelling homemade cigarettes that makes men get red eyes and look at girls in a way that makes them feel scared. Her Uncle Mike rubs his rough whiskers on little girls when he's trying to get a kiss from them.

Katrina is gone now because she moved away somewhere, just out of the blue. But wherever she is, I don't think it's good as long as her uncle is around, and maybe her daddy is just like him. She had lots of food in her house, I noticed. But now I think I know why she was so skinny even with all the food around. There's not much use in having all that food around if you can't ever sit down and eat without your uncle coming around and trying to get hugs and kisses from you while you eat, and your older brother is sitting there, not knowing a thing and your daddy or mama aren't there to keep you safe."

Evelyn's mama always says to us to pray for folks who need helping if you can't help them yourself, so I reckon I'll have to add her to my list.

And I do. But I wonder if it will help, because I still pray for Ducy Jones that his mama will stop whipping him, but that doesn't seem to change things. Even so, my prayer list is always growing and most every night I lay there and whisper to God and the moon about all the people I know who need helping.

Chapter Thirty-Five

It's a Thursday morning and I'm trying to wake up because Mama is telling me to hurry up and get up. "I overslept," she says.

I'm trying to get up and hurry, but my eyes are stuck shut with something like I had them glued while I slept. I don't want Mama to know because I'm thinking I might have pink eye and she'll get mad at me. If we get sick during the school year, she always screams at us, "but you *have* to go to school to get a hot meal!" or, "It's the only thing you'll have to eat today!" in a high-sounding shriek, like something wounded.

I'm feeling my way down the hall with the cinderblock walls that were once upon a time painted white, but got gray, after so many years of people living here. There are hand prints up high on these walls and I never could figure out how they got there. The paint is chipped right by the bathroom door on my right, so I know I'm by the bathroom when I feel the edge of the chipped part. I dip in fast before anyone can see me feeling my way down the hall.

I close the door behind me and I know I'm standing in front of the sink because I can feel the corner of the counter where I slipped and hit my head when I was getting out of the tub once and Mama screamed at me in that shrieky voice, but that time it wasn't because I wasn't going to get my meal at school, but because I was bleeding all over her new beige bathroom rug. "I can't have nothin'!" was what she shrieked that time.

There's a cloth hanging by the sink and I grab it and wet it with warm water and wipe the crusty stuff on my eyes. Mama's screaming at me again to hurry and I tell her I'm hurrying. I wipe my eyes with water as hot as I can and feel around for the soap that I know must be right here somewhere. There was a little sliver of Dial soap last night after we took our baths, so I just have to feel around for it and make sure I don't drop it down the drain once I do find it because that will be another thing that would make Mama shriek.

I found the soap, so I rub it on the cloth with warm water and wipe the crust some more. Wash, rinse, wash, rinse with warm, almost hot water to make sure I don't have soap on them, but the crust won't come off all the way no matter how hard I wipe my eyes with the cloth. I can finally open them, though, and I pry them open with my fingers. When I do, they sting and feel like someone just poured sand right in them like when I was little, and that boy threw a handful of sand right in my eyes when I was playing in the sandbox next to him at preschool. I want to cry, but I know everyone will know that something is wrong. Mama will come running and see my eyes and scream at me that I won't be able to have a hot meal today. I'll cry some more and I'm sure that will make the stinging in my eyes worse. So, I wipe them one last time, pry them open one more time and swallow hard to keep myself from crying from the pain when light gets in them. I'm peeking at myself in the mirror, but I can't look too long because the light bulb without a cover over it above the sink is making my eyes burn even worse. I can see that they're so red it looks like I have blood on the white parts of my eyes. I don't know how I'm going to hide this, but Stevie is knocking on the door now and saying Mama wants to know what's taking me so long and that she's getting mad. I can hear Joseph in the kitchen having a fit about something and I know that this would be the worst possible moment for me to walk out into the kitchen with eyes as red as blood and yellow crust all around the edges.

When I open the door, Stevie sucks in a big gasp like he just saw something scary, and says, "What happened to you?!" I shush him as fast as I can.

He's standing over me, shocked, with his hair hanging in his face. Mama says all the time that his hair is too long, and he looks like a juvenile delinquent with the way it falls in his face. One time I looked up the words "juvenile" and "delinquent," so I could see if that was a bad thing to be. I thought it was because Mama always follows it with telling him the "news" that he ain't never going nowhere in life with hair hanging in his face.

"Well, I got news for you, young man!" she says.

"Juvenile: Not fully grown or developed; young." That's pretty much what I thought about that word, but I wanted to be sure.

"Delinquent: Failing to do what law or duty requires." Is it against the law for a boy to have long hair? I didn't think so because the Lord had long hair and he would never break a law.

So, even after I looked up the words, I couldn't figure out why Mama called Stevie that just because his hair hung in his face, like it is right now while he's standing over me stunned quiet at the sight of my eyes.

"Don't tell Mama," I whisper to him. "She'll yell at me that I can't go to school and have something to eat today."

"I'm not going to tell her, but how are you going to get past her like that? Your eyes are red as a fire engine!"

"Shhh!" I shush him again. He's trying to whisper, but his whisper is still too loud.

"I don't know. I'll just keep my head down." That's all I can think of to do.

I go fast back to my room and put on some clothes and go out to the living room, keeping my head low and my eyes squinted. Stevie just left out the door with his army green book bag that looks like a pillowcase flung over his shoulder. He can't be late because he's in high school and he'll get in big trouble for being late to home room.

"Good luck," he leans over and whispers before going out the door.

It's at least good that Joseph is done having his fit and he's sitting now on the wooden rocking chair that I used to sit in backwards when I was his age and watch while Stevie went off to school in the morning. He's talking to me, but I'm not really listening to him since I'm trying to keep my head down and I'm having to peek with my eyes half shut to make sure I have all my papers and books in my bag.

I almost forgot my report that I wrote about dogs for my 4-H presentation that's due next week.

Mrs. Phillips said if we want to write it early and bring for her to look over, we'd get extra points for working so hard and being prompt. She said I could do my own research on dogs from the encyclopedia set in the library instead of doing like everybody else who got their information from the 4-H packets that came in the mail and were handed out to us in a 4-H Club meeting.

Two weeks earlier, we all got to write down the animal we wanted to learn more about because 4-H is all about animals and such. I chose a dog because I love how in every dog story I ever heard, they can near about read humans' minds and know how we feel at any moment. On that day, the packets came in, everybody was so excited. We were seated in long rows in the cafeteria while the 4-H Club leader, Mrs. Waynesly, handed out the packets.

"Look at the baby lambs!" one girl squealed about a picture on the inside of her packet.

"Ain't that little piglet so cute?" another girl said.

Before too long everyone's talking over each other so much you can't make out full sentences with the names of animals, "goat, rabbits, ducklings, horse, bull," being the only clear words that would jump out of all the noise. I was as patient as I could be, but I couldn't wait to get my information packet on dogs. Finally, after what seemed like a forever kind of wait, Mrs. Waynesly brought my packet. I was so excited, I didn't open the envelope in a neat way, but tore it open kind of raggedy. I could see the glossy edge of the paper inside and I slipped my hand in and pulled out my booklet. It was like my heart sunk right down to my stomach when I saw the heading in big blue letters, "The Dairy Cow," with a picture of a cow staring into the camera with its eyes all big and sad.

"Cow??" I asked to no one in particular, but Mrs. Waynesly was standing where she could hear me, so she came over and put her hand on my shoulder as if to comfort me. She leaned down a little to look at my booklet. "Oh, I'm so sorry, hon. I forgot to tell you. They didn't have any dog booklets, so they sent you a cow booklet instead. Now, doesn't that cow have beautiful eyes? Now, who knew that?"

I just shook my head like I agreed with her, but I didn't care how pretty the cow's eyes were. A cow is not the same as a dog and I wanted a dog booklet.

Well, after I recovered from my disappointment and my teacher said I could study about dogs and write a report on them anyway, I was kind of okay.

I'm putting the report in my book bag and making sure it's tucked in safe in its folder to keep it from getting crushed. While I'm doing this, the man on the radio, who Stevie likes to laugh at the way he always sounds like he's got his cheeks stuffed with cotton, is announcing the Dougherty County School District lunch menu.

"Mac-n-cheese, roast pork, hot rolls, and apple sauce. Chocolate milk to drink," he says, and I'm thinking that sounds like a fine lunch that I really don't want to miss, when all of a sudden there's a loud commotion, with Joseph letting out a scream and the rocking chair tipping over sideways. Joseph spills out onto the floor face first and bloodies his lip, so he's screaming even louder.

While this rocking chair disaster unfolds itself, Mama's in the kitchen where she's having a cigarette for breakfast. "All I need are my smokes, and my peace and quiet," she likes to say when we don't got much to eat, so she gives us the food as long as she has her cigarettes.

But right now, her peace and quiet and breakfast of Winstons have been interrupted by the howling of my little brother with his face slammed into the cement slab floor of the living room, that's not made soft at all by the old carpet covering it. The second Mama rushes through the doorway of the living room, she's screeching at me about how I should have been watching him, so he wouldn't hurt himself and "How many Goddamn times does she have to tell him how to sit in that Goddamn rocking chair anyway and what is he anyway?! Retarded?!" With the way he doesn't act like he understands much of what she tells him at all. She puts her cigarette from her hand to her mouth and scoops Joseph off the dingy green carpet of the living room floor. She props him up on her knee and he's still crying out loud throwing his head back so it's hard for Mama to hold him up. She tells me to run to the bathroom and get a cloth for her to wipe his lip before he bleeds all over everything. Her cigarette is hanging in between her lips and it bounces up and down each time she says something.

"Hurry up!" she raises her voice with her lips clamped on the cigarette.

She hasn't noticed my eyes yet and I turn toward the bathroom and she calls out, "Get me the cloth hanging by the sink! That yellow one hanging by the sink!"

I realize that she's talking about the one that I just used for my eyes and left in my room on the floor in my rush to get ready earlier. "Which one?" I ask, trying to think about what to do. If I tell her I used it, the world will stop turning, the sky will rip open and rain down fire, and it will be like the Armageddon brother Pritchard was always warning about when we went to church. And my mama will suddenly grow into a 20-foot-tall monster, the Beast, and she will eat my little brother in one gulp and finish off by eating me in two.

"The only one that's hanging over the sink! It's not like we got a lot of 'em!" Then she says something about how it's her new one that she uses for her make-up but "get it anyway."

"Ummm, it's not here," I say when I can't think of what to say or do. By that time, she comes into the bathroom to see for herself, holding Joseph on her hip. I turn fast toward the tub, still trying to hide my eyes.

"Where the hell is my cloth?" Mama is asking. Just then I see one on the tub that I know is not the one she was talking about. It's so used up, it's thin in spots and has holes in it.

"That will do," she says and grabs it from my hand. She's dabbing Joseph's lip and that's when she notices my fire engine red eyes with crust around them.

"Oh my God, Isabelle, what the hell? You got pink eye?! Oh my God! What now?! Can't nothin' go right?" Her cigarette bounces. I don't know if she's asking me or if she's asking God if nothin' can't go right, but if she's asking me, I'd have to say, "No, Mama, can't nothin' go right." But just as soon as I had that thought come to my head, she has taken the cigarette from her mouth so she can open her mouth wide enough for shrieking about how I won't have anything to eat today if I don't go to school. So, just as Joseph is done crying over his busted lip, I start crying over my stinging eyes like they got sand in them and my stomach burning from being empty already that morning.

Mama's got a remedy, though, to help get the redness out and get the crust off. She takes the last of the milk we have in the refrigerator and heats a little bit in a pot on top of the stove.

"It wasn't enough for nothin' anyway," she says and takes the cloth that I used earlier, the one that was supposed to be her make-up cloth and soaks it in the little bit of warm milk. I went ahead and told her that I used it a few minutes ago when I was in the middle of crying because as long as everything was already going bad, I thought I might as well let her know, so if she was going to get mad at me, it would just be once while she was in the middle of it, instead of telling her later so she would get mad at me all over again. At least right now, she might feel a little sorry for me with my red eyes keeping me away from my only meal of the day.

She sits on a chair in the kitchen where she says the light is good with the way it pours through the windows and tells me to lay across her knees, so she can squeeze the warm milk onto my eyes and dab them when the milk starts down the sides of my face. It's hard not to squirm or flinch with the milk dripping onto me and into my eyes, but she swears this will make them feel better, so I lay as still as I can while she tries to make them better.

She's breathing in my face and I can smell the cigarette she just finished and smashed the brown tip of it into an ash tray on the kitchen table. She never throws away the cigarette butts right away when she's finished smoking them, until she knows she can get a new carton. If she doesn't have any money when she runs out of them, she digs through an old tin can of smoked-up cigarettes until she finds one that's still got some left to smoke.

She finishes cleaning my eyes with the milk and it *did* get rid of the yellow crust, but they're still red and burning like they're on fire.

"You'll go on to school anyway," she says, "maybe no one will notice."

I try to open my eyes wider to try to make them look more normal. I look around the kitchen and blink to see if they get stuck anymore when I close them. Joseph has been sitting quiet, opening the little pink packets of liquid "Sweet-N-Low" that our neighbor, Mrs. Wallace, gave Mama for her coffee last night before she realized we still had a little bit of sugar shut up tight in a jelly jar in the back of the pantry behind the swollen cans of tomatoes. Mama keeps forgetting to throw the tomatoes out, so we don't accidentally eat and get ptomaine poisoning from them.

She lights another cigarette, puffs on it, and makes the smoke come out of her nose like a bull in a cartoon. Joseph laughs out loud at this and Mama does it again just to make him laugh. She said once that she loves how his eyes sparkle when he laughs. I notice that they're sparkling now, and he looks so happy, even with his lip all busted and swollen.

"You better get to school," Mama says. "If you walk fast, you'll still have time to get breakfast."

I get up from the table, grab my book bag, and step outside where the sunshine feels like pins in my eyes.

Chapter Thirty-Six

I'm just outside the lunchroom doors where only a few more kids are lined up for breakfast. Mrs. Tucker, the lunch lady, is telling some boys in the front of the line to pay attention and stop playing around because there is only "seven short minutes" until the bell rings to tell us it's the end of breakfast time.

Mrs. Tucker always announces the time like that.

"Okay boys and girls, you only have twenty short minutes to eat."

"We'll have some more hot rolls ready in four short minutes."

"In thirty short minutes, you won't be third graders anymore," she said at the end of the school year last year. We had gone to the cafeteria at the end of the day for an end of the year cookie party and she was telling us this as she was bringing out the last batch of warm sugar cookies she had made for us for the occasion.

I always wondered what was the difference between a short minute and a long minute because if all minutes equal 60 seconds, then how can there be long minutes and short ones? It doesn't matter. Right now, there's nothing but long minutes, while I'm standing in line here with my head hung low hoping no one sees my eyes.

It's my turn.

"What you going to have, hon?" Mrs. Tucker asks me. With my head down, it's hard to see what choices there are, but I see there are some rolls and scrambled eggs, so I just say that's what I want.

She notices that I'm not looking up at her and she says, "You alright, hon?" I just say I'm fine without looking up at her. I can see that she's wearing the sweater that's the color of olives that makes the green in her eyes really stand out, like the green in my eyes does every time I wear something that color. Mrs. Tucker and me like to joke that we're related since our eyes are so green, exactly the same color. I want to joke with her today, but of course, my eyes are more red than green today, so I just take my tray and slide it along the metal counter without saying anything. Mrs. Hershey is the cashier lady and she makes notations about who's paying for breakfast and who's poor enough to eat free.

My Aunt Gracie told me once that I'm lucky since I'm poor enough to eat free. I'm not sure about Aunt Gracie's idea of what lucky is because I'd rather be able to eat grits at home on a morning like this morning with my eyes on fire while I try to hide them for the few "short minutes" that Mrs. Tucker tries to talk to me.

Since I only have five short minutes left to eat, and I wonder now how minutes can seem long and short at the same time. I find a seat that is closest to the lunch line and I sit down facing Mrs. Tucker. I think to turn around with my back to her where she can't see my eyes, but I don't because I just want to sit down and eat as much as I can before the bell rings.

There's no one else at this table and usually I don't like having to sit alone to eat, but this time I don't care. There are only a few kids left in the lunchroom any way at this time since the group of loud boys who were at the front of the line earlier already swallowed their breakfast whole and went outside to be loud so the teachers outside can tell them to quiet down out there.

I'm sitting hunched over, scooping the scrambled eggs into my mouth and I'm happy to realize they have cheese in them. They're still hot, and I swallow them slow and it's almost like I feel them land in my empty stomach. "It's glorious," I think to myself, copying something my mother started saying lately whenever she has a first sip of coffee or a puff on a cigarette. I wonder why she says this since it doesn't sound at all like something she would say. But I like the sound of it, so I say it too, in my head.

I finish my "glorious" eggs and start on the roll. It's so warm and fresh, it's like it melts in my mouth. I want to close my eyes when I eat it, but I'm afraid they'll get stuck shut if I close them, so I don't. I'm letting the bite of hot roll melt in my mouth when I notice Mrs. Tucker saying something to the vice principal whose name is Mrs. Cartwright, but we call her "The Punisher" because it's her job to punish the kids when they act out at school. She walks around with a yard stick in her hand ready to use it if the need comes up.

I see Mrs. Tucker talking to Mrs. Cartwright and I think they're talking about me because they're looking this way and Mrs. Tucker is wrinkling her forehead like she's worried. I think it's because she's worrying because I didn't talk about her green sweater and instead just kept my head down.

"Oh no!" I'm thinking to myself, "don't tell her about my head hanging down!" Mrs. Tucker doesn't know that the vice principal isn't on our side, so she tells her when she's worried about a kid who's not eating or who's crying in the lunchroom or things like that. She doesn't know that we all hate Mrs. Cartwright and her yard stick and that she always comes over and makes things worse for any kid having a problem in the school.

I'm trying to focus on my hot roll even though I can see her and her yard stick walking toward me when I dare glance up for a second. "Keep your head down. Just eat," I tell myself and I can see the light blue of her suit jacket and even smell that powdery smell of old lady perfume when she comes over and stands over me. I'm not looking up at her. I don't care how long she stands there.

Just as I'm about to take another bite of my roll she stops me by laying the yard stick across my hand. I look up at her finally since it's like I got no choice now.

"Isabelle, you'll have to come to the office with me," she says, sounding like a policeman in a TV show telling someone "You'll have to come downtown with me." If it wasn't for the yard stick coming in between me and next bite of hot roll, I might feel like laughing right now at how much like a policeman she sounds.

I stand up, but I'm squeezing the roll in my fist because I have no plans of throwing it away.

"Why do I gotta come to the office?" I ask pretending not to know.

"It looks like you might have pink eye, which is mighty contagious, so we can't have you walking around here with that."

"No, I don't got pink eye. I got sand in my eyes this morning," I lie, even though I know she won't believe me, and she will drag me off to the office anyway.

"Well let's just go to see the nurse, just in case," she says. "Just leave your tray and toss that roll you have in your hand and follow me."

She guides me with her yard stick on my shoulder, like I saw a farmer do in the 4-H film when he was herding his cows with a stick in his hand.

I don't argue with her about going to the office because I know I won't win that fight, but instead of tossing the hot roll I have scrunched up in my hand, I stuff the whole half that was left, in my mouth and chew slow with my cheeks full. I swallow little bits of it at time and feel it going down and landing with the eggs in my stomach. I keep walking along, across the school yard, past the pile of coal next to the furnace room in the basement, up the three stone steps, and just inside the main school building, with "The Punisher's" yardstick against the back of my shoulder, guiding me to a chair just outside the nurse's office, which is right next to the principal's and vice principal's offices in the same waiting area.

The loud boys from the lunch line were there too since they were hauled into the office for being too loud outside and were sitting slumped over in their seats outside the principal's office waiting for Mrs. Cartwright to get back from dragging kids with sore eyes out of the lunchroom in the middle of breakfast.

When the loud boys are in with The Punisher, the nurse, Mrs. Marshall, comes out of her office and tells me to come in and have a seat. I do, and she takes a wooden popsicle stick thing and tries to open my eyes with it, so she can see how red they are. I squirm away and tell her that I can open them for her if she could take the popsicle stick out of my eye.

She says okay and I open them as much as I can but there is a bright light on the ceiling and it's making them hurt worse to open them. She puts on some rubber gloves and snaps them in place and then pries my eyes open to have a look and says, "hmm...mmm hmmm," and nods her head up and down like she's saying "yes" as if I asked her a question.

"Looks like pink eye for sure," she says. "Are you sure you got sand in them?" she asks but looks at me sideways. I know she thinks I'm lying so I decide to tell her the truth about how my mama thought it was pink eye too and washed them with milk, but they still hurt, but I had to come to school so I could eat. She's looking at me like she feels sorry for me and she shakes her head as if to say, "for shame, for shame", but then she says she has no choice though, but to send me home and she'll have to contact my mother to come and get me.

"We don't have a phone, so you can't reach her." I'm hoping that means I'll just have to stay right here at least until after lunch, but then Mrs. Marshall tells me that they have the neighbor's number, so they can try to reach my mother that way.

They can't find Mama since they called Evelyn's mama who went over and knocked on the door, but no one answered, so I have to wait in a room away from everyone else since my sore eyes are contagious, Mrs. Marshall says. I don't mind being here alone, but I don't like how the whole wall of this room is made of glass like a big window at the zoo, like I'm in a glass tank and everyone who comes by looks in at me like I'm some kind of animal. One of the loud boys even pressed his nose up against the glass and stuck his tongue out at me and licked the window after being let out of the office before he was dragged in to see Mrs. Cartwright to be taught a lesson again, since he didn't learn his lesson the first time.

I decide to put my head down on the table in front of me, so I don't have to see people looking at me. I fall asleep until I wake up with my eyes stuck shut again.

I keep my head down since I can't see anyway, and Mrs. Marshall comes in with gloves on again and washes my eyes with warm water at least so I can open them.

"Is my mama coming?" I ask, hoping she still hasn't reached her. I can see, now that my eyes are open, that it's about fifteen "short minutes" to lunch time and I'm surprised that I was sleeping all that time.

"We haven't reached her yet," she says. "If we don't reach her before lunch, we'll get someone to bring you some lunch. Okay?" She finishes cleaning off the crust from my eyes asks me if I need anything and I ask her if I can have some water and while I'm at it, I might as well go to the bathroom.

She shows me to a little bathroom that I never even knew was there. It's so tiny, I can hardly turn around, but it has a sink in it. After I use the bathroom, I wash my face with cool water, dry my face with the scratchy brown paper towels that are in the holder above the sink, and look at my eyes to see if they might look any better. There's a little clock on the wall so I know that the lunch bell will ring in about five minutes, so I'm really feeling hopeful that I might get to have lunch before I go home.

Just as I'm coming out of the bathroom, though, I can hear my mama's voice in the front office. The nurse is leading her to the zoo tank room where I was sitting earlier. I go back to the room and the nurse is telling my mother that she has no choice except to send me home with my pink eye being so contagious and all and that I should see a doctor first thing.

Mama says she figured that was the problem when Evelyn's mama caught up with her at home and told her that the school nurse was trying to reach her. She came right up as soon as she heard, she tells the nurse.

Just as my mother is finishing explaining how she, like a miracle, showed up without actually talking to the nurse, the lunch bell rings.

"I guess you'll get to go home after all," the office secretary says with a smile.

I don't think she knows that it's not a good thing for me that I'm going home now, just as the bell is ringing for lunch.

The nurse gives a look like she knows that I'm disappointed, and my mother helps me gather my books and put my jacket on. My socks are slouching around my ankles and usually I would bend down and pull them up, but I don't care right now about my socks and how they will slouch so far, they slip down into my floppy shoes if I don't pull them up.

We are walking down the hall toward the door and my mother is clicking her false teeth and holding her jaws tight and I know that means she's upset that I'm missing lunch. Mrs. Marshall rushes to catch up to us. "Isabelle," she says, "take this. I had it in my little cupboard." She presses a pack of peanut butter crackers in one of my hands and a little carton of milk in the other. "And I had this in my little fridge in my office," She finishes. "I hope you feel better."

"Thank you, ma'am," I say before my mama and me make our way to the exit.

We walk outside, down the three steps, past the heaps of charcoal by the burner room, and across the school yard where all the kids are lining up outside the lunchroom. The smell of lunch is floating up across the school yard, Macaroni-n-cheese, roast pork, hot rolls and apple sauce, with chocolate milk to drink.

Chapter Thirty-Seven

On the way home I eat my crackers and drink my milk that the school nurse gave me. Mama said it was okay to eat it because Joseph was at Evelyn's house with Barbara and Evelyn's mama. She said she would feed him something from her cupboard. I'm trying to be thankful to the Lord for what I have, but it's hard to be thankful for peanut butter crackers with the smell of food from the lunchroom still in my nose.

If I chew slow and really think about the taste of peanut butter mixed with cracker in my mouth, then followed by a gulp of the milk from Mrs. Marshall's little refrigerator, I feel pretty glad to at least have that. I eat the second to last cracker and I've spaced out the gulps of milk just right to have some after every cracker when it comes to me that maybe I should offer Mama one. I'm holding the last one in my hand and thinking this to myself while we walk along saying nothing.

Then it's like she knows I'm having some sort of thought like that because she suddenly stops and says, "Hold on," and she pulls her pack of cigarettes out of her shiny black purse that's made of patent leather. She likes this purse because it's fancy and she said it makes her feel rich with the way it shines and you can do a quick check on how you look in the reflection it makes. She said she likes this purse even if it was a "hand over" from Aunt Gracie who thinks she's better than us. Mama says it's a "hand over" not a "hand down" because if we call it a "hand down" it means we are lower than the person who gave it to us and Aunt Gracie ain't no better than us even if she's got a nice car and house and husband who makes a lot of money. Walking is better for you than driving in a car everywhere and she could have Aunt Gracie's husband if she wanted to anyway. That's what Mama says when she gets going on that subject.

"I could steal him right away. So what if she's got glamourous red lipstick on. Her teeth are yellow as this table," she says and slams her hand down on our kitchen table. No, she doesn't want Aunt Gracie's life, "Wouldn't trade with her for nothing," she says and clicks her false teeth hard.

"Hang on. Hold this." she hands me her shiny purse and smacks the half empty pack of Winstons on the palm of her hand, pulls one out, and strikes a match to light it. Just then a cool breeze comes along and puts the match out before she has a chance to light up.

I'm looking at my reflection in the purse to see if my eyes are crusty again. Mama's got the cigarette hanging from her mouth and she's trying to cup her hands over it when she lights the next match. She only has two matches left and along comes another breeze and blows out the second one.

"Doggone it!" Mama stamps her foot hard on the sidewalk and turns her back to where the wind came from and away from me, hunches over, and cups her hands around the cigarette and strikes the last match. For a second, I can't tell if it's lit or not and it feels like a long silence while I wait to see.

Finally, after the long second I can see smoke flowing in between Mama's fingers and rising up. She sucks in deep and lets the smoke come out of her nose and I feel like cheering for her because I know it makes her happy.

"There," she says, satisfied. "All I need is my smokes and my coffee and I'm alright and I'm going to have me a big ol' tumbler of coffee when we get home," and she winks at me. I know I can eat the last cracker that I'm still holding onto and chase it with the last bit of milk.

I hand Mama back her shiny purse and she hangs it on her left elbow. Every time she brings her cigarette to her mouth, I can see her glancing at her reflection in her purse. We're on our way walking again and I eat the last cracker since Mama has her cigarette. I chew it slow and keep the mushy peanut butter and cracker on my tongue for a minute, so I can taste it longer, then flush it down with the last swallow of milk that wasn't cold anymore.

When we get home, Mama has to go over and get Joseph. She couldn't bring him with her to get me, she said because he was screaming and crying that he didn't want to walk and even worse, he could feel the seams of his socks on his feet when he put his shoes on this morning, so he pulled off his shoes and threw them in the garbage. Now Mama will have to dig for them when she gets back from getting Joseph.

I'm alone here and it's so quiet except for the drip, drip, drip of the faucet in the kitchen sink and the rumble and whispery hum of the refrigerator. I sit at the window for a couple of minutes in Mama's chair and listen to the quiet.

Drip. Drip. Rumble. Hum. Drip. Drip. Rumble. Hum.

I think then to just look in the refrigerator just in case Mama got something and she was going to surprise me with it. In the three seconds that it takes me to get up and open the refrigerator, I've gone and dreamed up a whole smorgasbord of surprise food in the fridge; a chocolate pudding pie! A pot of beef stew with carrots and potatoes that all I got to do is heat it up on the stove! Cheese, the dark yellow kind with the red wax covering! Maybe even ice cream in the freezer!

In the excitement of my thoughts, I fling open the refrigerator door. Nothing... except for a lettuce leaf floating in the bottom. It's starting to get mold on it. And a half a slice of bread - an end piece wrapped up tight in the plastic bag it came in. Nobody likes the end piece, but Mama says the crust gives you a good singing voice if you eat it.

When the refrigerator is empty like this, I do this thing where I open it, look in, close it, and open it again. I look inside again, like maybe I was mistaken that there was no food waiting there or maybe there will be some magic when I open it back up or maybe even God would answer the prayer of a 12-year-old girl who was snatched up from her breakfast because of her sore eyes and was sent home with an empty stomach just moments after the lunch bell rang.

Maybe I'll open the door and there will be not just one end piece in the plastic bag, but a whole bunch of loaves of end pieces and Mama and Joseph and me will eat every last piece, except we'd save some for Stevie and later tonight all four of us will sing around the yellow table with our voices all clear and pretty as songbirds. And when we get tired, Joseph, Stevie, and me will drift off to sleep with our bellies still full of song bread and Mama would just keep singing and her songbird voice would be floating in and out of our dreams until morning.

I close the refrigerator door one last time and push it tight shut since it doesn't work right half the time and it pops open letting the cold air out. I take a seat back on Mama's perch again and listen to the quiet. Drip, drip, rumble, hum, drip, drip, rumble hum. The faucet is wasting water and the refrigerator is cooling a sliver of song bread and a moldy lettuce leaf.

Mama and Joseph come back and bust up the quiet of the house. Mama brought me a half of a peanut butter sandwich that Joseph didn't finish since he had some tomato soup too at Evelyn's house. Evelyn's mama gave us a few frozen chicken wings and some cornmeal and Mama puts it in the refrigerator until she's ready to cook it later.

Joseph runs through the house making a motor sound. He's an airplane with his arms out. He's a jumping airplane, jumping off the arm of the couch. He's barefooted and he's wearing Stevie's Flipper t-shirt inside out because he couldn't stand the feeling of the tag on his neck. The shirt is so big on him it looks like a dress, so the only way I know that he isn't wearing anything except underwear is that I see Mama has his pants in her hand until she tosses them over onto the couch, lets out a big sigh, and throws up her hands.

Joseph hardly ever sits still for even a minute and he's almost never quiet except when he's sleeping. He's always climbing or jumping or falling, making bruises and scrapes on himself. He's always running or screaming or crying or kicking or pushing or pulling or screaming again and crying again and sometimes laughing; laughing with his eyes or his whole body on the floor holding on to his stomach.

Mama says something's sure wrong with him with the way he can't be still, can't be quiet. I think that might be true and it makes me mad sometimes because all his fit pitching gets all the attention away from anything I might have to say to Mama. Sometimes I think I might hate him for it, but right now I'm watching him through my sore eyes that burn, and I think he looks beautiful with his eyes so brown, they're black and opened wide just before he jumps off the couch. He jumps over the coffee table and laughs while Mama shrieks at him that he'll kill himself if he doesn't quit it.

Right now, I don't hate him because I love the way his curly black hair is long and falling in his face while he laughs. I love the way his lips are red like a doll's lips or like he just had a red lollipop, but he didn't. I feel myself smile while he's laying on his back breathing hard and looking up at me to see my reaction. Right now, I don't hate him since he's making me smile with his little tan feet in the air.

"Izzee, you see me?" he sings, and smiles and his teeth are perfect little white squares behind his red lips. "Iiiizzeee! See me?" he sings louder.

"Yeah, I see you." I sing back.

"Your eyes hurt, Izzee? You got burny eyes?"

"Yeah," I say.

"Don't cry, Izzee, 'cause it gonna get more burny."

"I'm not crying, Joey."

"Okay." He's still on his back and pushing his feet up and almost over his head so that his voice changes. "Laugh, Izzee, laugh a' me."

I laugh. I still don't know where he came from when I was five years old and Mama somehow had a new baby even though she doesn't have a husband. I remember he came home screaming and crying so much it near 'bout drove Mama crazy. She said she was so worn out from hearing his voice always wanting something from her when she had nothing left of herself to give anybody. She was mad at him a lot for crying when lots of times it was just because he needed changing and his rash was burning his bottom.

Stevie and me would tend to him and Stevie would say to Mama, "He just needs a new diaper, Mama."

So, Mama would say, "Then put one on him. I ain't got time since I have to get dressed to go out and slave away to put food on the table." And then she'd mumble something down low about a "son of a bitch" whose name was Bento or Bernardo or something like that that I couldn't tell for sure. She'd put her red lipstick on thick, kiss at herself in the mirror, and go out the door to work. Sometimes she worked waiting tables at the Hasty House and sometimes we didn't know where she went. She'd go out when the sun was starting to go down and not come back until the middle of the night when she would come in thumping around and swearing away, picking up where she left off about this same "son of a bitch" whose name I couldn't really tell except that it started with a "B" for sure.

So, Stevie or me would change him and tend to him as best we could. As much as I felt like I hated Joseph sometimes for acting all kinds of wild, I felt bad for him too because it seemed like from the very start, he had to kick and scream for, or grab at and take anything he needed.

"That one there, he's like a storm," Aunt Gracie said once." A storm that came from out of nowhere." She wanted to know how Mama got him in her belly too, but Mama wasn't telling her anything.

Joseph hops from the floor and in two seconds he's over at the TV pulling the button to turn it on. He pulls it out to turn it on, pushes it back in, on, off, on, off. Mama can hear it from the kitchen where she's sitting with her cigarette and coffee.

"Leave it off or on, Joseph!" she hollers.

"Want it on," he whines.

"Then leave it on," I say and hold on to his hand, so he can't turn it off again. He leaves it on and then changes the stations really fast with the dial until it lands on a show called *Mr. Rogers' Neighborhood*. This show always seems to make a calm come over Joseph while he sits and stares at the screen and talks back to Mr. Rogers, who talks in a quiet voice right to the kids watching. He tells the kids who are watching that they are special and even fancy.

Mr. Rogers is singing that it's time to go and he's leaving out the side door of his house. Joseph's calm moment is over, so he starts turning the dial again as fast as he can.

"Don't turn it so fast," I say. "You're going to break it, then Mama's going to be mad." So, he turns it slower and stops on "Sesame Street" as it's coming on.

"Sunny day. Everything Aaaa okay," Joseph sings with the TV and runs around the room again, jumping on the couch until the music stops. Big Bird is telling us about the sound "sh" and I think, "I know a word that starts with "sh", but I can't say it out loud." and I have to laugh to myself. Joseph wants to know what's funny. I tell him "nothing." He doesn't believe me.

"What funny? What funny?" he asks over and over and hangs on my arm.

"Nothing, Joey. Get off me!"

"Get off her, Joseph!" Mama screams from the kitchen without even seeing what's happening. She doesn't need to see. She's always on the side of whoever Joseph is bothering.

He gets off me and goes over to the TV again and starts turning the channels again fast.

"Stop it!" I say mean-like, "You're going to break it!"

"Turn it! Sumpin else!" Joseph yells at me. I start to turn the channel slow until I get to something I want to see. It's a story, but it's not Mama's story. She likes to watch *Days of Our Lives*, but I know this isn't it because it's some other actors. This lady is crying, I think, because her husband left her or something. Joseph reaches up and starts changing the channel again.

"Stop it!" I snap, and whack at his hand landing a good solid smack on the top side of it.

He starts wailing like I just almost killed him and that about does it for Mama. She comes running in hollering in that high-sounding scream.

"What the hell happened?!"

"He won't stop changing the channel!" I whine at her.

Joseph is over on the couch now curled up with his knees tucked up in Stevie's Flipper inside out shirt that he's going to be mad that Joseph is stretching out. He's still wailing away and getting snot all over the shirt.

"Hate you!" he's crying, "She hit me, Mama! Hate you!" I don't know if the "hate you" is for me or for Mama, but I figure it might be for both of us because I slapped him and now Mama won't tend to him. She just leaves him there crying and tells me to come on in the kitchen. She'll make me a tumbler of coffee and I can have the last piece of bread that's in the refrigerator to go with it.

"Let him have the damn TV!" she says, and we go off into the kitchen. I

230

look back at Joseph who is still crying, but more quiet.

I'm sitting at the kitchen table drinking black coffee from a tall orange Tupper Ware cup. I don't like the taste too much, but Mama says it will take away the hunger some, so I drink it. We have a little sugar, so I'm allowed to put some in to take the edge off the bitterness of the coffee. I take the last piece of bread I got from the refrigerator and I dip in the coffee and imagine I'm having some kind of fancy tea and crumpets that my teacher says is a snack that people in England eat.

The coffee is hot, and I hold the cup under my nose to let the steam from it go into my nose. I'm starting to like the smell of coffee. I close my eyes and realize that my eyes are burning away like they're on fire. I hadn't noticed it so much while I was fighting with Joseph, who is being a little too quiet now for Mama's liking.

She gets up to go check on him and finds him sitting on the floor with a crayon and drawing away on her coffee table. It's a picture of Big Bird and even though he's not supposed to be drawing on Mama's table, I think it looks better than anything I could ever draw. I'm wondering if Mama's going to be mad or happy to see that he's such a good drawer at six years old.

I'm standing just behind her, so I can see that Big Bird has trees around him and the beginning of a truck or car or something with wheels on it that Joseph was working on in quiet before we came and discovered what he was doing. He's stopped drawing with the broken blue crayon frozen in motion on the back wheel of Big Bird's car and he's looking up at Mama with his eyes wide open.

"I draw Big Bird, Mama," he says, and I feel sad at the way he says it like he's begging Mama not to be mad. I'm afraid she's going to hit him for what he did and for a second, it's like no one is breathing between the three of us. The air in the room is just thick and hanging there and we're frozen right along with Joseph's broken blue crayon.

Then Mama doesn't say anything to Joseph, but she turns on her heels back toward the kitchen and starts smacking her forehead with the palm of her hand.

"I can't take it no more! I can't take it! I can't take it! I can't take it!" she screams and each time she says she can't take it, she smacks her hand on her forehead hard so there's big round red mark where the palm of her hand hit each time. "Goddamn it! I can't have nothin'! I can't take it no more! I work my fingers to the bone and we ain't got nothin! I can't take it no more!" She's screeching high now, and she puts her hands around her own throat to choke herself.

She's squeezing tight and her face is getting red. "Goodbye cruel world!" she's gasping.

"Mama! Don't Mama! Don't!" I rush up to her and pull on her arm to pull one hand free.

"Mama, don't!" I holler.

Joseph starts crying and saying he's sorry about Big Bird on her table. He's sorry he drew on her table. "Mama don't killed Mama, I good now, Mama!" he cries.

Mama stops trying to choke herself and hangs her head and goes off into the kitchen. Joseph is just crying now, and he doesn't care about snot on his face. He breaks the blue crayon some more and throws it across the room. My feelings for him are like they're on a roller coaster ride, because now I feel so sad for him and want to help him stop crying.

I have some Kleenex in my pocket that hasn't been used yet on my eyes and I take it out and wipe Joseph's face with it. He keeps crying and I shush him like I remember Mémère used to shush me when I was little like him. I take his hand and lead him to sit on the couch and he wants to sit on my lap. I don't know if it's such a good idea because I'm afraid he'll catch the sore eyes too, but I can't say 'no' to him when he climbs on my knees and curls up with his

232

head buried in my shirt. His tears are warm and soaking through, but I don't care right now.

I'm rocking him back and forth like a baby. He's stopping crying and he's reaching up and twirling my hair with his little fingers, "Mama hate me," he says in a whisper.

"No, she doesn't, "I whisper back but if I was to tell the truth, I'm not so sure. I just rock him to keep him calm. I can hear Mama in the kitchen knocking things around and swearing to herself about that son of a bitch whose name starts with a "B", Bento, or Bernardo or something like that.

Later that night Evelyn comes in on the Walkie-talkie and I hear it making a staticky sound from my room the while I'm in the kitchen, finishing up my chicken wing and fried cornmeal cake. I go grab my Walkie-talkie and flashlight from my windowsill and sit looking for the flash of Evelyn's flashlight.

"Come in Eagle. It's Sparrow here. Over," I say. I think I sound like an official on my Walkie-talkie, like a police person or a truck driver.

"Come in Sparrow. What you doin' girl?" Eagle says.

"I'm just waiting for your flashlight. Over."

"You ain't got to say 'over' every time you talk."

Eagle says, "I'm putting new batteries in my flashlight. Hold on."

Then she flashes it twice. Twice means "hello".

Three flashes mean, "really good day."

She flashes it three times.

"My teacher let me borrow her video camera for my project. We can make a movie when your eyes are better. When are your eyes going to be better?" she asks, with her voice staticky.

"That sounds like fun, making a movie. I don't know how long my eyes are going to be like this. I'm going to the doctor tomorrow."

"Okay. Hey, I gotta go, though. Mama's calling me. Flashlights," she says.

That means we flash our flashlights out our windows to say goodnight. She flashes first, then I do back. We do this for six flashes until we both take three turns. We don't remember why we started doing this and why we chose six flashes. We just did.

Chapter Thirty-Eight

Friday morning Mama let me sleep in a little bit since I have an appointment at the doctor's office for my sore eyes and I won't be going to school today. I woke up again with my eyes stuck shut. We don't have any milk now to wash them open with, so I just wash them with warm water from the faucet.

I don't know what I'm going to wear, but I don't care. It doesn't matter if my pants are too high or if I have stains on my shirt since I won't be at school for people to make fun of me about it. I just grab a pair of brown corduroy pants and a red shirt that used to be my favorite until a girl in my class told me it used to be hers, but she gave it to Good Will where my mama bought it for me. I tried to say that I got it from JC Penney, but then no sooner did I say that she was pulling at my collar from behind and showing everyone the tag in the back with her name scribbled on it.

"If you got it from JC Penney's, then why does it have *my* name on the tag?" She said, and she and her friends started laughing out loud and walked away leaving me standing there wilting like a weed.

Mama says she's sorry there's no breakfast. She saved some corn bread from last night and gave the last piece of it to Joseph for breakfast. Stevie left for school early, so he'll eat at school. She'll make me a tumbler of coffee, though, if I want it, but we don't got any sugar for it. I'll have a cup anyway, I say. I drink my coffee and listen to the radio telling what's for lunch today at school, "Spaghetti and meatballs, garlic bread, apple cobbler, white milk to drink."

My stomach is dying from being too empty and lets out a growl like it's angry and I take a sip of my bitter black coffee. Suddenly, I feel like I'm going to be sick, so I don't drink too much of the coffee, so as not to give me anything to throw up just in case.

Mama sighs a lot and says down low, "At least this morning Joseph ain't misbehaving like he usually does."

He's dressed in a purple sweat suit, that used to be mine, and sitting, watching TV. He's laughing at something. He doesn't care if his sweat suit is purple or a girl's sweat suit if he can't feel the tags in the back.

"This morning we're lucky," Mama says, "because Joseph don't seem to care if he feels the seams of his socks," and then "We gotta get going," and takes a long puff off her cigarette while she stands in the doorway signaling to Joseph to come on. She lets the smoke come out of her nose and he laughs out loud and throws his head back with his big black curls falling across his face.

I think for a moment that we look like a happy family in a magazine ad with Joseph laughing and Mama and me looking on with smiles on our faces. Except in an ad the Mama wouldn't be smoking a cigarette, the laughing boy wouldn't be wearing his sister's hand me overs and his sister, whose name is Isabelle, wouldn't be standing there wearing high water pants and a shirt with a tag in the collar that says the name "Sheila" in the back.

We walk to the doctor's office and I don't know what feels worse, my eyes or my stomach. They both burn. I think my stomach wins this one because it

236

feels three kinds of bad. First it burns from being empty, then it feels all stirred up like I'm going to throw up the nothing that's in there, then it feels like somebody punched me square across my stomach right where my belly button is. My eyes just burn. I could stand my eyes burning if I just had some food for my stomach.

Joseph is hopping and skipping a little in front of us and being careful not to step on cracks since Stevie told him that it would break Mama's back if he stepped on them. I know it's not true now even though I used to think that too since Stevie told me that. I let him think it though, since it seems to give him something to think about while he's going along.

We get to the doctor's and wait in the waiting room. I sit back in the chair and close my eyes and listen to the sound of the doctor's office phone ringing. The secretary answers it, "Dr. Roddin's office." And then, "Oh my! We'll see what Dr. Roddin has opening for later today," then I hear her tapping away at her typewriter.

Mama's sitting next to me whistling through her false teeth at some high-priced car ad in the magazine she picked up from the table. "Must be nice," she says and whistles through her false teeth again.

There's another mother here with her boy and he's at least two heads bigger than me, even though his mama said he's not but seven. I think he's awful big for seven, but that's not something you just say to someone, so I keep my mouth shut.

Then I hear the giant boy say to Joseph, "Are you a girl?"

Joseph says, "No. I not a girl."

"Why you wearin' girls' clothes?" the giant boy asks.

"This not girl clothes," Joseph says back.

"Yah huh. Purple ain't no boy color."

"Is too," Joseph says.

The giant boy's mother finally decides to chime in and tells him to stop talking about Joseph's clothes. He leans over onto his mama's knee and whispers out loud, "But he's wearing girl clothes."

"Shhh!" his mother says back at him.

Just then the doctor calls me back and we go back to a smaller room and Joseph throws himself on the floor and starts pulling at his shirt. He can feel the tag.

The doctor doesn't take long to tell my mother that I have pink eye and he gives her a tube of some medicine to put in my eyes and he gives her a prescription to fill for later.

"It will take a few days for her eyes to get better. She has a pretty bad case here," he tells my mama not to let anybody else get too close to me so nobody else catches it.

"How long has she had the symptoms?" he's asking questions and talking about me as if I'm not here.

"Well, just a couple of days," Mama says.

"This looks like it's been more than a couple of days," he says.

I answer that it has been only a couple of days, but he acts like he can't hear me, and she starts telling Mama how important it is to get this sort of thing treated quickly so others don't get it.

"Okay," Mama says. She's not arguing with the doctor. She just says thank you for the medicine and come on, Joseph. She reaches down to take his hand and he's pulled off his shirt. He doesn't want to wear a girl shirt, he says. I hop down off the table and follow Mama.

Mama's not arguing with Joseph. He can come on with his shirt off for all she cares.

"Better get your shirt back on," the smiling nurse says to Joseph when we get back to the waiting room.

"No!" Joseph says.

"Mama!" whispers giant boy, "He don't have a shirt on now!"

"Shh. Mind your business!" his mother whispers back.

"You want a lollipop?" the smiling nurse asks Joseph. I think she's kind of pretty, but she's got kind of a big nose. Not as big as Katrina Arnold's nose, but it's big enough so it's hard to focus on anything else on her face when she's talking.

Joseph is focusing on a bucket of lollipops that she's waving in front of him and nodding his head "yes" at the question of whether he wants a lollipop.

"Put your shirt on and you can have a lollipop," she says and looks at my mother to see if it's okay. Yes, he can have one. He lets Mama put his girl shirt back on him and plunges his hand in the bucket and grabs a hand full of lollipops.

"Just one. Okay?" the nurse says in a sweet voice. "Just one for you and one for your sister if she wants one." I nod my head, yes. Joseph takes a grape one and I take an orange one.

We step outside and the sunshine is sticking pins in my eyes again. I suck on my orange lollipop and think it's the best thing in the world. It tastes just like an orange. Then I wish for a real orange and it's not so great anymore.

By the time we are halfway home, Joseph has pulled off his shirt again and is walking bare chested and doesn't care that the wind is starting to blow cold making huge piles of leaves in people's yards blowing around like leaf tornadoes. Joseph wants to play in the leaves and he's pulling away from Mama and jumping in them.

While he's rolling around in the leaves, he pulls off his girl sweatpants too and shoes, so when he decides to get up and come with us, he can't find his pants in the leaves, so he has to walk with us all the way home in just his underwear and socks.

Mama is holding his shirt in one hand and his shoes in the other and she's wagging her head and walking ahead of us. She's got her shiny purse hanging from her wrist and I remember how she said it made her feel rich. I don't think it's making her feel rich right now. Because you can't feel rich when you fed your little boy the last cornbread there was, so there's no breakfast for your daughter who has sore eyes and then you had to walk to the doctor and all the way back with your little boy who won't put on his shirt and lost his pants because he didn't know they were girl clothes until a giant boy at the doctor's office told him so; so you wouldn't feel rich even if you had a hundred shiny purses to look into and see yourself in.

When we get home, Mama tells me I got to watch Joseph so she can go out begging for some food.

"I hate it!" she says with her head in her hands. I hope she doesn't start choking herself again. I don't think I can stop her from killing herself dead right before our eyes since I feel so shaky from being hungry.

"I hate this beggin' like some kind of white trash! How else we gonna eat? Somebody's got to do it. It might as well be me beggin' like some dog. It's because your father! That dirty dog! He ain't nothin' but a bum. No good for nothin'!" Even though it seems like she's talking to me because she's talking about my father who's not around, she's walking off into the kitchen leaving me and Joseph behind in the living room while her voice trails off behind her.

"Som' bitch! That som' bitch! Done did this to me. I hate you! I hate you!" she says. Now I don't know if she's talking about my own daddy or that other person she calls "son of a bitch" with a name that starts with a "B" that I can't quite make out.

I'm standing at the kitchen door and watching her walk back and forth with her head in her hands. I don't know why I'm standing here since I can't do anything if she starts to choke herself. I wish I could save her. I wish a lot that I could give my mama everything, so she won't hang her head and cry or smack her forehead with her hand until its red or near about choke herself to death. She stops walking back and forth and reaches in her purse and grabs something. It's her ID card.

"I need this in case they find me face down in a puddle of blood somewhere, so they'll know who I am."

A puddle of blood. That's how she always describes how someone will be found if they're lost and then found dead. When I think of a puddle, I think it's a lot and how much would someone have to bleed to make a whole puddle of blood? I know I'm not supposed to think stuff like this and if I was to tell someone, they would for sure say I'm crazy. I shiver myself away from my thoughts just as Mama slings her purse across the kitchen and all the stuff that was inside it spills out onto the floor.

"Take care of Joseph. Make sure he don't kill himself. Stevie will be home before too long," she says and goes out the door before I can say anything back.

I'm picking up the stuff from her purse from all over the floor. I can't help but cry right now even though I know it will make my eyes worse.

"You cry, Izzee?" Joseph is on his knees next to me. "You cry? You eyes burny?" he asks me.

"Yeah," I say, and I can see my reflection in Mama's shiny purse when I pick it up off the floor.

"No cry, Izzee," Joseph says and pats me on my shoulder. For some reason this makes me feel even more sad, but I wipe my face on my sleeve and try to stop crying so Joseph doesn't cry too.

"I'm okay, Joe. I won't cry anymore." My eyes are on fire and my stomach is stirring around in flips, then burning, then turning flips again and growling like it's mad.

Joseph is looking through the stuff in Mama's purse. He found a piece of Juicy Fruit and holds it up and breathes in deep with his surprise.

"Gum! Mama got gum! I can have it, Izzee?" he's asking, and I can't say no even if I think Mama would say no and that's *her* last piece of gum and can't she have *nothing* to herself, doggone it!

He chews the gum so hard and fast I'm afraid he'll bite his tongue.

"Mmmmm," he says, and he closes his eyes like he's in Heaven.

At 2:30 Mama isn't back yet, so I sit on the couch with Joseph and watch *The Brady Bunch*. Joseph sings with the song that's at the beginning. I like to watch this show and sometimes I like to imagine what it might be like to be in that family with a daddy who works drawing houses and Mama who's always in a pretty dress with her hair just right and she never tries to choke herself because she doesn't have worries like my mama.

Stevie said Mr. Brady makes a lot of money thinking up how to build houses and that's what he wants to do when he grows up. I think that's a good idea and ask him if he'll make a house for us. He says we'll be all grown up too with jobs of our own by the time he gets a job as an "architect". That's what he says it's called that Mr. Brady does. I think it sounds like a fancy job and I hope Stevie can have a fancy job someday.

Stevie says I'll have my own fancy job and that I can buy my own house, but he'll make one for my mama, so she won't have to worry any more about the rent like she does.

The Brady's maid, whose name is Alice, just called them all to dinner and they come running to the table all happy and I really wish I lived in that family, except I would want Stevie and Mama to be there instead of the Brady's mother and one of the boys, and Joseph too. He could take the place of Bobby and he probably wouldn't be so crazy like he is since everything would be perfect with the way they all get along so great from not ever having to be so hungry it makes you mad.

Stevie gets home and he comes in and drops his green book bag on the floor in the living room and sits cross legged on the floor to watch the perfect Brady family with us.

"You got sore eyes?" he asks me since he knows we went to the doctor this morning.

"Yeah, and I got some ointment stuff that Mama has to put in them later," I say.

"Don't get near me," he says. "I don't want to catch it. Where's Mama?"

"She go beg," Joseph chimes in. Stevie looks at me.

"Yeah. She went to try to get some food because there's nothing here." I knew he was looking at me to see if Joseph knew what he was talking about.

"Oh," he says and lets out a big sigh.

"You brought sumpin' Stevie?" Joseph's pulling on Stevie's bag to look inside.

"No, there's nothing in there," he says. "Just books and you can't eat those."

"Get sumpin in pantry, Stevie?" Now Joseph is pulling on Stevie's shirt and pulling him toward the pantry that's just between the kitchen and living room.

"Come see, Stevie. Come see," he says.

"There's nothing there, Joey, come sit with me and watch TV," Stevie answers him.

"No, come see, Stevie," he's pulling harder on Stevie's shirt.

"Why don't you have any clothes on? Why do you only have on underwear?" Stevie tries to change the subject.

"He took 'em off," I answered his question since Joseph wasn't listening.

"Come see, Stevie!" he's pulling Stevie's shirt harder.

"Stop, Joey! There's nothing there!" he yells at Joseph and Joseph lets go of his shirt.

"I go look!" He goes off into the pantry. We can hear him moving things around.

"Joey, you better not climb on anything!" Stevie yells and gets up from sitting cross legged watching the perfect Brady Bunch with their wonderful dinner.

Just at that time there's a great crashing sound and Joseph let's out a wail.

We both rush in to see what happened and find Joseph laying on his back right on top of the big metal bucket of dirty dishes that we keep on the floor in the pantry. I don't know why we have this giant bucket of dirty dishes in the pantry. I don't know how they got there and why nobody ever washes any of them or why we don't just throw them away. We never even use these dishes, and no one hardly ever dares lift the big top that's made out of aluminum because of the stink like something rotten that floods out from the bucket.

But Joseph was standing on it and it slipped open. The aluminum top crashed onto the floor and Joseph is laying in his underwear with his arms and legs stretched up and wailing and crying away on top of dirty plates, cups, pots, pans and bowls. Stevie scoops him up and Joseph is hanging on to Stevie's neck and burying his face in Stevie's shoulder.

"I told you not to climb," Stevie scolded Joseph.

"Want sompin' eat!" Joseph yells and starts crying so hard that he starts coughing and gagging like he's going to throw up.

"Here, hold him, while I look behind those boxes." Stevie hands Joseph over to me and he's still crying so hard I'm worried he's going to fall out from fainting if he doesn't throw up first.

"I'm looking, Joey, I'm looking. Shh. Shh," Stevie tries to hush him.

I sit with him right on the pantry floor until he hushes enough so he stops coughing. I hope he doesn't get sore eyes from being so close to me again.

Stevie puts the top back on the bucket of dishes and stands on it to reach behind some cardboard boxes up on the shelf. He pulls out a can of tomatoes and Joseph acts like he's just got some surprise birthday present.

"It's no good, though," Stevie says. "The can is swollen."

"Eat 'matoes," Joseph says.

"No, Joe, we'll get ptomaine if we eat that. We have to throw it out," Stevie says.

"No. We eat it! Want sumpin eat!" Joseph is kicking at the bucket of dishes and he starts crying full blast again when Stevie throws the tomatoes in a garbage bag on the floor.

"I'm looking for more food, Joey. Hold on," he says and digs some more behind the boxes.

"Hmmm," he says and pulls out a plastic Tupper Ware container with some flour in it.

Joseph stops crying and we both look on while Stevie opens the top of the Tupper Ware slow like something might jump out on him if he lets it out too fast. We are watching Stevie and it's like we aren't even breathing while we wait to see if he thinks we can eat this flour.

"Smells okay," he says after he sniffs in deep into the container.

"If it doesn't have any bugs in it, maybe I can make some pancakes," he says.

"Pancakes! Want pancakes!" Joseph is excited.

"Hold on. Let's pour it in a big bowl and see if there are any bugs in it. "

"Okay," we agree. So, we go around the yellow table and Stevie pulls out a bowl that we keep in the refrigerator, so the roaches couldn't get on it. He pours the flour into the bowl and we all hold our breath looking for bugs. Stevie stirs it with his finger and leans in closer to get a better look.

Finally, he says, "No bugs."

Joseph claps and cheers, "Yeah, pancakes! We have pancakes!"

Stevie finds a little bit of margarine in the door of the refrigerator and melts it in the bottom of a frypan. He let me stir the water into the flour after he made sure I didn't put too much in there. I let Joseph stir it some too since he wanted to help. We stand by the stove and watch the flour cook and sizzle and Stevie flips it with a spatula when it has enough bubbles on one side. The melting margarine mixed with the cooking flour smells like heaven, and I'm glad at that moment that Joseph made Stevie look in the pantry for something. There was enough flour to make three pancakes, just enough for us three.

Stevie said he only wanted a half of one and Joseph and me can have the rest.

We also found a little packet of grape jelly and a little packet of Sweet-N-Low from the bottom of the silverware drawer. Stevie ripped open the Sweet-N-Low and squeezed the clear liquid onto Joseph's pancake.

"Mmm!" Joseph says.

I squeeze the grape jelly onto my pancake and Stevie just eats his half a pancake in two quick bites, so he doesn't need anything on top of it, he says.

Joseph finishes his pancake so quick I don't know if he even chewed it up first before he swallowed it. He drinks water from the same orange plastic cup that I used this morning when Mama gave me some coffee. He has the cup over his mouth and he's talking into it.

"I still hungry," he says, and his voice is muffled in the cup.

I look at Stevie and he's putting his hand on his forehead and holding his head like a grown up does when they're worried about something. I still have some pancake left so, I break it in half and slide it over to Joseph. He eats it in a hurry and sits back and smiles with grape jelly smeared on his face.

I eat what's left of mine before he has a chance to say he's still hungry.

Stevie finds enough instant coffee to make a cup of coffee and he shares it with me. Joseph says coffee tastes yucky, so he doesn't want any. He just drinks his water.

We are sitting around the table with our flour pancakes just eaten and our unsweetened coffee and Joseph's tumbler cup of water. Stevie is telling a story about a hippopotamus that wears a polka dotted skirt and Joseph is laughing with his whole self. I think how my eyes are burning and I wonder how red they are now.

The Brady Bunch has long since finished their perfect meal their maid cooked up for them. The song is on again.

"The Brady Bunch, The Brady Bunch, That's the waaaay they became the Brady Bunch...dah duh dah daaaah daah dum."

Stevie takes the pan from the stove and finds a little circle of cooked flour left in the pan.

"Hey, a tiny pancake!" he says and pops it into his mouth.

Chapter Thirty-Nine

Mama comes home around five o'clock with a can of beef stew for us to have for supper. She puts it on the counter with a slam.

"That's all I could get," she says. "From all that walking around and begging, that's all I got. Don't nobody got nothin' to offer us."

"What about the food pantry?" I ask because I remember we went to the food pantry before when we didn't have anything to eat. They gave us some cans of corn and green beans and instant mashed potatoes. They even gave us some cinnamon buns.

"Do you think I ain't thought of that? For some reason they ain't open today. I walked all the way the hell over there and they ain't even open. I got blisters on my feet from these shoes rubbing my heels," she says and takes her shoes off fast and kicks them aside. She's sitting on the couch smoking a cigarette butt that she plucked out of her can of old cigarette butts.

Joseph is at Mama's feet asking if we can have the beef stew now and I can see her jaws get tight while she sits stiff and quiet. I try to get Joseph's attention away from asking for food right now.

"Joey, want to go outside?" I ask even though I don't know why I ask that, since I don't want to go out and I know that if he says "yes" I have to go out and watch him.

"No, I want eat." he says.

"We can't eat it now, Joseph," Mama says, "or there won't be nothin' later and you'll go to bed hungry."

He doesn't understand this. All he knows is that he's hungry now, so he starts up again.

"No, Mama, I want eat now," he says and he's still in just his underwear with his knees up against his chest and holding his feet in his hands.

"Can't you ever go play like a normal young'un?" Mama says to Joseph.

"My tummy mad, Mama," Joseph keeps on. I know what he means. When I'm so hungry I can't think of anything except how my stomach is growling at me like a mad dog. I can't play, or read, or run, or anything because my stomach is growling then turning flips and I can't even watch TV because they keep showing commercials with food in them and seeing food on TV makes me want to eat so bad, I cry and cover my face in my hands so Stevie won't think I'm crazy or Joseph won't see me and start crying too. All I want to do is put some food in there to hush it up. Then, I can play like a normal young'un.

So, I know that Joseph can't go play when his tummy is mad. And I know he's not going to take Mama's "no" for an answer right now of whether or not he can have the beef stew now. Mama takes one last suck on her cigarette butt and smashes it out in the ashtray that's overflowing with old cigarette butts.

She sighs all heavy and drags herself into the kitchen with Joseph right behind her.

"Get off my heels, like a dog, on my heels," she says to him. I try to keep him with me in the living room, so she doesn't get mad. I think she's going to open the can of beef stew now, so I tell him if he stays with me in the living room, he can have some beef stew after Mama cooks it.

I'm glad when he doesn't fight me about it and he turns on the TV and plops himself down in front of it on the floor. There's only news on, but he doesn't seem to mind. He just sits with his knees up to his chest again and his feet in his hands.

The news announcer is telling a story about a girl who was found dead in a creek and Joseph is looking up at it with a wrinkle in between his eyes and his mouth is in a big frown, like he understands just how bad this news story is.

"The young girl was taken from her bed while she slept one night two weeks ago while her younger sister, who slept in the bed with her, saw the abductor dragging her sister away." The newsman finished the story.

"Somebody kill girl, Izzee? Why somebody kill girl, Izzee?" he's asking me, and I don't know the answer. I can't believe he's asking me a question like why someone would kill someone else when I'm only 12 and he's only six. I'm about to tell him I don't know when Mama lets out a yell from the kitchen.

"Doggone it!" and we hear something slam. We go to the door of the kitchen to see what's wrong.

"The Goddamn can opener done broke! How am I going to open this now?! Where's Steven, Isabelle? *Now* what am I going to do? Ain't it enough that I had to go out begging and stealing to get one lousy can of beef stew?!"

"Did she say stealing?" I'm thinking to myself and hoping Mama don't get locked up for stealing something because I know that it's against the law, even if it is a lousy can of beef stew that you stole because you got to feed your three hungry children. I'm in my thoughts of Mama going to jail and I haven't answered her yet about where Stevie is. He's in his room probably reading like always. He can do that even when he's hungry.

"Where's Steven?!" Mama's screeching louder.

"He's in his room, reading," I say.

"Steven, get your nose out of that book for a minute and get out here!

Can't you hear I need your help?!" She's screaming at Stevie and she pushes past us and is standing in the living room and hollering down the gray hallway toward Stevie's closed door. He opens his door.

"Come help me figure out how I'm going to open this damn can of beef stew," she says.

"Use the can opener," he says and that sets Mama off into a rage.

"Don't you think I'm smart enough to know to use a can opener?! It done broke and now we ain't got nothin' to open it with! We ain't sufferin' enough with no food, now we ain't got no can opener! That cheap piece of shit can opener! Goddamn it! I can't take it! I can't take it no more! I hate my shitty life! Shitty life! It ain't shitty enough, I guess! We got it bad! We got it bad!" I'm thinking Mama's going to start smacking her head or choking herself because she usually starts that when she says she can't take it anymore.

I'm thinking too that Mama might wind up in Hell for taking God's name in vain like that, but Stevie told me one day you won't end up in Hell if you ask the Lord to forgive you.

"Well Goddamn! I said a swear. Lord forgive me ... Goddamn, I'm sorry, God. Please forgive me. Thanks," he said, and he laughed so hard he could hardly breathe. And he told this joke to Evelyn who thought it was funny too. I wanted to laugh at it too, but I was afraid Stevie might be wrong about the Lord forgiving you as long as you say you're sorry after you say "Goddamn." I just smiled instead.

Stevie doesn't know what Mama wants him to do about the can opener, so he goes into the kitchen and looks for something else to open the can with. He pulls out a small knife from the drawer and wedges it into the little hole that is already in the top of the can from the can opener before it broke apart making Mama's life more shitty.

"You can't use that! You'll break my only knife!" Mama's still screeching at Stevie.

"I don't know what to use then," he says and throws his hands in the air like he's done dealing with the can that's impossible to open now that we don't have a can opener.

"Go next door and borrow a can opener," she says.

"Send Isabelle. I don't want to go," he says back because I know he's embarrassed to go ask.

"She can't go, because she's got sore eyes," Mama answers. "Go on over. I ain't since I done walked all day 'til my feet were sore."

Stevie doesn't argue for long. He almost never gives Mama much of a fight about this sort of thing. I don't know why because I think he could get away with it since he's bigger now and Mama won't smack him or wash his mouth out with Dial soap. He just goes over and doesn't fight Mama on it. Mémère used to say that Stevie was like an angel and that he was going to be a priest someday. She could tell. That was before he started making jokes about saying "Goddamn" though, so Mémère doesn't know about that. So, I don't think he's an angel, but I think he just doesn't got much fight in him maybe because he's hungry.

Anyway, Stevie comes back with a can opener and he even has a cup of corn meal that the neighbors gave him. Mama's happy about that for a minute, until she needs some margarine to cook it with and looks in the refrigerator where she knows she left a little bit that was left over in the door of the refrigerator and where is it and did any of us touch it? Stevie steps up and tells Mama how Joseph was crying for food and how he found the flour and how we had pancakes and how he used the margarine that was in the door to cook it with. That's when Mama sits down in the chair next to the table. She's covering her face in her hands and crying.

"I can go back over and ask for margarine," Stevie offers because he can't stand to see Mama cry like that.

"Okay." Mama's voice is muffled in her hands.

"I go wif you, Stevie?" Joseph is hanging on Stevie's arm.

"Piggyback," Stevie says and turns so that Joseph can climb on his back. Joseph laughs. I'm glad that Joey is happy to have a piggyback, but I feel jealous a little because Stevie used to always give *me* piggyback rides, but he doesn't anymore since I got bigger.

When they are out the door it's quiet except for the sound of the refrigerator humming and thumping and Mama sniffling and whispering while she's crying.

"Oh. When is Jesus coming? Oh. Oh. My kids are starving, Jesus. Don't nobody care. Ohhh. Don't nobody... care..."

I wonder if I should pat my mama's shoulder like Joseph patted mine earlier. I remember how it made me cry more, but how I wanted him to stay right there with his little hand patting my shoulder in a rhythm like a heartbeat.

While I'm thinking about this, it's like I'm just pulled over by something invisible anyway and like I got no choice, I start patting Mama's shoulder in a heartbeat rhythm. She cries some more, and she says sorry to God for taking his name in vain. She's still burying her face, so her voice is still muffled, and she sighs heavy then wipes her face on the sleeve of her shirt. Her mascara ran down her face and is all over her sleeve. She sighs again and keeps wiping her face until the mascara is almost all gone.

"Is it gone?" she looks up from her hands.

"Yeah," I say.

She covers her face again and just sighs a lot into her hands now and I start patting like a heartbeat rhythm again.

"Thank you ... Isabelle," she whispers into her cupped hands.

"You're welcome, Mama," I say and at that moment I love my mama so much I wish I could buy her all the food in the world, so she wouldn't have to tell Jesus nobody cares if her kids are starving. I'd buy cans and cans of food and stock the cupboards to overflowing. And I'd buy a brand-new can opener that isn't a cheap piece of shit can opener so we can open the cans with no problem at all and eat to our heart's content.

Stevie and Joseph are coming back over from next door and we can hear them coming up on the porch.

"Do again, Stevie, do again!" Stevie must have done whatever it was again because Joseph is laughing hard when they come in the door. Stevie puts a whole stick of margarine on the table and a handful of lollipops too. They're all different colors and they look so shiny and beautiful to me laying out on the table.

"They gave us these too. She remembered she had these because Joseph chimed up and asked her if she had any candy."

Joseph wants to know if he can have one now. Mama says yes, he can and so can Stevie and me if we want to. We do. Stevie has a grape one and I have an orange one since orange is my favorite flavor. Joseph copies me and has an orange one.

Mama sets out to cooking the beef stew on the stove. "Let's count the lollipops," Stevie says and so we do. There are 12 of them, take away the ones we just had. I'm adding it up in my head and Joseph puts up his fingers.

"Firteen, fourteen, fiveteen," he counts and holds up the three fingers to show for the three lollipops we ate already.

"Wow! Good counting!" Stevie says. I'm surprised too because Joseph is so good with counting.

"Was that on Sesame Street?" I ask him.

He just shrugs his shoulders up and doesn't pay my question much attention since he's too busy now putting the candies in groups and dividing them up. He looks up and asks if Mama wants candy.

"Sure," she says while she's stirring the beef stew, so it doesn't scorch in the pan.

He thinks for a minute and puts them in four piles. "Mama, Izzee, Me,

Stevie," he says and puts a lollipop in each pile every time he says a name. He leans over the table and counts each pile. I can see the marks from the pans and dishes that he fell on earlier when he was looking for food. It looks like somebody beat him in the back and I wonder if the neighbor saw it and that's why she gave us the lollipops because she felt sad for him.

Mama says that she can't understand how Joseph can be so smart at math when he can't even talk right yet. She says he must have got it from his own daddy and that's the only time she ever said anything about where Joseph came from. But she seemed surprised at her own words after that and closed her mouth shut tight and looked over out of the corner of her eye at Joseph sleeping on the green couch.

Late in the night, Stevie and me are sitting and watching Johnny Carson since we can stay up late on account of it's Friday. Mama is sitting next to Joseph on the couch, taking her finger and moving over his curls from his face.

"He looks like a doll," she says in kind of a whisper. We thought she was talking to us, but when we looked, she didn't even look up at us. She just moved to take the orange lollipop from his fingers and set it down next to him on the coffee table. Joseph stirred a little bit, whined and turned on his side toward us where the TV light is shining on his face and we can see he's smiling in his sleep.

Chapter Forty

After Mama puts the ointment in my eyes I can't open them for a while, so I'm sitting on the couch next to her with my eyes shut tight. We're the only ones awake this early, and I think this would be a good time to have Mama to myself if things were better. But at this moment, things aren't better.

We ate our last can of borrowed food last night after Stevie was able to borrow a can opener, so we could get at it. We had beef stew, a little cornbread hoecakes and lollipops. Stevie and me ate all but two of the lollipops since Mama said we had to leave some for Joseph for when he wakes up because he'll surely be asking for them.

After midnight last night I was sitting up next to Stevie, with an orange lollipop hanging out of my mouth, forcing my eyes to stay open. I like to collect the orange sugary juice from it on my tongue and leave there for a minute before I swallow it. I couldn't keep my eyes open anymore and was awakened by Stevie laughing at me because I was drooling orange lollipop juice all down my chin and on to my shirt. I woke up and finished off the lollipop by crunching it down then fell back to sleep on the green couch with springs poking me in my back.

I even dreamed of lollipops, armies of them, marching across the yellow table in the kitchen while Joseph is standing in the sink wearing a doctor's coat and counting. He was on number 342 when my dream drifted to something else: a drain of swirling gray water and my mama screeching off in the distance that she "can't have nothin'!" I don't know what else I dreamed. I think it was just a fuzzy gray screen in my brain the rest of the night, like when the TV channel goes off the air so there's nothing but a mess of gray moving around on the screen.

So, I'm sitting here next Mama with my eyes shut tight and thinking about how things aren't better, mixed with thoughts of marching lollipops, when for some reason, I ask her if we got anything for breakfast. I know we don't. And I know that asking her can send her off into a fit of some sort, either screaming or crying or a mix of the two. The moment I say it, I wish I hadn't, but my mama surprises me by sitting silent beside me. She's not saying anything, and I would have thought maybe she just fell dead sitting up there next to me on the couch, but I can hear her rustling around in the ashtray that's full of old cigarette butts on the side table. I can hear the scrape of the match on the match box, making that match smell that I like. I can even hear the little flame light the cigarette butt when Mama sucks in on it to get it going. I can hear her breathe out the smoke. I can smell the smoke that smells different than a brand-new cigarette. Mama says low, "It's better than nothin'."

That's one of Mama's favorite things to say. When we have only a can of beef stew between the four of us to eat, she says it. When we have to borrow water from the neighbors, she says it. When we don't have money even for toilet paper and we have to use newspapers to wipe ourselves with, she says it. When the lights are turned off and we're seeing around in the dark with a candle at night, she says it. And if the utilities are cut off and we don't have a candle to light up the room, we just sit in the dark side by side on the couch, all four of us Mama on one end, then me next to her, with Stevie next to me, then Joseph draped over across me and Stevie's knees like a blanket. We just sit there like statues in a dark museum and listen to each other's lungs breathing and stomachs growling. Mama says, "Well, it's better than nothin.' It's better than dyin'."

And Stevie says, "Is it?"

Mama breaks into my silent thoughts and asks me if I want one of Joseph's lollipops. "He don't got to know," she says, "and besides it ain't like one piece of candy is going to make a difference." I know I shouldn't take it, but I tell her I do want it. When she puts it in my hand, I open my eyes a little to see what flavor it is, and I can see it's orange and can't help but smile while I tear the wrapper off and pop it in my mouth.

I close my eyes again and let the sugary juice collect on my tongue. I imagine it tastes like those orange slice gummy candies I like with the sugar all on them. Then I imagine it tastes just like a real orange from Florida with juice that squirts out and into your eye if you're not careful. It's a wonderful imagining, but at some point along the line it goes from being a thing of pleasure to a thing of yearning because I already crossed the line in my brain that goes from thankfulness to want and suddenly, I'm sitting there with an orange lollipop in my mouth, with my eyes shut tight and tears streaming down the sides of my face.

I think at that moment Mama might get mad at me for crying when she just gave me a candy, but at this moment, she doesn't. Instead, she pulls out a tissue from her purse and puts it in my hand. I can feel her do this and she wraps her fingers around mine for a couple of seconds and doesn't say anything. She doesn't need to. For the first time in my life, I feel like my mama really understands what I'm feeling without even a word.

I dab my face dry and finally Mama says, "You can open your eyes now. You want a cup of coffee? I got enough. That's about all we got right now." I say yes, even though I know according to a song I learned at school, coffee isn't supposed to be drank by young'uns. "C-O-F-F-E-E, coffee is NOT for me," the song says. I remember when I heard it the first time, I thought in my head that this song wasn't talking about me or any other young'un whose mama gives them coffee in the morning when there's nothing else in the house to eat or drink.

She brings it to me steaming hot in a plastic Tupperware tumbler she got when she was trying to make some money selling Tupperware dishes. The company let her hold on to some sample dishes that Mama was supposed to give back when she wasn't selling it anymore. Mama tried to have some Tupperware parties, but no one showed up, so she just kept the dishes and said, "It ain't nothin. I gotta get something for my troubles of trying to sell those dishes. They're too expensive, that's why. It's like highway robbery."

I'm planning on sipping my coffee, black with a packet of Sweet-N-Low Mama picked up from the counter at Kress' department store diner and stuffed in her pocket with a couple of packets of salt and pepper and a box of matches someone left behind on the counter.

I hold the cup in both my hands just like I see the teachers do when they're on recess duty out in the school yard huddled up in a circle off to the side talking and hugging their cups of coffee. I put it under my nose and breathe it in before I take a sip. It's bitter even though there's Sweet-N-Low to take the edge off and it's just hot enough from the spigot to not burn my mouth and throat when it goes down. So, I start off with a sip but pick up speed when the warm liquid slides down the back of my throat and gives me a sudden burst of energy, like a little bolt of lightning through my brain. Mama reminds me that it's a good appetite killer too, which comes in handy when there's no use to having an appetite you can't fill.

I figure whoever wrote that song, "C-O-F-F-E-E, coffee is not for me" to teach kids not to drink it, never had coffee from a Tupperware tumbler flowing down their throat making a lightning bolt in the brain and an appetite killer in the stomach when they were 12 and had nothing to eat on a Saturday morning sitting on the couch with their Mama; their mama sitting there puffing on cigarette butts and sipping her own coffee all quiet except for the clacking sound she makes with her false teeth. I know that means she's plenty worried about something or mad. She's not mad, because she gave me a tissue to wipe my eyes. No. She's not mad, but she's got a world of worry behind her teeth.

Mama finishes her coffee and says she's going out to look for food. She wants to try to get something before Joseph wakes up, crying that he's hungry. She says I can give him his lollipop to keep him quiet if he was to wake up while she's gone. She's not worried about Stevie because he has to get up and go cut the grass at Mrs. Parker's house. He'll make a couple of dollars to give to Mama and Mrs. Parker will cook him a nice dinner or buy him a burger and fries from the Burger Chef and then sit him down in the living room with Mr. Parker in front of the TV with a stack of Oreos and a glass of milk. He'll sit and stuff his cheeks with cookies and drink milk while Mr. Parker carries on about how he "can't stand the Blacks taking over the television channels." Stevie doesn't like this kind of talk, but he loves him some Oreo cookies, so he doesn't say anything about it to argue. And when he finishes that stack, Mrs. Parker will ask him if he wants some more. And, why, yes of course, he does. Some days he brings me and Joseph a cookie or two and some Grape-Nuts cereal boxes with some cereal left in them. So, Mama says it's okay even if we got this rule that says when there's no food at the house for your brother and sister, you're not allowed to fill your stomach at someone else's house. This is different because Stevie worked for it and he might well be able to bring us something too.

After Mama goes, I go sit in the kitchen on the chair by the open window like Mama does when she's waiting for the Lord to come back. The sun is already making wide ribbons of light pouring down on my face and it feels so warm and comforting and I close my eyes and raise my face toward it. I still have a little coffee in the bottom of my tumbler so I'm cherishing the last bit of it by drinking it real slow.

I'm finishing it and just about that time my stomach lets out an angry growl because I haven't put real food in it for a while now. I hope Mama comes back with some food because I don't know how much longer I can last without eating. My eyes seem to burn less since Mama's started putting the ointment in them last night, but I can't tell if they burn less, or they seem to because my empty stomach burns more. My head is starting to pound like a hammer in my skull and it makes me want to cry. I know that crying won't help, and it will make my eyes burn again, so I keep myself from crying. The one thing I don't want is eyes and stomach burning and my head throbbing in three equal parts of pain.

Maybe if I drink some water it will help, I'm thinking. So, I get up to fill my tumbler and drink down the water so fast, it makes my head pound faster. I take the cloth off the side of the sink, run water over it, and put it across my forehead. I know I'm not supposed to be using Mama's good dishcloth for my forehead, but my head hurts so bad I can't worry about that. Though, I do hope mama doesn't come back and start screeching at me because I used the one decent thing she has to wash dishes with.

I sit still in the chair by the window and close my eyes again. I'm thinking of food that I hope Mama brings back, maybe some more beef stew in a can or some bread and ham or some chicken to fry up and some self-rising flour so she can make some fluffy biscuits. Somewhere in the middle of my thoughts of food, the thought creeps in of Mama waiting for Jesus by this window. I think that'd be okay too, but I think it'd be better if I combine the thoughts and think it'd be nice if the Lord *does* come back right now, if he brings us something to eat first before he takes us all up to Heaven in the Rapture. I imagine being raptured away into the heavens might take a lot of energy and I don't have any energy and I don't want to get to Heaven and the first thing I do is ask for something to eat like I don't have any manners at all.

I'm in the quiet of the kitchen with my thoughts of the Lord coming again in glory carrying a sack of groceries when Joseph startled me by tugging on my shirt. I didn't even know he was standing next to me and I wonder how long he's been standing there. "How long you been standing there?" I ask him. I know he doesn't know about time measurement, so I don't even know why I asked him that.

"Mama gone?" he asks.

"She went to look for food," I say in a flat tone.

"I want sompin' eat. You cook sompin', 'kay?" He doesn't understand that we have nothing to cook. Just then, I remember the lollipop Mama saved back for him, kept in the refrigerator so roaches don't get at it.

"Hey, you know what Mama left for you?" I move the wet dish cloth away from my forehead, and right at that moment a breeze is coming through the window, making a cooling sensation. I don't want to move from this spot right now. "Look in the fridge," I tell him because I know he'll have fun finding the lollipop himself.

He can't miss it since it's the only thing there on the shelf. "Waaaaaoh!" he hollers when he sees it and takes about two seconds to unwrap it and pop it in his mouth.

"Now, don't bite it," I remind him. The idea is to make it last long enough for Mama to get back home because it will keep him from crying for food we don't have until then.

We hear the toilet flush and Joseph takes his lollipop from his mouth for a second.

"Stevie awake!" he says and trots off into the living room with the lollipop in his mouth.

"Don't run with that in your mouth!" I screech at him and I can hear my mama's voice in my voice with the fear that's in it. I imagine in one second flat the whole terrible scene of Joseph who fell on the lollipop in his mouth and it got shoved down his throat 'til he choked and Mama came home to an ambulance in the front yard and maybe even policemen telling her she's got one less child this morning.

One time, Evelyn told me I think bad thoughts too much and it's amazing how I can cram a whole hour's worth of horrors in one lil' second of time. I said she's right, but I don't know how not to do that when most of the time it's not really me thinking of bad things, but bad things finding me and working their way into my brain, like a worm. Evelyn told me I might be plum crazy for that thought. Then I explained what I meant by reminding her of the story of the time I was watching a pretty little bird singing on the line stretched across the alley, when suddenly a boy with a BB gun came up behind me and shot it dead, silencing its song in a single second. She said, "Okay. I get you now. But the part about a worm in the brain? Girl, that's just weird! Where you come up with that anyhow?" I shrug my shoulders because I don't know.

Stevie comes into the kitchen with Joseph taking a ride with his feet on Stevie's feet. Joseph is laughing with the lollipop in his mouth and I'm thinking again that he might choke.

"Come sit down," I say, "Stevie's leaving anyway. Right, Stevie?"

"Yeah, I gotta go cut some grass for Mrs. Parker."

"You bring cookies?" It seems Joseph is always thinking of where his next bit of food is coming from. He's not like other little kids that ask for things like toys. No, he always asks for candy, cookies, or crackers or he pulls on my or Stevie's shirt and asks, "Make sompin' eat? Make sompin'?" I can never get him to understand when there's nothing. I'm glad right now that he has that lollipop to keep him happy for a few minutes.

"Yeah. I'll bring some cookies, Joey. Okay?" And Stevie drinks some water from the kitchen faucet with his cupped hands.

"Where's Mama?" he asks like he just now noticed she's not here.

"She went to look for food," I answer. "She should be back soon, because she's been gone a little while." Stevie wants to know where she went exactly. I don't know. I don't know where a person goes to look for food. When I was little, I used to think it meant she went looking in the trees and shrubbery bushes up and down the alley because sometimes wild fruits would grow there. I wonder if that's what Joseph thinks when he hears us say Mama's gone looking for food.

"I gotta go because Mrs. Parker wants the grass cut before noon. Tell Mama, I'll be back before 3:00." With that, he slides his feet without socks into his tennis shoes with the laces permanently tied in knots and the holes on the sides so you can see his little toes on both feet. When he cuts Mrs. Parker's grass, he gets grass in his shoes by those holes. He said it makes his feet itch like crazy, but he figures it's worth it for the burger and fries and the mountains of Oreo cookies alongside cold glasses of milk that he gets for doing it.

Stevie tussles Joseph's hair the way Aunt Monique used to do to my hair when we lived in Maine. Joseph is sitting at the table resting his head across his arm with his lollipop still in his mouth. He's making his fingers walk across his arm with his left hand and humming to himself like he's in another world. I don't know where he goes in his head when he does this humming thing. Wherever that is, there's singing there. With Stevie out the door and off to cut some grass for a bite to eat, I'm left here with Joseph and his walking fingers and the drums still pounding on the inside of my skull. I want to go lay down, but I know I can't because I have to watch Joseph to make sure he doesn't do something like play with the gas burners on the stove and blow up the whole apartment.

I'm lucky because there wasn't much more time before Mama came back. I could see her coming down the alley with a paper bag in her arms. I right away started dreaming about what she might be bringing in that bag. Maybe enough food to have lunch and dinner and then maybe even breakfast again. I know that I can tell if she found a lot of food by the way she's walking. If she has a good find, she walks in kind of a light skipping motion. But if she didn't find much, her steps are quick and hard almost like she's stomping. Today, she's stomping with her head down like a person who just lost a fight.

As soon as she comes in the door Joseph is jumping up and down. "You find food? You find food?" he wants to know.

"Calm down!" Mama says like she's barking and puts the bag on the table. In the bag she has three oranges, a can of SpaghettiOs and a can of cream style corn.

"That's all I could get. The Lord's Pantry is closed on Saturdays. Don't they think people gotta eat? Just because it's Saturday don't mean people don't eat. What are we supposed to do?"

"I have orange, Mama? Can I?" Joseph is grabbing at the bag still with the lollipop stick hanging in his mouth. When he talks the stick moves up and down like Mama's cigarette does when she's talking with one clamped in her lips.

"Hold on a second! Don't grab at the bag like some kind of animal!" Her voice is getting higher and I'm afraid she's going to start smacking the palm of her hand on her forehead again if she gets too upset.

Joseph sinks down in the chair and starts crying out loud. "I hungry, Mama!" And when he opens his mouth wide the lollipop stick falls out of his mouth and the little bit of candy that was left on the stick breaks in two on the dirty kitchen floor. Joseph cries louder.

Just then in all the commotion, I tell Mama I can peel the orange for him if she doesn't feel like it and does she want some coffee, I can make it for her, I tell her. "Yes," she says, and I reckon she means yes to both things I just asked, but I'm not sure which one I should do first, make the coffee or peel the orange. I decide to peel the orange because I figure the sooner I can get Joseph to stop crying, the better.

"Look, Joseph. Smell it," I say, holding the cool orange in my hand. I dig my finger into it and pull the peel back and juice squirts me in the face. Joseph thinks that's funny and now he's laughing and throwing his head back with his hair falling in his face. Though I'm glad the orange juice didn't go in my eye, I almost think it would have been worth it to see Joseph laughing like this. When he laughs like this, there's no way Mama can keep a frown in between her eyes. Her red lipsticked mouth is turned like a bow and I think we look like a family in a commercial where they're the happiest people on the planet with perfect lives and wonderful oranges any time they want them.

I divide the orange slices and Mama says she doesn't want any, she'll just have her cigarette butt, and that Joseph and me can have the oranges. I'm biting into one and I think I'm in Heaven with the juice of the orange washing over my tongue and down my throat. I remember that I told Mama I'd make her some coffee. I also remember I had Mama's good dishcloth on my forehead because of my headache and I'm thinking that she might ask me why it's on the table. I will tell her I was washing the table for her. I know this will be a lie, but I think I'll take my chances on Hell, so Mama won't yell at me for ruining her only good thing in the house.

Without her really noticing, I grab the dish cloth and go to the kitchen sink to put it back and turn the water on so it will get real hot for her coffee. Mama keeps her coffee tumbler in the refrigerator away from the roaches. I leave the water on while I get her tumbler and steam is billowing up like smoke the way Mama likes it when she makes her coffee. She used to be afraid I would burn myself with the hot water like that, but now that I'm older she knows I'm almost an expert at handling the hot water even though it gets so hot it could burn right through the top layer of skin if someone was to put their hand in.

She likes the spoon of instant coffee in before the water, so the coffee smell floods up right.

"There's a right order to this," she said, when she showed me how to make it. When we have Coffee Mate, she lets Joseph put the spoon of Coffee Mate in the coffee, so he can dip the spoon to the bottom of the cup and watch the clump of Coffee Mate float to the top in a bubble. But today, she says she's fine if it's just black.

I bring Mama her coffee and she's gone ahead and moved over to the window where she sits to wait for Jesus. I put it on the table and ask her like a waitress "Will there be anything else?"

"No thank you," she says and gives me a little sideways smile and I feel really good that I can get that out of her.

"You'd make a good little waitress, Isabelle," she says. It makes me proud when she says I'd be good at something.

We sit again in quiet, with Joseph stuffing his cheeks with orange slices, me eating my half of an orange slow one half a slice at a time and letting the juice sit on my tongue like I do the orange lollipop juice when I have one. Mama has turned toward the window to look at the sky and smoke and sip her coffee with the steam rising up.

It's late in the afternoon. Mama took Joseph with her to walk in the alley and pick some wild onions and honeysuckle from the edge of the field where we play stick ball. I don't feel good, I told Mama, so I was going to stay back and lay down. I thought my head pain was on the way out after I ate the orange and Mama let me have a half a tumbler of coffee, but it's back again full blast. My stomach has that feeling like someone punched me. I lay down on the couch in the quiet and try to fall asleep, so I won't know how I feel, but it's no use. I can't sleep in the middle of the day.

I turn on the TV, smack it on the side, like you have to do sometimes to get it to turn on and arrange the coat hanger around, so the picture comes in clear enough. I'm laying on the couch watching a cartoon on our black and white TV about a panther who's pink. I know he's pink because that's the name of the show, *The Pink Panther*, even though on our TV he looks gray. I like this show because the panther is always sneaking in places and stealing expensive jewelry. Even though he's stealing, I root for him to get away with it. So does Mama, who watches this cartoon and says it's her favorite. She says the rich got it all and they won't even miss them anyway if the *Pink Panther*, who is gray on our TV, takes the jewels. The times when we're all four laughing in the living room, it's usually because we're watching *The Pink Panther* on a Saturday afternoon on the black and white TV that works just fine once you whack it good on the side.

Mama and Joseph come back just as the show is ending and Joseph is all excited to tell me that they came across a lady that gave him a doughnut. Mama struck up a conversation with her because the lady was curious about the wild onions they were pulling up and collecting in a paper bag. She wanted to know if they were going to eat them. When Mama said yes and Joseph was standing beside her pulling apart a honeysuckle and sucking the honey off the stringy stem from the middle, the lady thought correctly that maybe they were pulling wild onions and eating honey suckles because they were desperate for something to eat. That's when she asked Mama if it would be okay if Joseph had one of the doughnuts she had in the grocery bag she was carrying.

"Of course, he can. Why thank you very much!" Mama said and told us she believes that lady was an angel with the way she just appeared like a miracle from out of nowhere to offer a doughnut to Joseph like that. I don't know if she was an angel or not and I'm glad for Joseph, but I wish the miracle lady had given Mama a doughnut so she could bring me one too.

We can't eat the SpaghettiOs and corn until later for supper, so I'll just have to wait to put something in my stomach. I don't have any strength to do anything but lay around. I'm thinking it's almost a good thing I got the sore eyes, because if I didn't Evelyn would want me to come out and play and I'd have to tell her I don't have energy for play and she'd ask her mama if I could eat with them. Even though they don't have much food either, her mama would let me, but then the whole time, I'd feel guilty like I'm taking food away from them all while my own family is hungry at home.

Stevie came home before 3:00 and put the stack of four Oreo cookies and a half a box of Grape-Nuts Cereal on the table.

"I kept my promise, Joey," he said to Joseph who was already climbing on Stevie like he was a set of monkey bars.

"I eat now?" Joseph asks while he's hanging upside down and Stevie is holding him up by his legs.

"After supper," Stevie answers. He knows this will be what Mama says.

Just before it starts to get dark, Mama heats up the SpaghettiOs and corn. She uses a bit of margarine to cook the cut up wild onions that she and Joseph pulled from the field.

"It's plenty enough margarine to cook 'em," she says and, "The Lord provides."

I think the Lord might provide sometimes, but I'm blaspheming in my head because I'm thinking for a Lord who is supposed to see to it people receive when they ask, he's coming up short on the providing. We got one can of SpaghettiOs and one can of cream style corn to split up four ways. Mama says we have to save the other two oranges for tomorrow morning. We'll have them and the dry Grape-Nuts cereal for breakfast before Mrs. Gunnels comes to get us for church.

"We're going to try church again," Mama says. And tells us that last week after she ran into one of the ladies from church downtown, she figured enough time had passed since that last thing that happened when we went before.

Stevie looks at me out of the corner of his eye. He doesn't like to go to church and still feels guilty about that time he tricked me and made me think the Lord was there. But the last thing that happened took the cake, Mama said. We don't even talk about it really, but we call it, "The Squawking Incident," if we ever mention it. Or Stevie laughs and calls it, "The Squawking." It's always said in a whisper like you do when something is shameful. In time, everybody at church forgot it, except us.

But, after church there will be doughnuts and coffee to be had. That's enough to make us not too upset to go again. Stevie calls the doughnuts and coffee, "The Lure," and he and Mama laugh, and I do too and pretend I understand what's funny.

We all get just a little more than a couple of tablespoons of each thing on our plate at supper and we eat as slow as we can and drink water in between spoonfuls to fill us up better," Mama says. Joseph mixed his SpaghettiOs with his corn and Mama acts like she doesn't even notice. Nobody is saying anything. All we can hear are the plastic spoons tapping on the plates while we eat.

Afterward we each have an Oreo cookie. Mama says even though Stevie had some already at Mrs. Parker's house, he can have one too.

"He worked for them, after all," she says, "and it ain't right if he don't get one."

Me and Joseph pull ours apart and lick the frosting off of them.

"Don't let me forget to put more ointment in your eyes, Isabelle," Mama reminds me.

"I won't," I answer, but I'm hoping she forgets and if she does, I will too. I hate having that stuff squeezed in my eyes.

When the sun is sinking down in the sky, Joseph falls asleep on the couch and Mama says just to leave him there. She hopes he sleeps on through the night, so he doesn't wake up and realize how empty his stomach is. Stevie and me are sitting on the floor watching TV and Mama's sitting on the end of the couch where Joseph isn't. I know it's just a matter of time before I'm so hungry I want to cry again because I'm already feeling it. I can't tell Mama because she'll get mad. She can't take it when we tell her we're hungry and there isn't a thing she can do about it, so I figure I might as well keep it to myself.

Before too long, Stevie goes to his room because there's nothing on now except a show called *The Lawrence Welk Show*. Mama likes this show, but I don't know why. It has this guy who talks funny and bubbles floating all over from a bubble machine and he introduces people that sing songs that only grownups like.

I get the mind to go to my room myself to color or write on the piece of cardboard Mama gave me from her panty hose package since my diary I got for Christmas is full up and out of space. I turn on my Walkie-talkie in case Evelyn calls me on it or maybe I'll call her. But I can't think of anything except how hungry I feel since I didn't have but a few spoons of hot food today and hardly nothing since Thursday morning when The Punisher, Mrs. Cartwright stopped me cold in the middle of breakfast and sent me home before lunch because of the sore eyes.

I'm laying on my mattress and my stomach hurts so bad, I want to cry, so I do. It doesn't matter if it's making my eyes and head hurt too. I can't keep myself from crying because my stomach is so empty, I could have sworn somebody punched me square in my belly button. I just want to fill my stomach with something, anything so as not to feel the emptiness.

That's when I get the idea that I could drink enough water to fill my stomach and kill the pain. I got an empty mayonnaise jar on the windowsill in my room and so I take it and go into the bathroom and fill it to the brim with water and drink it down. I feel so thankful for the water. I fill the jar again and drink it down fast. I drink another full jar and another. I already drank four whole jars of water, but I can't stop, so I drink more. If I keep filling my stomach with water, I can pretend it was food and go lay down and go to sleep feeling all full and comfortable while I fall off to sleep whispering "The Lord provides," just before I close my eyes.

My stomach is so full of water now, I almost can't tell from what, except I'm shaky and weak while I walk down the hall to my room, lay down and try to think my stomach is full of food. I'm laying there, though, and suddenly my face feels hot like it's on fire and the water in my stomach is churning around in circles. I'm trying not to think of it, but the churning is getting worse.

"Mama!" I call out, "Mama!" and I sit up just in time because I suddenly throw up all the water all warm and foamy on the slick cement floor. At that moment, Mama appears at my door to witness the whole thing.

"I'm sorry," I start to cry and Mama calls Stevie to get her a towel from the bathroom and the washcloth on the sink and wet it with cool water, she says.

Stevie is pretty fast with it. "What happened?" he asks and gives Mama the towel.

"Isabelle threw up," she says. She dries my face with it and then tosses it on the floor to clean up the mess. Then she puts the cool cloth on my forehead and lays me back on the pillow and puts the sheet over me. I'm shivering, and Mama wants to know if I think I might get sick again. I don't think so, but she makes Stevie bring a bowl from the kitchen anyway, just in case. He gives me a pitying look when he brings in the bowl, but I can tell he's nervous it might be something catching by the way he puts down the bowl and steps back quick. "Do you need anything else, Mama?" he asks.

"No," she says and scoots onto the mattress beside me. She's rubbing my hair back from my forehead and I ask her to play with my fingers. For as long as I remember, I've always asked my mama to play with my fingers when I'm sick and she does. It always makes me feel comfort. She's sitting next to me, and she takes my hand and threads her fingers in and out of mine until I'm drifting off to sleep.

I wake up later to the sound of my Walkie-talkie making static-y sounds. Mama isn't beside me anymore and it's almost completely dark out. I grab the Walkie-talkie and mess around with the volume and channel nob. "Come in, Sparrow. Where you at girl?"

It's Evelyn. "I'm here, Eagle. I got sick. Over." Click.

"Girl, you ain't got to say 'over'. What you mean you got sick? Come to the window. What's wrong with you?"

I get up and go to the window, even though my head still hurts and I feel like I got hit by a Mack truck. I turn on my flashlight, even though the battery is weak so the light from it is looking kind of orangey-pink, and flash it out the window.

"Eagle to Sparrow. I'm at the window." She flashes her flashlight. It's nice and bright enough to make a stream of light across the grass outside.

"What you mean you got sick, girl?" she asks.

"I threw up water," I say.

"Ooooh ... that's bad. Why did you throw up water? You got the flu?"

"No. I'm okay now," I say. I didn't see any point in explaining the whole drinking all that water and then getting sick from it.

"When are you going to be able to come out? Tomorrow after church?" she wants to know.

"I think so, maybe," I say and remember that Mama never did put the medicine in my eyes.

I hear Evelyn's mama saying something to her about letting that girl sleep and then Evelyn says she has to go.

"Okay, over," I say.

"You ain't never going to learn that you don't have to say 'over' are you? Say goodnight, girl."

"Goodnight, girl ... Over," I say it now just to joke and I hear her laugh and say, "Goodnight, Sparrow."

She flashes her bright white light of her flashlight three times at me, and I return flashes with my weak faded orange light at her. I sit there at that window staring up at the stars for a few minutes thinking how lucky I am to have a friend like Evelyn just across the driveway to tell me good night over a Walkie-talkie and flash her flashlight across the yard. I think no matter how bad my days are, they always seem better at the end of the day as long as I have Evelyn's light blinking across the driveway at me.

Chapter Forty-One

It's Sunday morning and we're getting ready for church since I'm better from the throwing up and not contagious with the sore eyes anymore. We already ate the oranges that were left and we each had a pile of dry Grape-Nuts cereal to eat. Stevie says we all look like birds around the table eating little bits of dry cereal off pieces of paper that we're using as plates. Joseph leans over and eats it with his mouth. "See? I bird," and he acts like he's pecking at his cereal. Mama is trying not to laugh, but I see that she is behind her tumbler of coffee, while she sits in her chair by the window. She's got a cigarette she pulled out of her cigarette can and she's puffing away at it. Everybody is dressed for church except me. Joseph is being good because he knows that he gets to go to the nursery while Stevie and me go with Mama to worship since we're big enough to know how to take part in proper praise and there, he will have Lorna Dune cookies and Kool-Aid. I wish I could go to the nursery, and I ask Mama if I can go help out there instead of going to worship. She won't let me, though, and tells me she needs me in church with her and Stevie to add more prayers for our case.

So, I'm in my room and trying to find a dress to wear and I turn on my Walkie-talkie. I wonder if Evelyn is awake. "Sparrow to Eagle, come in." No response.

"Sparrow to Eagle," I say again. Then I hear static and then Evelyn comes over the Walkie-talkie.

"I'm getting ready for church," I say. "Y'all going to church this morning?" Evelyn and her family go to another church called Ebenezer Baptist on the South side of town. Evelyn wanted me to go with her sometimes, but Mama won't let me. She says it's not that the folks that go there are all Black that's the problem, but it's because she thinks that neighborhood is dangerous. She said this and Stevie, who was listening from the other side of the room, came back with, "Yeah, because this neighborhood is so safe." I don't think he meant it was actually safe because his tone was smart-alecky, as Mama calls it.

"Don't go gettin' all smart-alecky with me. I wasn't even talkin' to you no how," Mama said, and that was the end of that, except I always had to make up some excuse to tell Evelyn why I can't ever go with her to her church. So, every time she asked me, I really wanted to, so I said yes, but then the next day, I had to tell her something like I suddenly wasn't feeling good and I was sorry, but I was going to have to do it another time.

"You sure do get to feeling sick a lot," she said. Before too long, she stopped asking and we forgot about it. Since we are starting back going to Albany Gospel Chapel again. We have to go there, so I wouldn't be able to go with Evelyn to her church.

Evelyn tells me they aren't going to church this morning because Barbara isn't feeling good, and she has a great idea that she can go with me instead. I know I have to ask my mama and I hope she won't say no. At first Mama says she doesn't know if there will be room in Mrs. Gunnels' car and that she didn't want to impose on Mrs. Gunnels. "Please, Mama," I beg. "We'll make room in the car because Joseph can sit in my lap."

Mama's just looking at me and she's not saying anything, but she's pursing her lips around the bit of cigarette that's left. "Well, I reckon so, but you do know she'll be the only Black there. You don't think she'll be uncomfortable with that?"

"She doesn't care about that, Mama. She's going to be with us." I give my mama a hug and almost knock her off her chair.

"Can I go over and get dressed over at Evelyn's? She said she has some hand me over clothes she wants to give me."

"Well, I reckon," she says. Mama is in an easy mood this morning. I'm so excited, she hardly gets the word "reckon" out of her mouth before I'm out of the kitchen and in my room telling Evelyn over the Walkie-talkie that I'm on my way over.

At Evelyn's house, Barbara is curled up with her mama on the couch watching a preacher on TV. "Good morning, honey. How you doing? You all better from the sore eyes?" Mrs. Williams says to me all cheerful.

"I'm doing fine, Mrs. Williams. How are you?" I use proper manners and ask Mrs. Williams how she's doing without even giving a hint that last night I was about to die from being too hungry and I'm hungry now, but I'm not going to let on.

I don't have to say it anyway since Mrs. Williams asks me if I want a biscuit because she cooked some a little while ago. I do. She tells Evelyn she can have another one if she wants to because Barbara wasn't wanting hers this morning. Evelyn sets me a little plate and says if I want, I can put some butter on it and a little molasses over it. I do.

Evelyn and me, we sit at the table and eat biscuits. I'm so happy at this moment, even though I remember our rule that I'm not supposed to fill my stomach while my brothers are at home without anything much to eat. I tell myself, I'm not exactly filling my stomach, but just having a bit. Biscuits and molasses are about the most delicious thing to eat on the planet. I'm so hungry

I want to eat fast, but it's such a slice of heaven, I think I might have reached the promised land and I don't want this moment to end. I peel the top of the biscuit still warm from the oven and it's got so many layers of fluffy biscuit, I can't even count them. I take the butter knife and put me a pat of butter on it and it starts to melt right quick and it slides in little yellow streams all down the sides. And if that ain't enough, Evelyn hands me over the molasses, and I pour it on my biscuit, a steady little flow of shiny, brown bittersweetness joining the melting butter and dripping down on the sides of that beautiful biscuit.

I heard it said once by my Aunt Gracie that to lust after food in such a way is gluttony of the ardenter sort, which means "eating with an eagerness." She likes to spout Bible words at us, Mama says, to show off. Aunt Gracie says ardenter sort of gluttony has its own built-in punishment because that's why folks choke on their food. Then after they choke from eating too fast, they go straight to Hell for gluttony. Well, I reckon I'm fixing to land me in Hell then, because I'm fixing to glutton this right on up here ardenter style while I let it melt on my tongue. And Evelyn, she's right here with me. She's decorated her biscuit just the same.

"Look how that molasses flows down off the sides!" I gasp.

"Girl, that's not flowing. That's straight up cascading!" Evelyn's got a thing for being precise. So, we're sitting here with our mouths full of promise land and the only thing we can say is, "Mmmmm-mmmmmm-mmmmm!"

"Oh Lawd, that's good!" Evelyn finally says.

"Evelyn, don't you be taking the Lord's name in vain!" her mama hollers from the living room.

"Oh…I'm sorry, Mama!" she says.

"Don't be sorry to me. You'd best be saying sorry to the Lord."

"Ok, I will," Evelyn says, but I don't think she's really sorry because she's laughing into her cup of orange juice, and I hope she doesn't end up in Hell for taking the Lord's name in vain and not being sorry. But then I remember how I'm going to be there too for committing the sin of gluttony and I figure at least we'll be in good company.

Mrs. Gunnels shows up right on time at 9:00 so we can get there in plenty of time before services start at 9:30. We're all ready and sitting on the steps of the porch waiting. Evelyn and me are sitting on a towel she brought over so we can sit on it and not get our dresses dirty. I'm wearing a dress Evelyn gave me from that box of clothes she was so excited to give me. It's sky blue with daisy flowers around the waist. I love how flowy the skirt is and when I spin around, it does too. I feel like a rich girl in this dress and Evelyn says it looks great on me. I tell her I love her dress too. She's wearing a pink dress with a white collar, and she has her hair up in a pink bow to match. We both got white doilies pinned to the tops of our head after I told her how we wear it at Albany Gospel Chapel.

"Mrs. Gunnels is here, Mama!" I holler into the screen door to let Mama know.

She comes out quick with Joseph and Stevie behind her. Mama's wearing her favorite red dress that fits her backside right snug and her lipstick is red and shiny like she likes to wear when she goes to see Allen at the Pac-A-Sac store when we go see him to ask if we can have some credit to get some food. Aunt Gracie, who, according to Mama, thinks she's an expert on Godliness, says only a harlot would wear red to church and it just isn't done. I guess it *is* done because Mama is doing it. Aunt Gracie says a woman is supposed to be modest in the house of the Lord. Mama says Aunt Gracie's just jealous because she doesn't look so good in a dress like that, and besides, she's got her lace doily on her head to show she's plenty modest.

We're about to pile in the car, and Mama leans in and says to Mrs. Gunnels that Isabelle's, friend, Evelyn here, would like to come with us if that's alright. "Why, of course, that's right fine," and, "Oh the Lord is always happy when we carry more of his children to his house!" She's smiling big at us and saying, "Hi" and, "How y'all?" I can see she's wearing some lipstick too, but it's kind of like a pale pink and not red, like Mama's.

At church we file in the pew and I can feel the people looking at us and wondering why we have a Black girl with us. They aren't saying anything like that, but the way they're looking tells us that they're shocked by what they're seeing.

Mama comes in after bringing Joseph to the nursery and she slides into the pew next to us on the other side of Stevie who's sitting on the other side of Evelyn. Mama's shifting herself like she's nervous and looks at Stevie sideways. "I can feel folks staring at us," she leans towards him and whispers.

"Umm hmmm," is all he says, and he's got a closed mouth smile on his face like he's enjoying seeing Mama squirm in her seat. He knows she doesn't like to be the center of attention, not in this sort of way at least.

"Folks looking at us?" Evelyn whispers to me.

"Yeah, I believe they are," I say.

"They ain't never seen a Black person?" she whispers a little loud, so Mama shushes us and turns red. That's when I get the big urge to giggle, and let out a snort from behind the Good News tract the man at the door gave me when we came in.

Now none of us in our pew can resist the urge to giggle, even Mama whose face is even redder, but there's no way she can hide that she's laughing too with her Bible opened up in front of her while she's burying her face on the page where John 3:16 is. I can tell because I see a book marker where she keeps it because it's her favorite verse.

Evelyn turns around and flashes a big smile at everyone and waves like those Miss Albany pageant girls on the float last summer in the fourth of July parade. I take my cue from her and do the same thing. Stevie turns and nods a friendly "Howdy, partner" nod like they do in that show *Bonanza* that he likes so much.

Well, the singing and preaching got underway, and Brother Pritchard comes up to the podium and preaches about Jesus and the loaves of bread and the basket of fish. Stevie whispers to Evelyn that all this talk about bread and fish are going make him hungry and she giggles behind the song book and bats her eyelashes at him. I can't tell if she's doing this on purpose or if it's just her natural way when she's sitting squeezed in next to a boy she thinks is cute. Mama shushes him and shifts in her seat again.

Brother Pritchard is banging on the podium for affect. Mama said that was to wake people up when they fall asleep during his sermon. I don't know if that's true, but it sure does get our attention when he does it. We look up and blink every time he pounds on the podium even if we know it's coming and it's not a surprise anymore after the first couple of times he does it.

Brother Pritchard stops talking, and we stand to sing and follow along in the song book. I'm sharing one with Evelyn and Stevie is sharing one with Mama. Evelyn says she doesn't know most of the songs, so she just pretty much listens along. Then a song starts to play, "His eyes are on the sparrow ..."

"I know this one," she whispers, and she straightens up tall and joins in song, "and I knoooow he watches meeee!" She's singing loud, almost like an opera singer. Mama's smiling over at us because Evelyn sounds so good, and Stevie raises his eyebrows in surprise. I knew Evelyn could sing like this because we sing together lots of times when we're walking together or sitting together on the porch. It was at that moment I think I might well be the happiest I can remember being. I'm glad Evelyn came to church with us and I'm making plans to see if we can do this every Sunday. Though, I don't think her mama would let her, because that means she'd have to choose between going with me or them, so I think I'll just have to try to see if she can come with me sometimes and be happy with that.

After church, Mama sends Stevie to fetch Joseph from the nursery and we all meet for fellowship in the hall, and this is our favorite part. We mingle around and Mama pretends like she's interested in what the other ladies at church are talking about, but just until she's had her doughnut and coffee. They all compliment her on her commitment to bring us to church again even though we don't have a car and it must be hard getting all those young'uns ready without a daddy around. And oh, isn't Joseph a lovely little fella with the way his hair is so curly and wild like that and wherever did he get those big black curls ... and dark eyes to boot? At this part Mama looks at the floor and laughs a little, not like it's a real laugh, but a laugh that comes from nerves. She changes the subject, "Wasn't Brother Pritchard's sermon beautiful?" and, "Oh and Mrs. Ida Flo, wherever did you get that pin?"

"Like I give a shit!" She later adds when me and her make a pit stop in the lady's room during fellowship.

"I don't care about no pin! Those women at the church are a bunch of hypocrites with the way they make little jabs at me because I got young'uns and no husband to help me with 'em," Mama says and peeks under the bathroom stall to make sure we're the only ones in there.

We have had our fill of doughnuts and now it's time to go. On the way home, Evelyn asks me if we all want to come over for supper with her family if her mama says it's okay. I say yes, before I even ask Mama.

"Now, hold on," Mama says. I'm afraid she's going to say no, even though I know we don't have anything for supper.

"You need to ask your mama first," she finishes her statement.

"Please, Mama." I ask.

"Quit begging, Isabelle. It ain't polite," she tells me and I'm thinking I know my mama begs sometimes for food for us, but I never thought it wasn't polite. I know it's because she doesn't have another way. I forget all about what I was thinking when she says "Yes, if it's alright with Mrs. Williams."

It's alright with Mrs. Williams. She's cooking a whole chicken and some collard greens. She's made some sweet corn bread with some real corn in it. For dessert we're having chocolate cake with creamy chocolate frosting all on top of it chased down with cold milk. We're all eating and talking and laughing and I'm looking over at Mama and I'm watching her laugh with Evelyn's mama, and I don't remember the last time I saw her laughing like this.

After the supper dishes are cleaned up because everybody pitched in to help, we all sit around the table and play cards. We play Go Fish so Barbara and Joseph can play too. Before too long the kids leave the table and Barbara and Joseph go to play in the living room with Barbara's play dough on the coffee table.

Stevie is curled up on a chair in the corner of the living room with his nose in a book. Evelyn and me are in her room talking. We're in front of the mirror with me sitting and she's standing behind me doing my hair in a braid. We look at each other by looking in the mirror.

"I'm glad y'all came for dinner," she says and slides a hair pick through my straight hair. "Ain't nothing to this," she adds under her breath about my hair because the pick just glides right through it.

"Me too. It sure was good," I say. "Your mama can cook."

"She sure can. Hey, you know that boy in my grade named Eric?" Sometimes it's hard to keep up with Evelyn because she changes subjects without a warning.

"I don't know him but, I know who he is. What about him?"

"He says he likes me. He wants to know if I wanna go with him.

"What you going to tell him?" Now I know that to "go with a boy" doesn't mean you go anywhere with him. It just means you like him, and he likes you, so you can't like anybody else.

"I don't know. I think he's kind of cute and all, but I like me somebody else."

"Who you like?" I'm looking at her in the mirror and she's looking downward at my hair and braiding it with a dreamy looking smile across her face.

"Who you like?" I ask again.

"I don't know if he can like me back," she says, finally.

"What you mean? Who is it? Why can't he like you back? Is he a grown up or something?"

"No, girl. It ain't anything like that. Dang. Well, he's older than me by a bit, but that ain't really the problem." Evelyn is being mysterious and now I really want to know who she's talking about. She's got that dreamy look on her face again while she's making a braid in my hair.

"Well, you going to tell me who it is?" I'm losing my patience.

"I like your brother, Stevie." She's not looking at me in the mirror, so she can't see that I'm smiling because I knew it. I could tell by the way she laughs at all his jokes and she tries to have an excuse to sit next to him all the time. "But I reckon he can't like me back," she finishes.

"Why not?" I want to know.

"In case you ain't noticed, girl, y'all are white and I'm Black. It's okay if you and me are friends, but nobody is going to like it if a Black girl and a white boy go with each other. Mama says some folks even think it's a sin." She's looking at me now in the mirror and she's stopped braiding my hair.

I don't even know what to say, because for some reason, that didn't even cross my mind. I guess I just forget sometimes about the whole Black/white thing. Evelyn says it's hard to forget when it's your face that's Black and it wasn't too long ago that Black folks couldn't even go to school with whites. "Not too long ago, we couldn't even be friends. That's the truth."

"I guess you're right about that, but when's the last time you cared what anybody thought?" I ask her because usually she doesn't care. Usually she says, "I ain't studying that mess," which means that she doesn't "give a shit". That's what Mama says when she doesn't care about something like the church lady's pin or Stevie says it when Mama's not around to threaten to wash his mouth out with soap for swearing.

I don't dare say swears, because once when I said a swear word Mama washed my mouth out with Dial soap. She held me right down across her legs and breathed cigarette smell in my face and then washed my mouth out. Now when I give my mama a hug and she smells like Dial soap and Winstons, it makes me think of that bar of soap golden and slippery in my mouth and I feel sick.

So, I'm here with my thoughts drifting away from Evelyn liking Stevie because I've got in mind the taste of Dial soap and Evelyn makes the decision right then and there that she won't pay any mind to folks that got a problem with the Black/white thing.

"But don't say anything to Stevie," she says. "Let me work it out." Now she's back to braiding my hair with that dreamy smile on her face again.

"I ain't going to say nothing," I say, and we do a pinky swear, because everybody knows a pinky swear is solid.

Chapter Forty-Two

I'm not supposed to be walking alone, but I *am* because I wanted to go collect some pecans from underneath the giant tree down the street. Fall is coming in, so that means all the pecan trees around are dropping their pecans. Mama loves this season because that means we can have all the pecans we want, and it doesn't cost a thing and what's better than that? I got this idea to go collect some to surprise Mama for later. I brought my paper sack to fill up and it's nice and full right now. I was lucky to find a ton of big, ripe pecans that already shed their outside peels that cover the brown shell.

One time a couple of weeks ago Evelyn and me collected a bunch of pecans, but they still had the outside peels and we had to remove them. So, we sat on her back porch most of the afternoon peeling the greenish brown covers from off the shells, making the palms of our hands and underside of our fingers turn brown. It wasn't that easy to see on Evelyn being as her skin is already brown, but on mine, it looked like I put my hands palm down in some brown ink.

Out on the schoolyard a whole big group of Black kids made a circle around me and gawked at my hands.

"Girl, look at your hands. You turning Black?" one girl asked.

I tried to explain it was because I was peeling all those unripe pecans, but they wouldn't listen.

"Yeah, she's turning alright. What are you gonna do now? That's from being around all those Black folks in The Projects. Your whole family's gonna turn," one all-knowing girl declared without so much as a single doubt.

I tried again to explain about the pecans.

"What? You got a problem with being Black? You ain't peeled no pecans. See? That won't come off for nothing." One girl pulled at my hand and tried to rub my palm to see if the brown would come off.

"That's because it's stained on there," one little girl named Requetta chimed in. I remembered her name clear as day because she's the girl from down the street who has an extra little finger hanging on the side of each hand and you don't forget someone who has an affliction like that. If you forget everything else about her, you're going to remember her sitting next to you at school assembly, writing her name over and over again on the front of her composition notebook, with her little finger useless and dragging across the surface while she wrote.

One blond haired, Nellie Olson, *Little House on the Prairie* looking girl, asked her one time why she doesn't just get those ugly extra fingers chopped off. She just shrugged her shoulders up and said she didn't know and went off about the business of jumping rope with her extra fingers flopping around every time she jumped up and then landed.

"It's because she's too poor to get them chopped off," one other girl, who was best friends with the Nellie Olson girl, said. I remember wondering why those girls were even troubling themselves to come clear across the school yard to say anything to us anyway, being as we were from The Projects and they weren't. They didn't usually have anything to say to me, except to remind me that the pants I'm wearing on any old day look just like the pants they gave to the Salvation Army because they didn't like them anymore.

So anyway, at that moment in the middle of this declaration that I'm turning Black, everybody turned from gawking at my hands, to telling off Requetta for disagreeing with their explanation for my brown palms and fingers.

"You shut up ole nappy head, girl! Besides what you know, with your extra finger self?" the other Black kids yelled at her.

Just then the bell rang, and recess was over. I was glad because I didn't know if those other kids were going to beat up on Requetta for daring to disagree with them when it just isn't something that's done. And if you got extra fingers flapping around on the end of your hands, it really isn't something that's done on account of you don't want to call attention to yourself.

Today I'm walking down the sidewalk with my ripe pecans feeling pretty happy about bringing them to Mama when I know how much she loves pecans. Maybe she won't even mind that I walked by myself once she sees all these.

I'm most afraid of running into Ronny G. who lives across the field out front from us. His mama is nice, and she even lets us get water from her outside spigot when our water is off, but her son is mean and well known for beating up folks with sticks and rocks. When we see him coming along the sidewalk, we go quick to the other side of road then dip off somewhere out of his sight because if you make eye contact with him, he says something like, "What you lookin' at, bitch! I'll kick your ass, mother fuckah!" And we know he will.

He isn't that tall, but he's all muscled up and mad. I saw him once hit this other boy across the head with a stick until he was bleeding and then drag that boy along the sidewalk making a trail of blood on the concrete. That boy's mama called the cops, but nothing happened to Ronny G. for that. Everyone is afraid of him, even kids that are bigger than him because he doesn't have any bounds and no fear. I'm scared, but I just keep on walking and imagining how happy Mama will be with a whole bag of pecans just to herself.

I'm right in the middle of my thoughts about Mama being happy when all of a sudden, a bunch of kids, both boys and girls, just come out of nowhere and surround me. I don't know what to say because I don't know what they want or why they're making a circle around me. It's at this moment that I notice one of them, a girl, has pot pie in her hand. I'm thinking this is a weird place to be eating a pie, when she raises her hand with the pie and throws it right in my face.

I drop my bag of pecans and they spill out all over the sidewalk. I right quick pick up the bag with what's left inside and in the very next moment, I've got a hot rage heat in my face and pot pie sauce and peas dripping off my chin and covering my eyes. I wipe the sauce away from my eyes and I see the kids all running away from me. I should just let them go, pick up as many pecans as I can save, and go on home wearing chicken pot pie on my face, but I don't. Instead, I clutch the tattered bag and set my eyes like a target on the back of the head of the girl who threw the pie and run after her. The other kids are running alongside her, but I only really see her and her yellow barrettes wagging back and forth when she runs and her red sweater flowing back like a flag from behind her.

I don't know what I'm going to do if I catch her, but it doesn't matter, I just move like some kind of machine without a brain. I reach up to her and grab her by her sweater with the hand that's not holding the half-empty bag of pecans and slam her hard on the sidewalk. She starts screaming out loud for her mama and her friends scatter in all directions.

That's when I leave her right there and I take off running too. I know if her mama comes out, she'll beat me like I was her own young'un. Because that's how folks do around here.

Grownups will hit young'uns even if they ain't their own kids. The first time I figured this out we were in a war with the next-door-neighbors. Their cousin, Gail, called me a honky and I didn't really know what to say because I didn't know what a honky was. I just tried to ignore her, but she wouldn't let me.

"Hey girl! I'll kick your ass!" she threatened for no reason that I could think of.

I was about to just go inside instead because I wasn't in the mood to have my ass kicked, but just then Joseph noticed that Bookie was playing with his firetruck that he left over on their porch the last time we were friends with them.

"Hey, my fi-tuck!" Joseph whined.

Just then, Gail grabbed it from her cousin and threw it hard on the cement porch and it cracked the window and side.

"Hey!" Joseph screamed and headed over toward their porch to get his busted-up firetruck.

Of course, I couldn't let him go alone so I followed him.

Just before he could get to the porch to try to get his truck, Bookie picked it up and brought it inside.

"She 'teal my tuck!" Joseph was climbing onto their porch.

Gail went inside, but I wasn't sure why. I don't know why I thought it was to go get Joseph's truck.

Just then Joseph grabbed Bookie's mama's new mop down from a nail it was hanging on and dropped it hard on the cement porch.

That's when their mama came running outside with her hair up in curlers.

"Don't fuck with my mop! I *will* break it over your fucking head!" she screamed and waved the mop around fast making whooshing sounds where it was cutting the air.

Joseph had jumped off the porch quick as lightning and called Bookie's mama a bitch, except he can't really say it right, so he yelled "bits!" while he was running away and back over to our porch.

Gail came back out and then I saw why she went in when I saw she had a board in her hand. Everything after that happened so fast, it's almost like a blur how the scene unfolded itself.

I was standing in the yard, just between our porch and their porch. Joseph was behind me, I think, and suddenly Gail came flying off the porch with her board and gave me a solid whack on my right hip with it. I wanted to cry, but I just stood there with my feet planted on the earth and grit my teeth. I didn't want her to know that what I really felt like doing was dropping to the grass and wrapped up like a baby inside its mama's belly like I saw in that biology book at the library.

So, I stood there, what seemed like a long time, but was probably only seconds, holding in my cries, bracing my body with my arms folded in front of me. Then, strange as all get out, Gail just turned around and went back inside the apartment without so much as a peep or a "bitch" or "honky," whatever that is.

The next day Gail left town and two days later, Bretta and Sephina invited me over for dinner and to play paper dolls. I went, even though Mama warned me that they might poison the food on my plate when I wasn't looking. It was my choice, she told me, since we had some food at home, I could accept a meal somewhere else if I wanted to.

At dinner I stayed nearby watching their mama cook. She didn't even seem like the same woman at all who was screaming about my brother fucking with her mop. Even though I didn't really think they would put poison in my food, I felt like I should keep an eye out for it just in case.

There was no poison. Just a hot plate heaping with macaroni and cheese, turnip greens, cornbread, fried pork chops falling just right off the bone, chocolate ice cream for dessert, and a tall glass of root beer to chase it all down with. We sat at the table and I let them start eating first for good measure and then decided it was safe.

"You sure can cook, Mrs. Johnson." I told their mama.

"Well, thank you, Isabelle. You are welcome anytime," she said, like there was never any warfare between us at all.

After dinner us three girls washed up the dishes, laughing and talking the whole time. And then we played paper dolls until it was time for me to go home. I left with the question in my head about how people can be such different selves from one day to the next. I wondered too, which of the selves was the real ones.

So, this day when I was walking just as peaceful as ever and minding my own beeswax and this girl throws a chicken pot pie in my face, I guess my usual self just couldn't take it. I chased her and slammed her hard on the sidewalk. I had never hit anyone like that in all my life.

I'm running home as fast as I can and a whole mix of thoughts are swirling around in my head. First, I got to get home fast because that girl's mama might catch up to me and whip up on me. Then, I'm puzzling why in the world she would throw a pie at me in the first place and wasn't that a perfectly fine meal she threw away? Then, in the middle of all this, I got a little creeping feeling of shame for slamming someone on the sidewalk and what if I hurt her bad? Because I didn't stick around to make sure she wasn't hurt bad.

"What if I killed her?" I gasp in my head just when I'm reaching my front porch.

Inside, I fling myself breathless on the couch and Mama and Joseph and Stevie gather around me all puzzled.

I hand Mama the crumpled bag with only a few pecans left inside.

"You had food?" Joseph asks.

"You could say that," I answer in between breaths.

"What happened?" Stevie wants to know.

I tell them about what happened and about the girl I might have killed on the sidewalk.

Mama tells Joseph to run and get a towel from the bathroom to wipe my face.

"Wet it first," she tells him.

He brings out a towel all sopping wet and drips water all over the place. Mama has to get up quick and go find another towel to dry up the mess. She's on her knees drying up the floor and carrying on about how there's no rest for the weary.

I wash my face with the sopping wet towel, Joseph tells Mama he's sorry for making a mess, and Stevie tells me it's a good thing the pie wasn't hot, "It wasn't, was it?" he adds, "because if it was, you'd have scars like little pock marks from hot peas in your face for the rest of your life," he's laughing.

"Yeah, good thing," I agree and with my face buried in the wet towel, I can't help but laugh myself, but I sure hope I didn't kill anyone with the body slam to the sidewalk.

I can hear the news report on the TV about it now. "A local girl was killed by another girl today after she shared her lunch of chicken pot pie," the reporter would say.

And they'd have the witnesses saying, "We don't know what happened. She was giving the girl her lunch and suddenly that girl went crazy and body slammed her like a wrestler on the sidewalk. I reckon she ain't liked chicken pot pie," the witness would say.

I figure I'll watch the news later to see, just in case.

Chapter Forty-Three

Well, I guess I didn't kill anyone since it wasn't on the news, so I'm happy about that. I might have wanted to get that girl back for throwing a chicken pot pie in my face, but I wasn't trying to kill anybody.

Besides, today is a glorious morning because the sun is shining bright even though the air is cool with winter coming in soon. We get to eat cinnamon buns and milk for breakfast, since we just got our food stamps yesterday, and Mama got a few things to hold us over.

Aunt Gracie is going to give us a ride to the grocery store, so she can watch over what Mama buys. She said if we want a ride, though, we have to be up early, and we can't be lazy and expecting her to go get the groceries for us. Mama says Aunt Gracie just wants to run her life. So, Mama always sneaks a goody or two in the cart when she isn't looking. "Because it ain't none of her business!" Mama always says.

I'm thankful that she's taking us to the store, but I don't like how she's always telling Mama that without her, she would be nothing and wouldn't know what to do with herself and makes Mama look down at the floor.

After Aunt Gracie let us off and we unpacked all the groceries from the trunk of her car, she takes a seat on one of the chairs that Grandma let us use "out of the goodness of her heart", she always reminds us. Then she calls Joseph over to sit on her knee because she "never really got to know him, or his daddy," she says and looks at my mama like she's waiting for an answer to a question. But Joseph isn't interested in that and moves away from her.

Mama says, "Well thanks for taking us to the store, Gracie," but Aunt Gracie doesn't act like she's going anywhere fast. Instead, she asks me to come have a seat on her lap being as she doesn't see me much anymore and look at me, I'm light as a feather.

I sit in her lap, but it feels strange and what Mama calls "phony" because that's what it's called when someone pretends something like they like you, but they don't really. That's what it feels like. Like she's pretending because she never asked me to sit in her lap before, but I go sit there because I want to know what it's like to sit on your aunt's lap since I kind of forgot that part of Aunt Monique. I sat in her lap sometimes when we all played cards when I lived with Mémère. Besides, I didn't want to hurt Aunt Gracie's feelings even though she doesn't seem to mind hurting Mama's feelings.

I'm sitting there and she's talking away to Mama while she's leaning over and looking past her out the kitchen window.

"The Blacks are as thick as fleas around here now. I don't know how y'all stand it." Then just as quick, she changes the subject.

"My, my, Isabelle, you sure have a sharp rump!" she says laughing. That's when I get the idea to shift my body, so my rump bone is pushing into her leg harder because I don't like how she's saying Black people are like fleas because it's like she's talking about Evelyn too and she isn't like no nasty flea.

"Ouch! Now that hurts! Hop up!" she snaps at me and I hop up. My back is to her so she can't see my face and I smile at my mama, who I know is smiling but she's hiding it behind her tumbler of coffee because it ain't just her mouth that's smiling but her eyes too.

"Well, I'd best be going. Oscar and I have to get to church." Then she stands at the door, turns, and puts her hand next to her mouth like she's telling a secret. I always notice the same thing about how her hair doesn't move because it has so much hairspray in it and she says, "Look out for the niggras, ya heaaauh." Then she tiptoes out to her yellow Grand Torino and drives off fast as she can down the alley with red clay dust rising up all over.

Then Mama says how she can't stand her and how she'd like to grab her by her hair and swing her around. And "ain't her teeth as yellow as this table?" That's what Mama says every time Aunt Gracie comes and goes.

With Aunt Gracie gone, Mama takes out of the grocery bags and thanks the Lord for each item.

"Thank you, Jesus, for the peanut butter. Thank you, Jesus, for the bread. Thank you, Jesus, for the Coffee Mate. Thank you, Jesus, for the coffee... Thank you, Jesus. Thank you, Jesus."

We have to all gather around the table while she prays and thanks the Lord for the food.

She's on a big sack of vegetables that she got because she knows I like them. We got some cucumbers, celery, carrots, and tomatoes and I like to eat them raw. Mama says I'm a strange young'un for liking uncooked vegetables like that and where did I get that highfalutin way of eating anyway? I'm glad she got them, though, and I can't wait to eat me some sliced cucumber later on today.

She pulls out a bag of apples and Stevie whispers to me that she has to thank the Lord for each apple.

Mama hears him and tells him to hush because it's impolite to interrupt when she's talking to the Lord, don't he know?

I'm glad to see she only thanks Jesus for the whole bag of apples and I see we're almost finished.

Joseph is sitting at the table with a string of lollipops in all colors and he's thanking the Lord for each color.

I want to ask if we have to wait for him to finish since Mama, the official prayer sayer in our family, is done, but I don't dare because I'm afraid I'll disturb the peace by asking and Joseph will have a fit and maybe even have to start all over.

He's on the last lollipop and there's a knock at the door. Mama says that he said a fine prayer and we could all learn to pray like that too and it wouldn't kill us.

It's Evelyn and she wants to know if I can come out and play. I think Mama's going to let me, but then she surprises me by saying we're going to church this morning. Two Sunday's ago, she said we were done again because the ladies at church are nothing but hypocrites. Now she decided this week we're going, and Mrs. Gunnels will be here in an hour, so we need to get dressed.

"I don't want to go to church, Mama!" Stevie is arguing.

"Tough. We're going. We're going to give it another chance because we need to 'preciate the blessings we have."

Stevie storms off into his room and Mama yells at him like she always does, that he's going to turn into a regular juvenile delinquent if he doesn't change.

"I don't have anything to wear, Mama," I say, and Evelyn tells me right quick that I can come borrow a dress of hers, because she's sure to have some that could fit me.

"Can I, Mama?" I ask.

"Go ahead, but don't be long. We don't want to make Mrs. Gunnels wait."

I grab a couple of lollipops for me and Evelyn and Barbara too and we're off across the driveway. I lay the lollipops on the table in the kitchen at Evelyn's house and Barbara is all excited to see them and she picks up a couple of them and holds them up to the sunlight pouring in the window and squeals. It feels good to make your best friend's little sister so happy over lollipops on a Sunday morning when you have food enough at home, so you can share.

The dress I'm borrowing is dark purple and Evelyn says it's the color of royalty and I look like a princess in it.

I stand in the mirror and look all dreamy at myself. "I reckon I do."

"You sure do that dress right! You can keep it if you want, because it doesn't fit me anymore really and it'll be years before Barbara can use it."

I do want it, so I twirl in the mirror and tell her thank you very much.

"It's nothing," she says.

Since I don't have any church shoes and tennis shoes will look silly with this dress, Evelyn said I could borrow her church shoes since they aren't going to church that morning and she won't need them.

They're big on me and they try to flop off my feet, but Evelyn's got a trick. She stuffs the toes with tissue paper to make them tighter and it works, but it's uncomfortable on my toes. I just don't pay it any mind, though, because I like the way the shiny black shoes look with the purple of the dress.

I'm getting ready to go so Evelyn and me give hugs. I'm thinking, at that moment how Stevie says girls are silly because they always need to hug before going different ways. Mrs. Williams comes out into the living room and tells me I look real pretty and I say, "Thank you, Ma'am."

Mama's calling so I have to go, and I make my way back over to my place to wait for Mrs. Gunnels.

We're sitting around the table waiting. Nobody's saying much since we all have lollipops in our mouths. Joseph is counting the lollipops left in their shiny plastic wrappers and putting them in color groups and counting them again. Stevie has his face in his book, like always and Mama reminds him that he can't bring it and disrespect the Lord by reading it in church. He doesn't answer anything back, but I know he won't dare bring it and bring about the wrath of Mama and the Lord at the same time.

Mrs. Gunnels pulls up in the driveway and we go out like we're in a parade to get in her new car. It's a big shiny Buick that's a pretty blue color. The neighbors all around are looking at us while we duck into the shiny car like a bunch of movie stars ducking down into their limousines while everybody looks on pointing with their mouths hanging open. I imagine for a minute that we're a famous family and this is our limo. Our Mama is a famous movie star, and we sing in a family band, but we also play in TV shows too when the producer man is willing to pay us enough.

At church we all file in the pews toward the back in case Mama has to scoot out with Joseph on account of he's coming into church service with us today. He didn't want to go to the nursery and Mama wasn't in the mood for him to pitch a fit like she knew he would if she didn't just let him come with us.

So, after the opening prayers, we're all sitting there just as quiet as we could be, the whole church, because we're in the middle of a few moments of "reflection." I don't know what they mean by reflection because the only reflection I know is when you look in a mirror or in a window, but I don't see any windows around. I try to ask Stevie if there are mirrors we're supposed to look in, but Mama throws a dirty look at me, so I know I better shut up.

It was in that moment when I figured I had better shut my mouth when Joseph figured he should open his.

"Mama, yook!" he says pointing toward a man who doesn't have any hair so the lights from the ceiling are reflecting on his head. I'm thinking to myself, "There's the reflection they were talking about," and Joseph says at that same second that thought was in my head, "Dhere fly on dhat man's head!"

The whole church, bursts out laughing, and Mama turns beet red and covers her face with her song book. She keeps her head like this for a minute until the congregation starts singing a song and she feels like it's safe to look up again when folks aren't looking at us anymore.

About halfway through church Brother Pritchard announces that the sermon will be short because there's going to be a "calling up" today.

He's going to invite us up to be saved just like they do on the Billy Graham show that Mama likes to watch because it makes her feel so close to the Lord to watch it.

The choir starts singing and we're invited to sing along. It's the same song they sing on the Billy Graham show and it gets Mama emotional. She loves when they have a "calling up to Christ" at church and she'd go up again and again, but she's already saved, she said, and you can only be saved once.

"Just as I am, without one plea,
But that Thy blood was shed for me,
And that Thou bid'st me come to Thee,
O Lamb of God, I come! I come!

Just as I am, and waiting not
To rid my soul of one dark blot;
To Thee whose blood can cleanse each spot,
O Lamb of God, I come, I come!"

Folks are singing, and Brother Pritchard is talking into the microphone.

"Come as you are. He's calling you to come up and receive him as your personal Lord and Savior. Come, receive him and there are people waiting right here to pray with you," he says.

People are getting up from their seats and going forward up to the stage. Some of them are looking around first as if they aren't sure if they should go up, but then Brother Pritchard's words make them want to go ahead and get up. There are so many people, two long lines are forming on both sides of the stage where the alter is.

Some people are coming back with smiling and crying at the same time and whispering, "Thank you Jesus. Yes, Jesus."

"Just as I am, and waiting not
To rid my soul of one dark blot;
To Thee whose blood can cleanse each spot,
O Lamb of God, I come, I come!

Just as I am, though tossed about
With many a conflict, many a doubt;
Fightings within, and fears without,
O Lamb of God, I come, I come!"

Brother Pritchard is laying more words on top of the singing, "Yes, come one and all. No matter what sins blot your soul. Come and ask the Lord into your heart and he will forgive you. If you feel it in your heart, don't wait. Tomorrow might be too late. The Lord is calling you to come forward."

I'm sitting at the end of the pew with Stevie next to me and Joseph on the other side of him. I'm looking over at Mama out of the corner of my eye and I'm thinking how I want to get rid of the "blot on my soul" that I got from almost killing that girl the other day. I'm thinking Mama would be so proud of me if I go up to be saved. Then we'll be saved together, and we can talk about how it is to be washed of our sins and how we'd love to go up over and over again but can't since you can only get saved once.

My heart is beating fast because I'm not sure if it's okay if I go up, but I know I'm moved to go up. So, I think maybe the Lord is calling me like Brother Pritchard says. That's when I stand up and get in the line that's going down the aisle beside our seat. The line moves forward and I go with it. When I walk forward, I don't know what to do with my hands so I'm glad that my new hand-me-over dress from Evelyn has little pockets in the sides, so I put my hands in my pockets and make my way up the stairs to the crowded stage with all the prayer ladies who will pray with me so I can erase my sins.

Some space cleared up in front of a kind looking lady with silver hair and a dress that's blue like the sky. I step forward and for a second, we're just looking at each other because I don't know exactly what to say when you're going up to receive the Lord as your Savior.

I think I'm supposed to say something like, "I want to receive Jesus into my heart," or something like that, when the silver haired lady smiles and bends down to me and says, "Shuuugh, you're too youuuung," and she stretches out the word "young" like it's a mile long.

I try to tell her that I'm 12 and plenty old even though I look younger, but she's already on the next person who came up to get saved so I just turn and walk back to my seat with my blot still on me since that lady thinks I'm too young for the Lord to be my Savior.

Back at my seat, nobody says anything to me, but Stevie is looking all shocked at me. Mama is staring straight ahead and clacking her false teeth. Joseph is dozing off with a lollipop in his mouth.

After church, there's supposed to be fellowship with doughnuts and we want to go, but Mama says she has a terrible headache and "Stevie go find Mrs. Gunnels too, so we can ask her if she'll bring us on home."

"Why, of course, Jolene!" Mrs. Gunnels says all cheery, so we pile in her car to head back home. This time I don't feel like we're famous and everyone is looking on like they're amazed. This time, we're all quiet and looking down, and I think it's because we all know when we get home Mama's going to have one of her mad outbursts.

I'm right. We get in the door after our polite thank you's to Mrs. Gunnels, and Mama lets loose on us.

"We can't go nowhere! Every time we try to go to church y'all have to make me the laughingstock! Joseph, you know better than to point at people!"

Joseph is looking up at her, stunned, because I think he has no idea he did anything wrong since everybody laughed when he told the whole church that the man sitting two rows up had a fly on his head. It's not long before his shock turns to crying because he didn't know.

Mama doesn't care. Now, she's yelling at me.

"And Isabelle, what was that? What kind of stunt were you trying to pull?! Trying to make me look bad, is all!"

"No, I wasn't, Mama! I was just tryin' ..." I try to explain, but she tells me to be quiet and stop talking back.

"I just wanted to be saaaaved!" I cry and hide my face in my hands on the yellow Formica table.

So, Joseph and me are sitting side by side at the table crying and Stevie tells us to come in his room and listen to a story he could read to us. Joseph doesn't want to, but Stevie tells him he can have another lollipop if he comes with us and stops crying.

We go into Stevie's room and he reads to us, but we can hear Mama out in the kitchen talking away to herself about how she can't have normal young'uns, no, they got to embarrass her. And that's it for church, she says. She really is finished now. She hasn't been so embarrassed since that whole crying and nursery incident I pulled a few years ago.

She's talking about the time we were in church and I fell asleep right in the middle of Brother Pritchard's preaching and Mama pinched me to wake me up. I woke up alright. I woke up squawking like a baby and Stevie had to carry me off to the nursery and put me in a crib because there was nowhere else for me to lay. I didn't care when he put me in the crib, but when I woke up, I felt plain foolish. There I was, a big ole seven-and-a-half-year-old child sleeping away in a crib like some kind of newborn.

Stevie pauses his reading for a minute.

"You know, Isabelle, you *did* look kind of funny walking up there today. The way you had your hands in your pockets, looked like you were a farmer." He's laughing and trying to get me to laugh too, but I'm not sure I want to. It's hard to think it's funny when you're at church and the Lord is calling you up to be saved, but then a silver haired lady tells you you're too young for that and on top of it all, you walked like a farmer all the way up there in front of the whole church, embarrassing your mama to death.

Chapter Forty-Four

Mama calmed down from her after church fit so there's peace in the house. We're sitting around the table about to eat a lunch of ham sandwiches and potato chips. We have some cookies for dessert, but we can't have them just yet, Mama says. We got to eat our sandwiches first.

I invited Evelyn and Barbara over to eat with us and they're playing a game of cards with Joseph while I'm making our sandwiches. They're playing Go Fish and Joseph thinks he and Barbara get three turns to Evelyn's one, just because she's older, and we all know it isn't right, but we let it go. Because that's what you do when you're sitting around the table like this on a Sunday afternoon with a peaceful feeling since you got plenty to eat, even enough to share.

Mama says poor people share more than rich people and I think I understand what she means by that. It's like when we have nothing to eat, or hardly anything to eat, and we go for days scraping to find food. Then, the first thing I think of when we finally have a refrigerator full of groceries, is who I can share it with.

Having food to eat makes everything different. Mama got mad at us this morning, but now she isn't even thinking about that. She's sitting by the window munching on chips and she said she made herself a potato chip sandwich. Evelyn and me decided that we don't like sandwiches made of chips because of the way the bread is so soft and sweet in your mouth and then suddenly you bite down on hard chips. It's like someone slipped something that wasn't supposed to be there in your sandwich.

When we tried it once, we ended up taking the chips off and eating them separately. And since we didn't want to waste, we ate the bread plain because we didn't have any ham or anything else to put on it. Mama said if you chew the bread enough it turns to sugar because it's got sugar in it. So, we chewed and chewed until it disappeared in our mouths, but it didn't turn to sugar.

The sandwiches are ready, and Joseph and Barbara aren't upset one bit about having to put the cards away before we eat. Mama sends Joseph to get Stevie because I made his sandwich too. I know he likes mustard, so I slathered it on and cut it in half just the way he likes it.

We're sitting and eating, and I can see plain as day now that Evelyn likes Stevie with the way she keeps looking at him and laughing at everything he does to show off. He's bitten all the crust from the edges of his bread and then went ahead and bit off all around the two sides of the sandwich until they're shaped like two ears, that he holds up to the sides of his head in front of his real ears. He's flapping them back and forth and we're all laughing, even Mama. We're all laughing, but the way Evelyn is laughing has something special to it, because I saw her touch his shoulder while she was laughing. That's what she told me once was a trick you could do if you like a boy, so he can know that you like him. You touch his shoulder or maybe his hand.

Before too long Joseph wants to make his sandwich into ears too and that's when Mama has to put her foot down. Well, she's in such a good mood right now, she doesn't yell, but instead she tells Joseph he needs to go ahead and eat his sandwich, so he can have some cookies.

This is the way I wish it always was. But I know that this is how it goes: We get our food stamps. Mama buys all kinds of groceries. We sit around the table while she thanks the Lord for each thing. Then we eat like royalty for a week. Then by the second week, things are starting to get low again. Mama tells us to go easy on things.

"I think we can stretch it this time," she says, but she wrinkles up her forehead when she says it like she doesn't believe herself.

By the end of the second week, she has to ask the man at the Pac-a-Sac for a store credit. He winks at her and says she can pay it back in the usual way that I don't know what that means. Then she goes back to the little room with him while we pick out the usual things and she comes out just in time for us to ring up the food and put it into bags. Except one time, she took a little longer than most times.

That was that time that I was standing in the aisle where the SpaghettiOs were because Mama said we could get some on account of Joseph likes them so much. We forgot them but remembered them just in time. While Mama was back in the room, Stevie sent me to get them. I was standing there next to the canned peas and carrots and just down the aisle from the potted meat. I saw Ronny G. there stuffing a can of potted meat in his sock.

At first, he didn't see me, but he looked up just as my eyes were zoomed in on the can of meat being slipped inside his sock and that's when our eyes met up. For about two quick seconds, it's like our eyes were stuck on each other. Then he looked away and straightened up his body, tugged on the waist of his pants and made his way out the door with his potted meat tucked safe in his sock.

That day in the Pac-a-Sac, he didn't look so scary like usual because I knew why he was stealing food. He knew I knew that too. I could tell how he looked at the floor all shame faced. I don't think it was the stealing that made him that way, but the hunger does that to a person. It makes you shame faced. Except I don't understand why a person has to feel ashamed of being hungry like you've done something wrong. But that's how it feels.

Since that day, Ronny G. doesn't mess with me or anyone I'm with if he sees me. It's like we have a secret understanding. I won't tell anyone about how I saw hunger kicking his ass so he had to steal to eat and he won't kick my ass or anyone I'm with when he crosses our path. Evelyn wonders why he doesn't bother us anymore. I just say I don't know and maybe he just got tired of it.

So, now we're sitting with our stomachs full of sandwiches of ham and chips. Evelyn tells us that her family is going to the fall carnival up Slappey Blvd. this evening and we can all come too if we want.

Mama says maybe we'll go if it's okay with Evelyn's mama. Evelyn says it is, even though she hasn't asked yet. We can all fit in her Mama's Chevy if Barbara and Joseph can sit on someone's lap.

We all say it's a good idea and now we *have* to go because Joseph has his heart set on it, so that's that. We're going.

Mama counts her tips that she made last night from work and says she has enough so that we can play some carnival games if we want.

"But isn't that throwing away money?" Stevie asks.

"We gotta have some fun while we can. It ain't every day we get the chance. We could be dead tomorrow," Mama says, and I think she's right. Though, I hope she's not right about the being dead tomorrow part.

It's not dark yet and the sky is looking all orange and yellow mixed with gray blue while the sun is starting to sink down below the trees in the alley. We were playing stick ball with a tennis ball in the fenced area beside the alley until some kids came along and said it was their turn to play in that field and we needed to go and that stick we had was theirs too.

"That's our stick," one boy said.

We didn't think it was their stick, but we just let them have it instead of fighting to keep it.

"I'm not fixin' to fight over a stick when I see a whole alley way full of sticks we could just as easy get," Evelyn said. I agreed with her about that. and we just left the field to those kids who only stayed there for a few minutes anyhow, but they took the stick when they left.

We could go back over to the field, but we don't feel like it now that our game was interrupted. We just decide to throw the ball back and forth across the driveway from Evelyn's yard to mine. We have teams. Me and Evelyn and Barbara are on one side and Stevie and Joseph are on the other.

We have to throw the tennis ball across the driveway and the other team has to catch it without letting it bounce more than once. If you catch it without it hitting the ground, you get two points. If it bounces once, you get one point.

Anyway, Stevie can throw the ball high and he likes to throw it almost straight up, so we have to run and try to catch it. It was then that he threw the ball so high and lopsided that it landed on the roof of the apartment next door to Evelyn's house.

We can see it sitting there right at the bend in the roof where the cover to the porch is. We know that if somebody can climb up on the railings of the neighbor's porch, we might be able to get it back.

We don't know these new neighbors, though, since they just moved in. We don't know if they're nice or not. We know there's a couple of big boys that like to listen to loud music sometimes because Evelyn says it's so loud it shakes the cinderblock walls to their kitchen and living room.

We don't know what to do, so Stevie goes to ask Mama if we can climb up and get the ball. She doesn't know if it's a good idea, but she figures if she goes over and helps him that it might be alright.

She's standing on the edge of the steps to the porch next to Evelyn's place and holding on to Stevie's legs while he tries to pull himself up onto the roof, so he can reach it.

"I can almost reach it without even climbing up," he calls down to Mama while he's stretching his body as far as he can.

We're all standing around in a circle around Mama and Stevie. Suddenly somebody yells at us from inside a dark kitchen.

"Hey! What y'all doing on my porch? Hey! Get your ass off my fucking porch!" She's yelling, and she turns on the light in the kitchen and on the porch at the same time. For a second, I think it's Ducy's mama because she's just as big and yelling and cussing at folks just like she does.

Stevie jumped down from the railing right quick and Mama said to that woman that we were just trying to get Stevie's tennis ball that was on the roof.

"You ain't fixin' to get shit off my roof!" the angry woman cusses away.

"You ain't got to get so mad. We's just trying to get a ball down," Mama says back at her. I never saw my mama get into a fight and I'm wondering if this might be the day that I do.

"I said you better get your white scraggly ass out my yard before I make you skeet shit up in here!"

Mama tells us to come on and let's just go, forget about the ball. So, we go over to Evelyn's house next door with the woman yelling after my mama some more.

"I will make you skeet shit!" she's hollering.

Evelyn's mama says there wasn't any call for that, and Mama agrees. The two of them sit at the kitchen table drinking a cup of coffee while us kids are in the living room playing Go Fish on the floor in a circle.

"Well, I reckon they ain't so friendly," Mama says.

"Don't pay her no mind," Mrs. Williams says. "We're fixin' to go out to the carnival anyway."

We all pile into Mrs. Williams' car. She turns the key and nothing happens but a little click.

"Damn. Now what?" she says under her breath and she tries it again. Nothing.

Barbara and Joseph start to whine and cry from their places on Evelyn and Stevie's laps. I'm sitting right in the middle of them so it's like a stereo with two kids crying out about wanting to go to the carnival.

"Oh, we can still go," Mrs. Williams says. "We'll just have to walk if we want to go bad enough."

"But ain't it far up Slappey to walk?" Mama wants to know.

"Well, it's not right close. We could put the young'uns in the wagon and pull them and the rest of us can just walk. That is, if y'all really want to go."

"We wanna go!" Barbara and Joseph start whining again.

"What do y'all think?" Mama is asking us older kids. Stevie says he wouldn't mind too much, although he'd be just as happy inside reading his book. Mama says if we go, he needs to come with us to help out pulling the wagon.

Evelyn and me say we want to go even if we have to walk.

"Okay. Then, I reckon we're going," Mama says, and Barbara and Joseph are happy.

We pile them in the wagon with a blanket and everybody's got their jackets on since the night air is starting to get a bite to it. We head out all together, walking up Society Avenue and then up Slappey Boulevard with all the loud traffic and lights.

We're all walking, and Stevie is pulling the wagon, Evelyn and me are in front of everyone walking arm in arm. Mama and Mrs. Williams are behind us all so they can keep an eye out on everything. Up and down the street we can smell fried food from the restaurants all down the boulevard.

We all say how we love that smell.

"Makes you want some French fries or something, don't it?" Mrs. Williams says.

"Sure does," Mama agrees.

"Can we get some French fries at the carnival?" Stevie wants to know and so do I.

"Maybe. We'll see how much they cost," Mama says.

We're okay with that. I just love walking on the busy street with all the lights and cars whizzing past. That's when Evelyn and I plan to go to college together in a big city and then get an apartment with big windows that look out over the city lights. She'll go before me because she's older and then when I get there later, we'll be roommates until one of us finds a boy to marry, but that won't happen for a long time after, we say.

At the carnival, there are rides that spin around with loud music and lights flashing, and games for people to play, like bobbing for apples, pin the tail on the donkey, and coloring pages for little kids to color. There's even an old swayback horse that kids can ride, as long as they're under a certain height and weight.

Stevie says he bets this is the horse's last chance to keep him away from being sent to the glue factory. I want to know what he means by that, but Mama tells him to shut his mouth with that story.

There's a sweet smell of dough frying and French fries and hot dogs. There's some fiddle music playing loud over the speakers on poles all around the carnival grounds and I think it's pretty okay with how it's got a happy sound to it. We're walking by a pumpkin carving table. We have to stop here and let Joseph and Barbara carve little pumpkins. It only costs fifty cents each to carve one and Mama and Mrs. Williams think that's a pretty good deal. That's when we notice that there's a dance floor where they're showing people how to square dance. It doesn't cost anything because we see a sign plain as day that says, "FREE Square Dance Lessons." Evelyn and me think it might be fun and we bug our mamas to let us go over. They say we can as long as Stevie goes with us. Of course, he doesn't want to go and at first, he says there's no way.

He doesn't have much choice, though, because we start teaming up on him begging him to come with us. It doesn't take too long before he gives in because he can't take us begging him in both ears to please come with us.

We go over and notice there are no Black folks over here at the square dance floor. All the white folks on the floor and around the edges watching are looking at us out the corner of their eyes or staring straight at us.

"Why is everybody looking at us?" Evelyn asks Stevie.

"Why you think?" he asks.

"I don't know. I got something on my face?" Evelyn says. I think I know why folks are looking at us strange and Evelyn is acting like she has no idea and I can't tell if she's just pretending or what.

That's when we overheard this white woman with a giant head of blond hair say to the man she's with, who's white too but beet red with a sunburn, say, "Oh here comes the niggers. We can't have nothing to ourselves no more."

The sunburned man laughs and says, "You know once there's one nigger, there's going to be others. They're like cockroaches."

The woman thought this was so funny she just about fell off the wooden stool she had half of her backside hanging off of.

"Careful now, Beverly, you going to hurt yourself," the sunburned man says and laughs so hard he's losing his breath and sounding all whistley in his lungs. I could see when he opened his mouth wide that he had a whole mess of cavities right square in the front.

I feel my face getting hot and I'm pretty sure Evelyn heard what they said, but she just ignores them, if she did, and grabs both me and Stevie by the hands and says, "Come on! Let's do the steps."

Stevie tried to pull away, but we were both pulling on him so instead of calling attention to himself from having two girls pulling on him, I guess he figured he'd just cooperate.

We try to follow the steps that the girl is trying to lead everybody to do, but we aren't any good at it. So, we just decide we'll just do our own kind of dance. We hook our arms together and spin around in circles and hand each other off to one another.

I don't know how it looks, but if I have to guess, I'd say we're doing pretty good at our own little made-up square dance steps. That's what Mama and Mrs. Williams say when they come and join up with us.

They park the wagon off to the side with Joseph and Barbara's jack-o-lanterns in them and every one of us are on the square dance floor. We make a circle around Joseph and Barbara while they hook up arms like we show them how to and we go around in circles. With the little kids in the middle doing their thing, we invent some more moves, with Mama and Mrs. Williams going around in the circle toward me and Evelyn and Stevie. Then, we hook arms and twirl around and pass on the next person, which was either Mama or Mrs. Williams.

We are going around like that with Joseph and Barbara in the middle for a good while and I notice at some moment, that every one of us is laughing and smiling, even Stevie. I love seeing Mama laughing so hard, it's like she's laughing with her whole body. I've never seen Mama laugh like this ever.

So, after the dancing is done, we're all hungry and that's when Mama figured it'd be a good idea to think about getting something to eat before Joseph gets too hungry and starts getting ornery. That's what Mama was saving her money for, so she hadn't spent any more than 50 cents so far, so Joseph could carve a pumpkin.

Just at that moment, that blond woman that was calling Evelyn names before the dance yells from her perch on the fence, "Now, get on, niggers!" The rotten teeth man laughs all whistley again.

I think for a moment we're just going to ignore them and head over to get some food, but suddenly Mama is stepping up toward that woman and telling her to shut up.

"Wasn't nobody bothering y'all! Y'all are the ones that need to get on!" Mama yells and she's pulling up her sweater sleeves.

"And who's gonna make me? A bunch of nigger lovers?" The woman is laughing now.

Evelyn's mama is tugging Mama around the elbow, but Mama ain't backing down.

"You need to shut up with that talk!" Mama steps closer to the woman who's still laughing, with her whistley laughing man.

She's still laughing and yelling, "Niggers and nigger lovers! Nothin' but nig-" and suddenly before any of us knew what was happening Mama shut her up in the middle of the N-word by slapping her square across the face.

The woman's laughing stopped and turned into a scream and a cry and her man's whistley laugh stopped and he swore, "Goddamn y'all!" but didn't come after us because the woman hid her face in her hands, hopped off the fence, and rushed away with her man trailing behind her. "Come on, Beverly. Hold up!" he yelled after her.

We are all stunned, even Mama, and standing without saying a word for a few seconds. Barbara and Joseph are hiding behind Stevie, Evelyn, and me. People around look at us, but no one has stepped up to defend the woman Mama slapped. Just as quick, they go back to acting like nothing even happened.

Mrs. Williams pulls Mama by the arm. "Come on, Jolene. I don't think they want to fight us anymore. Besides, we still got some hungry young'uns who need feeding."

Evelyn's mama and my mama walk arm in arm like Evelyn and me do all the time and we head over to the hot dog stand.

We get to a hotdog stand and all us kids are begging for French fries. Mama says we have to go easy and see what we can afford for all of us and she keeps looking nervous over toward the square dance floor.

Mrs. Williams puts her hand on Mama's shoulder and winks and says we should put our money together and share everything, so we can afford more.

"That's a good idea," Mama says and relaxes a little, "but y'all might get shortchanged because I think y'all got more than I got."

"No. We won't get short changed. We're in it all together. We *all* going to get our fill," Mrs. Williams says.

"Well okay. If y'all are sure," Mama agrees.

So, we put our money together and that was enough to buy everyone a hotdog and a whole mess of fries for us all to share. We even got little cups of soda to go with our food. We're glad that we have the wagon too because it's easier to carry all that stuff over to the little round picnic table we found left empty like it's waiting just for us. We squeeze in, all of us, around that little table and eat our food without saying much, but not because we're mad or anything like that. It's because we're all so happy, there isn't much to say, but we're still smiling at each other while we fill ourselves.

After all that, we still had enough left over for dessert. We have the choice of fried dough or candy apples. Joseph and Barbara want the fried dough cake.

"One of them is about as big as a grown man's head," Mama says, "so one is enough to split for them."

As a matter of fact, she'll have fried dough too, on account she can't eat candy apples since she's got false teeth that might get stuck in the apple and come loose from her mouth while she's in the middle of eating it "and

316

wouldn't that be a sight." That's what Mama says when she talks about something that would be strange to see.

So, Mrs. Williams, Stevie, Evelyn and me, we get us some shiny red candy apples. I knew from the moment I had the choice, what I was going to pick. I've got my apple in my hand and before I start to eat it, I want to admire it a bit with the way the lights around are bouncing off of it.

It's time to go because it's getting a little late, our mamas point out and we have a long walk ahead of us to get home. We pile Joseph and Barbara back in the wagon with their jack-o-lanterns and wrap the blanket around their shoulders while we all take turns pulling the wagon. Mama's finished with her fried dough cake, so she says she'll pull it for a while so the rest of us can eat our candy apples in peace without having to pull on the wagon.

We're on the long stretch of Slappey Blvd, all of us walking along. It's all the way night out with the streetlights and cars going by. Me and Evelyn in the front, Stevie behind us, Mama and Mrs. Williams in the back with the wagon being pulled along like a little train caboose.

Before too long Joseph and Barbara finish their dessert and fall asleep with their heads leaning on to each other's head and their arms wrapped around their jack-o-lanterns like they were doll babies or teddy bears.

"Ain't that sweet?" Mama says while she stopped to take a little break pulling.

"That *is* sweet," Mrs. Williams agrees.

"Mama, I'm done with my apple, so I can pull the wagon for a bit if you want," Stevie says.

"Oh. That'd be nice. Then I can have me a smoke while I walk. I can't smoke and pull the wagon at the same time. I don't know why. It's just hard," Mama answers and laughs a little and Evelyn's mama laughs too.

Mama and Mrs. Williams walk ahead, and Stevie's in the middle pulling the wagon of sleeping young'uns. Me and Evelyn walk behind everybody, side by side, both of us biting into our candy apples. The cool air from the nighttime is blowing in our faces that are all wet and sticky from the red candy over the apples and apple juice is dripping down our fingers.

We can hear our mamas talking and laughing mixed in with the sound of the traffic going by. I got half of my shiny candy left on my apple still and I can see my face in it when we pass under a streetlight.

"I love that red," I say to Evelyn.

"Me too," she says. "It's like a race car."

"Yeah, or a firetruck," I say.

"It could be like a rose flower," she says.

"Yeah, I reckon," I say, "but maybe it's more like a valentine."

"Sure enough a pretty color, no matter," she says and then takes a last big bite out of her candy apple.

"Sure is," I say and go for the last giant bite of my own.

Chapter Forty-Five

Mama's leaning over the kitchen sink washing her hair with Super Suds Soap Powders because we don't have any shampoo and she said she can't be going into work at Joe's Cellar with greasy hair.

She got her old job back there after she lost all her baby weight from having Joseph. She said it's about time, since he's almost seven years old now and it must have taken her so long to lose on account of she had a baby right about the time middle age spread came creeping up on her.

"I got it bad!" she cried out when she hopped on the scale over at Evelyn's mama's house. "I have got to lose me some weight!" So, she started smoking more to curb her appetite.

"I don't hardly got to eat nothing no more since I picked up my smoking level," she said.

"Now, Jolene, you know that ain't good for you. It'll give you cancer, it will." Evelyn's mama warns.

Ever since we went to the carnival that time, Evelyn's mama and my mama have become friends. Evelyn's mama doesn't smoke, but she drinks coffee and sometimes they sit out on the porch and drink coffee and Mama smokes until sundown.

"You need to cut back," she told Mama once when Mama was having a coughing fit.

"That stuff is going to kill you, Jolene!"

"Well, I'll make a good-looking corpse!" Mama said and they laughed so hard they were *both* losing their air.

"You're crazy!" Mrs. Williams said to Mama.

So, Mama lost all that middle age spread from a combination of smoking like a chimney, that's what she called it, and standing in the doorway from the kitchen to the living room and pounding her hips back and forth, from side to side, on the door frame.

She said that's how you get rid of saddlebag thighs, like she said she had, and she did this every day for a while, even if it made sore bruises on her thighs from doing it.

When she was back down to 115 pounds, she put on a tight dress and red lipstick and marched herself down to talk to the manager at Joe's Cellar and came back all smiles saying, "I *knew* he was sweet on me. He gave me my job back lickety split once he saw how good I look now."

Once she was back at Joe's Cellar, church was out. That's the way it was when she was working there before and then I didn't know why, but now I do, because I'm old enough to know that it's a bar where people drink alcohol and I'm pretty sure it's a sin to drink alcohol. Except it's a little confusing because I know that Jesus turned water into wine at a party once, and wine's got alcohol in it, so I don't know how it can be a sin to drink alcohol when the Lord drank it himself.

I asked Mama about this once and she said she didn't know the answer to that since she ain't a preacher or anything. Stevie chimed in the conversation with a story about Jesus being invited to all the parties around since he could do that trick of turning water into wine and folks invited him, so they could save on the wine budget, even though they thought Jesus was weird with all this "son of God" stuff he was saying all the time.

Mama told him to shut up, just because we don't go to church doesn't mean we got to bring the wrath of God upon us with that kind of blasphemy and she quoted the Bible, "He that blasphemeth the name of the Lord, he shall surely be put to death, and all the congregation shall certainly stone him. Leviticus 24:13-16," complete with the name of the book and exact chapter and verse where you can find the proof that she didn't make it up.

After she said that, I was worried because I did laugh at it and I wondered if that meant I blasphemed too.

"Well, I guess it's good we don't go to church anymore so there's no 'congregation' to stone me for it." Stevie, who actually wants me to start calling him Steven, smarted back, making quotation marks in the air when he said "congregation."

Steven laughed to himself and went off to his room while Mama carried on something about sparing the rod and spoiling the child.

We didn't have to go to church anymore, but Mama said I could go with Evelyn to church if I want to. I can't wait to tell her. She'll be so happy when I say I can go and I don't come up sick.

Mama said you don't got to go to church to be a Christian anyhow. Just after she got her Joe's Cellar job back, she told Mrs. Gunnels she wouldn't need her to come get us for church anymore, because she was going to be working late Saturday nights from now on and won't the Lord understand?

Mrs. Gunnels said, "Of course the Lord will understand," and convinced Mama to at least to go to Bingo with her and the other ladies from church on a Wednesday night once. Mama came back that night all excited about what she won.

"Isabelle! Steven! Joseph! Come into the kitchen!" she called.

We came running all excited. In the 10 seconds it took me to get from my room all the way down the hall and into the kitchen, my imagination ran wild about what it could be. A new TV! Brand new shiny dishes! A record player! A bunch of money!

She made us gather around the table where she had set a box in the middle. It looked sort of like the kind of box Aunt Gracie wrapped a whole year's worth of socks in for Steven on his last birthday. That's when I thought it might be socks for the whole family or something, but then I thought she wouldn't be so excited about socks since she said about Aunt Gracie's gift to Steven that it was about the most tacky gift you could give a 15-year-old boy, since Steven was turning 15 at that time.

We looked on while Mama opened the top to the box slow and then pulled back the newspaper covering what was inside. We leaned in, holding our breath. That's when we could see it was a painting of Jesus looking up to Heaven. His hair was brown and flowing and glowing where the light in the painting shines on it. His skin was perfect and smooth looking.

We don't really know what to say, except Steven said, "oh" like he was disappointed.

"Oh? Is that all you can say? That's the Lord, you know!" Mama snapped at Steven.

"Well, it's not actually the Lord, Mama. If it was, we could ask him for some miracles, you know, like to not be poor anymore," he says back.

"You'd best watch your mouth, Steven!" Mama scolded. "You're going to mess around and end up in Hell! You're old enough, you know."

"I'm just saying, it's just a painting of what someone thinks Jesus looked like, that's all," Steven said and rolled his eyes.

"Well, it ain't just any old painting. I've been praying for blessings and asking the Lord if I should've gone back to my old job at Joe's Cellar. I asked him for a sign, and this is a sign," Mama explained. I didn't say anything because I was afraid I might say something wrong and Mama would remind me that I could end up in Hell alongside Steven.

"How is it a sign?" Steven wanted to know.

"It just is. What do you think, Isabelle?" Now she turned to me. If I told the truth, I would have said I was disappointed it wasn't something more useful like a stereo or at least a new set of dishes or something, but I also knew that if I said, "well, *I* like it, Mama," I'd be on Mama's good side and the Lord's good side at the same time.

"Well, *I* like it, Mama," I heard myself say, covering up my disappointment.

"Good, you can help me hang it over the couch," she said. We found a nail in one of the kitchen drawers. Mama climbed up on the couch to hammer it in the wall with an iron skillet her mama gave her when she first came here to Georgia. The nail bent and Mama got upset and started to swear.

"Sumbitch! Doggawn it! The devil's trying to stop us from hanging it up!" she declared.

"He is?" I didn't know the devil would be looking in on us and knowing what we're doing enough to know we're trying to hang a picture of the Lord.

"Right he is, but he ain't going to win," she said and hammered the nail again even though it was bent. It popped out from under the frypan and went flying across the room like a bullet. Joseph took off after it.

"I got it! I got it!" he yelled and slithered like a snake on his belly to get it out from underneath the rocking chair.

"Steven, I need you to come help us out here!" Mama called out to Steven who had already gone back to his room to pick up whatever it was he was doing before he was called into the kitchen to be disappointed about the Lord in a box, since it wasn't the real Lord, but a painting.

"Come on. We're in a battle with the devil and we ain't going to let him win!" Mama continued.

"What do you need me to do?" Steven asked while he stood by the living room door.

"I need you to take this skillet and flatten out that nail."

"What? Don't we have another one?"

"No. We don't. That's the only one we have, and the devil knows it." Mama was holding the frypan out to Steven and Joseph brought the nail to him in his hands cupped together like someone who is taking the Body of Christ at Mass.

That's the moment the first Bible talk sentence came into my mind.

"And he brought forth the sacred nail unto Steven," was what the thought said. I didn't know where that came from because that's not the way I talk for real.

Steven put the nail out on the floor and slammed the frying pan down on it so hard it dented the floor.

"That's okay," Mama said, "don't worry about the floor. That's just the devil trying to make us think twice't."

Steven slammed the frypan down one more time on the bent nail and then held it up to Mama.

"Behold! The sacred nail!" another Bible talk thought in my head said.

"Oh, thank you, Steven! It's a miracle!" Mama gasped, "You hammer it in. We'll stand back and tell you when it's straight since you're so good with that thing."

Steven and Mama switched places and the three of us watched while Steven gave the nail three solid whacks and the nail was stuck good in the concrete.

"Wow! You *are* good at that!" Mama cheered and clapped and so we clapped too, Joseph and me. Steven took a bow and started to climb down from the couch until Mama told him to hold on. She said he deserved the honor of hanging the picture since he was such an expert at straightening the nail and then hammering it solid in the concrete cinderblock wall with a frypan.

We watched while Steven hung the picture. Mama held her mouth open and inhaled like when Steven performed the miracle of the straightened nail. She said again how it was a sign that she was making the right choice to go back to work at Joe's Cellar, even though Aunt Gracie and the ladies at church said it was surely a den of iniquity. I didn't know what "iniquity" was, so I asked Steven to help me look it up in the dictionary and I found out it meant sin.

I asked Steven what sins they did at Joe's Cellar.

"I guess it's because of the drinking," he said, which brought me back in my mind to the little puzzle of why Jesus would turn water into wine if it was a sin to drink it.

"Or maybe it's the smoking," Steven said.

Steven hopped down off the couch and we all stood looking up at the Lord with his eyes turned toward Heaven. That's when Mama declared that we were going make up for not going to church by kissing the picture of Jesus every night. Starting tonight. Each one of us was to get up on the couch and give the Lord seven kisses on the cheek.

"Why seven?" Steven wanted to know.

"Because it's a lucky number," was all Mama would say to explain it.

"Another thing we're going to do is read three chapters in the Bible every day," Mama went on to say. "That way, the Lord knows we ain't forgot him. And we'll all say our prayers before we sleep, since we got out of doing that."

We used to kneel beside our bed and pray,

> *"Now I lay me down to sleep,*
> *I pray the Lord my soul to keep,*
> *If I should die before I wake,*

I pray the Lord my soul to take."

Then we would ask the Lord to bless a list of folks. Who was in the list of folks depended who we knew that needed prayers. It wasn't always the same folks, except at the end we always would say, "and God bless papa, wherever he may be."

I think Mama forgot that only me and Steven have the same papa when she told us to say this because Joseph wanted to say it too because he didn't understand that he had a different daddy than us. She started to tell him he didn't have to say it, but he wanted to, so she just let him at first. But then, after a while, she told us none of us had to say that part if we didn't want to.

I didn't mind the asking blessings for folks part and the "God bless papa, wherever he may be" part, but I asked Mama if we could have another prayer that didn't talk about dying in our sleep. Mama said it's a fine prayer and there's nothing to fear because Jesus is with us, but if we got a different one we want to say, that would probably be okay with the Lord.

Since then, every evening, we huddle around and Mama reads from her old red Bible with the pages falling apart in chunks, three chapters even if the electricity is off, she reads, and we listen by candlelight and sometimes she convinces Steven to do the reading since he's the man of the house. Then we all line up and climb on the couch to do our duty to give Jesus seven kisses each.

So now Mama's finished washing her hair and she's got her short skirt and those stockings that look like finishing nets on like before when she was working at Joe's Cellar. I'm watching her put on her make-up, so I can know how to do it when I'm grown up.

I ask Mama if I can work at Joe's Cellar too when I grow up. And she turns and looks at me hard, straight in my eyes and says in a voice almost like she's mad, "no!"

"Why not, Mama?" I want to know.

"Just no, is all. You're going to do something else when you're grown up."

"Can I have the cardboard from your stockings, Mama?" I ask, because I always get the cardboard from her stockings so I can write on it. "I want to write," I always say when I ask her for it.

So, she gives me the cardboard and I write a story or a poem on it for her and she keeps them in a box under her bed with the red Bible. It's where she keeps her treasures, she says to us. And tucked in the Bible is a stripper's feather that Mama's friend named Gigi gave her when they worked together at Joe's Cellar before.

"What's a stripper?" I asked Mama when she first showed me the pink feather and told me where it came from. She was resting on her bed that evening next to me when I had a fever that came along just out of the blue, so neither Steven nor Joseph were allowed to come in just in case I was contagious.

I was laying with my head tucked under her arm and she played with my fingers, threading her fingers in and out of them. The sun going down was stretching out orangey pink light across the room and our hands threading in and out made a shadow on the wall next to us. Mama noticed the shadow and laughed a whispery laugh and made her hand like a duck beak shadow and it made me laugh too.

"Mama, what's a stripper?" I asked again. Since she didn't answer me before, I thought it was something I wasn't supposed to know, so I wanted to know it more.

"Well, a stripper is a lady that does dances for men and sometimes they take off some of their clothes just to make the men happy."

"You mean a lady dances to make her husband happy?"

"Not exactly. Well, sometimes ladies dance in a bar on a stage, because they have to make money to feed their young'uns," she said in a whispery voice.

"Oh. Do they like to do it?" I wanted to know, because I think I wouldn't like it at all, and I can't even use my imagination to think of liking taking my clothes off in front of a bunch of boys.

"Hmmm ... Not really. At least Gigi didn't like it, but she didn't have no choice really."

"Mama? Do you...?" I started to ask her if she dances on the stage for men and takes off her clothes, but she answered me before I could get my question out.

"No...no...I don't. I bring them their drinks."

"Mama?" I had some more questions. "What happened to Gigi?"

"We don't know. She just went away one day, and no one heard from her since," she sighed heavy at that. "She just pretty much disappeared like she never existed...except I have that feather that was hers."

"Oh, you must have been sad. I'd be real sad if Evelyn ever just up and went away like that," I said.

"Well, baby, it's a good thing, she ain't going nowhere. Why don't you try to sleep now? Everything is okay," She told me, because she knows I'll worry about what ever happened to Gigi who had no choice but to dance and take her clothes off in front of a bunch of men for money.

Chapter Forty-Six

It's the third day of summer after sixth grade graduation. We're waking up to one of those fierce Georgia thunderstorms, the kind of storm where it's so dark you could swear it's nightfall. The thunder is crashing so loud I can feel it in my chest like a drum.

Mama's usually got strict rules for how we should behave during this kind of weather.

"Y'all sit down in the hall, now. And be quiet! No talking 'til it's through!" Mama orders us and she huddles down next to us and wrings her hands around each other. I got my Walkie-talkie with me, and I want to try to reach Evelyn, but Mama said, "No" and to put it away.

I reckon if we make any noise a tornado would hear us and find its way right to our place and rip the roof right off the building and take us all along with it because one of us kids didn't see fit to obey our mama and spoke.

Anyway, the storm passes quick, but then after that one, another passes through and then another. It's just that kind of morning all the way into afternoon. But no one got sucked away in a tornado, apparently since we were all quiet when Mama told us to be. After the sky cleared itself, I went out to the red clay alleyway, down at the other end of it where the clay is the best, with Evelyn to build some rivers and streams out of the water that had collected there. We squat in the orange mud and make long curving streams that seem alive and flow downhill.

Evelyn plucked her some purple lilacs, and I plucked some mimosa flowers and we stuck them in the mud beside the streams.

"I wish I could shrink myself down real small and take a seat right under one of those lilacs or mimosa flowers," I say, and Evelyn laughs a little.

"Oh, I know! Let's make a big old mountain off to the side and put some trees on it too!" she says while she's pushing clumps of clay together off to the side next to the tangled shrubbery bushes hanging into the alley.

I like that idea and I start raking up clay too and we pat it down and put some more until it's solid.

We break some branches off the hanging shrubs and stick them in the mountainside.

"We could have a house right here!" I say, pointing to the top of the mountain.

"Yeah! And let's make a little lake next to the mountain!" Evelyn suggests and scoops a little clay out to make the lake and smooths it down on the inside, just like we do when we make dishes out of the clay, so when she puts water in it, it won't sink through. She finds an old plastic cup someone threw out and cups some rainwater into the lake.

"How we going to make the house?" I ask.

"We'll make it out of clay first. Then we can stick little sticks in it like a log cabin." Evelyn is so fast with the ideas.

"Yeah!" I agree and we start building our mountain top house.

Just then Evelyn remembers she has to get cleaned up in a minute for her piano lesson with Mrs. Washington.

"Oh shoot! I near 'bout forgot about that!" Evelyn says.

I had forgotten about that too. Mrs. Washington, who was her English teacher last year, is teaching Evelyn piano and "she's doing it out of kindness," Evelyn told me once. I was thinking at the time maybe I could come too, but then Mama said it wouldn't be polite for me to ask to go over to someone's house that I didn't even know, just because Evelyn was going.

So, the minute turned into more than a minute because we got all caught up in the house building with the smells of the mimosa and lilacs all mixed together with the smell of rain and wet clay and the sounds cicadas make when the sun is getting real hot and high in the sky.

Suddenly, we hear a snap of branches in the shrubbery bushes beside us. No sooner than we can turn our heads toward the sound we see three big boys staring at us through the leaves.

I know one of them is "bloody valentine" Willard, who lives across the field on the other side of the front porch, and I think the other boy is Willard's cousin. The other boy with them is a Black boy that I don't know.

"What y'all doin?" Willard's cousin asks us.

"Nothing," Evelyn says and puts down the little pieces of branches she was about to put on our house. She moves her hand close to mine, so her fingers are touching mine.

I got a feeling like I'm afraid to make any noise, like I'm hiding, but I know they can see us. We aren't exactly hidden. There's something in my stomach that's shaking like something real wrong is going on.

"Y'all come play with us," Willard's cousin says.

This is when Evelyn takes hold of my hand and jumps up.

"Run, girl!" she yells, and she pulls me by the arm quick as lightning and we run down the alley way splashing orange clay mud in our faces while we go.

I look back to see if they're after us and see they are.

"Don't look back, Isabelle! Run!" Our hands lost each other's grip and we keep running, but Evelyn trips on something and gets behind me.

I turn around to see her get up and start running again.

I'm going as fast as I can and take a quick turn right to dip out of the alley way and back toward the rows and rows of apartments where there are people, so we'll be safer.

Just as I'm running through, a bunch of bushes a branch swipes me across the face and cuts me making me bleed.

I'm out of breath, but I yell to Evelyn to watch out for that branch, but she doesn't say anything back. I don't stop because I figure she must be right behind me and didn't feel like now is exactly the time to chat.

I keep running until I'm finally in the driveway in between our apartments. I'm standing there breathing real hard. I wipe the blood from where the branch scraped me on my face with my shirt sleeve that's all muddy anyway.

"I can't believe we outran those boys!" I say and turn around to tell Evelyn, but she's not behind me.

It's at that moment, that I get a hot rush of heat washing over me like a wave because I see that she's not been behind me all this time like I thought. I can hear my heart thumping in my ears while I go fast around the front side of her apartment, thinking, somehow, she went a different way and ended up on the other side of the building.

She's not there.

That's when I start knocking hard on the door. Mrs. Williams comes to the door and flings it open.

"What is wrong, child? Where's Evelyn? She got a piano lesson with that nice ..." She's looking behind me. "Where's Evelyn? She with you?" she asks, and she's got a confused look on her face.

"Those boys...those boys chased us," I said in between breaths because I still haven't caught my breath all the way from running.

"What boys?! Where did they chase my baby?!" Mrs. Williams screams, with her eyes looking scared and now Barbara's standing behind her with her fingers in her mouth with her eyes wide too.

"We were playing and all of the sudden those boys. Willard and his cousin and one other Black boy I ain't ever seen before, they chased us all the way down the alley. I thought she was right behind me but ...."

I was still talking when Mrs. Williams suddenly let out a holler that made me jump. I think she's about to lose her mind and she starts yelling, "Oh, Lord Jesus! They're going to get my baby girl! Oh, Lord! Where did they go, child? Which way they go?!" She's asking and walking back and forth with her arms crossed over the front of her, rubbing up and down all frantic on both arms.

"I think they went that way," I say, and point out toward the alley where we were building a mountain out of clay.

Then Mrs. Williams turns and says to Barbara, "Stay here with Isabelle!" And she cuts out the back door toward the alley screaming Evelyn's name.

It wasn't too long before Mrs. Williams came back all hysterical and crying. She called the police when she got back inside, and I thought she was going to have a heart attack waiting for them because they were taking so long. She was back to pacing the floor and rubbing her arms again. Her hair is loose from its hair bob and it's falling in her face.

I'm trying to keep Barbara busy with some coloring books so as to keep her from sitting and staring at her mama all upset and scared like that.

The police finally show up and Mrs. Williams explains what happened. Then the police want to talk to me being as I was the last one with Evelyn before we saw those boys. So, I told him about what happened. There were two policemen there, but only one of them was doing all the talking while the other one just stood off to the side with his hand on his belt, saying nothing.

"Now, was one of those boys her boyfriend?" the talking policeman asked.

"No sir. We don't know those boys, except one's name is Willard, who's white and his cousin, who's white too, but I don't know his name or the Black boy that was there too," I say.

"Now, I thought you said y'all didn't know those boys," the policeman says.

"I know one of their names, but we ain't friends or anything," I tell him.

"Is one of them her boyfriend?" he asks again.

That's when Evelyn's mama can't take anymore, and she chimes in, "What's wrong with y'all police? My baby's been chased by some big boys. They ain't her boyfriends!"

"Now, Mrs. Williams, you are going to have to stay calm or I'm going to have to take you downtown," the policeman says in a robot voice.

"You gonna take *me* downtown?! Why? My baby is gone! We need to find her! We are wasting time!" Evelyn's mama is crying now with tears rolling down her face.

"Well, Mrs. Williams," he says in that robot voice again while he's looking down at his clipboard and writing something, "You have to understand, we get these kinds of calls all the time. Some young girl runs off with her boyfriend and everyone thinks she's in danger and she's just off fooling around with him all day. That's why we have such a high teen pregnancy rate these days."

"We told you, that wasn't none of her boyfriend!! Y'all going to look for my baby?"

"Well, yes ma'am we're going to go out looking. Now you give us a call, though, if she comes home."

And with that, the policeman leaves and Mrs. Williams sits down stunned in a chair in the kitchen for a few minutes and she hangs her head in her hands and cries and so do I except I'm trying hard not to let it show.

Then suddenly she hops ups from her chair.

"Come on. We'll get folks around to help us look."

I run across and get Steven and Joseph. Mama's not home because she had to go off to work.

Mrs. Williams takes Barbara by the hand and goes next door to ask the new neighbors that just moved in if they wouldn't mind helping. Those neighbors send their son over across the way to ask the neighbors there.

Next thing we know, we got a whole army of us walking up and down the alley calling out Evelyn's name. We go up and down and then over to Society Avenue.

We look inside an empty apartment across the field.

We look in some of the lean-to shacks down the alley, but there's no sign of Evelyn, nor those boys.

Hours pass and even as the sun is starting to go down you can still hear folks calling her name and it sounds to me like a Black-capped Chickadee. I usually love that bird call; with the way they call out like they could be calling out anyone's name. Now, I'm thinking I might not like it so much anymore because then, it will remind me of this day.

But then I tell myself to stop that thinking, because it's going be just fine when Evelyn finally shows up. Then I'll tell her about how we looked for her and then I can like the Chickadee song again.

So up and down the street "Eeeev-lyyyn! Eeeev-lynnn!" the birds in my head call out, "Eeeevlynnn!"

But Evelyn doesn't answer, so the Chickadee sounds sadder and sadder each time he calls.

When the sun goes down, there's a kind of quiet in the neighborhood. People got their windows and doors open, but there's no sound coming out of them like usual.

The police came by one time to ask if Evelyn had showed up yet and then left without really saying much when they found out she hadn't.

I'm sitting in the grass in the backyard with my Walkie-talkie and staring at Evelyn's window. I keep thinking at any moment, her light is going to come on and she's going to flash her flashlight out to me. She's going to tell me she just went down the alley and got lost or something when she was running, but she's back now and everything is fine. She's sorry she scared us so. She's going to appear right there any second. I know it and tell me all this is just something I imagined. She's going to...

My thoughts drift around in circles. "She's gone. Where's my friend?" I say out loud into my knees while I bring them up close to my chest. I bury my face and cry.

Just then, Mama comes to the door since she's back from work.

"Come on in, Isabelle. Sitting out here by yourself is dangerous," she says. "Come on. We'll all sit together on the couch and watch a show and you can keep your Walkie-talkie right there for when Evelyn comes back." Mama comes out and sits cross legged beside me in the grass and smokes a cigarette.

She puts her arm around me and says, "She'll be back. There must be some reason she ain't show up yet, some reason that ain't serious."

I lean over and lay my head across my mama's knees and she brushes my hair back with her hand until she finishes her cigarette.

Chapter Forty-Seven

I wake up to the sound of screaming around 3:00 in the morning. I sit up straight on my mattress and rub my eyes to see blue lights going around and around across the wall of my room through my opened curtains. A screen door slams. I jump up and go to my window and that's when I see the police car in the driveway, and I see some policemen standing in Evelyn's yard talking to her mama and Mama is next to Evelyn's mama, holding her up 'cause she looks like she's about to fall out on the sidewalk.

"Steven!" I call out. "Steven!" and run out into the hallway.

"What's going on?" Steven asks, standing in his doorway in his short pants and no shirt, rubbing his eyes.

"The police are outside. Mama's out there with Mrs. Williams," I answer quick and go out the back door too, leaving Steven there blinking his eyes.

I'm standing on the sidewalk on the edge of the driveway close enough that I can hear some of what the police are saying to Mrs. Williams.

I know I heard him say "body" and I know that when somebody is dead, they are called a body. I feel a chill go up my back like something is crawling on me.

I look at my mama and our eyes lock for a moment. She's gasping to herself with her mouth open and that's when I hear the word "body" again. Mrs. Williams lets out a loud wail and breaks free from Mama's arms and runs right past me. For a second, she looks right at me, right in my eyes, but then, she doesn't even act like she sees me and runs down the alley in the pitch dark, making a horrible shrieking cry, "My baby! My baby! Oh Lord, my baby!"

Some of the neighbor ladies that had gathered around ran down the alley after her and another neighbor lady went inside Evelyn's place, I guess to stay with Barbara, who is probably sleeping away in her bed.

The police get back in their car and head back down the alley, going slow and silent with their blue lights still on and shining on the shrubbery bushes and the trees on the side of the alley.

It's at that moment that I think I must be dreaming this. Or maybe I'm dead too and, somehow, I'm just a ghost watching this scene unfold around me and that's why Evelyn's mama didn't see me.

As quick as these thoughts are filling my head, I hear the voices of the women coming back down the alley with Mrs. Williams. There are two of them on each side of her holding her up while she's throwing her head back and crying for Jesus to help her.

Mama's beside me, touching me on the shoulder and calling out my name, but I can't say anything. The ladies and Mrs. Williams are getting closer until they're crossing the driveway just in front of us and the two ladies on each side of her go with her into the house. The other lady comes over toward us and it's like she's walking in slow motion. She's talking to Mama and Mama's talking to her and their voices sound like they're under water in my mind.

"Isabelle, honey," the lady says, and I turn to look at her and it's like I'm moving in slow motion too and I look at her face, but I fix my eyes on her mouth. From above us, the dim yellow lamp light that's been about to go out forever, is flickering on her while she speaks.

"Yes, ma'am?" I say, and my voice sounds under water too.

She put her arm on my other shoulder.

"It's Evelyn, baby. She ain't alive no more," she says, and I can't speak, but I'm just staring straight ahead at Evelyn's dark window.

I hear the lady say something to Mama about praying and I see Mama out of the corner of my eye nodding her head, "yes," like she agrees. Then the lady goes inside where Evelyn's mama went with the other ladies and where Barbara is sleeping without knowing anything.

I stand there on the edge of the driveway for what seems like a long time. I don't even know if I'm breathing because my chest feels stiff and heavy like the trunk of the mimosa. My arms feel cold and unbendable like the branches of the mimosa on the shady side of the tree in the late afternoon when me and Evelyn sat with our legs dangling off the sides for hours. I'm frozen here on the edge of this driveway beside the garbage can with the sleeping morning glories all around it and my feet are in the ground like roots sinking deep into the concrete. I think, at that moment, in my mind's eye, maybe I'm the mimosa and I have been a witness and what I have seen and what I know tonight made all my flowers fall off all at once and they spin around me like twirling pink dresses.

And then in a moment, I know I'm not the mimosa, but I am me, and Mama is beside me calling me back to the world again and she's telling me about having faith. I just look at her and nod, "yes", but I know that tonight I left my faith right there on the sidewalk, on the edge of the driveway, like some material thing, a useless old pair of boots that don't fit anymore and got holes in the soles, so they don't do anyone any good.

Chapter Forty-Eight

It's the day of Evelyn's funeral and I'm over at Evelyn's house, well, her mama's house, sitting on the couch in my hand me over dress that Evelyn gave me last year. Mama said it was kind of weird to wear a dress of a dead friend to her own funeral, but I don't know what else to do since I don't have another dress and it wouldn't be fitting to wear just any old thing to see her off to be with the Lord. This one is just the right amount of somber to wear on a day like this because it's dark gray with little off-white satiny flowers around the collar. Mrs. Williams said it was okay and that though my mama means well, she ain't right on this one and that she's sure that Evelyn will be smiling down on me from Heaven, and she'll say, "Girl, you do that dress fine!", like she always said when she gave me hand me over clothes.

So, I'm sitting here, thinking how Evelyn would approve of my dress and I suddenly hear Mrs. Williams crying out. "Come on, child! You need to come on out of that tub. We got to get on down to the church!" She's yelling at Barbara who's in the tub and won't get out. I can hear Barbara starting to cry too.

"Noooo! Mama, I don't want to go see Evelyn dead in a box!"

"Come on now! I got your dress. Look, at your dress. Ain't it pretty? Evelyn is going to love this on... She's going ...Evelyn's... going to... oh, Lord, Jesus... Evelyn...Lord Jesus...Evelyn...why, Lord Jesus...why did you take my baby? Why?" And then I hear a crash.

I get up and rush to the bathroom doorway and I see Evelyn's Mama sitting on the floor with tub water all over her and her hair is falling down in her face. "I can't......can't..." I don't know what she "can't" and this whole time Barbara is sitting in the tub naked and shivering with her knees pulled up to her chest and staring straight ahead at the wall like she's in some sort of trance, like there's no life behind her eyes. She looks like a doll just staring ahead at nothing.

Just then I step forward and a jagged part of the door frame catches hold of my dress and snags a hole in it. This alone is enough to make me cry, and I got Mrs. Williams there on the floor and Barbara in the tub in a trance, so I don't know what to do. I got tears coming down when I'm trying not to and then Mrs. Williams notices and with that, she changes from needing help to helping and she pulls herself up from the floor, "Don't you mind that now, we'll sew that right up." She's wiping her face with the back of her sleeve. She hands me a strip of toilet tissue to wipe my face and turns to Barbara. "Come on, honey. We got to get going. You're going to have to get out the tub, baby." Barbara doesn't say anything.

Then Mrs. Williams tells me to go ahead and take off my dress and that she'll sew it up, while I see if I can get this child out the tub. I take off my dress and I'm looking in the mirror at my white skin, with the tattoo that Evelyn drew with an ink pen on my shoulder. It says "best" inside half a heart. On her shoulder I wrote "friends" and put the other half of the heart that would go with mine. We thought it was nice how one half of the heart was white, and the other half was black. Evelyn said it was kind of like a Chinese "yin and

341

yang." I thought so too, even though I didn't know what that symbol meant, just that it *did* have black and white sides that fit perfect together just like a puzzle. So, I keep this drawing on my skin by being careful not to wash it when I take a bath. It still keeps fading even though I don't wash that spot, so every so often I trace it back over where Evelyn drew, but it's not so easy because it's on my right shoulder and I'm right-handed. You can tell where I traced it over because the lines get kind of squiggly in places.

I'm in my thoughts about my half a tattoo and I realize I need to try to get Barbara out the tub, so I get down on my knees next to her. I'm trying to think about what to do next when I get the idea to show her my tattoo and tell her the story of how me and Evelyn got matching ones. I got to get her to look at me, I'm thinking. That's how they say you get somebody out of a trance.

"Barbara, look at this half a heart Evelyn drew on my shoulder." Next thing I know, I think I'm a genius because I offer to draw one just like it on her shoulder and I tell her it's her job to pick up where Evelyn left off and be the other half of that heart. She's looking at me now and I can tell she's interested.

"You want one of these on your shoulder ... just like Evelyn?" I ask, and I can feel a lump up in my throat and kind of a feeling of a flood behind my eyes, but I'm trying with all my might to hold that flood in so it doesn't get Barbara upset more. It's no use, though, because Barbara is looking up at me and saying nothing, but she's got big tears streaming down her face making wet tracks of darker brown all the way to her chin. She's shivering like crazy because the bath water has gone cold.

"Come on, let's get you out of this water," I say, and I hear my voice sounding all grown up and I wonder who this girl is that's me, but in a different kind of way. I turn to grab a towel and wipe it on my face first because I'm not doing too great holding back my own tears that I don't want Barbara to see.

"Come on." I'm sounding like a mama now and holding the towel out to her to wrap her up. She stands up all soaking wet and shivering so bad I think she might fall out. I wrap the towel around her body and lift her from the tub. I remark to myself in my head how she's not much heavier than a bag of feathers, and I'm glad of that because I don't think I could have picked her up otherwise.

So, I sit on the toilet seat with the lid down like a chair and sit there with Barbara wrapped up snug and rock her back and forth like a baby while she cries tears all on my shoulder blade. While I'm rocking her, I notice on the bathroom window a stained-glass paper decoration that Evelyn put up last Christmas. It's a drawing of a white dove with a branch in his mouth and the words "peace on earth" written across a dark blue sky. I don't know if it was left up there on purpose or if it was forgotten when all the Christmas decorations were taken down, but seeing it is giving me a wish so big it makes my chest hurt.

I'm still rocking Barbara while she's resting her head on my chest with my chin resting on her head. She's got two fingers in her mouth like she used to do when she was little lying across Evelyn's knees while Evelyn and me stayed up until sunrise sprawled out on the living room floor on pillows because there was more room there than in Evelyn's room. When she breathes in, she's gasping in air and shaking the air out. Her hair feels woolly and thick against my neck. I'm crying so hard right now I'm dripping that flood of tears that was behind my eyes right down on top of her head. She doesn't even notice so we sit there just like that until Mrs. Williams comes in with my dress in her hand.

"Oh, it's as good as new now, honey. You can go on ahead and put it on now." And so, I do after I hand Barbara off all bundled up in a towel to her mama. I wipe my tears off my face with some more toilet tissue and comb my hair back with Mrs. Williams' hair pick she keeps on the side of the sink. My hair's got nothing to it compared to Barbara's and so it just slips right through it like I'm combing with my fingers. I pat some water down on some hairs that stick up like a cow licked in the front of my forehead. I know that as soon as it dries that cow lick will pop right back up but I'm not going to worry about it. I stand back and look in the mirror with my hand me over dress and I look for what seems like a long time.

I remember the last time I saw Evelyn wear this dress. It was at my 6th grade graduation. I remarked in my head how pretty her skin looked against the silky off-white flowers and then how the gray in the dress seemed to make any specks of gray in her eyes just jump right on out. I must have been looking at her hard when I was doing all my admiring because she asked me if something was wrong about the dress.

I told her, "Nothing's wrong at all. You look real pretty in it, that's all." I wanted to ask her if I could have it when she outgrew of it, but it was like she was reading my mind because that's when she said, "You can have it when I'm too big for it." She brought it over to me right after that saying she thought it might already fit me, since it had a belt around the waist.

That's how we did. Evelyn and me. We knew each other's thoughts lots of times. So, while I'm standing here looking at myself, I don't know why, but a little smile comes across my mouth. At that moment, I swear I hear Evelyn's voice. "Girl, you do that dress fine!" she says.

Ebenezer Baptist Church is on the Southside of Albany six city blocks from the park with the rickety seesaw that fell apart one time when Evelyn and me were on it right in the middle of see and saw. When we fell to the ground I landed on a jagged piece of glass and cut my leg straight through my favorite pair of jeans. Evelyn made a bandage with her over shirt to try to stop the bleeding like she learned about in health class. She pressed down on it while I yelped out loud. She said she was sorry, but she had to get the bleeding to stop so I didn't bleed to death on our way home. She was able to slow down the bleeding, so I didn't die that day. When we got home, we went to her house and she washed it out with warm saltwater and put a real bandage on it.

Since that time she bandaged my blister that I got from holding Steven's record player, Evelyn said she was going to a be a doctor when she grew up.

"I'm serious, Auntie," she said when she told her Auntie Nina about her plans.

"Now, girl, you got a big old dream in your head. How are you going to go to college when your mama's going to need you to get to work first chance you get to help out around here?"

"Hey, now, you let my baby have her dreams, ya hear. She can be what she puts her mind to," her mama took up for her. I was glad of that, because I was of the mind that Evelyn sure would be a doctor if that's what she wanted to do.

So, we're on our way to the church, driving on a bumpy street with holes all in it. We're all piled in Evelyn's Uncle Tyrone's big old Ford and every time we roll over those potholes, we're being all shaken around like on those rides at the fair that's supposed to be so fun. Evelyn's Uncle Tyrone is driving, and Mrs. Williams is in the front seat just in front of me. While he's driving, he keeps having to comfort Mrs. Williams every couple of minutes when she breaks out crying right in mid-sentence and hangs her head and cries out loud. Every time, Uncle Tyrone reaches over with his big hand and pats his sister on the head like you do when you pat a cat. When Mrs. Williams is sobbing, all I can see of her is the top of her head from over the seat in front of me, with Uncle Tyrone's dry fingers snagging up in her hair every time he rubs her hair down. "It's okay, now, Ruby," he says. "Evelyn's with the Lord now." Then he closes his jaws shut so tight his jaw muscles are flexing and his little gray curls on his sideburns are moving along with the flexing jaw muscles.

I've got Barbara perched on my lap asleep against the door and Steven is next to me with Joseph on his lap. Joseph doesn't seem to understand exactly where we're going or that anything so bad has happened with the way he's playing with a little plastic car, making it ride over his knees and crash onto the seat. He's making little whispery car crash sounds and smiling up at Steven every time. Steven just looks blank, like he doesn't know what's the right look or sound to make at a time like this when you're piled in the car on the way to the funeral of your little sister's best friend, who just last week in the evening on the back porch laid her head on your shoulder so you let her keep it there because she fell asleep like that.

Mama's sitting by the window behind Evelyn's Uncle Tyrone, staring out at the passing clouds and cars. She didn't wear any mascara on account of she figured there'd be crying that would make her cry too and she didn't want it running down her face, making a mess out of herself. I think she forgot, though, that make-up gets tracks down it when tears roll over it too. I can see the tracks on the right side of Mama's face, and they go all the way down to her neck where the make-up stops in a straight, pink line.

At the church, we separate from Uncle Tyrone and Mrs. Williams who go off into a room behind the alter, after an usher shows us to our seats in the front where family is to be seated. Mama tries to whisper to the usher that we aren't family, but he says he has instructions to put us here. So, Mama just closes her lips tight and gets a little worry wrinkle between her eyes.

"It's okay, Mama. Besides that, we have Barbara with us and she's family," Steven says. Mama looks like she just realized this and agrees quick, which I was glad about because there was a clog of folks building behind us and I didn't want Mama to make a scene by keeping it clogged.

Organ music is playing, and it feels like it's running electricity through my head and chest. The church is filling up as we take our seats in the same order we were in the car. I'm looking around behind us while Barbara is holding tight to my hand with her face buried into my shoulder. Steven is keeping Joseph busy by showing him things around the church, pointing at flower arrangements and a big wooden cross above the alter.

Mama says to stop pointing. "It's rude enough on any day, but even more rude to point at folks grieving in church. People can't even grieve in peace without having someone pointing at them," she says.

Steven tries to whisper that he's not pointing at people, but she shoots a look at him that says for him to keep his mouth shut, so he does.

"And don't be staring at people," she leans over past Steven and Joseph and whispers at me. "We don't want them to think we're uncivilized."

At that moment I wish my mama didn't come with us. She's acting like this is a regular church service with the way she's all worried what people are going to think about us.

I'm getting lost in my thoughts in my head and the next thing I know I'm thinking how the only thing that people here care about is Evelyn dead in the casket up in front of the church. The casket is open, and I know that she's laying in there with her eyes closed like a doll and her arms are probably crossed in front across her chest. I'm looking at the casket and I can't take my eyes away and I'm hoping it's not rude for me to fix my eyes so hard like that and Mama's whispering something with a question sound at the end of it but it's like I can't really hear her because the organ music feels like it just got louder in my head when that's all I can hear. I feel Barbara burying her face more in my shoulder and that's when I realize I got another flood of tears flowing down my face and I can't make it stop.

That's when all of a sudden there's a bunch of ladies I don't know around me patting my head and offering me Kleenexes. I look over at Mama and she's got tears too. She's saying she's sorry and that I can look all I want behind us and she didn't mean to make me upset like that. The ladies tell me that the Lord is going to see to it that we pull through this and he's right here in the middle of all this.

I want to believe that, but at that point with the church all full, that's when Evelyn's Uncle Tyrone and Mrs. Williams come into the chapel with a whole crowd of Evelyn's aunts and some more uncles holding Mrs. Williams up. She can hardly even stand up to walk to her seat over at the other end of the pew from me.

At that time, Evelyn's Auntie Nina comes over and scoops up Barbara, who had only just now taken her face from my shoulder leaving it wet with tears. She took Barbara onto her hip and Barbara hung on like she was hanging on for dear life around her aunt's neck. Auntie Nina took Barbara to the end of the pew next to her mama, leaving me with an empty space where she was sitting beside me until Stevie noticed and slid himself and Joseph over next to me.

The choir is singing now, a slow song about going to Heaven. It's like the song was made to sound just sad enough to make a person cry no matter if he wants to or not. Some people are looking down at song books and singing through the tears. I'm trying to do the same thing, but I can't. I can't see the words on the paper for the flood that's flowing from my eyes now. Steven hands me a wad of tissue and I cover my face in my hands and lean over toward Steven with Joseph nestled in between us. With my head resting on Steven, I can see my mama who is steady crying and dabbing her face with tissue. Any make-up that was on her face is on the tissue making it all peach colored. I can see Evelyn's mama with all of Evelyn's aunts and uncles surrounding her for comfort. Everybody in our pew has got somebody to touch and hang on to except Mama. That's when I reach out my fingers behind Steven's back toward Mama and she takes my fingers and kisses them, dripping tears on my hand and my sleeve.

The funeral seems to go forward in phases and goes from slow music to faster music as the preacher tells us that this is a celebration of Evelyn's life and we are going to rejoice. We are to lift our voices in rejoicing for God has called her home. Amen. Amen. And people in the congregation said, "Amen. Praise Jesus. Yes, Lord." Some people are clapping in rhythm to the music, but I can't get up any strength to clap when my arms feel again like they did that night when I stood on the curb side of the driveway and watched the scene unfold when the policeman was telling Mrs. Williams that her daughter was just a body.

After a fast phase where we're supposed to praise God for taking Evelyn home, Evelyn's Auntie Nina gets up to the podium and tells some stories about Evelyn when she was a little thing, and how she was a friend to everyone who needed a friend. "Even from an early age, that girl was special, Yes, Lord. Yes, Lord! She was. She sure was. She was drawn to those who suffered and with her sweetness she was there, yes, she was! Like the Lord himself had sent her."

"Amen! Amen!" the congregation agrees. Her aunt goes on to tell how Evelyn rescued me from the hands of some angry young'uns and she points me out. Everybody is now looking at me through their watery eyes and praising the Lord. "And that child right there turned out to be just like a sister to our Evelyn, praise Jesus! If you saw a little Black girl and a little white girl walking arm in arm down Society Avenue, chances are it was them on any day. That, all by itself, was a testimony to the love of our Lord, working through Evelyn and Isabelle to show us all how it can be in this world, if we only let it. Praise, Jesus!"

"Amen! Thank you, Lord!" everybody says and some ladies behind me leaned forward to hug me and tell me, "Praise Jesus."

After Auntie Nina is done, a lady starts singing a song, "Precious Lord, take my hand …" She's singing and coming down from the pulpit to where we are, starting at the end of the pew where Evelyn's mama is. She's looking at everybody right in their eyes and singing, "Lead me on. Let me staaaaaaaaaaaand." She's stretching out the words in song. "I'm tired, I'm weak I'm worn, through the stoooooooooorm, through the night." She's right in front of Steven and me and Joseph. We're looking up at her and she reaches out and touches Joseph on the hair and makes him smile. She moves over and looks me right in my eyes and sings the next part.

"Lead me on to the light. Take my hand precious Lord, lead me hooooooome." I can't keep from crying again and she pulls me up to her in a big hug and I can hear my own voice sobbing over the speakers in the church because when she's hugging me, the microphone is close to my face enough to pick up every sniffle. Any other time, this would have embarrassed me so bad I'd want to crawl up in a hole in the ground and hide, but at this moment, wrapped up in the arms of this woman I don't know while she sings about the Lord taking Evelyn's hand, I feel a wave of emotion that's so big I don't have any control. I'm crying out loud in between the lines of the song and the whole congregation is moved to cry out loud along with me.

After I quiet my cry a little bit, the singing lady loosens her hug and lets me sit back down next to my brothers, who are ready with another handful of tissues and my mama reaches over from behind Steven and rubs me on my back. I peek out from the tissue covering my face and see the faces of people joining me in sorrow and I feel a wave of comfort. I know at that moment that Evelyn is here with us in spirit, like she's not even really dead. It's not something you can really explain, but I can feel the energy from her right next to me, and she's telling me, "We got this, girl. This ain't no thang," like she always said when she was convincing me I can do something that takes a lot of courage or go-to-itness.

We all go through this funeral like we're all riding on some wave together, moved about by the words and song that's happening. It's time to file out of seats. The preacher man says, "All those who wish, to gaze upon her lovely face and say goodbye to our child and sister in Christ, until we see her again in Heaven." This is the part that, when I heard about it, I wasn't sure I could do it. I'm like Barbara with that feeling I don't want to see Evelyn dead in a box. But at the same time, I need to tell her "goodbye" to her face.

So, the choir is singing, "His eye is on the sparrow... and I knoooooow he's watchinnnnng meee!" And we're lining up like we used to do in the Catholic Church when I went up with Mémère to get the body of Christ. It's strange to have that feeling like you're in Mass with your Mémère, in line for the Holy Eucharist when you are really in line to look into the face of your best friend who is dead, and on her way to be with the Lord. I'm confused because I thought she was already with the Lord because that's what they've been saying for the last couple of days, "She's with the Lord now." But we're here, saying our goodbyes to see her off to be with the Lord.

Joseph is staying back in our seats with Mama on account of he's too young to look at a dead body without giving him nightmares, and Mama is scared anyway to look upon Evelyn that way because she's never seen a dead body before and she doesn't plan to, ever. Steven is going up with me and a couple of Evelyn's aunts and uncles are in line in front of us.

Each person in line is stepping forward and looking in the casket. Some people exclaim how beautiful she looks. Some people say a prayer over her. Everyone tells her, "Rest in sweet peace with the Lord."

There are only two people in front of me and I'm feeling my heart pounding like a drum in my chest. Steven has his hand on my shoulder and he's telling me it'll be okay. When it's now my turn to step forward, my feet feel planted in the floor. I know there are people behind me who are ready to move forward and can't because it isn't polite to skip someone in line to view a body at a funeral.

A couple of ladies behind me encourage me that I can do it and Steven says in my ear that he'll step forward with me. So, we do, and I'm looking down into the casket with the song about sparrows in my ears and the white of the covering up to her waist is satiny and glowing and her hands are crossed on her chest just like I imagined. Her face is like a doll with a smoothness like clay and she's more still than any object ever on the planet. I want to touch her, but I don't think I'm supposed to. I feel my brother's arm around me and he's whispering something to me, but I don't know why I can't make out what he's saying. I'm just leaning in and staring hard at Evelyn's eyes and mouth and hands and back at her closed eyes again and I've got a whole river of tears coming down dripping right down onto her satiny covering, making wet spots on it and her hand. Now I'm whispering something that I don't know what and suddenly the room is spinning, and my face is hot like it's on fire. It's like someone's pulling the shades down on my eyes because a curtain of dark is coming into view and the dark is spinning.

When I wake up, I'm in a little room with a couch off the side of the chapel, with my whole family around me and a couple of ladies from the church wiping my face with cool wet cloths. My mama is standing off to the side holding Joseph in a loving way like I'm not sure I've ever seen her do before. Just behind her is a light, making a glow around her head, and she and Joseph look like Mary and the Baby Jesus with the light making a halo around them.

Steven is sitting on the edge of the couch with his hand resting on my shin looking at me with no look on his face. "What happened?" I ask. "How did I get here?"

"You fell out, baby," one of the ladies says while she's leaning over me to throw open the window just above the couch. "There, now. The natural air will do you good," she says. Steven tells me that I fell over, right on top of Evelyn like I was going to lay right on in the casket with her. He said the whole congregation gasped all at once and the music stopped with the choir looking on with their mouths hanging open in the middle of a word. He reached over to pick me up, but I was dead weight, so he couldn't do it like he used to do. So, a man in the church that Steven didn't know rushed up to help and carried me off into this little room with my family trailing behind him all in shock and not sure if I was dead or just fainted.

Steven asked me why I was saying "sorry" to Evelyn because he says that's what I was whispering just before I fell out. "Oh," is all I can say, because I didn't know I was even saying it, so I don't know why I was saying it. I guess it must mean that I'm sorry that I was the lucky one and that she had to die alone without me the way she did. I guess I was sorry I took off in a different direction than her that day and that if we had stayed together maybe we could have fought those boys off. I'm too tired to tell all that to Steven though. I'm just fixing my eyes on a pink mimosa tree out the window. It's not as big and beautiful as the one that we have in our back yard, but its flowers are in full bloom and are swaying in the breeze. I'm just going to lay right here and stare at the dancing flowers and breathe in that smell like fresh peaches. How long can I stay here like this? Can I get the vision of Evelyn as a lifeless doll out of my mind if I try hard? Can I close my eyes and go like I'm riding on mimosa breeze and be back on my roof laying up there for hours with Evelyn there talking and laughing and watching the clouds move by behind the pink flowers?

Evelyn said one time that the flowers looked like ladies' dresses spinning around in a waltz when the wind moved them in circles. She said that mimosa I had by my porch was a real gift from the Lord. And then she'd say like the ladies at church, "Praise Jesus."

"Praise Jesus." I must have said it out loud because Stevie said, "Huh?" and the ladies from the church said, "Yes, Lord" and nodded down at me and Mama over in the corner, now sitting with Joseph in her lap said, "Amen. Amen," and stared at the floor.

Chapter Forty-Nine

Evelyn's mama didn't bury her in the ground like other folks who I heard of who died, but she had her body burned to ashes. I couldn't think about Evelyn being burned up like that, even though she did say one time that when she dies, she wanted to be cremated and have her ashes spread out on a breeze off the side of a mountain somewhere. She said this way, it's like she'd be flying, and she always thought it would be a wonderful thing to fly.

They put her ashes in a fancy container they call an urn and Mrs. Williams keeps it on her dresser surrounded by pictures from Evelyn's life. It was beautiful and sad at the same time. Mrs. Williams said I could come over any time and visit Evelyn in the urn and talk to her and it would bring me comfort. I did, but it didn't bring me comfort. It just made me ache bad in the center of my chest like it did that night the police came and told Mrs. Williams they found Evelyn dead.

Most of Evelyn's family didn't like the idea of there being no burial stone to lay flowers on. They said it's like there's no sign she ever was. Evelyn's Auntie Nina said it would be fair if Mrs. Williams let everyone have a little bit of the ashes so they could have her with them too. Mrs. Williams wasn't too sure if that was a good idea, but then her brothers and their wives and her sisters and their husbands wouldn't quiet down about it, so she decided it would be the Christian thing to do, to share Evelyn's ashes.

It's been 2 weeks since the funeral and I'm at Evelyn's mama's house because they're going to divide the ashes amongst the aunts and uncles. Mrs. Williams said I could have some if I promised to take good care of them. My mama said I couldn't have any, though, because she believes having ashes of a body in our house would invite spirits, and she doesn't want spirits coming around from the afterlife scaring us and throwing things around.

So, we're here with the urn on the kitchen table and some little Tupperware containers laid out on white paper napkins. Since they only have one urn to put Evelyn in, they're going to have to put her ashes in something else for everyone to bring some with them. Evelyn's Auntie Wanda said she had just the perfect thing from her Tupperware collection. I knew where she got them too because she was the only one that bought any from Mama one time when she was selling Tupperware. Evelyn brought home the catalogue because she bet Steven she could sell some and so she did, to her aunt.

Gospel music is playing loud on the stereo and everybody is gathered around to eat some cake and drink some Kool-Aid. Uncle Tyrone is drinking a bottle of whiskey that he's willing to share, but nobody wants any.

"Now, you know it's too early in the day for drink, Ty," his wife says and tries to grab at his bottle of whiskey.

"Don't tell me when I can drink!" Evelyn's Uncle Tyrone starts yelling.

All the other uncles surround him and tell him, "Calm down. You can keep your drink, man."

"Damn straight, I'm gonna keep my drink. Because I'm a grown ass man! Goddammit!" Uncle Tyrone snaps back and takes a drink to show he can if wants.

When he was yelling, Barbara started crying and all the women made a circle around her to comfort her and coo at her and tell her that everything is going to be alright and that Uncle Tyrone just ain't sure how to deal with his sadness over Evelyn. They prop her up on the couch next to me where I'm sitting and writing "Rest in Peace" on little pieces of papers because we're going to stick them on the sides of the containers with some Scotch tape to show respect for the ashes and so nobody forgets what's in there.

It's at that time I remember that I asked Barbara if she wanted a heart tattoo like I told her before Evelyn's funeral I would do. She does, and I draw the heart to make the other half of the heart to go with mine, with the word "friend" in the middle of it. I ask her if she'll trace mine in fresh and she does her best to make it neat. The lines are kind of squiggly, but I tell her it's great and that Evelyn would be happy about it.

"Look, Mama! Look at our tattoos!" Barbara says.

Her mama and her aunt come over and make a big fuss over how cute it is that the hearts fit together and say, "best friends." Mrs. Williams tells everybody that Evelyn had the other half of the heart tattoo on her before and Barbara's picking up where she left off. Everybody says if that isn't the most touching thing they ever heard, they don't know what is. We put our heart halves side by side and everybody except Uncle Tyrone is looking on and sighing and praising Jesus for this sweetness. Uncle Tyrone is sitting in the corner of the room on the floor with his back against the wall. I'm looking at him and I can swear I see tears on his face, but I don't say anything about it, because I don't know what's the right thing to say to my best friend's uncle when he's sitting in the corner of the room with tears on his face instead of thanking Jesus for this, the most touching moment ever.

Mrs. Williams breaks up the moment to say it's time to go ahead and divide the ashes. Auntie Wanda turns the music on the stereo down to a whisper in the background. So, we all gather around the table with me and Barbara leaning over the table on our knees on Mrs. Williams' kitchen chairs. She never would have let us sit in those chairs like that before because it wasn't a proper way to treat your belongings, she always said. But right now, she doesn't care about those chairs.

The sun is pouring in through the window in wide rays of sunlight across the table, on the empty Tupperware. "Come on over, Tyrone," they say. But Uncle Tyrone says he'll just sit there. Evelyn's mama and aunts and uncle around the table just look at each other like they don't know what their next move should be concerning Uncle Tyrone until Mrs. Williams shakes her head as if to say "no."

They just let him be and we're all having a moment of silence before Mrs. Williams takes a plastic scoop and reaches in the urn and comes up with some ashes. Everybody gasps all whispery. Mrs. Williams' hand is shaking while she's pouring little bits of ashes in each little plastic bowl.

"You want me to take over?" Evelyn's Auntie Nina offers.

"No, honey, I got it," Mrs. Williams says.

"Just don't nobody breathe hard," her Uncle Willie says. And everybody looks at him like they're telling him to shut up. He shuts his mouth tight and doesn't say anything else and I suddenly can't stop worrying that I'm going to breathe hard on the ashes or worse, let out a sneeze and scatter Evelyn all over the kitchen.

Nobody breathed hard or sneezed on Evelyn's ashes, so they were closed up tight in the little plastic bowls with little "Rest in Peace" labels we put on them. Barbara brought a container over to Uncle Tyrone who took it in his hand, looked at it, and put it in his shirt pocket.

With the ashes all divided up, Evelyn's mama says I can put the ones left in the urn back in its place on her dresser. I bring it to Mrs. Williams' bedroom and put it back in place and arrange the pictures around the urn, so they're all facing out. I'm taking a long pause to look at one picture of us one Halloween when we both were dressed up like angels. We made wings out of cardboard and painted the wings gold colored. Both of us are wearing white dresses and we've got halos on our heads that Steven made for us out of aluminum foil.

"You looked so pretty with your angel wings," I say out loud to Evelyn. I heave a big sigh because I got that feeling of want so bad it hurts. Everybody says we'll see Evelyn again, but while I'm standing here in the quiet of Mrs. Williams' bedroom talking to Evelyn's ashes, I'm thinking that just isn't enough.

Chapter Fifty

Five days after Evelyn's ashes were divided up, Mrs. Williams and Barbara come over to say they're going to be moving out. They're moving in with family up in Macon because they'd be better off there. She has a little box in her hand with some glassy something clanking around.

"I got something here I'm sure Evelyn would want you to have, Isabelle," and she hands it out to me.

I take it and look inside to see the most beautiful, delicate little set of dishes. These are the china dishes she told me she had when we first met, and she was going to show it to me, but we kept forgetting about it. Before too long, I think she might have forgotten about it altogether, so I always wasn't sure in my mind, if I remembered it for a second, whether that just was a story.

"Thank you, ma'am," I whisper, and put the dishes out on the table. I run my fingertips around the smooth edges of all the pieces.

Mama is giving Mrs. Williams a long, quiet hug standing in the middle of the kitchen. They aren't saying much of anything, just holding on to each other in this moment. I'm not sure if I should say anything or just let the silence stay until Mrs. Williams says, "Jesus got her with him now. She's alright, now."

"We know that's right," Mama agrees, and they smile at each other. It's then that I think it's okay if I say something.

"Can Barbara come and play dolls with me before y'all go?" I ask.

"We don't have time, baby. We're going now up to my sister's house. The men from the church, along with a couple of my brothers, are going to come back and move our things," she says.

Just then Barbara taps on the door.

"Come on in, honey," my mama says, and Barbara comes in and walks right into my arms. I wrap myself around her and we hug too, just like Mama and Mrs. Williams. Next thing I know Joseph and Steven come in from the other room.

"Y'all come on in and get in this hug," Mrs. Williams says with a kind of a sad laugh, if you can imagine a laugh being sad.

So, we stand in the kitchen hugging just like that time we went to the carnival and made us a circle on the dance floor, with, all of us there in a circle, except Evelyn, of course.

And, just like that, they're gone.

Joseph and me watch from our back porch while all of the Williams' things were loaded onto a truck and taken off. The apartment across the way is so dark and still, it's like they were never even there. I imagine in my head that maybe the whole thing was a dream. The whole thing, right from the start from the day Evelyn stumbled upon me with those kids shoving me around until she stepped in with her imaginary crazy brother that would kill them all just for looking at him wrong. Looking at the quiet of that apartment across the way, I can't believe how one day just a while ago we were playing in the alley after a hard rain, laughing and building little villages out of clay, with rivers flowing through them. We could just say the word and mold life out of nothing, like we were goddesses. And today, there's nothing but a dark, hollow space where Evelyn used to live.

I don't have words for how that feels. I guess I'd say the biggest thing is the want that comes up like something swelling up from in my chest. It's a want that I know won't be filled no matter what I do. There's no person, no angel, or even a god that can bring me what I want. And the more I realize that it can't be filled, the bigger that want gets. I feel like it might well kill me or turn me into a girl who can't do anything but sit there and cry, cry, cry for a wish that will never come true.

I don't want Joseph to see me cry, so I'm slumping over with my head across my arm in my lap, and I'm pretending like I fell asleep right there on the porch.

"Izzee, you sleep?" he's nudging me.

"Oh, I reckon I did fall asleep," I say, and keep my head down being as I need to get a hold of myself before I raise my head.

Joseph hops up from the porch and starts climbing the mimosa. He likes to climb up it and jump down into the grass and do a little tumble and a roll like he was in some cop show on TV. I'm glad when he gets up and gets occupied, so it gives me some time to dry my face.

I want him to go inside because I got me an idea to go over and see if I can go inside Evelyn's old apartment, just to have me a look around. I don't know why, but I just want to. I tell Joseph I heard Steven calling him from inside. I know it's a lie, but if I want to go over there, I don't have much choice but to tell him something that I know will make him go in, so I can sneak away. He can't come with me because he'll tell Mama. Then not only will I get in trouble for going over there, but I'll be in double trouble for bringing him with me.

He doesn't believe me at first, but I convince him that Steven said he was wanting to read him a story. "I heard him earlier ... and I believe he might've said he had some candy." I hear myself cranking up that lie higher, so the story doesn't have a word of truth in it, even if we pick it apart. The last thing Steven wants is for Joseph to come knocking on his door expecting to be read to and given candy.

Steven's been hiding out in his room most of the time since the funeral and I can't even get him to read to me either like he still likes to do, so I know he doesn't want to read to Joseph.

I think for a short moment that maybe I should tell him that I was mistaken, that I didn't hear Steven calling after all, but when he jumps down off the mimosa with a thud and a tumble and heads for the door to go in, I can't bring myself to tell the truth. The moment he goes in and fades into the gray light of the kitchen, I'm off across the driveway.

I can't believe my luck when I try the door and find out they left it unlocked. So, I slide in quick and quiet. Standing in Evelyn's empty kitchen, I right away imagine how it was, how many times we all gathered around the table and Evelyn's mama hollered at us about how not to sit in her chairs. We made cookies for Christmas and Evelyn made a giant Christmas tree-shaped cookie that she cut out of the dough with a butter knife. We decorated it with green colored sugar and M & M's for lights on the tree. We took a picture of it and then in no more than two minutes, we cut that cookie up and ate it, us kids and our mamas, while it was still warm and soft. Mrs. Williams said, "Now we can't have a cookie without nice cold milk to chase it," and she pulled out a gallon of milk from the refrigerator and filled six empty jelly jars she used for glasses. Everyone got some. Mama was amazed that someone could be so generous with what must be a precious supply of milk since she knew Mrs. Williams didn't have much money either and sometimes had to borrow from her sisters to get by.

Knowing Mrs. Williams changed my mama for the better. She wasn't ever a person who hated folks deep in her heart for their skin color, but she seemed she was stuck in between two places and didn't know before which place was the right one to be. She grew up with an uncle that used to brag about his KKK connection and how they used to burn crosses in the yards of Black folks to chase them out of white neighborhoods and keep the neighborhood "pure." She had been told all her life that Black folks were dirty and some of the "laziest and greedy sum' bitches on the planet with how they want rights, but don't want to pay for nothing."

Then she got to know Evelyn's family. She saw that Mrs. Williams is house proud and keeps her place so spic and span, you could near about trust eating on the floor if you had to. She saw that Mrs. Williams worked every day more than nine hours most days, cleaning houses across town, and came home just in time to feed her own young'uns and see to it they had their homework done before she got them off to bed. Mama remarked how when she saw Mrs. Williams walking home down the driveway, she saw that she had the same bend in her back like she does after a long day of waiting on tables at the Hasty House or Joe's Cellar. I think that's what finally pulled Mama over to the side of not hating Black folks. She saw that Mrs. Williams had that same back ache, she said.

I leave my thoughts about Mama and Mrs. Williams with the same bent back on the ghost of a table in the kitchen and go through the living room without stopping and I go straight down the long hall to Evelyn's old room. I hear my heart beating in my head now and that wish is there, swelling up again. I stand in the middle of her room and turn myself around to look out at every corner, every line of the walls. Then I run my finger along the wall where we hung posters late into the night standing on her bed and then laying side by side and telling each other secrets we were sworn to 'til the death, we said. But we didn't think we needed to mean real death. We didn't know that. I feel the walls all the way around until I come across a spot just by the closet door where me and Evelyn kept track of how tall we were. I was always so much shorter than her, she used to like to call me Lil Bit, just to tease me. I can see where she wrote "Lil Bit" next to my measurement, the first time we did this, marked February 26, 1978.

I remember that day there was a real cold snap coming through and we spent the day mostly in her room where we had made a tent on her bed with an old sheet and covered it with a blanket. We had our flashlights and sat under there reading and talking until we got bored of the dark and came out. That's when Evelyn had the idea to measure how tall we were. From then on, we measured every couple of months, even though we knew it takes more than a couple of months to grow any. I just wished to be taller so much that I wanted to make sure if I was, I'd know it right away.

I'm running my fingers along the measurements in pencil to the last time we measured ourselves, June 7, 1981: two days before we were chased down the alley. Two days before I made it home and two days before Evelyn didn't. Two days before Evelyn was dragged off into an old lean-to down the alley...two days before...I can't even say, even though I know what happened. It was written three days before the time the police came and told Mrs. Williams they found her dead. Three days before Mrs. Williams went running down the alley screaming for her after she just about lost her mind over that news.

We got into the habit of writing some little something next to our measurements about how we felt on that day, kind of like a snapshot of a shared diary on the wall. On that day, I wrote, "I feel tall," because I had grown a little bit.

Evelyn wrote, "Love." That's all. I asked her why she only wrote "Love" and she said, "Because that's all I can think of. Besides that, what else we need? Mama says that's all folks need."

I reckoned that could be right when you think of it since love is what makes good things happen most of the time.

I'm feeling the pencil marks with my fingertips and I stare at the word "love" for a long time and suddenly I feel like something weighs a ton in my legs, and I lean my back on the wall and slide down it to the floor where I sit and sigh out loud for I don't know how long. I got that ache in my chest that feels like it's a part of me now. I figure at that moment Mama might start wondering where I am, and I pull myself up, take one last look around the room and leave into the living room.

I figure I might want to leave out the front door in case Mama is looking out for me from across the driveway. Just as I'm reaching for the doorknob, I see out of the corner of my eye, something that I can't believe I'm seeing. It's Uncle Tyrone's Tupperware container with Evelyn's ashes in it tucked over in the corner on the floor where he went to sit after we all divided up the ashes that night, drinking his whiskey and crying.

"Oh my God!" I hear myself say out loud, while I rush to my knees on the floor to pick it up.

I cup it in my hands and hold it close to my heart and close my eyes. "Thank you, Jesus," I say. I'm not sure what I'm thanking Jesus for. I'm just thankful Evelyn's ashes didn't get thrown away in the Dixie Dumpster by the next people who move in here and toss it out without knowing they just threw somebody's ashes in the garbage.

Chapter Fifty-One

I know she won't come back, but I sleep with my Walkie-talkie on next to me when I go to bed. What if she wants to contact me from beyond? Maybe she'll call to tell me what Heaven is like. I don't know if I believe in Heaven, but I have to. If I don't believe in it, then Evelyn is nowhere.

Her Walkie-talkie is in the box with her things up on my closet shelf with no batteries in it because I needed them in mine. Hers has "Eagle" written on it in faded magic marker.

I didn't mean for anyone to know about my strange Walkie-talkie habit, and I had been able to keep it to myself until Joseph came in my room this morning early and wanted me to read to him. He came bounding in and onto my mattress and bumped his knee on the Walkie-talkie that was under the covers. The channel switch flipped to another channel and made a staticky sound and I grabbed it to turn it off.

"Evelyn's calling!" Joseph said with a big smile. He still doesn't really understand that she died and when someone dies, they are gone for good.

"No, Joseph. Evelyn's gone. She died. You know. She went to Heaven and once you go to Heaven you can't come back."

"Maybe God gonna let her use the Heaven Talkie-talkie and then she call," he said and lifted his eyebrows.

"Maybe," I said, knowing that's a lie.

"'Cause I sawed her though. 'Member?" Joseph said.

He was talking about the other day when he got up in the morning and told Steven that he saw Evelyn.

"You mean you had a dream about Evelyn?" Steven asked.

"No. I sawed her. She was smiling at me and she said I can play cards with Barbara and then she flied away," Joseph said.

I admit when he said this, I was thinking maybe he saw a ghost and it gave me a chill up my back. But then I thought it wouldn't make sense for her to tell Joseph he can play cards with Barbara when they don't even live nearby anymore and if Evelyn was a ghost, she would surely know they don't live there anymore.

"It was a dream, Joey," Steven told him.

"No. I sawed her," Joseph insisted.

"Okay, but let's tell Mama it was dream if you tell her about it. But don't tell her, though. Okay? Cause it will scare her. Okay?"

Joseph agreed not to tell her anything about the dream in case it scared Mama, but he told her anyway. Now, Mama is convinced Evelyn visited Joseph because she knew it wouldn't scare him since he's still little and doesn't know it's a scary thing to see someone who died.

"Don't tell Mama or Steven that I have the Walkie-talkie in the bed. They'll think I'm crazy," I told Joseph.

"Okay," he said.

Around 6:30 Mama calls me out for dinner, and I sit and play with my

SpaghettiOs and take tiny little bites off my slice of buttered bread.

"You need to eat to keep your strength up, Isabelle," Mama says.

"I know," I say and shift my SpaghettiOs around and put some in my spoon to show that I'm going to eat, even though I probably won't. I keep asking myself what kind of person eats when their best friend is dead. I don't know the answer, so I only really eat when I have to when I get too hungry or if Mama looks like she'll be upset if I waste. If I don't finish tonight's dinner, Joseph can eat the leftovers tomorrow for lunch, so she knows they at least won't go to the garbage.

"Eat just a couple of spoons full and half your bread and we'll save the rest for Joseph for tomorrow," Mama says.

"Evelyn gonna call on the Talkie-talkie," Joseph says out the blue.

"What?" Mama asks.

"What are you talking about, Joey?" Steven wants to know. "She can't call, Joey. She's in Heaven."

"Izzie got the Talkie-talkie in bed with her so if God lets her, Evelyn can call," Joseph says.

Mama and Steven are looking at me for an explanation, but I don't offer one. I'm shifting the food around on my plate with my spoon and pretending not to be listening.

"What's he talking about, Isabelle? Why would you have the Walkie-talkie in bed with you? Where's the other one that Evelyn used to use?"

"It's in a box in the closet in my room," I answer.

"But why do you have one in bed with you?" Mama looks worried.

"I don't know. Just because," I answer and shrug my shoulders like it's no big deal.

"Well, Isabelle, I'm starting to wonder if it's okay how much time you spend in your room just laying on the mattress staring at the ceiling all quiet. I mean, it's not like you're reading or listening to music or nothing. And now, you got the Walkie-talkie like you think Evelyn's gonna call?" Mama says and wrinkles up her forehead.

"It's nothing, Mama. You're making a big deal out of nothing. Joey, I told you not to say anything," I say, annoyed.

"Uh Oh. I forgotted," Joseph says and shoves a heaping spoon of SpaghettiOs in his mouth.

"What do you think, Steven?" Mama always gets Steven's thoughts on matters such as this, but I don't think he knows anything about what's a normal way to act when your best friend is killed.

"Maybe you need some distractions, Isabelle," Steven says, sounding all wise and like a grown up so much I almost don't know what he means. "Like you need some hobbies or things to do to get your mind off stuff," he suggests.

"Maybe that's it," Mama says. "Why don't you draw some pictures or write some stories? I got a pad of paper you can have that somebody left at their table I was waiting on and the boss said I could keep it."

"Maybe I could. But I don't know. That's kind of boring since I've done plenty of that before Evelyn died," I say back.

"How about I give you some books that are your favorite ones? You could now read them yourself since you're older. Stories seem altogether different when you read them yourself," Steven offers.

"Okay," I say, kind of mopey.

"Or ..." Steven says with a little closed mouth smile across his lips. "Or ... I could give you my little record player and you can choose some records that could be yours and you could also borrow some of mine."

"Really?" I ask.

"Yeah, really. I hardly use it anyway since I got the other one that's not portable from Mrs. Parker. Come to think of it, I don't know why I didn't give it to you sooner. Anyway, yeah, you can have it if you want it," he says.

"Of course, I want it," I say, and I get a sudden urge to give Steven a hug and jump up from my seat to hug him with wet in my eyes.

"Thank you," I say through my tears, with my arms wrapped around his shoulders from behind him and my head resting on his back.

"You're welcome," he says and pats my arm.

Mama smiles over at us and Joseph asks if he can have the rest of my SpaghettiOs.

Since I got the record player, I play it all the time. Steven let me have his album of Beethoven's Ninth. I've played it so many times, I bet I know most of the notes like they're words of a song. It was hard listening to it at first because all I could think of was how much Evelyn loved it that day when I "borrowed" Steven's record player and took it to the park.

I was going to stop listening to it even though I love it, but it's like I could hear Evelyn telling me, "Naw, girl, you gotta go ahead through it," like she would say sometimes when I would try to keep from doing something I had to do because it was hard to do. Like when you have to go get your shots at school.

I remember that one time when it was shot day and I told Evelyn on the way to school that I thought we should go play hooky so we wouldn't get the shot. "Nuh-uh. We got to go ahead through it, girl. We got no choice," she said.

At school they lined us up in the hall to get our vaccinations. The smell of rubbing alcohol floated all up and down the hall on the breeze that came in through the double doors to outside and joined up with the sound of kids crying from the needle stick.

Afterward, they marched us back to our classrooms and gave us ice cream to help us calm down. Before afternoon whichever arm we got the shot in would get stiff and painful like a big old bruise when we went to move it. That's when the pain from the shot went from being something scary to something like a badge of honor. If your arm was super sore and stiff, everyone would be impressed. So, everyone was trying to say their arm was the sorest of all.

This summer went by in kind of a blur with everything in life kind of happening all around me. But it's like I wasn't really a part of it. I haven't really shook off the feeling from that night they found Evelyn and I was all mixed up about whether I was dead or alive or a mimosa tree or a girl named Isabelle who just that afternoon was building mountains and rivers with her best friend in the alley.

The world is moving around me. It's loud and yelling and ringing and storming with thunder clapping and days that are dark as night with threats of tornadoes. The world is laughing and crying and talking and jumping and spinning and running and splashing and sometimes it's singing. It's a train whistle sound blowing way far off. But in my head, even when Beethoven's Ninth is playing for the one hundredth time, notes I know are coming, there's a dull buzz that never stops. Its tone is never higher, never lower. In my brain and through my whole body, if the sad I feel was a sound, it would be that humming that doesn't have an ending.

Chapter Fifty-Two

I'm sitting in Mrs. Washington's homeroom class on the first day of eighth grade. A whole year has gone by since I had to go back to school without Evelyn. Last year, I was so disappointed when I didn't get to have a class with Mrs. Washington who was Evelyn's most favorite teacher ever. I can't believe I lucked out and got to have Mrs. Washington for a teacher this year when I had no idea that was even possible since I knew she taught seventh grade English before. She's telling us about how she jumped at the chance to teach eighth grade this year because she was excited that she would get to teach us about Shakespeare who was an "exquisite playwright and poet whose words were like pure gold".

I'm listening to her and noticing how elegant she is from the very top of her hair that's an almost perfectly round neat little afro to her high heeled boots. Evelyn told me all about this teacher, how she's so smart and how she cares about her students enough to tell them the truth about themselves. That's what I'm thinking while she's standing up there by the black board giving us all a talking to. When she reaches up to write, the sun's rays pouring in the window and across her forearm, make her dark brown skin look like satin.

"Now, sometimes you might not want to come to school. You might think you have better things to do. Let me tell you something, ladies and gentlemen," she says.

"Ladies and gentlemen." We are ladies and gentlemen, not boys and girls. Right away, I feel like I need to think more like a grown up in this grade.

"*This* is when it begins to count, big time! *This* is when you start to make choices that are truly going to affect the rest of your lives. If you don't care now, you are going to have a *very* hard time in your life later on down the road. Right *now,* is the time!"

I'm listening. I like the way she speaks with grammar that's perfect. I know right away that I want to talk just like her.

At this moment, she's telling us that there are teachers who will help us in life and that she cares about each and every one of us. She knows we all have problems in our lives, but we don't have to *stay* in those problems. We can rise above all that because we are about to have more control of our destinies.

"If you need help, come and talk to me. If I can't do something for you, I will find someone who can. You have my word. Now let's do roll call," she says.

Mrs. Washington is calling out the names on the roll call and she comes to my name right in between Lane and Little and she pauses for a moment. "Isabelle Letourneau." She calls out.

"Here," I say in a shy voice.

"How *are* you, Hon?" She asks and she's sounding more like a mom of a friend or an aunt than a teacher. I tell her I'm okay. "I'm glad to hear." She smiles at me and I think she must know I was Evelyn's friend. Evelyn, who died a year and a half ago. Evelyn who everybody knows by now, was fighting those boys who were trying to rape her. Evelyn, who was murdered, maybe on accident, but murdered, nonetheless. And then moves on to the next name, because what does a teacher say when she realizes that a new student in her homeroom class is the friend of a murdered girl?

"Josephine Little...Josephine." She's scanning the room, looking for a Josephine who's not answering.

"She ain't here," a tall, Elmer-glue-white boy with hair the color of rust who is slouched down low in his seat, answers in her place.

"You mean she *isn't* here. She *isn't*. Everyone repeat after me, she isn't." The class repeats it like a chorus. "Good." She says and she's smiling out at all of us.

"Now, if you'd sit up straight in your seat, young man, you'd be just about perfect." He sits up straight and smiles down at his desk while the class laughs.

"Now, no one in here can laugh at anyone else because not one of y'all are perfect either. As a matter of fact, I'm going to go ahead and point this out. Some of y'all in here are coming in all funky. Now, I'm not going to point anyone out on that, but I'm going to tell you, you need to wash up and put on some deodorant. If you don't have what you need to keep yourself from smelling funky, you come talk to me in private, and I will see to it that you have what you need. It's important, young people. Important!"

No one is laughing now. I'm sitting here thinking how glad I am that I just washed up this morning and even put on some of Mama's Tigress cologne, so I *know* she isn't talking about me. I do smell the cloud of onion funk and hope that whoever it is will take her up on her offer to get them what they need to get rid of that smell, because I like onions okay, all fried up right, but *this* smell is enough to make a person hate real onions even.

Mrs. Washington gives us our schedules of classes. This is the second year we change classes for each subject instead of staying in one classroom all day. I like it because it makes me feel grown up to get to go on my own and change classes, but I'm a little nervous about being able to find my classrooms on time in this bigger school. Mrs. Washington tells us not to worry and that we will all be fine in time, that the teachers all understand it might take a little time for us to get used to the layout of the school. I'm looking at my schedule and I can see I have her for my English class. I can't believe my luck because I already like this teacher a lot.

We're all filing out and some boys get up too fast and slide the desk loud on the hardwood floor. "Oh, no, no, no! Stop right there!" Mrs. Washington is raising her voice. Everyone freezes like they're afraid to move an inch, even those boys, who seem like they wouldn't be afraid of anyone. She points out the boys who dragged the desk and tells them to get back in the classroom and the rest of us can go.

I can hear her while I'm walking away giving those boys the gospel over how they aren't supposed to be dragging desks around like this is some kind of playground. I go on to my first class, which is math. I know I'm going to hate it. I hate numbers with all my heart because they make me feel stupid. I'm in the low-level math, but high level everything else.

In math class the students don't care one bit about listening to this teacher. He's wearing all brown, brown jacket, shirt and even his tie is brown. All brown, right down to his socks, which we can see when he sits on the edge of his desk making his pants look like high waters. He even has brown hair. If it wasn't for his white skin that turns red when he raises his voice at some boys in the back of the class who are talking over him, he'd blend right into the light brown wall behind him. He turns red and the boys snicker at him, which makes us all want to snicker, even though I know you're not supposed to act like this to your math teacher just because he blends in with the wall. To top it all off, his name is Mr. Brown.

I'm sitting here thinking about how I can't wait to tell Steven about this teacher so we can laugh all out loud about it and not worry about being rude because it's okay to laugh at someone, as long as that person has no idea, so it doesn't hurt their feelings.

My second class is with Mrs. Washington and I think I'm going to like her class. I sit in the back, but she calls out my name and tells me she'd like me to sit up toward the front. I wonder why, but I don't ask because I think it's not something I should even question. She doesn't seem mad at me or anything, and I wasn't talking to anyone when I wasn't supposed to, so I don't think she moved me as a punishment.

So, my first English class in eighth grade is going along and we're talking about the syllabus. That's a new word I learned. It's a paper that tells us what all we're going to study in that class and when. She tells us that the syllabus is like a contract and when we get to college, we'll have a syllabus for every class. College. I've never heard a teacher talking about students going to college as if it's as natural as anything. Most people in my neighborhood don't go to college. It's not something I really thought I would ever think about seriously. Even when Evelyn used to talk about it because she learned it from Mrs. Washington, I didn't really think it was something that was possible for me. For some reason, I thought maybe it was possible for Evelyn, but not me. I never told Evelyn I thought that because she used to say when she went off to college, she could make sure that when I went, that I would be able to have a room with her, so she could look after me. In her mind, I was going to go to the same place as her. So, then, I didn't tell her I thought I wouldn't be able to go because she would have told me, "Girl, hush!"

So, Mrs. Washington is telling us that we're going to be reading Romeo and Juliet by Shakespeare. I'm so excited. I know it's because we're a high-level class that we are reading something hard to understand. I'm a little worried that I won't understand it, but when another student asks her how we're going to be able to understand that old English, she tells us she will help us. Believe in ourselves, we'll be able to understand it and appreciate it for the beauty of the language. At this moment, I'm not so sure, but I'm willing to try.

I'm chosen, along with one other student, to hand out the paperback books about Romeo and Juliet. I haven't seen this boy before and I'm thinking he's as beautiful as a doll, with a perfect mouth that opens slightly into a shy smile, that he flashed and made my face go hot when he accidentally touched my hand when we were reaching for the piles of books to hand out. His name is Roderick and I wish at this moment so much that I could tell Evelyn about him.

I think this class could be the perfect convergence of things. Convergence, that's a word I learned this last summer when Steven was reading a short story to me called "Everything that Rises, Must Converge." Come together. Not only do I get to have class with Mrs. Washington, who Evelyn said was the best teacher on the planet, but I get to read this romantic story, alongside this boy that I'm thinking I might be *liking,* liking soon if everything works out right.

Mrs. Washington dives right into reading out loud to us. She's throwing her hands in the air when it's right for expression. Now she's calling on us all to read a bit. She's calling on us at random and my heart is thumping in my throat because I know she's going to choose me at some point. I hate reading in front of people, although, in my head I really like to read. I'm always afraid I'll pronounce words wrong or people will know that I don't understand some of the words I'm reading. All my classmates will know I'm not so smart and I'll be found out. They'll know I'm some sort of imposter. That's what I felt like last year when I got the invitation to join the National Junior Beta Club.

"They must have mixed me up with someone else," I said to Steven when we stood looking at the letter; me, in disbelief, he, in a burst of pride that he couldn't help but exclaim to Mama that all that reading he'd been doing to me must be paying off.

"Maybe. I reckon that could be it," she said, with her lit cigarette bouncing up and down while she responded without looking up from the newspaper she was reading.

"No, they don't have you mixed up with someone else, Isabelle. You'll have to face it. You might be smarter than you think," Steven said, beaming like a proud dad down at me.

"But how can I be in a smart kids' club when I'm in dumb kids' math?" I asked.

"It's not about the level class you're in. It's about the grades you get in all your classes," Steven answered. He knows about this stuff, since he's always been a part of the smart kids' club.

So, I accepted the invitation, went through the initiation, and was in. I got to go to smart kid meetings, and I had a football jersey with my name across the back of it. But I always felt out of place, like I'd fooled everyone into thinking I was smart. I kept it a secret that I was in a low-level math.

Here I am, in a high-level English class, with the world's best English teacher and a boy that I was hoping I might see if he could *like*, like me, and I'm about to be found out. I've got my thoughts divided between me being an imposter and me not understanding at all what is being read. I should have known I couldn't do this. I'm trying to keep up with my finger following along when it happens. She calls on Roderick to read the part of Romeo and I'm to read the part of Juliet, Act two Scene two. Roderick begins reading.

> *"He jests at scars that never felt a wound.*
> *But, soft! what light through yonder window breaks?*
> *It is the east, and Juliet is the sun.*
> *Arise, fair sun, and kill the envious moon,*
> *Who is already sick and pale with grief,*

That thou her maid art far more fair than she:
Be not her maid, since she is envious;
Her vestal livery is but sick and green
And none but fools do wear it; cast it off.
It is my lady, O, it is my love!
O, that she knew she were!
She speaks yet she says nothing: what of that?
Her eye discourses; I will answer it.
I am too bold, 'tis not to me she speaks:
Two of the fairest stars in all the heaven,
Having some business, do entreat her eyes
To twinkle in their spheres till they return.
What if her eyes were there, they in her head?
The brightness of her cheek would shame those stars,
As daylight doth a lamp; her eyes in heaven
Would through the airy region stream so bright
That birds would sing and think it were not night.
See, how she leans her cheek upon her hand!
O, that I were a glove upon that hand,
That I might touch that cheek!"

He's pausing now and glancing at me when he reads this part and I think for a second, it's because it's my turn. And I see it *is*.

"Ay, me," I say in almost a whisper and see that it was supposed to be an exclamation and I don't know what it would mean to say "ay, me" anyway. I think I messed it up, but Roderick keeps reading.

"She speaks:
O, speak again, bright angel! for thou art

As glorious to this night, being o'er my head
As is a winged messenger of heaven
Unto the white-upturned wondering eyes
Of mortals that fall back to gaze on him
When he bestrides the lazy-pacing clouds
And sails upon the bosom of the air."

It's my turn and my heart is thumping in my ears, but Mrs. Washington is smiling down on me again like a mother and I feel mixed in with my fear a sudden strange surge of a feeling like I can do this, so I start:

"O Romeo, Romeo! wherefore art thou Romeo?" I'm terrified, but I'm trying to read it right with the exclamation where it's supposed to be and I can tell Mrs. Washington likes it because she's nodding her head like she's saying "yes", so I keep on reading. I can't believe how much confidence I have in myself at this very moment, so I continue, "Deny thy father and refuse thy name; Or, if thou wilt not, be but sworn my love, And I'll no longer be a Capulet."

"Shall I hear more, or shall I speak at this?" Roderick reads.

The next long part is mine, so I read and hope my voice doesn't shake.

"'Tis but thy name that is my enemy;
Thou art thyself, though not a Montague.
What's Montague? it is nor hand, nor foot,
Nor arm, nor face, nor any other part
Belonging to a man. O, be some other name!
What's in a name? that which we call a rose
By any other name would smell as sweet;
So Romeo would, were he not Romeo call'd,
Retain that dear perfection which he owes

Without that title. Romeo, doff thy name,
And for that name which is no part of thee
Take all myself."

Hmm. Take all myself. I'm thinking how interesting that sounds and Roderick continues reading. Mrs. Washington is letting us read more than the other students read, so I guess she thinks we are doing a good job of it.

"I take thee at thy word: Call me but love, and I'll be new baptized; Henceforth I never will be Romeo," Roderick reads and puts his hand to his heart like he's acting it out. I don't want to lose my place and be embarrassed, but at the same time, I can't stop myself from looking at Roderick's mouth, especially when he reads a string of words that seem to make sense in the most romantic of ways, with phrases like, "with love's light wings ..." and, "but thou love me, let them find me here ..."and, "...lovers' tongues by night..."

I'm lacing my lines in between his and it almost feels like it's turning into our story, even though I just met him and hardly know a thing about this boy. And we continue reading as long as Mrs. Washington doesn't stop us.

By the time I get to my last part, I'm feeling dizzy from Shakespeare's words that I don't really understand, and Roderick's mouth saying words strung together like a necklace of charms, "with...love's...light...wings..." and "...I would I were thy bird."

I catch my breath to finish my part.

"Sweet, so would I:
Yet I should kill thee with much cherishing.
Good night, good night! parting is such
sweet sorrow,
That I shall say good night till it be morrow."

And Roderick finishes.

> *"Sleep dwell upon thine eyes,*
> *peace in thy breast!*
> *Would I were sleep and peace, so sweet to rest!*
> *Hence will I to my ghostly father's cell,*
> *His help to crave, and my dear hap to tell."*

Mrs. Washington stands up quick from her chair and starts clapping, which gets the class to clap too.

"Bravo!" she says. "That was wonderful! Bravo!" And she tells us we should stand and take a bow. So, we do.

We are standing side by side and just as natural as sunshine or rain we reach out at the same time and hold hands. My face is hot and flushed and I think at that moment it is the most perfect feeling in the world to start off in the smart kids' English class with the best teacher in the world, scared and insecure and to finish feeling good and holding hands with a new boy I just met, but makes me feel like an electric current just shot straight through me.

I think this is the kind of class I would run and tell Evelyn about first thing after school. I decide I'll have to tell her spirit that I'm sure must be alive somewhere, watching out for me anyway.

Chapter Fifty-Three

Dead cat smells like metal. I know because one time, Evelyn and me came across one under the bushes on the other side of the alley. Someone had shot the poor cat through the eye with a BB gun. It upset me so bad I had to throw up in the bushes right there.

Evelyn held my hair back while I threw up that morning's Apple Jacks mixed with last night's macaroni. Then, we dug a hole as deep as we could and buried it in a proper grave, complete with a cross out of sticks and morning glories from around our garbage can by the driveway. We had to sneak the morning glories because Mama doesn't allow anyone to pick them.

I don't know why I'm thinking of that poor dead cat with the BBs in his head right at this moment, except I just woke from a dream of Evelyn. First, she was running, like on that day, and then she was in a box in the shrubbery by the alley. In my dream she was beside me alive, but she was also in the box. I used to have a thought pop up in my head sometimes that Evelyn smelled like that cat when they found her in the lean-to dead that night. This thought would come out of nowhere and I had to throw up the first couple of times it popped up.

Mama thought I had the stomach flu the first time and I let her think it, so I could stay out of school that day. I hate school since Evelyn died. There's nothing I like about it since I don't really have any friends on account of how shy I am.

Actually, shy isn't the right word. How I feel is like a small nobody. I only have two pairs of pants, and they're too short, so people laugh at me. In the cafeteria, some kids ask me why I wear the same thing all the time. I just shrug my shoulders and stare at my free lunch on the tray in front of me.

That's another thing they laugh at, that I have the green lunch card that means it's free. I tried to hide it while I'm passing it to the lunch lady to stamp, but it's impossible. Everyone can see the green card from clear across the room. The same girl that's so curious about why I wear the same clothes is also curious about why I get free lunch. She knows it's because I'm poor and can't afford to buy my own lunch, so I don't know why she asks me. I know if Evelyn was here, she'd stand beside me and tell that girl it ain't none of her Goddamn business, except Evelyn would never say Goddamn like I do. I started saying it that night god let those boys kill my best friend.

They said they didn't mean to kill her, that they were all trying to have sex with her when she fell and hit her head hard on the fireplace hearth that was made of jagged edge bricks. That's what they said in the court room.

I had to go testify since I was the last one to see her alive. When I got on the stand, I pointed out two of the boys I was sure I recognized as "bloody Valentine" Willard and Willard's cousin, but I wasn't sure about the other one.

It was said that they thought she was just knocked out. They didn't know what to do with her, so they put her in an old trunk that was there. And that's how the police found her: laid in a heap in that old trunk.

So, that's the picture that pops up in my mind sometimes when I have that weird thought that dead cats smell like metal and when I have the most bizarre wonderment about Evelyn smelling like that too after being dead for hours there. That's when in my head I hear Evelyn saying, "Girl, now you *know* I don't smell like metal!" I shake that thought away. I push it out of my head, but it always pops back up at the weirdest time and makes me wonder if I'm going crazy.

I wanted to tell someone, so I thought to tell Mrs. Washington since I got to know her so much. We were sitting at her kitchen table one day after we had our English lesson. I've been going to her house every Saturday afternoon and she's helping me get better grammar habits.

"That's all it is," she says, "habits. We all speak how we are accustomed to speaking. It doesn't have anything to do with how smart we are."

I go over and we talk for a couple of hours and read lots out loud. We're reading Pygmalion, which is a story about a girl who has horrible grammar until a professor helps her correct it so she can be more classy. Mrs. Washington, says I'm a regular Eliza Dolittle, who is the character whose grammar the professor is helping, with the way I'm picking it up so quickly and changing my habits.

She was working this way with Evelyn too. That's why right before she died, she was going through this kind of change herself. She was going to go to college and improve her life. She just couldn't decide between music and film because she wanted to do them both, or maybe she would be a doctor. Mrs. Washington was teaching her piano too, and on that day, she had a lesson planned with her, but of course, she didn't make it there.

Mrs. Washington is sipping her tea and telling me how that afternoon, how strange she thought it was that Evelyn didn't show up.

"Because I knew that child would *never* miss a piano lesson, unless something terrible was going on," She said and stared through the steam swirling up out of her teacup and off across the room at the wall of bookshelves stuffed full of books of every kind.

"I didn't know how I could get in touch to find out what was holding her since Evelyn's phone was like it was stuck on a busy signal. I had a mind to go by their place, but I thought it might be too forward of me. I thought the busy signal was strange, but I just put it out of my mind as best I could and figured it would all be explained soon enough."

I'm sitting here listening and I actually like that Mrs. Washington is sharing with me what she was thinking and feeling that day. It makes me feel like a grown up in a way and I'm sipping my tea like she's sipping hers and thinking this. I nod my head to show her I'm listening.

"I'd been writing this piece of music, you know. And I was teaching it to Evelyn as I was writing it."

"Can I hear it?" I ask.

I don't know. *Can* you?" Mrs. Washington smiles. I knew I should say "May I."

"May I?" I correct myself.

"Yes, you may," she says, so I follow her over to the piano.

She starts playing this beautiful, sad piece that sounds like the piano is whispering some parts, she's playing it so soft. She plays, and her face is serious and at some parts, the whispering parts, she closes her eyes and looks like she's in a combination of peace and sorrow. I wonder how it's possible that a person can feel both at the same time, but I see it is when she plays this.

She finishes, and we sit in quiet for a few moments.

"It made me think of Evelyn," I told her.

"Funny you should say that." She continues, "I named it *Evelyn* after her. That night around a quarter 'til three I suddenly woke from a sound sleep and just felt so stirred up inside, I got up and came out to the piano. That's when I was moved to finish this piece. I don't really know where the inspiration came from, but there I was at 3:00 AM, inspired by some invisible force to write this music and it just poured out of me."

I'm listening to her story with my eyes opened wide at what she's saying, and she says, "What's wrong, Isabelle?"

"Mrs. Washington, 3:00 in the morning is when the police came around and told Evelyn's mama that they found her body."

"Oh my! Is that the truth?!" Mrs. Washington gasps.

"Yes, ma'am. It is the honest to God truth."

"Oh…Oh," Mrs. Washington says, looking down at her piano keys like she's stunned. I can't tell if I upset her.

"I'm sorry," I apologize.

"What are you sorry for?" she asks.

"I don't know. I just figured I upset you is all because you look shocked," I explain.

"Shocked, yes, but upset, no. It's beautiful. Strange, but beautiful. I can't help but believe now that that piece of music *was* inspired by Evelyn herself," she says.

I agree, and we sit thinking that thought for a few more minutes before we move on to the next chapter of Pygmalion.

That's why I didn't get a chance to tell her about Evelyn and the metal smelling cat and that thought that Evelyn smelled like that while she was in that box. That's just not something you say when you just realize that your friend that died was the true inspiration for a beautiful piece of music at the very hour the police found her dead.

Chapter Fifty-Four

I'm sitting on the back porch doing my homework from Mrs. Washington's class. We have to write a poem in Shakespeare style and I actually love this kind of homework. I decided I want to be a writer when I grow up. Mrs. Washington tells me I've got natural talent.

I never knew that before since I've always felt so shy and a lot like a nobody to ever really have a natural talent. Since I was little, I've always thought of stories and sometimes I wrote them down when I learned to write. The only person I ever told about my stories other than Mama is Evelyn and she said she liked them, but I wasn't sure if it was because she was my friend and that's what you say when you want to make your friend feel good when she's telling you her made up stories.

So, I'm here, trying to think up some Shakespeare-like poetry, when I see Roderick come of out his apartment across the way. They moved into the apartment where Ducy used to live, after Ducy's mama up and left him one day all alone. He came home from school to find her gone one day and Ducy came running up to me and Evelyn, saying he thinks his mama left him. He showed us a note she left saying she needed to be moving on, "Take care of yourself and here is the name and address of some kinfolk you ain't seen in a long time but they're kin, so they can take care of you if you ain't grown enough to take care of yourself," the note said. When he read it to us Ducy had a smile on his face that he was trying to keep from spreading because you aren't supposed to smile when your mama disappears.

Folks around here don't think anyone took her because like folks said, "Who's going to mess with that mean ass bitch?" Besides, she took her purse and a few things with her and left that note for Ducy.

"Maybe I can just live by myself!" Ducy exclaimed.

"Maybe, since you know how to take care of yourself pretty much," Evelyn and me agreed and we started in saying we could always check in on him and we're right here if he needed some advice because we know a lot being as we're older than him.

But then Evelyn's mama set us straight after we told her what happened, and she said we had to call Child Protective Services.

"No!" Ducy yelled and threatened to run away if Mrs. Williams did call the Child Protective Services. But then Mrs. Williams soothed him by making him some cookies and giving him a nice tall glass of milk to go with it. So, with our bellies full of warm chocolate chip cookies and milk, we were all able to sit around the table and talk about what was best for Ducy.

We decided that Ducy could spend the night on the couch at Evelyn's house so he wouldn't be alone in that apartment and Evelyn's mama would call Child Protection tomorrow. So that night I stayed the night at Evelyn's house and Ducy, Evelyn, and me sat up later than we're usually allowed on a school night since this might well be the last time we saw Ducy. We were playing cards and Ducy was laughing. I never saw him laugh before. I hadn't even seen him really smile before then, so I feel like I must have been dreaming. Then I was happy when I realized for sure it wasn't a dream because the laughing Ducy is more like a young'un should be.

Before too long though, Evelyn's Mama told us we'd best be getting to bed since we had school tomorrow. We whined a little, but she told us "hush now" and that we should be happy we could have a sleepover during the school week.

"Here you go, now sugar," Evelyn's mama said when she brought Ducy a pillow and a blanket to sleep with on the couch.

Later that night, after everybody was sleeping Evelyn woke me up to say she thought she heard Ducy crying to himself out in the living room.

"What should we do?" I whispered to her while we sat up in bed and listened for a minute.

"We should go give him some comfort," she whispered back.

"What if he doesn't want us out there?" I asked because I was worried he'd be embarrassed.

"Well, we gotta do something. Let's go and if he doesn't want us there, we'll just come back." Evelyn had a good idea like always.

We tiptoed down the hall, so we didn't wake up Evelyn's Mama and we could see the light from the front porch falling across Ducy while he was laying there quivering and crying down low.

"Ducy," Evelyn said in a very quiet voice, "you okay?"

We moved in closer, so we could talk to him and he rolled over and cried into the pillow. Evelyn put her hand on his back, and I did the same.

"Ducy, you can talk to us if you want," I said and Evelyn nodded, yes, because that was true.

"My mama never loved me. First, she beat me, then she left me. Why?" He rolled over and looked at us like he really thought we could give him an answer to that.

"I don't know, Ducy. My mama says she must be sick in the head, you know, like maybe she's crazy. That ain't your fault." Evelyn was doing a good job answering his question because I didn't have any idea what to say to him.

"You think so?" he asked.

"Yeah," Evelyn and me said at the same time.

At that moment I thought to go get some tissue for Ducy, so I hopped up and tiptoed into the bathroom as quiet as I could. When I brought back the tissue Evelyn had gone to the kitchen and got Ducy a glass of milk.

"It's going to be okay now, though, because your Mama won't be able to hurt you anymore. Do you got any aunties or uncles around that you could stay with?" Evelyn asked while she handed him the milk. She was so wise with the things she was saying to Ducy, I thought she would be a really good counselor lady, like that lady at school that helps kids calm down when they're upset.

Ducy said he had an auntie and uncle who had a farm in Leesburg and they have four young'uns who are Ducy's cousins. His auntie was his mama's sister, but they stopped talking to each other a long time ago when Ducy's mama said she didn't want nothing to do with her sister nor her husband because they were too bossy.

He said his auntie was sweet and funny and always had a big laugh and a smile, but he hasn't seen her since he was about five. We said maybe he could go live with them on the farm and wouldn't that be fun? He agreed it would be and then drank his milk before he curled back up with his blanket and closed his eyes and fell asleep. We figured we could go back to bed then since he was calmed down, and we were out in no time too.

The next day after Mrs. Williams fed us a breakfast of grits and eggs, she called Child Protective Services. They were going to send a social worker right out. We wanted to wait until they came to go to school, but Mrs. Williams told us to go ahead and give Ducy hugs and get on to school. She and Barbara would keep him company until they got here.

We gave him hugs and told him everything was going to be okay and if he wanted, he could send us a letter later to tell us how he was doing. He said he would. And that's the last time we saw Ducy.

It's been almost a year since Ducy's mama up and left and Child Protection came and got him. We don't know where he went to live, but I like to imagine he went to live on the farm with his auntie with the big laugh and he helps his cousins with the chores because he likes it and the whole family sits around the table in some farmhouse kitchen, eating and talking and laughing, with Ducy laughing right along like he never had a mean mama that beat him.

That's what I imagined in my head every time I looked over at the empty apartment where Ducy used to live. That apartment stayed empty for near about a year until Roderick's family moved in. I didn't even know they moved in until after that day when we read Shakespeare in Mrs. Washington's class. His family moved in in the middle of the night and there he was the next day at school.

So, I'm here on the porch and I was trying to write a poem, but Roderick just came out to hang clothes on the line so I can't think of my homework right now. He smiles and waves at me and then looks down at his feet like he's not sure what else to do.

I want to say something to him, but I'm not sure what's okay for a girl to say to a boy she's taken a liking to and I wish Evelyn was here, because she'd have some idea of what I should do.

"Go on over there," I hear her say in my mind's ear. "Talk to the boy. You *know* he *likes* you, likes you."

I get up from the porch and pretend like I'm fixing to climb the mimosa tree, because I'm not sure I got enough courage to just go over there and maybe he'll see me and want to climb up here too.

That's when I notice a tennis ball in the grass, and I hop down from the tree and go get it. I go over to the side of the apartment where I'm closer to him and I start bouncing that ball off the side of the building. I look over at him and notice he's smiling at me. I smile back.

"You got a good arm for throwing!" he calls out.

"I do?"

"Yeah. You wanna play catch when I'm done hanging these?" he asks me. I do.

In the field on the other side of where Evelyn used to live, we throw the ball back and forth and Roderick says he's getting hot, so he pulls off his t-shirt. Now, I don't know if this is proper because I've never quite had these kinds of thoughts about a boy before, but I like the way the sun shines on his skin that's shiny wet with sweat. I mean I've thought a boy was cute before, but this is different how I'm thinking when I'm looking at him now and think it must be something to do with what they told us is called hormones in sex education class last year.

Just then we decide to take a little break from playing catch. Roderick puts his shirt back on and we sit down shoulder to shoulder underneath a pecan tree that hasn't started dropping its pecans yet since it's just now fall coming and it's still plenty hot. The gray moss hanging down from the tree is swaying in the breeze. It always reminds me of old ladies' hair hanging in grief off their heads, but I push that thought away. It's not really the thing to be thinking at this moment with our outstretched legs touching and the skin of my leg has never touched the skin of a boy's leg before and the dragonflies are flying all around every which way like they usually do in the middle of summer.

We sit and talk about all kinds of things. He tells me about how his family moved here from Macon when his mama found a job she liked. His daddy is nowhere to be found. He tells me that he has a little sister named Jacqueline who's eight years old and that his daddy up and left after she was born. His mama says he ran off with some hussy. I tell him about Maine, what I can remember of it, and the snow and that my Northern grandma used to speak French, but I hadn't seen her since I was five. And my daddy, who speaks French too, but I hadn't learned much from him since I haven't seen him since I was little too. I tell him about Evelyn, that we were best friends, and she lived in that apartment right across from us. I point it out.

"Did she move away?" he asks.

"No, she died," I say and there's a silence hanging in between us like he doesn't know what to say, because what do you say when you're sitting under a pecan tree in early fall with a girl you like in the eighth grade and she tells you her best friend died.

"That's sad. What happened to her? She got sick?" Now he's asking questions and I wish I could back up and undo that I said anything about what happened to Evelyn, but of course you can't unring a bell once it's rung.

"She was killed by some boys after they chased us. I got away, but they caught her. I can't really talk about it much, though, okay? It makes me too sad," I say right out. I figure that would be easier than having him ask more questions.

"I'm sorry," he says and leans his head toward mine while we both rest our heads on the craggy trunk of the pecan tree.

I've never been this close to a boy before, well except for that time when Ricky Adair forced a balogna smelling kiss on my mouth, but I hated that. But this here, this is alright. Real alright.

Chapter Fifty-Five

Roderick is standing outside my window whispering my name. I rush quick to the window, so he knows I hear him. We've been doing this late at night on weekends. He comes over to my window and calls my name in a voice that's loud enough for me to hear, but quiet enough not to wake folks up. It's kind of a whispering yell. So, I answer him and then on those nights I climb out the window onto his shoulders and he helps me down to the grass and we sit side by side talking until almost morning and then he helps me back up to my window so I can climb back in and crawl into bed and curl up so Mama or no one else knows I was even outside.

It all started after that day we played catch and then he leaned his head next to mine underneath the pecan tree. It wasn't too long after that we decided we might well be in love with each other.

"I got something I want to tell you," he said one day after English class.

"What? Tell me then," I said back.

"I can't tell you here. I'll tell you later," he said.

"Come on. You know I hate waiting. Is it bad or good?" I was getting impatient and then the second bell rang for the next class period.

"Oh, it's good. Don't worry," he said and smiled at his feet. I liked the way one side of his mouth always went up a little higher than the other when he smiled.

Just then the science teacher who was standing just outside the lab barked at us that we'd best be getting on to class, so we had no choice but to split up and go our separate ways.

For the rest of the day, I couldn't concentrate on anything else except what it might be that Roderick wanted to tell me. What could it be that was good and why couldn't he tell me here? I was sitting in my history class with my mind drifting all over the place.

I was deep in thought of what it could be, when suddenly I heard Mr. McCloud's voice say my name with a question inflection at the end of it. That's all I heard. The question mark. My face went hot with embarrassment when he called my name again in a question?

"Well," I looked at the page in my book for a clue of what on earth we might be talking about and what that question could have been about.

"Well," he copied me, and the class laughed. "Well, Miss Letourneau, it seems as though your head was way up in clouds."

"I'm sorry, sir," was all I could think of to say because it was true. Mr. McCloud didn't say whether or not I was forgiven for having my head in the clouds. He just went on to the next person to answer the next question.

Later that evening, just before the sun was starting to sink down and the sky turned all pink at the horizon, I went outside and Roderick came over and asked me if I could go for a walk with him in the alley.

"Why we gotta go over there?" I wanted to know.

"Privacy. Because I don't want anyone else to hear us, you know because I have that thing to tell you," he said.

I said I guess I could, but I'd best not ask Mama because she might say no, so I just took it upon myself to make that decision for myself. We went out into the alley.

We went just beyond the fence where we play stick ball and Roderick always hits the ball far and high over the fence and I watch him run around the bases with his shirt off. I think he looks as graceful as a gazelle with the way his body moves so smooth. I have some thoughts sometimes about him and it's lots of times when I see him run around the bases like this on a hot day.

So, we went out by the fence and Roderick asked me if he could hold my hand.

"Yes," I said, and he reached over and took hold of my hand.

I looked at our hands wrapped around each other with our different skin and I thought it looked like artwork, but I know some people wouldn't think so. I must have had a little look on my face because he asked me what was wrong.

"Just ... just ... people are probably going to say mean things about us. You know...because you're Black and I'm white," I said.

"I don't care about what people say. Don't worry about that," he said.

"Okay," I said, but I wasn't too sure I wasn't really going to worry, but I just left that thought there.

"What were you going to tell me, anyway?" I was still waiting to know what the big secret was.

"Well, you know how both of us are shy in class? I mean, we're near 'bout the shyest two people in class, isn't that right?"

"We are," I agreed, but I still don't know why that's such a secret.

"Well," he continued talking and we walked with our hands still wrapped up together, "isn't it funny how the two shyest people in the class ended up falling in love?"

My mind was racing around because I was sure I just heard him say we were in love.

"Yeah," I said, and I was too nervous to look up at him, so I looked down at ground.

"You in love with me too?" he asked and pulled me to stop walking and face him.

"Yeah...yeah...I am," I said, and I shifted my feet around in the dusty clay dirt.

"Then, will you go with me?" he asked me and touched my chin to get me to look at him. His eyes were so deep and black, I can't believe how I felt, like I could just fall into them and swim. I was thinking of his eyes so much I forgot to answer him.

"Will you go with me?" he asked again and this time I was watching his mouth.

"Yes. Yes, I will," I said.

Umm, could I kiss you then?" Now he was the one shifting his feet in the dirt.

"Yes," I said and that's when he touched my chin again and kissed me slow while my head was spinning around with his mouth on mine, our hands, both of them wrapped together, and the lilac bushes and wild berry smells all around us, and an electrical current going up and down my body like a wave of heat and a tingle and I swore I felt his heart beating in my own chest ...or was that my heart beating in his chest? I have no idea because everything, all the sensations were all mixed in together like one giant whirlwind of sensations all blended up.

That night, I wished so bad that I had Evelyn to tell about my first real kiss, because I'm still not counting that balogna kiss by Ricky. I know she would have been so happy for me and maybe by now she would be going with my brother because she always had a crush on him. And I would be happy for her too, but she couldn't tell me too much about their kisses and such being as he's my brother and I don't really want to hear such stuff about my brother. And she would probably tell me anyway and we would laugh when I cover my ears and say "la! la! la! I'm not listening!"

I'm laying here thinking for a while about this and it comes to my mind again how strange it is that we can be happy and sad all at once because at the same time I was staring at the ceiling daydreaming about Roderick's mouth, I had the biggest feeling in the pit of my stomach like I wanted to bury my face in my pillow and cry from missing Evelyn so much.

Chapter Fifty-Six

It's Saturday afternoon and Roderick's Mama and sister have gone over to his auntie's house for the day.

"Hey, girl, come on over," he says, and smiles sideways at me from the driveway in front of my apartment. "It's just you and me."

That's what we do ever since that day when we kissed. We just want to be alone so we can kiss some more and sometimes we do other things when we get the chance. Like once we even touched each other where our privates are. We kept our clothes on, though, so I guess if this sort of thing can send a person to Hell, maybe we won't go straight to Hell since we kept our clothes on.

We don't go to church anymore, so I'm not around a lot of church folks that seem to have a habit of worrying if they're going to Hell and they make sure they warn everybody else about it too. But Mama still makes us climb up on the couch and kiss the picture of Jesus seven times each night. Steven flat out refuses and he's too big for Mama to make him, so he's free of it finally. Mama screeched at him that he was probably going to wind up in Hell if he didn't change, but he doesn't care. I try not to care too, but I can't seem to just shake it off like Steven does because I can't just ignore Mama's screeching.

But even the worry about Hell isn't enough to keep me from doing things with Roderick, so when he says, "Come on over, girl," I go over.

Today we're listening to music on his stereo in his room. We listen to a little Michael Jackson, a little Marvin Gaye and even a Kansas album that I "borrowed" from Steven's room.

"That's all nice," he says, "but *this* here, this *here* is our song." And he puts on a song by Teddy Pendergrass called *Close the Door.*

In the song, the man is singing to his girl how he wants her to close the door, so he can give her what she's been waiting for. Roderick sings along with it in my ear.

We close the bedroom door just in case his mama comes home by surprise.

"If she doesn't see us doing anything, she can't be sure so we can always say we weren't," he says.

We kiss and Teddy sings on...

I don't know if it's the song making us crazy or what, but it doesn't matter what it is. We are alone, and the door is closed, and we are pressed right up to each other so there's no space between us and we fall onto his bed.

Everything happens so fast at this moment because the next thing I know he's got his shirt off and we are there on his bed and he asks me if he should take his pants down and I say yes in my head because I do want to see. "Well?" Roderick is asking me again in my ear because I thought I answered out loud. His mouth is soft on my neck and I say, "Yes!" And I almost can't catch my breath and Teddy sings on...

And when Teddy sings, "Come here, baby!" Roderick sings it along with him in my ear and then just when he's telling me that he loves me and I'm breathing how much I love him too, we hear his mama's car pull up in the driveway.

"Oh shit!" Roderick jumps up from the bed and fumbles to pull his pants up and then throws his shirt back on. He pulls his shirt down over his pants zipper without zipping it. I sit up and put my dress over my knees while I sit with my feet dangling off the side of the bed looking innocent.

Roderick rushes over and pulls the record needle over the record with a scratch to stop from singing that song that makes teenagers do things they aren't supposed to be doing anyway. In the same five seconds he flings open his bedroom door, so his mama won't know what we were up to.

She comes in with Jacqueline, his little sister, and they're clinking some things around in the kitchen, putting some groceries away.

"Rod!? You in your room?" she calls out.

"Yes, ma'am," He answers back.

"What you doing? Come and h-," she comes and stands by the door to Roderick's room and stops talking right in the middle of her sentence when she sees that I'm here with him.

"What y'all doin'?" she wants to know and she's looking at me and then at Roderick's shirt because I think she's noticing right about the same time I'm noticing that his shirt is on inside out.

"We just listening to music. That's all," he lied.

"Mmmm hmm ... yeah ... and I'm the Queen of Sheba. I don't hear no music. Y'all come on up out your bedroom. Now you know you ain't supposed to have a girl over to the house when I ain't home and especially not in your bedroom. Your mama know you're over here, Isabelle?"

"Yes, ma'am," I lied.

"Y'all come help us put these groceries away," she says still looking at us sideways while she's walking away.

"Yes ma'am," Roderick answers and I tug on his shirt that he still hasn't noticed is inside out.

"Oh damn!" he whispers. "You think she saw it?"

"I don't think so. Wouldn't she say something?" I'm not really sure of my answer.

That's when Roderick's mama calls out, "Oh, and fix your shirt, boy. It's inside out!"

Chapter Fifty-Seven

We learned our lesson that day, that we can't trust that someone won't pop up on the scene right at the moment when things are getting good. So, we find ourselves sneaking down the alley on his bicycle, him driving the bike standing up and me sitting on the banana seat. At first, I don't want to go there because the alley makes me think of what happened to Evelyn. I don't tell Roderick about that, though, and I try to put it out of my mind. When we're on his bike, I just close my eyes and rest my head on his back with my arms around his waist.

At the far end of the alley just beyond Davis Street, tucked in behind a mess of tangled shrubbery bushes and grass growing wild and high, we found an abandoned shack that became our favorite secluded spot.

Today, we spread a blanket down on the dusty floor and lay there together all quiet, listening to the sound of cicadas getting louder and louder as the day gets hotter. We lay there for a long time which leads to all sorts of exciting things, except we say we won't go all the way because I'm scared of getting pregnant.

"Babies always bring people closer," Roderick says, and I think for a second, he might be right, and I imagine myself all swelled up with his baby in my belly. For a very quick second I get all lovey feeling inside, but that's when we both hear a commotion coming up to our shack.

There's a big group of boys pulling on the front door of the place.

"Why's it locked?" we hear one of them say.

"I don't know. I ain't locked it," another answers.

"Just pull on it hard. It ain't nothing but an old lock anyway."

Roderick gets up quick and puts his finger up to his mouth to say "shhh" and we grab the blanket off the floor, and he pulls me into a closet, where we sit huddled together, afraid to move or even breathe.

The boys make their way into the shack. It sounds like they're having some sort of meeting while they're talking about somebody that was going rat them out and how they were going to have to kill his punk ass.

"We'll jump his ass. He knows it. I'll gut him like a fish," they laugh.

"No, seriously, we gonna kill that motherfucker or what?" They must be smoking some reefer because we can smell it and one of the boys starts coughing like it choked him up.

"That's some nasty ass shit, y'all!" he says after he catches his breath, and the other guys laugh at him and call him a pussy.

We sit huddled there in that closet in the dark for what seems like a long time, but it's only about ten minutes or so until that gang of boys leave. Ten minutes can seem like a whole heap of time though, when you're afraid to move or even breathe, but you're so scared you want to cry.

After that gang leaves, we hop up and leave by the window of the room we're hiding in. We're glad that this time we left the bicycle out back against a tree instead of out front. If we had, those boys would have surely known we were there and found us.

"No telling what they would have done to us," Roderick says. "I'm strong, but that was a whole gang of boys, and they could have kicked my ass no matter if I was going to fight back."

We decided from that day on, we'd never go back to our favorite hide out anymore. We had to find another one.

Now Roderick comes calling after midnight at my window in the summer and I sneak out and we go out to our little hide away in the bushes beside my apartment. There's a hollowed-out space right in the middle of the bunch of shrubbery bushes, like someone carved it there just for us. We bring a flashlight, so we can see where we're going, but once we're there, we don't need any light because we can feel each other.

We also decided that that day in the shack when we were thinking maybe having a baby wouldn't be so bad, that maybe the Lord himself sent that gang of boys to scare us, since we were about to make a bad decision. Maybe I would be pregnant now and we'd have a world of trouble when the reality hit that it ain't all sweet and lovey warm to have to take care of baby when you're 15 going on 16.

So now we sit in the dark in the bushes and kiss and feel each other and sometimes we even fall asleep there. It's like we got our own little Eden right there in the shrubbery bushes.

We had our own little secret Eden until one day, for some reason, we have no idea why, the Housing Authority comes around and chops down all the shrubs on the sides of the buildings, destroying our little piece of paradise.

"We can't have nothin'!" I say, copying my mama.

That's when me and Roderick take our love to the roof top since it's near about the only place we can be alone now. Late in the day after we get rid of my little brother and his little sister by sending them inside, we climb up the mimosa tree and lay side by side on the slant of the roof. Our favorite time is when the sky gets pink making the light all around us look like champagne.

We kiss and talk and hold hands and still sometimes we feel each other, hidden by the mimosa tree. But you can't go getting all carried away with that too much because we might lose our senses and go sliding off the roof and wouldn't that be something to explain how it happened?

Well, it wasn't too long before even our pink champagne color rooftop paradise got taken away from us when the Housing Authority came on another path of destruction by cutting down some trees in the neighborhood.

It was early on a Friday morning when I woke to the buzz of chainsaws outside. I got up and made my way down the hall to the kitchen where Mama was standing by the screen door holding a tissue up to her nose and crying.

"What's going on?" I asked.

"They're cutting down our mimosa," she choked.

"Why?" I wanted to know.

"I don't know. They said the branches was too tall up to the roof. I don't know why that means they got to cut it down. I love that tree! The sum' bitches! Gotta go take every bit of joy we got away!" Mama cried into her hands.

I sighed and stood next to Mama while we watched.

They cut that tree down to a stump.

Mama walked around for days grieving like she was grieving a dead person and she kept saying under her breath, "We can't have nothin'. We can't have nothin'."

"You're telling me," I said in my head because I knew that not only did this mean the end of the beautiful pink blossoms in the spring that we could see from a whole block away, but it also meant the end of Roderick and my ladder to our last place we could find to be alone.

We had to settle for going back to sneaking little kisses here and there like we did in the beginning when we first said we were in love. Not being able to touch each other so much put a craving in me, like it was deep in my soul. I wanted to be alone with him so bad, I found myself daydreaming about it all times of the day or night.

He felt it too. I know because he said so in his little love notes that he gave me. My favorite one read,

"Dear Isabelle,

I wish I could touch you and feel you next to me in the dark. I wanna feel you, baby.

Girl, you so fine. I think about you all the time. Maybe one day, we can be together, like in the same house. You know, like married. I will love you up so right then.

Love,
Roderick."

But that one day won't be coming because Roderick just found out that they're moving back to Macon because his Mama is getting married to a man she met not too long after she divorced his father who ran off with a hussy.

Roderick says he knew she had this man friend up in Macon that she would go see once in a while, but he didn't think they were getting married.

"He's some lawyer man that she met up to the courthouse when she went to file for divorce," he explained.

"And we're moving before school starts back up in two weeks, so we can start school in a new place," he says and sits down on the porch next to me hanging his head down. He's sitting so still and not looking up at me. I'm not sure if he's crying until I'm sure I see a tear rolling down his face and land on the cement stairs. One tear turns to two and then too many to count follow.

I got this big knot in my throat that I get when I'm trying not to cry, like

I've had so many times. I lay my head on his shoulder and reach my hand up and around his head and rest my hand there. I love the feel of his hair in the palm of my hand. I nestle my nose up to his neck and breathe in the summer smell of Roderick's skin. I can't help but to let myself cry.

He reaches for my other hand and cups it in his hands and kisses my fingers, and his tears that were dropping onto the steps are dropping onto my fingers.

Chapter Fifty-Eight

It's been a while since I've been over to Mrs. Washington's house. I don't know when I'm going to get over there again because I think I might have other things to concern myself with other than my grammar.

I come home today, and Mama is sitting at the table crying with Joseph sitting next to her with his arm around her like he's trying to comfort her like a little man. He's nine years old now and he's calmed down some since those days when he used to pitch a fit about near about anything at any given moment. Now, he still does pitch a fit sometimes because he still has a temper, but in between those times, he's calm.

Mama said it was the drawing gift the Lord gave him that calms him. At school they put him in special education, so he has to go a few times a week to a classroom down in the basement of the school, where all they do is give the kids comic books to read to keep them quiet. At first Joseph hated it and it used to make him mad that he had to go down there, until he realized that he could use that time to draw and paint.

So, he started drawing every day and painting, things like landscapes and skies and oceans. Mama was amazed, especially since Joseph hadn't even been to the ocean.

Today I ask mama what's wrong and I think somebody died or something, because that's the first thing I think anymore at a time like this.

"They're throwing us out on the street," she says and shows me a letter we got from the Housing Authority in the mail today.

We got three months behind on rent and Mama just couldn't catch up, no matter how many hours she worked at Joe's Cellar. My little job 2 days a week in the school library after school barely helps out either. Sometimes it helps buy groceries, but usually Joseph or I need something for school, so it goes for that. Mama doesn't know how she got so far behind, except maybe because of those times she had to pay reconnect fees to get the lights turned back on. Then also when you're late with the rent you have to pay late fees for that.

"It just piled up," she says and cries hard with her mascara running down her face like it does.

I don't know what to say, so we just sat here still and quiet, the three of us, staring at the kitchen walls and comforting each other in silence.

We stayed like this for a long time, until Steven came home from cutting Mrs. Parker's grass. It's the day before he's going to college up in North Georgia. Mama's so proud of him for being the first person in her family ever to go to college.

"And on a full scholarship!" she'd marvel to the neighbor lady next door.

"What's going on?" he asks as he laid the usual donations from the Parkers on the table, a halfway empty box of Grape-Nuts cereal and a couple of boxes of crackers, and $5.00 to help Mama out. Steven brought an Oreo cookie for each of us too this time.

Mama shows him the letter.

"What are y'all going to do? Or should I put off college so I can stay and help out and get a job?"

"No, no...you gotta go on to college. You already put it off once't," Mama says, because last year Steven didn't go so he could work in the town library and give his earnings to Mama. It wasn't enough though because halfway through the year they didn't need him anymore and let him go. He tried to find another job, but just couldn't seem to find more than jobs cutting grass here and there.

Mama insists that he go ahead to college. A selfish part of me wants him to stay. Somehow, I think if he stayed, we wouldn't be thrown out. It doesn't make sense of me to think that because I know that isn't true. What could he do about it anyway? He might as well be at college so maybe he can have a chance at a better life, Mama says.

The next morning we're all up before sunrise, lined up on the couch waiting for Steven to come out of his room with his bags packed for college. His friend from high school is coming to pick him up with his parents. They're going to the same college together and they're going to be roommates this year.

When Steven told me about this, I got a flashback in my mind of the night we all went to the carnival together and Evelyn and I were walking behind everyone else, making plans for college and we were going to be roommates after I got there too, to catch up with her. I can't take these kinds of thoughts and when I get them, I have to go be alone somewhere because I just want to curl up and disappear from the pain of missing Evelyn.

Steven finally comes out of his room with his clothes in a pillowcase. He sounds like his nose is stuffy and Mama says she's worried he's coming down with something.

"No, I'm not, Mama. I was sneezing because of dust or something."

I step closer to him and I see in the pink and gray of the morning that his eyes are puffy too. That's when I realize he's been crying. I've only ever seen Steven cry once and the thought of it makes a bad feeling swell up in my chest. It's like he knows that things are fixing to get real bad here or maybe he's scared because he's going away from us. Either way, I feel like I'm the only one here that knows he's been crying aside from him and it makes me want to cry too.

I'm sniffling and Joseph hops up off the couch and nestles himself under Steven's arm.

"Why you gotta go? Who's gonna read stories to me?" Joseph asks.

"Isabelle will, won't you Isabelle?" Steven answers.

"Yes, I will," my voice cracked out the words. I feel like I lived this scene before a long time ago.

"You going to take care of yourself and study hard, okay? Make something of yourself," Mama says.

"When are we going to hear from you?" I want to know.

"As soon as I get settled, I'll send a postcard," he says, and I know he will. "Just let me know where to send it," Steven turns to Mama and says with his forehead wrinkled.

Just about that time, Mama lets loose with the crying and then, like dominoes, we all follow suit, with Joseph next, then me, and finally Steven. We're all standing in a circle with our arms around each other bawling our eyes out when we hear a little tap at the back door. It must be Steven's friend.

"Just a minute," Mama calls out and goes to the bathroom to fetch a roll of toilet paper for us all to wipe our faces with.

"Good thing I just bought this yesterday," she says with a little nervous laugh.

"Yeah. Good thing," Steven says through a stuffy nose laugh and goes into the kitchen with the three of us following behind him. The little lamp mama put on the counter is on, giving the kitchen a warm orange glow so Steven can see to make his way to the door to open it.

"Hey! You ready?" Steven's friend Paul asks and quickly turns to Mama. "Howdy, Mrs. Letourneau," he says in a happy tone. I think he's too cheerful for this time of the morning.

"Hey, Paul. Thank y'all for taking Steven with y'all."

Paul nods at Mama to say it's no big deal.

"Yeah, I'm ready," Steven says and throws his pillowcase of clothes over his shoulder like Santa carries his bag in those cartoons we see around Christmas time.

He turns to us one more time. "I'll be in touch. Behave, Joseph and Isabelle, do your best in school." He knows I've started hating it.

"I will," I lie, and we give him one more group hug, quick though, so no one has a chance to start crying again.

He and his friend go out the door. Mama turns off the lamp, so we can see out the window better into the dark morning. We all watch them shuffling down the sidewalk looking like shadows underneath the flicker of the lamp post light. We can hardly make them out to see who is who when they get to the car where Paul's parents are waiting. We hear car doors open and close. A car engine starts. They back out and for a moment the car lights are shining right on Evelyn's old window. Someone else lives there now, but I don't know their names or even really what they look like.

That night after Steven left for college, Mama said the quiet was too much without him here. I didn't know what she was talking about since Steven was always in his room as quiet as he could be with a book in his face. He used to play record albums kind of loud sometime until the needle arm came loose from the hinge and Steven couldn't fix it with the Scotch tape like he tried to do. He thought he had rigged it up just right and put on his newest record album, by a singer named Linda Ronstadt. She was singing away something about being cheated and mistreated and when will she be loved? Just about that time the tape gave way, and the arm broke off, scratched across poor unloved Linda, and flung by the spinning record, across the room.

"Well, I reckon it ain't today, Linda." I thought, and I laughed in my head at how clever I am sometimes.

I guess that's what Mama means by it's too quiet. She must be remembering the music that used to be coming from Steven's room and she would yell at him to turn it down. I agree that it's too quiet. Joseph asks me if I want to read, and I say I don't feel like it. I just go to my room to lay down and think.

I lay here and think and wish all kinds of things. I wish most of all that Evelyn was alive. Then I wish that Roderick never left. Then, of course, Steven. I wish I had some nice clothes to wear to school tomorrow. I wish I didn't have to get free lunch and feel like a speck. I wish we had a nice house. I wish we had food and running water all the time. I wish. I wish. I wish.

It's a month after the eviction notice came so, I know it will be any day now that we'll be kicked out. Today at school I just feel like keeping my head low, so nobody will say anything to me. If I keep my head down, maybe I'll be invisible. No such luck. The teacher calls on me in History class and I just mumble "I don't know," and everyone laughs. I don't know why it's so funny that someone doesn't know something. I keep my head down and say nothing. I know I'm like some kind of weird freak with the way I don't talk to anybody and the way my hair is so stringy and unkempt and often times not even washed because we don't have running water lots of times.

Anyway, I'm at school and I'm sitting here eating my free lunch by myself like I want to, and along comes Miss Curious, the one who was asking me why I wear the same thing all the time and why I get free lunch.

"Hey!" she says all smiles like we're best friends or something, "I've come to sit with you!" she's almost singing it now.

"Huh?" I ask, shoving a spoon of mashed potatoes in my mouth.

"I've come to sit with you," she sings out again and I'm not sure what she thinks I'm supposed to say to that. Am I supposed to be happy? What made her think I wanted her to sit with me? I don't know what to say, so I focus on my food and then I open one of my books to pretend I'm reading, except it's a math book and no one opens a math book to read while they're eating lunch, so she *must* know I'm not really reading.

She doesn't stick around long though. She must have figured I didn't care that she was there, so she got up to go sit with some other girls two tables over. I hear one of them asking her why she was sitting with that weird girl.

"I was doing an experiment to see if it talks," she says, and they all laugh out loud.

"I heard she was pregnant from a Black boy," one of them whispers loud enough for me to hear it.

"She's a nigger lover on top of being so weird," another says.

At that moment, my face goes hot and I feel a mix of wanting to kill someone and wanting to die myself. I can see in my mind's eye, I go over in a rage and hit them right across the temples with my math book or the corner of the tray. I know that can kill someone. I see them crying and saying they're sorry.

But then it's like I wake from my imaginings and I know they aren't sorry because they're still over there laughing at me. They're never sorry.

That's when I get up from my seat, leaving my lunch tray right there, even though you're supposed to empty it, and somehow without thinking too much, it's like my legs are just taking me over to their table and I stand there in front of them with my stringy hair in my face and my hand on my hip. They all stop laughing and they're looking up surprised at me. They didn't expect this.

"No, I'm *not* pregnant!" I say out loud so the whole cafeteria can hear me.

Everybody turns to look. "And if you ever use that 'n' word around me again, I'll..." They're all looking at me as if they're waiting for what it is I'll do. "I'll whip all y'all's asses!" I finish. After a couple of seconds, they start laughing again and I turn around and walk right past the table where I was sitting and past a group of mostly Black students looking on, shocked. I don't know if they're surprised because I just threatened those girls, or if it's because they probably never even heard me talk before since I'm so quiet at school. Maybe they thought I couldn't talk.

"You tell 'em, girl!" one girl calls out at me as I walk past.

"They know they don't want us to come over there!" another girl says. And she's followed by a rumble of comments from her friends loudly agreeing with her.

A teacher turns the lights in the cafeteria off to try to signal to the students to calm down before the ruckus gets any bigger.

I just keep on walking, right out of the cafeteria, ignoring a teacher who is asking me where I'm going, right down the hall and out the side door, past the smoking area, across the field until I'm on the edge of campus. I don't look back. I'm never going back there again, I decide.

I'm almost 16 and in Georgia, a person can decide to drop out if they want. I'll just tell Mama that I'll go look for a job, like a waitress job, that pays more than they pay me to put books away in the library. I'll tell her that, so she won't be mad.

I get to the street where I can see my apartment and I see my mama and Joseph standing out on the sidewalk. Joseph is near about walking in circles and Mama's standing there with her arms crossed. I come closer and I see she's crying, with black streams of mascara running down her face. Joseph is crying too and then I see men in Housing Authority shirts dragging our things out of the house and piling it on the sidewalk for all the neighbors to see. Joseph is screaming that they're throwing his favorite car that Steven left for him. It's already under a bunch of things. He's heading for the pile when Mama grabs his arms and tries to keep him back, but he breaks free and starts digging through the growing tangle of our things until he finds his car and pulls it out, clinging to it so tight his knuckles are white. He grits his teeth and makes growling noises with tears coming down his face. I think he's gone crazy right there.

That's when suddenly I get a hot fear flooding over my face when I realize that my Evelyn box is up in the closet with her ashes and things that were hers, that tea set and some writing papers. I rush inside and past the men, to my room and to my closet. I'm relieved when I see they haven't gotten to it yet and I climb up on a plastic crate I have in my closet and grab the box. I hold onto it tight and go back out with my brother and my mama. Mama has, by now, been able to get Joseph to come stand with her.

I notice at that time, there are Sheriff's Department officers standing off to the side, I guess to keep order. There's nothing we can do to stop what's happening. Our pile of things has grown into a mountain, a heap that looks a lot like a trash heap. Right on top, they tossed the picture of Jesus, with the paint worn off his cheek from all those years of kisses, and the edges of the picture tattered and curled up from being without a frame for so long after it broke. The nail is still in the hole we made just above his head to hang it up after that. He used to hang there and stare straight across the room at the dingy curtains, but now he's looking straight up at the sky, until a man piles the rocking chair right on top, blocking the Lord's view to the Heavens.

"My Jesus. My Jesus," Mama whimpers.

That night, we made our way to the Salvation Army to have something to eat and a place to sleep. The couple that looked after the place were Christians and told us that the Lord would provide. She showed us to a room where we would sleep on some cots lined up next to other cots, where other people were going to stay.

"And young fella, you come with me," she says to Joseph.

"What do you mean, he goes with you?" Mama asks, confused.

"Oh, the men folk sleep on one side and the women folk sleep on the other." she says.

"He ain't no man,' Mama argues. "He ain't but a boy who just lost his home."

I've never heard Mama make this much sense before and I find myself wishing she had because maybe we wouldn't be homeless now.

"Well, those are the rules, Mrs. Letourneau. Now, come on with me, young fella," she calls him again.

"I don't want to, Mama!" Joseph protested. "I won't!"

"Come on, now Joseph. It's going to be okay. You can go with the lady and she'll get you a nice bed." Then she turns to me and says, "Help me out here. Talk to him."

"I can't, Mama," I say and stand holding Evelyn's ashes and things in the box. I don't want to lie because I don't believe things are going to be okay.

That's when that lady offers Joseph some nice milk and cookies if he'd come with her. "And your mama and sister will be right on the other side of the wall. It's no different from being at home, really."

Joseph went for the milk and cookies, still holding on tight to his car, after Mama gave him a kiss goodnight.

Later, with all the lights off in the place, we can hear Joseph crying on the other side of the wall. Next thing we know, the lights are on in the hall and Joseph is in a full wail.

The Christian couple both come rushing in their house coats.

"What's the trouble?" the husband asks. By that time Mama and I and all the other women in our room are out in the hall too.

"He don't want to sleep in a room with a bunch of strange men," Mama says. "He just lost everything he had, except for his toy car."

The other ladies started chiming in. "Come on! Let the young'un come in the room with his mama and sister!" they all say.

"We have rules," the Christian lady says.

"We need to sleep! We can't sleep with a young'un squawking all hours of the night! Come on, let the boy go be with his mama! Please!" the men all plead.

The Christian couple bends the rules and lets Joseph come in with us to the lady's sleeping section. All the ladies there said that that's what the Lord would have done in the first place. The nerve of those folks taking that boy away from his family at a time like that, they said.

Chapter Fifty-Nine

The next day, Mama didn't make us go to school, nor did she go to work because we had just been through such a shock and we needed some time to adjust, so she lost her job at Joe's Cellar. Her personal problems weren't his problems, her boss told her. And he needed someone who could come to work regular and not be fretting about her young'uns.

The days after that, though, Mama took Joseph to school because she needed him to have somewhere to be while she went to try to get her old job at Hasty House back even though she wouldn't make as much money as she did at Joe's Cellar. She figured I was going to school, but I told her I wasn't going anymore, and that I was going to get a job instead. She just sighed heavy and told me I was going to have to go somewhere during the day and not to let the Salvation Army couple know I wasn't going to school. So, I packed my book bag with my Evelyn box because I was afraid to leave it at the shelter, and I roamed around the town, just walking and going to the park laying in the sun and talking to Evelyn, who I could just hear telling me I need to be in school like we planned.

"But you aren't here like we planned," I told her. "I'm going to get a job," I told her. But when I stopped in the bakery shop to ask to apply for a job, the man there told me I need to be in school instead. And so did the lady at the flower shop where I stopped in.

I didn't know it, but Mrs. Washington got wind of what was happening with me and was trying to find me. One of the neighbor ladies told her that she told us to go to the Salvation Army for shelter and food. She hadn't heard from us, she said, but she reckoned that would be the place we'd go.

Three days before we were supposed to be out, I was going out to do my roaming, when I was so surprised to meet up with her on the sidewalk outside the Salvation Army.

"Isabelle! Oh my! What's happened to you all?" she held her arms opened, and I ran to her.

"We got kicked out of our apartment," I said and then I spit out, "and I quit school. I couldn't stay there any longer, Mrs. Washington!" I broke down.

"Now, now, come on! Let's go somewhere and talk. We'll figure it out, honey," she was so kind to me, and I wished at that moment that I was her daughter, that I had always been her daughter, and that I had grown up in her house with her, and the piano, and surrounded by books. I had this thought but at the same time I had felt guilty for having it because I felt like I was betraying my own family with that kind of wish.

We shuffled into a booth at the little coffee shop on the corner and she asked me if I would like some breakfast. I would, I said. We each ordered a stack of pancakes and a cup of coffee.

"Don't you have to teach today?" I asked.

"No, I'm newly retired," she said. "I'm going to travel the world this year," She smiled across the table at me.

"Not much here for me to stick around for since my husband's been passed on for years now and my son has moved out to California," she continued.

"I see," I said, thinking how mature I sounded. I knew her husband had died before and she had one son who was really smart and always super busy, so I never even saw him when I went over to her house.

"Are you going to Paris, France?" I asked.

"I sure am. I'll send you a postcard from there. How about that?" she said. "Now, let's talk about what you're going to do though, Isabelle. You have to get an education."

"I know. I want to, but I can't go back to that high school. I just can't, Mrs. Washington. "

She's sitting and biting her bottom lip and looking at me like she's thinking.

"I might have a suggestion," she says.

"Okay?"

"There's an alternative education program. It's like a little school where you go and you study and you get what's called your General Educational Development certificate or GED for short," she explains.

I never heard of this before, but it sounds interesting.

"What's that?" I ask.

"Well, it's kind of like a diploma. You go to this little school. You study with a teacher there. You have to take exams. You have to work for it. It's not so easy. Then you have to take a very big test after it's all done. If you pass that test, you get your GED. Does that sound interesting?" she asks.

Yes, it does.

Mrs. Washington popped back into my life that day and rescued me and pretty much my whole family because after hearing how we had three days to be out of the Salvation Army, she made a couple of calls to a friend of hers who worked at the welfare office. Within two days, we had some emergency help and a voucher for an apartment, an apartment that just happened to be within a city block of the Alternative School. That's the way it is with that sort of thing, I guess. If you know someone, like if you have special connections, you can get help fast.

We got through that terrible time and, after all, we got out of The Projects. The apartment we had wasn't fancy at all. It was small, and we were kind of cramped up and Mama had to sleep on a couch in the living room, but she didn't mind. In a way, we were starting over. Mama said that being evicted was a blessing in disguise.

It's the end of the school year and I'm so proud because I got my GED. Steven is home from college. Mama says he's a grown man for sure and he's got the moustache to prove it. Joseph has been showing him all his drawings and paintings he's been doing in the special ed classroom. They are hung all over the walls in the apartment, but there are more that Mama keeps in a box. Steven tells Joseph he's a little Rembrandt and he explains who that is and that he learned all about him in an art history class.

There's a little ceremony Friday evening for graduation from The Alternative School and Mrs. Washington got back from a trip to Mexico just in time to come to the ceremony. She sat with Mama, Steven, and Joseph. When I walk up to get my diploma, I feel giddy with pride in myself. It's a funny kind of happy feeling that makes you cry even though you don't feel sad.

Saturday afternoon, Steven and I are across the street at the laundromat. Sitting and watching the clothes go around and around in the giant dryers, he's telling me all about his first year of college. "You have to stand on your own and there are rules and some professors are strict and if you get in trouble or miss class it's your own problem and if you miss a day you have to make it up or you'll fail. And no one is going to tell you to do it. You do it because you have to be responsible. It's not all work, though. I went to some parties and drank some beer too," he says, with a sly smile.

"Really? You drank beer?"

"Yeah, but don't saying anything about that to Mama," he adds. "So now what are you going to do since you got your GED?"

"I guess I'll go to vocational school," I say. "I don't know."

"Why don't you go to college?" he asks.

"What?"

"Yeah. Why not?"

"I don't know. I just didn't think I was smart enough," I say.

"Of course, you are."

"Hmm…maybe I'll think about it, then." I hadn't really thought about it since Evelyn died. I guess I got sidetracked. I stopped believing I could even go to college and then I kind of accepted it like it was some impossibility.

Chapter Sixty

I'm on the city bus on my way to Albany Jr. College to take a placement test to see if I can score high enough to be accepted into college. The bus is half full of nervous students who are on their way to take the same test. Some of them are trying to get some last-minute studying in so they have their heads buried in their notes.

There's an old man sitting across the aisle from me and he winks and says, "Oh yeah, college placement test time. I remember that feeling." I smile at him.

I lean my head back and close my eyes, thinking about all that's happened to me in the last few years, and I almost can't believe that I'm here, on my way to take this test, headed off to college somewhere soon.

The bus stops at a stop and some other people file in. There's a mama and five little kids, with one boy who's older than the other four, helping his mama look after the two youngest little boys. The littlest boy is about two and wants to bounce around everywhere.

"Come on now, Chris, you gotta sit here," the big brother says and struggles to hold on to him. The mama takes the little wild acting one up in her arms and sits him in her lap next to the window on the other side of his only slightly older, but much quieter brother, who is looking out the window in kind of a daydream.

"Sit like Timmy. See? Look out the window," the mama says and sighs, exasperated.

"Y'all sit here," the mama says to the two little girls who are dressed alike in brown sundresses with daisies sewn around the waist. She motions for them to sit next to their big brother.

They keep turning around and waving at me and giggling while they say "hi" at the same time. "Y'all quit that, Celeste," the mama says.

"She was doin' it too," one of them whines and points at the other.

Then my attention is shifted away from the frustrated mama and her five kids when a young man wearing military fatigues gets on. For a second, I think my eyes are playing tricks on me when I think he looks an awful lot like Roderick.

It *is* Roderick! And about the same time, I'm feeling sure about this, he's looking at me and the biggest smile comes across his face.

"Hey girl! I can't believe it's you!" he says.

I hop up from my seat and he hugs me right in the aisle. People trying to get by want to be annoyed because we are in their way, but how can you be annoyed when you see people so happy to see each other they have to hug, no matter if they're blocking the aisle of an Albany city bus? So, they smile and wait for our hug to end.

He sits down next to me and I feel like I must be shaking.

"I didn't think I'd ever see you again," he says, "with the way things went. I sent you a letter, but I didn't hear back. You still live there?"

"No," I say. "We moved. That must be why I didn't get it if you wrote a letter in the last school year." I skip the whole eviction and Salvation Army part of the story.

"What are you doing?" I ask, tugging on his shirt sleeve.

"Oh this? I'm in the military," he flashes one of those shy smiles where he looks downward. "We're shipping out in a couple of days, to Germany," he says.

"I see," I don't really know what to say.

"I'm on my way out to my auntie's house. Mama's going to have a little party for my going away and she told me to come in my fatigues so my auntie can see."

"Mmm...hmm," I say, again at a loss for words because I'm thinking what could be the purpose of running into him like this here? I'm confused because I'm so happy to see him, but at the same time, I got this feeling like I just want to be scooped up in his arms to a Teddy Pendergrass song playing and there's nothing I can do about that. I wonder if he remembers all that.

"What are you doing?" he asks me.

"Umm, I have to go take a placement test for college."

"Oh, good for you! You were always smart. I could see you in college," he smiles at me sideways.

The bus moves along stopping to let people off and on and I'm wondering how far his stop is from where we are.

"Where do you get off?" I ask.

"In a few blocks. You?"

"I have a few more than that, so you'll be off before me," I say.

"Yeah," then he notices my Walkman. "What are you listening to?"

"Oh, it's a bunch of mixed hits, Michael Jackson and Laura Branigan and stuff like that," I say.

"Hey, you remember 'Close the door?'" he asks.

"Yeah, how could I forget?" I say, feeling flush.

"Me too," he says, and he slides his hand onto mine. "I didn't forget *any* of that."

I'm feeling a sudden rush of a familiar feeling and I put my head, just for a moment, on his shoulder and smell his neck, his skin.

He's holding my hand tighter. "My stop is coming up. Here. Take my address. This is my mama's house." He's writing it quickly on a little piece of paper and he folds my hand over it.

"You'll write to me?" he asks.

"Yes. I will," I say.

"Promise?"

"I promise," I say.

"Here's my stop," he says, and leans in and gives me a quick kiss on the mouth just before he gets up to go. Some of the college hopefuls whoop and holler when they see us kiss and the old winking man woke up from his nap he fell into after the bus got rolling along.

Roderick hops off the bus and turns to wave at me through the bus window. I get a mix of sweetness and sorrow and I got an ache that makes me wish with everything I've got to be back in a moment with Roderick, curled up together under the shrubbery bushes in the dark on the side of the house. I fold my fingers up tight around the paper with his mother's address on it.

Chapter Sixty-One

Things seemed to move pretty fast after that day I took the test. I scored well. I'm going to college, but I don't know where. This is the way it happens sometimes, though, just when you're worrying yourself about what is the right thing to do, something happens that makes that decision for you.

I came home from work at the little bakery shop down the street, the same one where the man told me to go to school that day, and Mama had some news that we had heard from my Aunt Monique.

We were not that easy to find, she said, but she kept looking until she found an address of one of Mama's family members from Aunt Gracie's side, even though they weren't on speaking terms with us anymore since Mama finally told her off one day. Aunt Gracie said since she was a Christian woman, who likes to help folks, she could put them in touch with someone who might know where we were. It was surprising because Aunt Gracie actually went into The Projects alone to ask the neighbor lady across the way if she knew where we were. Mama gave that lady our address when we got this apartment, so she knew it and gave it to Aunt Gracie, who gave it to Aunt Monique. Mama kept saying for days how she couldn't believe Gracie went into The Projects to look for her.

Anyway, Aunt Monique wrote to us. She was glad to find us. Things had been okay until then, but now Mémère is sick with cancer. She gave us a phone number and told us we could call collect. Mama did. We talked for a long time on the phone with her and Mémère, taking turns handing the phone around. We told her about how smart Steven is and that he's in college. Mama told them all about our eviction "adventure." Of course, she had to tell them that her other son, Joseph, that they never met, paints like Rembrandt. I told them I was going to go to college. Aunt Monique asked me if I might consider going there to the University of Orono. She would send me money for the bus fare up, and Mémère would sure like to see me.

So, that's what I was saying earlier. Just when you're going in circles worrying about what you should do, sometimes, just maybe, the fates or whatever, have it already figured out and all you have to do is follow along.

So, that's why I'm on this Trailways bus on my way back to Maine. I'm watching Highway 95 stretch out as far as I can see in front of me, with my backpack beside me. Tucked in a dark compartment inside it, is a box, with a china tea set in it, some Walkie-talkies, and a Tupperware container of ashes zipped up safe and sound after it was rescued from off the floor by a kind old lady sitting across the aisle from me.

Chapter Sixty-Two

Mémère is telling me how life goes like it's in a circle. I'm sitting at her feet with my doll, Soleil, and I notice how what she says is true. I have come back around to this moment like all those other moments when I was little. I'm looking across the room at us there in the mirror, Mémère, me, and Soleil and I see us as our younger selves. Mémère is talking about her favorite saint, who is Saint Francis, for how he was kind to animals. Just then her old tabby cat climbs up in her lap like he knows what she was talking about. The cat purrs out loud and Mémère winces in pain with her eyes closed.

When the dim light of evening pours in the living room, I see Mémère turning to a silhouette on the couch. She asks me to help her to bed, so I do. I fluff her pillows and get her a drink of water.

"You're a good girl," she says.

"Yes, Mémère, I reckon I am," I say. And she laughs at how I say "reckon" like she always laughed when Steven and I said "ma'am" because that's what we learned from Mama.

I sit next to her bed in the too small chair that was mine when I was here with her so many years ago.

"Come here, dear," she says and pats the space on the bed beside her. I'm three, going on four again and I climb up on the bed next to my grandmother.

"Rest your head here," she says with her eyes closed and pats herself on the shoulder. I do as she says with Soleil in my arms. I close my eyes and listen to her breathing slow and labored. I'm listening to her heart and I'm afraid it will stop. Before I even know it, I've got a steady stream of tears flowing onto Mémère's shoulder.

"Shhhh shhhh...everything's alright, dear," she's shushing me like she did when I was little.

It's at this moment Mémère opens her eyes and takes my left hand in her right.

"Hold up your hand," she says, and she places her hand on mine. "It's like a reflection."

I see it's true. Our hands, placed like that, look like mirror images.

Hmmm......what do...........ya....... know?" Her words are spaced out far from each other and she smiles a little with her eyes closed again.

I remember how she used to say, "I'm just resting my eyes," when I used to tell her not to go to sleep before me.

"Mémère!" I want to cry out. "Don't go to sleep before me. Mémère don't go to sleep!". This feeling is swelling in my chest, but I have to keep it in. Because you don't disturb your grandmother when you're 17, going on 18, and laying in her arms like you did when you were three and you feel in your heart that this is a last moment, a last moment that your Mémère has made peace with, while she's resting her eyes before dying.

Aunt Monique, who has been in the kitchen washing dishes, comes to the door of the bedroom wiping her hands dry with a dish towel that she has draped over her shoulder. She smiles down on us with our mirrored hands clasped together.

"Not much changes in life sometimes. That's how you used to always fall asleep when you lived here just before you went to Georgia." Her voice is just above a whisper.

"Our hands are exactly the same size," I say, and Aunt Monique leans in closer to take a look.

"Well, how about that?" she says, and reaches over to turn off the lamp, but I stop her mid-reach.

"Aunt Monique, can you leave the light on?"

"Oh, of course," she says with a knowing smile. She must remember how I always needed the light on to sleep. She didn't know I still do. Not much changes sometimes. There is still an uneasiness between me and darkness.

"Let me know if you need anything," She says and touches my head before she goes back out to the kitchen. I hear her putting dishes away in a deliberately quiet way and I can tell how the plates are laid down slowly on each other with careful little taps of glass on glass. I feel myself drifting off to sleep and I'm dreaming about my own mother putting dishes away and talking to God in the kitchen on Society Avenue.

I'm awakened to hushed voices and stirring around us.

"Isabelle," Aunt Monique is calling my name and touching my shoulder.

I rub my eyes and look around the room where my uncles and aunts are in a circle around us.

"She was calling out to her mama," my aunt Therese said, crying.

I sit up and realize they're saying she died right there with me on her shoulder. I never heard a thing and I wonder how it is you can lay on your grandmother's shoulder and sleep so deep you don't hear her calling out to her own mama when she's slipping off into the afterlife.

Chapter Sixty-Three

I'm sitting in Mémère's living room, with a mess of her unwanted things around me. A few days after she was buried, the family came and went through her belongings in a frenzy to see who could get their hands on what first. All that's left is stuff that nobody wants, save the TV one of my cousins I don't even know staked a claim on. At least I *think* he's a cousin. He could be a stranger off the street, for all I know. He couldn't bring it with him that day on account of his truck being broken down.

Somebody took my doll, Soleil, that Mémère kept for me all those years. I didn't even get a chance to say I wanted it. It was on that Saturday I had taken a stroll up Sand Hill all the way to the cemetery to sit and talk to Mémère. I sat in the cool grass and then I lay my head right on Mémère's tomb stone that was flat and slick and had a sad looking Mary, Mother of Christ on it. I lay my head down and I cried on Mary until I felt a great comfort when I could hear in my head my grandmother talking to me.

"You're a good girl, Isabelle. You're a good girl." I could hear her say. I never knew why she used to say that to me all the time, because I'm not so sure

435

I'm such a good girl. I'm as full of sin as the next person. But at that moment, that's what Mémère wished to tell me while I cried on her tomb stone. A wave of calm washed over me like she was right there with me. I picked myself up and decided I was going to go to her place and sit in quiet. I wanted to be surrounded by her things and I had plans to lie down on the couch and wrap myself up in her blanket that she knitted herself, the one with the cats on it.

So, when I got to her place, I could hear a commotion as I was going up the stairs. Folks were loud in there and the door was halfway flung open. I couldn't believe my eyes when I got to the door and just stared in disbelief. The place was full of folks I hadn't even seen before, not even at Mémère's funeral, except for this one uncle, one of my father's brothers. He was grinning from ear to ear and he hopped up to come and greet me as if it was a party that was happening there.

"Well, hello there, Isabelle! I haven't seen you since you were just a baby! Now, look at you all grown up and quite the looker, I might add!"

His wife, and I guess my aunt by marriage, slapped him on his shoulder and said, "Hey, now! That *is* your niece, you know!"

I just ignored him and walked straight through the living room and into the bedroom to see if my doll was in her place and maybe my little rocking chair I had when I was little. The bedroom had been stripped of furniture and Mémère's clothes were in a heap in the corner where the rocking chair was sitting before with Soleil resting there for the last twelve years. I rushed over and dug through the mountain of clothes like those people in a search and rescue operation I saw on the news after a building collapsed in Beirut, Lebanon after it was bombed.

I scooped up dozens of pairs of polyester pants with matching flowery blouses and put them aside, on top of another mound of polyester pants and matching flowery blouses. When I was finished digging through one pile, I'd dig through another pile until I got to the point when I couldn't remember what piles I had already dug through. My doll was gone. I felt like crying like a three-year-old as I just sat in the middle of all the piles of clothes. I was the sun in the middle of Mémère's universe of matching clothes, surrounded by thirty years' worth of Mémère's Sunday-best and the lingering smell of incense from the thousand masses she had attended over the years, incense that had seeped in and become part of the fabric, and even a part of her skin ... but there was no Soleil and no little rocking chair.

Everyone cleared out by the time the sun was casting slanting shadows across the hardwood floor of what used to be Mémère's living room.

I don't know what will become of the things that are left here, but I'm sitting here thinking there's no way I can clean it all up.

I decide I'm just going to get up and walk out and I'm thinking I'll walk up sand hill, or maybe down it toward the traffic circle. If I go up Sand Hill, I know I'll be pulled in to sit by Mémère's grave again where she'll remind me that I'm good while I lay my head on Mary, carved in her headstone. If I go down it, I'll end up at the traffic circle and I'll cross over it to the other side, down Western Avenue going nowhere special.

I think I'll keep the blanket Mémère made with the cats on it, even though the cats aren't even my style. It smells like her, and I imagine I can wrap myself in it every night when the sun goes down. I'll curl up and close my eyes and feel the comfort in knitted cats and incense.

I stumble out onto the sun porch for one last glance and feel a weight in my chest when I see the chair that Steven and I sat curled up in, waiting for spring so many years ago. He read to me and I watched the ice melt, spring dripping closer and closer, and the coming of the time when they would leave me here.

There's a mark on the arm of the chair where I colored orange flowers with crayon. Mémère got mad at me, but then later changed her mind and decided that orange flowers looked good on the blue background of the painted wood of the arms. She laughed and told me I was a good artist. Here I am, running my fingers across the crayon and making tracks where my fingertips go through the dust collected there.

Sunlight is flooding in from every painted-shut window on the porch and it's so hot, I think I could bake here if I stay too long. There's a fly way up at the top of one of the windows banging himself over and over against the ceiling, making a panicked buzz that makes me feel sorry for him.

How long could a being survive in this heat if it got locked in? What if a stray cat had gotten trapped in here, or a bird? I realize I've been looking at each dusty corner, my eyes peeled for some suffering creature that might need a hero, but it seems I'm alone with that unreachable fly. I kick a couple of half empty cardboard boxes left there to see if anything rustles out.

At this moment, a box catches my eye. It's tucked in the corner next to the chair, and it's marked on the top in big black marker, "to the dump." I imagine that inside the box I'll find my doll, Soleil, and I'll recover her and wrap her up as if she were a real baby and I'll push her hair back, dust off her clothes and even wash them in Aunt Monique's fancy new washing machine.

I open the box and dust flies up, making me sneeze. I can see there's some kind of electronic thing in there. When I dig it out, I see it's Mémère's old projector. I can't believe they were going to just throw this thing out. I'm pulling it out, and I see it has all the parts, even the instruction booklet that came with it. Besides the projector, there are a bunch of old religious booklets. "Our Blessed Mother. – The Sanctity of Mary", it reads, with a painting of Mary looking downward and sad like she always does on the front of it. And another, "The Sacrifice of Saints", with a painting of one of the martyred saints looking up toward Heaven in agony with blood on his face. I shiver and wonder why a god would want his saints to suffer.

That's when I notice a manila-colored envelope addressed to Mémère. It has flowers, hearts, a smiling sun and rainbows drawn on it with waxy, faded crayon. My heart is thumping fast because I remember drawing those. I know Joseph's rainbow, colored just in the correct order of rainbow colors. I know Barbara's smiling sun. I recognize the handwriting addressing the envelope as Evelyn's. I glide by fingers over the writing.

"Ohh," I hear myself say, in a pained whisper.

There is something boxy in the envelope and for about two seconds I think it might be a book or something, until I remember in a rush of memory, a film that we made one time for Mémère when Evelyn's teacher had loaned her a movie camera to do a project for her history class. I can't remember what the project was anymore, but I remember now that we used the camera to make a film for Mémère.

My hands are shaking, and I empty the packet onto the dusty wooden floor and sit myself down to look at it. A film cartridge and a cassette tape land with a crash followed by a piece of paper folded up. I unfold it like it's some kind of relic or precious paper document you might find in a museum in Philadelphia or somewhere else more ancient and maybe even biblical. It's a five-and-a-half-years-closed-up-in-a-manila-envelope, kind of yellow.

The letter my 12-year-old self wrote to Mémère is laid out before me, the writing slanting upward to the right.

> *"Dear Mémère, here is a film we made for you. It's starring me and my friend, Evelyn, Stevie, and my little brother, Joseph, who you never met.*

> *We hope you like it.*

> *Stevie and me miss you a bunch. Don't tell Mama I said this, but our Southern grandma is nowhere as good a grandma as you."*

Then even though it was my note, we all signed it. "Love, from Stevie, Isabelle, Joey, Barbara, and Evelyn," with Evelyn's drawings of a little heart on each side of her name. I'm remembering now that she said she was going to make that part of her signature and it makes a half smile come over my face.

I continue my inspection of the contents of the envelope. One film cartridge and one audio cassette. I'm thinking I'll watch the film, but I don't know about the cassette that I know goes with it. I remember we had to make the audio cassette separately. Evelyn was in charge of the video.

I'm glad there are instructions for the projector because I'm pretty sure I wouldn't have known how to put this thing together without them. I follow the steps to get the movie ready, threading the film through on each end. I flip the switch and the old machine makes a loud whirring noise and stirs up a smell like ancient books and oil you use to fix a squeak. I switch it off before the pictures get going, because I don't want to watch it without the sound. I'm wondering if there might even be a cassette player in that box, underneath the other stack of religious books.

I'm digging through and praying out loud, "Lord, please let me find a cassette player."

No sooner do I get those words out, I realize how silly I must sound, as if the Lord has time to worry about me finding a cassette player or not. Then, like a miracle handed to me by Jesus himself, I spot a cassette player just under a booklet called, "A guide to the Holy Rosary, with Sister Sophie Pelletier. Cassette Included!" Sister Pelletier was in the picture smiling with a rosary draped over her hand. I didn't see this cassette that was supposed to make me so excited to find included. There was just the empty space where it should have been.

I pull the cassette player out and realize there were no batteries almost at the same exact time that I found there was an adapter that plugs into the wall included.

"Thank you, Lord!" I say. When I think about it, I can't be sure the Lord had anything at all to do with me finding a cassette player, complete with power adapter, mind you. But it sure was a big coincidence, so I figure it won't hurt to say thank you, just in case.

I opened the cassette player to remove the cassette that was there. "A guide to the Holy Rosary, with Sister Sophie Pelletier," it read on the label.

So, I've got the film ready to go in the projector. The cassette is ready in the player right at the beginning. The projector is pointed toward the wall. I've got my finger on the "play" button on the cassette and the "start" button on the projector because I have to push them at the exact same time for the voices to be matching with the video.

I'm remembering how long it took us to match it up exactly when we watched it before sending it off to Mémère. I was upset then because I wanted it to be perfect. I remember how Evelyn told me how it would be as perfect as it needed to be, which wasn't perfect at all. She said that grandmas love to see little mistakes her grandkids make when they make something for her. Steven agreed with her, so I calmed down.

Anyway, I'm sitting here poised just right to start the film onto the wall in the living room, when I think it would be much better if I could cover the windows to make it darker in the room. I need something to hang on the hooks that are left in the wall. I've got Mémère's knitted blanket, but I don't want to use that because I have plans to keep that as a keepsake and I don't want to hang it on those rusty hooks in the wall.

I go into the bedroom where I think I remember seeing an old sheet amongst all Mémère's Sunday-best collection. It's a pink sheet and not as a dark a color as I wanted, but it will do. When I climb on the old chair that was left by the window and hook the sheet up to cover it, the sun coming through is filtered to make a pinkish gray dim across the room. I don't mind the color, so

I sit on the floor on Mémère's knitted cat blanket, with my back against the wall and push "start" and "play" at the same time.

It starts with me and Steven sitting side by side. I'm holding the tape recorder in my hand pushing the button. The video starts before the sound does and Steven is talking away. We're in the back yard on the grass in front of the pink mimosa. The sound comes on while he's in the middle of a sentence so it's a little off, but not too bad, "and so Isabelle's friend, Evelyn, got a camera from her teacher."

I can hear Evelyn say, from the other side of the camera. "I'm your friend, too, boy!" And he stuttered, "Of...of course," and smiled.

In the film, I smiled and waved and said hi to Mémère and told her that we missed her. I put the cassette recorder down beside us and I reached for a flute recorder I was really excited to show her. I picked it up and told her I wanted to learn to play music and Steven was showing me how.

Evelyn said, "Show her what you can play!" I played *Hot Cross Buns*.

That's when Joseph came bounding into the line of view. "I want sing! I want sing!" he whined.

"Mémère, this is our little brother, Joseph," Steven said.

"Sing, Stevie!" Joseph said and started to sing. "One penny, two pennies, not cross buns!"

I was playing the recorder and Steven was laughing because he knew that Joseph was making a mistake and it was okay.

I hear Evelyn laughing too and she said, "Hold up. Hold up. I'm putting the camera on the stand so I can get in the picture," and the picture got all shaky while she was adjusting it to the tripod.

I'm in Mémère's living room watching this film through watery eyes and laughing to myself while I hear Evelyn fiddle with the camera stand.

"What's wrong with this ... oh ... okay ... I got it," she said and popped into view waving and smiling.

"Hi Mémère! How you doin?" She said and plopped herself down on the ground in front of me and Steven.

By that time, I had stopped playing the flute recorder and Joseph was making himself comfortable on Evelyn's lap.

"Where Barbara? Where Barbara?" he was trying to get Evelyn's attention with his hands on her face.

"Joseph, I'm trying to talk to your grandmama, now," she said.

"Where Barbara?" he asked again.

"She's in the house with Mama. You can go play with her. You want to?"

"Yeah!" I think he forgot about the camera.

"Go knock on the door. Mama's just inside there. We'll watch you go," Evelyn said, and Steven said it's okay, so Joseph was off, leaving the three of us in peace.

Evelyn was squeezed in between me and Steven on the film and she was telling Mémère how she hoped to come to Maine with us some day to visit her.

About that moment, Joseph could be heard whining for Steven to help him with the door at Evelyn's house, so he said, "Mémère, I gotta go help Joseph. Bye!" And he blew her a kiss and went out of the frame.

Then Evelyn and I sat with our arms draped over each other's shoulders, and Evelyn told Mémère how she sees me like her sister, except there's one problem. She can't be my sister because that would make her Steven's sister too, and she wanted to tell her, woman to woman, that she actually thinks she might well be in love with him and that maybe one day they'll go with each other, you know, like boyfriend and girlfriend.

"But... shhh ... it's a secret between us women, okay?" She was winking at the camera.

By this time, while I'm sitting with my back to the wall and watching this, tears are streaming down my face and I'm laughing at the same time, because I had forgotten that she had said that to Mémère. I've got my eyes fixed on our arms draped across each other and I remember that so clearly, I feel like I could sit back against this wall in Mémère's old apartment for a hundred years and make a flow of tears all the way to the Kennebec River for missing Evelyn so bad.

Then that's when, in the film, I nudged Evelyn to show her Steven was coming back.

"Oh, look, Mémère, you have *got* to see this mimosa behind us! It's not bloomed now, but you should see it when it is!" Evelyn suddenly changed the subject and motioned to the tree behind us.

We laughed, and Steven can be heard asking, "what's so funny?"

"Nothing," I said, and Evelyn and I smiled and looked at each other sideways and then back at the camera.

"Oh! We're about to run out of film! We have to say goodbye now, Mémère," Evelyn said as if she just remembered. Steven popped back into view. We all squeezed in the camera and waved and blew kisses at Mémère. Steven's head was up against Evelyn's and she had the biggest smile on her face. Then the film stops.

I'm sitting now with my knees pulled clear up to my chest and I'm wrapping my arms up tight around my legs, sobbing into my knees. I feel so sad, I could just wrap myself up tighter and tighter into a ball until I disappear.

The cassette keeps on going. I listen through my own sobs. I can hear Evelyn talking about her project for class, the one that she borrowed the camera to do. She needs to make sure she gets more film so she can film the gravestones.

That's when I remember that she was doing a project on the oldest graves in Albany. On the cassette, that I apparently forgot my duty to turn off, Evelyn goes from talking about filming gravestones and "wasn't anything going to be moving, anyhow" to how she wouldn't want to be buried when she dies. No sir. She wants to be "cremated like old lady Watson down the street. Only she wants her ashes scattered off the side of a mountain and not held up for all eternity in some fancy container like old lady Watson."

That's when she realized the cassette was still recording. "Ooh, girl, that thing still on? Your grandmama is gonna think I'm crazy. Talking about some ashes being scattered off a mountain top."

"Oops! I forgot!" I said on the cassette. "I'll cut that part out," I promised, but then forgot before we sent it to her. Evelyn laughed and that's the last time I hear her voice in the tape.

I rewind it once to listen to her laughing again.

After watching this film, I sit in the dim light and cry. I run my fingers along the letters on the envelope, tracing Evelyn's handwriting. It's like I'm grieving all over again for her. And while I'm at it, I cry about Mémère, newly dead. And from there, I get a parade of thoughts, like an old film .... all of it, everything from when Mama and Steven left me here to all the stuff that happened in Georgia. All of it was playing in my mind and I cried and cried until the pink light of the living room turned dark and blurry.

I finally pick myself up from the floor, wipe my face with my shirt, collect the film and cassette, the projector and cassette player, and Mémère's knitted blanket, and put them all in a box that I found in the corner of the room. I walk to the doorway and turn to look at the mess that was left behind. Mémère's clothes in the other room, the chair that Steven and I sat in while we watched spring arrive.

I don't know who is going to clean it, or if anyone will. I only know I can't bear to stand here any longer. I tighten my hold of my box with my treasures inside, look around the room one more time, and make my way out the kitchen door and into the stairwell.

The stairwell smells of 100-year-old wood and varnish. In my mind's eye, I see my three-year-old self, sliding down these stairs giggling and getting dirt on the back of her pants with Mémère chasing after her, frustrated, but laughing just the same. I leave them there; the three-year-old and her laughing grandmother. That's how I want them to stay.

Chapter Sixty-Four

Last night, I tossed and turned and couldn't sleep. I got up and opened the curtains so I could see the moon and lay there for what must have been a couple of hours just staring at the moonlight spread across my bed like a blanket.

Eventually, I drifted into an uneasy sleep where I was dreaming that I was my 13-year-old self, running terrified through a forest alone. Someone was after me. I was calling out to Evelyn and my voice changed from my own voice to that of a Black-capped Chickadee, calling out what I understood to be Evelyn's name. The next thing I knew, I reached an opening in the trees and a flood of white sunlight burst through. Suddenly, everything fell eerily silent, except for the low howling of wind while I stood, frozen in place, trembling and staring at an abandoned old shack, covered with vines.

In my dream, I knew that Evelyn was dead in there.

I woke up with my heart beating a hundred miles a minute. Realizing it was only a dream and that it was actually morning already, I was able to calm down. In that still moment, an idea came to me. It was like somewhere in between my running, calling for Evelyn, and coming across the place where she died, I had a discussion with someone about what I was going to do with her ashes. Maybe that someone was me in my sleep deciding or maybe that someone was Evelyn. I don't know. But whatever it was, the moment I thought about it, the plan was in place. I was going to take Evelyn's ashes and scatter them off the side of Cadillac Mountain in Bar Harbor.

It was a perfect plan. I could use Aunt Monique's car on account of today is her day off from work. I'm pretty sure she'll let me since she let me drive after she helped me get my license a couple of weeks ago. I'm guessing if she doesn't need the car and I put gas in, she won't mind at all. I still have $5.00 from the last time I babysat my cousin's daughter, so I've got gas money.

I figure I'll go ask Aunt Monique before I get Evelyn's ashes out. No sense in taking them down from the closet if I can't go. I've been hanging on to her ashes in that little Tupperware container for all these years. I can't believe I'm actually going to part with them. I tell myself out loud it's what she'd want.

"Who you talking to in there?" Aunt Monique calls out from the living room.

"Talking to myself, Aunt Monique. Nothing new there," I call back.

Aunt Monique appears at the bedroom door. "You want some breakfast? I can make some biscuits," she offers.

"Sure. Thanks," I say and give myself a good stretch before I crawl out of bed and follow behind her into the kitchen.

I'm sitting at the table watching my aunt making the biscuits, with Mémère's tabby cat, who lives with Aunt Monique now, curling himself around and around my ankles. I'm thinking about how I always feel like a little kid when I'm around my aunts and uncles.

She starts humming some tune to a song that I don't know, but I think it sounds lovely and the sound of it takes my thoughts over to the window and out and up, carried off on a breeze where I can see the world from a bird's-eye view. It's beautiful up high in the trees, even if it's a bit cloudy. I think I might perch myself on a branch way up, like I used to do, Evelyn and me on those great magnolia trees in South Georgia.

In my mind, I've got me and Evelyn sitting up on a branch looking down at everything with the breeze in our faces when I hear a question inflection coming from Aunt Monique. I hadn't even noticed her humming had stopped.

"Right?" she's asking.

I don't know what she's asking about, but I say, "Right," anyway.

"Well, that's not a very nice thing for you to agree to," she says.

"I'm sorry, Aunt Monique. I didn't hear what you were asking me, actually." I don't want to hurt her feelings or get her mad at me for answering wrong.

"It's okay, dear. You were just daydreaming out the window, so you didn't hear me. I said you might as well find something to do anyway instead of spending your whole day with your boring old aunt. You might want to find something to do today because even though it's my day off, I've got to babysit for Kathryn again."

Kathryn is my cousin who has a little girl named Ellie who is almost two. She needs lots of help right now from the family since her baby's father took off with some other girl. We're all glad to help, although, sometimes, according to Aunt Monique, that little daughter of hers can be a handful.

"Oh. Yeah, I'm sorry. I don't think you're boring at all," I say and try to think of how I can ask to borrow her car so soon after I insulted her. She says not to worry and that she understands that my mind must be elsewhere, what with all that's been going on in my life.

She's talking away and I'm just listening, and she brings over a plate of biscuits with steam rising off the top of them. I'm reminded of when I went over to Evelyn's and had biscuits before we went to church that time I brought her with me. I'm sitting here staring at the heap of biscuits and here comes the familiar lump in my throat. I feel like I just might cry. What kind of person sits at the table in her aunt's house and starts tearing up over a heap of biscuits?

"What's the matter, dear?" my aunt is asking, but quickly answers her own question. "Oh, I know. We're all still torn up over your Mémère. It'll be a while before we're able to think of her without wanting to cry," she says.

Of course, I'm sad about Mémère, but at this moment, the thing that's making me want to cry is thinking about Evelyn and the Sunday morning biscuits. I don't know if that's something I should tell my aunt or if I should just let her go on thinking it's about Mémère that I'm looking so down at this particular moment. I'm thinking about it while I pour my molasses and take a bite of biscuit.

It's so good, it's like it melts in my mouth. I decide I'm going to let her think my glum look is for Mémère.

"Yes, it will be a while," I finally say after I've swallowed my first bite of biscuit.

I figure since Aunt Monique already suggested I do something else other than hanging around with her today, I should just come out and ask if I can borrow her car. But how will that sound, "Yes, I'm sad about Mémère ... can I borrow your car?"

I let a few moments of quiet pass before I start in telling Aunt Monique about my plan to scatter Evelyn's ashes.

"Aunt Monique, you remember that I had a friend that died four years ago?"

She nods her head "yes" while she wipes her mouth with a napkin and furrows her brow.

"Yes. I remember you told me about that. Just terrible."

"Well, you know, I've had her ashes since I found them left behind and forgotten in the apartment where she used to live," I began.

"Right. That's terrible too, that someone would leave the poor girl's ashes like that." She's shaking her head to express how shameful she thinks that is. "And I never heard of putting something as sacred as someone's ashes in plastic containers like that," she adds.

"I'm pretty sure her drunk uncle left them right where he was sitting that night on the floor. He was sitting in the corner crying when Evelyn's little sister, Barbara, brought him his. I mean, they thought it would be fair to separate the ashes, so everyone could have a little and the only thing they had to put them in was some Tupperware containers," I explained to Aunt Monique. I didn't want her to think that Evelyn's family meant any disrespect for her ashes. I know they loved her with all their hearts.

"Yeah, I suppose I can understand that," Aunt Monique finishes off saying, and she reaches out and touches my hand while I talk. That's one thing I always liked about my aunt. She's always been so warm-hearted. She always knows what to say, when to touch someone, so she's not all too touchy-feely, but just right. She makes a person feel comforted in general.

"So, I was thinking today that I would take Evelyn's ashes and go show my respects by scattering them off the side of Cadillac Mountain, but I would need to see if I can use your car to do it." I went right in on asking her if I can use her car.

The question floated in the air for about five seconds, but it seemed like a long time. I raked my molasses around on my plate to try to distract from the awkwardness of the moment. I didn't know if she would think my idea was crazy. For those five seconds I envision the words to my question floating around and twisting up in the sound of the clock that's hanging just above us on the wall, making sure and sturdy ticks like it was counting down. Five ... four ... three ... two ... Then the phone rings, startling us both.

Aunt Monique jumped up to catch the phone in the living room. I sat with my thoughts and my molasses streams and biscuits. I take a bite and chew slowly because I'm listening to her from the other room, and I don't want the chewing sound in my head to be too loud.

"Oh, sure. You can bring her by about ten o'clock."

I know she's talking about Ellie, and I'm hoping she doesn't need the car.

"You might want to bring some of her toys, some coloring books and things of that nature. Yeah, her little pail and shovel will be good. No ... no ... she won't need her bathing suit. We aren't going to the beach. I just thought we could play in the park. No ... no ... I won't have the car today. I'm letting Isabelle use it for a bit."

I smile to myself over the last bite of biscuit and molasses dribbles down my chin.

Then I hear Aunt Monique talking to the mailman who's telling her that we have some mail from Dixieland. That's what he says every time we get a letter from Georgia.

When she comes back in, I pretend I didn't hear her. I don't want her to think I was eavesdropping.

"That was Kathryn. She's bringing Ellie around ten. And look what the mail man brought you!" she says cheerfully and lays two letters addressed to me down on the table. One is from Steven and the other one is from Mama.

"Oh Cool!" I say, wanting to get on to opening the letters, but I wish we'd first clear up this matter about the car.

"So, yes, as we were saying, you can use my car," she finally says. "I won't need it. If we have an emergency, there are plenty of neighbors around that can give us a ride somewhere."

I turn around quickly and wrap my arms around my aunt. "Thank you, thank you, thank you!" I say.

"Oh, it's nothing, dear," she responds, "You go and do what you need to do for your friend. But first, open those letters." And she pinches my cheek like she used to do when I was a little girl.

"Of, course," I chuckle and tear into the one from Steven. It's short and sweet and I read it out loud.

> *"Hey, Isabelle.*
>
> *I was just thinking I can't believe my little sister has her driver's license! Before too long, you'll be an independent woman, with your own apartment and everything.*
> *Things are going great here. I'm going to start taking my architecture classes finally next semester. Can't wait!*
> *I'm working hard to be able to build Mama that house someday."*

"Awww! He's always been so sweet!" Aunt Monique cuts in with her hand to her heart like you do when you hear of something that's just too darling.

> *"Anyway, I gotta get. I'm meeting some friends for a hike in the woods. I'm not exactly a woodsy person, but I do love the smell of pine. Write me back. Okay?*
>
> *Love,*
> *Stevie"*

"That's funny," I say. "I haven't called him Stevie for years. Wonder why he signed it that way."

"Probably just being cute," Aunt Monique says.

Then I tear into the letter from Mama.

"*Dear Isabelle,*

We sure do miss you. I hope you're settling in real good and getting ready for your first year of college. I'm so proud of you!

I got a new job as a silver wrapper at a steak house on Slappey and sometimes I wait tables. The tips are pretty good too. I even get to eat steak for free because I get free meals on my lunch break. Imagine that! Who'd a thought your ole mama would be eating steak several times a week? Of course, I bring some home to for Joseph too almost every time I have me some. That boy loves him some steak!

Speaking of Joseph, take a look at the picture he drew on the back of this letter. I can't get over how good he can draw and paint! He's reading and writing pretty good now too with some extra help at school from the teacher's aide. He's always been good with his numbers. That boy can do math in his head like it ain't nobody's business.

By the way, the next part is his part of the letter, so I'm gonna say bye for now.

Love always,
Mama. (By the way, would you look at his writing? Can you believe it?!)

Hi, Izzy. It's Joey. Are you having fun in Maine? Is it cold there? Mama forgot to tell you I can read now too. I'm reading stories about a girl named Alice and a boy named Jerry. My teacher says I'm smart. I did a picture for you on the back.

Love,
Joey"

And he drew four red hearts and labeled them, "Izzy, Joey, Steven, Mama."

I flip the page over to see in color pencils, the most beautiful drawing of a mimosa tree, full of fluffy pink flowers and sitting on a branch, are two of the most perfect little birds you can imagine.

Aunt Monique is sitting with her hand still on her heart. "Well, that's so good for your mama! And your little brother is just cunnin'," which I know means cute up here in New England. "And such a good artist!" she adds.

I feel all teary eyed from seeing Joey's drawing and get up fast to put my breakfast dishes in the sink.

"I can wash the dishes for you before I go, Aunt Monique," I offer.

"No ... no I'll get 'em. You go ahead, so you have plenty of time. I'll want you back before dark, so I don't start worrying, okay?"

In my bedroom, I tape Joey's picture to the wall above my bed. I sit cross-legged looking at it, especially the two little birds perched side by side.

As I'm sitting there, it's suddenly occurring to me what I'm about to go do. I've been holding on to Evelyn's ashes for four years and it feels strange to think of throwing them out somewhere, even if it is some grand gesture that I know Evelyn herself would approve of. Will I regret it once I throw them?

At that moment, I imagine myself on the edge of a mountain, losing my balance and falling over after I reach in vain to try to catch the ashes. I see the ashes floating upward, while I'm falling downward toward the craggy Maine coastline at the foot of Cadillac Mountain.

I put my face in my hands and breathe in and it's at that moment I can hear Evelyn ragging on me like she used to do. "Girl, why do you gotta go thinking things to death, dang!"

She's right.

I pull down the box labeled "Evelyn things" from the top shelf in the closet. Back on the bed, I go through the box. I hold each thing in my hand and close my eyes. I see her and hear her voice with each object in my hand. A picture she drew of the peace dove, a "stained glass" window hanging made of cellophane for Christmas that time, a couple of her hair bows. I cup the hair bows in my hands and breathe in deep. I can't believe I can still smell her hair lotion on these. Then there are the Walkie-talkies. I turn hers on and off when I realize I took the batteries out of both of them some time ago. There are some pictures of us, the colors fading from them from the years they spent in a frame on the Mrs. Williams' dresser, where the sun beat down on them. And the delicate china teacups. I remember how the sun shined on them when I was holding them in my hands by the window right after Mrs. Williams gave them to me that day, three weeks after Evelyn died. I think it's funny how now, at this very moment too, when I'm holding them in my hands, the sun is suddenly shining in straight bright rays through my window, right onto them. I think it's funny how, now, they're making the same little reflections right in my eyes like they made that day, with the same little pin prick feeling in my eyes, making them get watery.

I had tucked the Tupperware with her ashes at the very bottom of the Evelyn box. I hold it in my hand and stare at it. "Rest in Peace," reads the piece of paper we had put on the side of each container, still attached, barely. The tape that holds it there is yellow and dried. I clutch the container in my hands and bring it close to me.

"What if ..." I start to think again. "Girl ... stop!" I hear Evelyn say.

I wonder if I'm crazy with the way I hear her voice like that. It's like she's here when her voice just pops into my head like that. The first time it happened was when I put on the dress that used to be hers and looked at myself in the mirror. I was planning to wear it to her funeral. I looked at myself hard in the mirror and that's when I heard her say, "Girl, you do that dress fine!"

So, at the time, I thought, "Of course, I still hear her voice. She hasn't been long gone yet." But now, it's been four years. A lot has happened in my life. So many pages have turned since that day, but she still chimes in when she wants to. And I've started to talk back to her when she does. I'm careful not to let anyone hear me do it, though.

Once my mama overheard me talking to Evelyn, though she was already long gone by then. She told me I'd better knock that off or I might well find myself in the Milledgeville Mental Hospital.

"You don't want to go to Milledgeville!" Mama told me. "There, you don't get nothing but mushy oatmeal to eat, so you can't hurt yourself on your food. Except..." she continued, "at least oatmeal is something when we ain't got nothin'. Ha. Ha. Ha."

"Okay, let's go." I hear myself say out loud after I put everything, except the ashes, back in the box and tucked up away again in the closet.

On my way out, I stop to thank my aunt again for letting me use her car. She's sweeping up the floor to make sure there's nothing Ellie can swallow since she still puts a lot of stuff in her mouth. Aunt Monique tells me that the biggest goal with any little kid is to keep him from killing himself, because they're accidents waiting to happen. All of them.

I nod in agreement, as if I know. Well, I do know, sort of, on account of Steven and I had to always keep Joseph from swallowing things like Mama's bobby pins or a stray penny that had somehow not gotten counted into our budget. I remember one time I brought a stray penny to Mama.

"Look, Mama! Look what Joseph could'a got hold of!" I exclaimed.

And she said, "Oh, gracious! How in the hell did I miss a penny? It's a good thing he *didn't* swallow it. I need that for tax!"

"Huh?" I remember, was all I could say.

"Oh, and it's good that he didn't choke, of course," she added.

So, my aunt is going on and on about how little kids got a death wish and all and how we have to stay a step ahead of them. Meanwhile, I'm eyeing the keys on the hook by the door and trying to think of how I can make my way over there without being rude.

I'm glad when she suddenly changes the subject, "Okay, so you ready to go?"

"Yes, ma'am," I say, and she laughs at how I say "ma'am."

"Well, you drive careful. There's enough gas in there to get you to the mountain and back, but if you can put some gas in, so I'm not surprised by a bone-dry tank, that'd be good enough."

"I will," I promise, and give her a quick hug and make my way to the door.

I head down the walkway, or the "door yaahd," as they say around here, to the car. Just as I'm leaning in to take the driver's seat, she hollers from the doorstep, "Now, you drive careful!"

"I will!" I say, smiling and waving at her.

"Wear your seat belt!" she hollers out again.

"Okay." I clamp it on, and she's satisfied because she can hear the click all the way up to the door. For about two seconds I hope the seat belt isn't making a dirty mark on my white sundress. Aunt Monique goes inside, and with that, I'm out of the driveway and headed down the road toward Highway 95 North.

Chapter Sixty-Five

Autumn 1985
Augusta, Maine

The highway is laid out ahead of me straight and wide with the sun peeking in and out of the clouds, some of them dark gray and threatening rain. Driving with the windows down, quick gusts of autumn are pushing through the car from one window and out the next. Just ahead a huge flock of geese are flying in V formation, casting their shadows on the grass beside the highway. They honk with excitement and I find myself looking hard at them, even turning my head to keep them in view as long as I can when I pass.

At that moment I realize that I'm daydreaming. Daydreaming about geese going South. South. I watched the geese going South when I was dreading my mother and brother leaving me in Maine when I was four. I watched the geese coming back when I was five, waiting for my mother to send for me. Standing in a field of tall springtime grass, I waited and watched for the geese.

"They'll make a V in the sky," Steven said.

"Look for it in the spring and that means Mama will be sending for you soon," he wrote in a letter.

I watched the geese fly over when Evelyn and I lay on the roof top in fall. We wondered where exactly they had come from. Where, exactly were they going? We wanted to fly with them, we said. We wanted to ... we wanted...

I shake myself from my daydreams and wind blowing cool across them. I wipe my tears on my sleeve and pull myself together. After all, what kind of person breaks down and cries over the sound of geese?

I'm approaching Bangor, and this is where I know I need to get off this highway and turn onto Route 1A toward Bar Harbor. I get off the highway and decide to stop at McDonald's for a cup of coffee and a toilet break. I'm thinking I'm going to have to break my five-dollar-bill because I suppose I have to buy something in order to use the toilet and I think it's an odd arrangement. "We'll let you pee in one of our toilets if you buy something from our menu."

I understand they don't want a line of homeless people taking up residence outside the bathroom doors, so they have to have rules like that, but then, again, I wonder how many people would actually be taking advantage of them and their glorious McDonald's toilets and would it kill them if every once in a while, a poor homeless person got to take care of a natural bodily function without paying them for it?

I'm wondering all this to myself, and I'm wondering why I'm wondering about such things as where a hobo gets to take a piss and whether or not he should have to pay for it. At that moment of wondering, I happen to glance down on the floorboard and notice four shiny quarters. I have another moment of wonder when I'm trying to figure out how in the world I didn't see those earlier. I mean, they're shiny and they're money, and I *always* notice if people leave it laying around, even coins.

I always wish I could be so careless as to just leave piles of quarters laying around or jars of coins used as a paper weight on a desk, like I've seen in the English professor's office at UMaine. I think I want to be a college professor someday so I can have an office and a big jar of coins holding my papers down and students can come in sit in a shiny leather chair across from me and admire how much I don't really need my coins and think how they, too, can be on the other side of a desk like this someday, with a paperweight of unnecessary coins, if they work hard enough.

Anyway, I snatched up the quarters from the floorboard and said out loud, again, in the voice of my mother, "The Lord provides." I hop out of the car and lock it, since I don't want to leave Evelyn alone in the car unlocked, just in case. Although, I can't imagine why anyone would take a plastic container out of a parked car in the McDonald's parking lot.

Then I have a second thought that maybe it's not right to leave her ashes in the car at all, so I get back in the car and put her in my purse.

Two steps toward the door later, I think, wait, maybe it's not appropriate to bring ashes like this in a restaurant, not that anyone would know except me. Then I try to think what Evelyn would think. "Leave me in the car, girl. What's wrong with you?"

I put the ashes back in the car, but under the car seat.

"Why you going to go ahead and leave your friend in the car like that?!" I imagine her saying now, just as I'm about to open the door to the restaurant. If there are any folks watching me, they must be having a laugh over this crazy girl going back and forth from her car because I turn around again and reach under my seat and put Evelyn in my purse.

"Now, why you ...?" in my mind again, she's playing tricks on me.

"Oh hush!" I say out loud and head into the restaurant, with a nice family of four walking past me with the mother looking at me strange and pulling her kids to the other side of her, to shield them from me, a crazy girl talking out loud to herself. The father doesn't think I'm too scary crazy since he's too busy staring at my breasts in my sundress because it's sleeveless and my unbuttoned sweater I'm wearing over it is sliding off my left shoulder, just enough to play peek-a-boo with that woman's husband.

The last leg of the trip seems short. I'm driving down route 1A, again with the windows open. I've got Evelyn's ashes on the passenger's seat next to me. I've found some beautiful music on the public radio station. I turn it up, a swell of violins and a blend of piano and it sounds triumphant. I think it's a perfect soundtrack for what I'm doing right now.

I'm driving along with my own soundtrack in my ears and Evelyn there beside me, about to be set free, and I look up and see more geese forming a giant V. They seem to be flying along in the same trajectory as me for the longest time. Perfect.

I come to a slow down and a stop in one of the small towns along the way. Just beside me on a signpost, a seagull's eyes meet mine. We are looking at each other for at least five seconds before the seagull takes off in flight almost exactly at the same moment the light changes. The seagull soars and joins with others going in the same direction, toward Bar Harbor, toward the mountain.

Then I see a flock of sparrows flying, by the hundreds, or maybe even thousands, like a cloud moving in one direction and then shifting all at once in the other direction toward the coast.

I can't believe my eyes, and I'm wondering if I'm imagining all this, since I'm prone to daydreams and imaginings of the "most amusing sort," my Mémère used to say.

No matter. At this point I'm driving with the music blaring out, autumn wind streaming through my hair, and we are all on the same trajectory toward the mountain, me, Evelyn, and my escort of birds, imagined or unimagined.

The drive up the mountain is slow and winding with the clouds above getting darker the higher I climb. The wind is whipping leaves around, getting a couple of them stuck in my windshield wipers. There is hardly anyone going up the mountain, but lots of people driving down with their lights on. The looks on the faces of a lot of people is tense. One man passing me going in the other direction is hunched over the steering wheel, staring intently ahead with his knuckles so tightly wrapped around it, they looked white enough to be gloves.

The rain starts tapping on my window with full bodied drops. Tap! - Tap! - Tap! - Tap! I stop at an overlook to roll up the windows. I continue on, determined not to let a little rain stop me from achieving what I set out to do. Tap! - Tap! - Tap! Quiet. Then, Tap!Tap!Tap! Tap!Tap!Tap!Tap!Tap!

Now *my* knuckles are glove white while I grip the steering wheel, and tell myself, "It's okay, it's okay."

The rain is over in less than a minute and the sun is shining again, peeking out from behind the clouds. As I drive up, I see people still descending the mountain, frightened away by a little rain.

I find a place to park, in a parking lot just before the top of the mountain. Even though the rain has mostly stopped, people are still scurrying to their cars as if they're escaping Armageddon. I take the Tupperware tight in my hands and make my way up the pathway to the top, passing by people looking at me, a family with a whining child that I can't make out if it's a boy or girl because they have the child so covered up with a giant towel as if one drop of rain will destroy him or her. A lovey-dovey couple locked in a full-bodied embrace even while walking, a couple of parents nodding at me, with the mother covering the head of her child and the father shielding his camera from the rain underneath his Kaki jacket. How odd they must think I am for going up, when everyone else has deemed it necessary to go down.

I'm at the top of Cadillac Mountain now, and the crowd cleared out, just in time to give me this moment alone up here. The sun is shining in straight, glorious rays on the mountain, the rugged rocks on the shore, and the blue green water below. I believe it may be the most beautiful sight I've ever seen.

I remember how my mama always gasps in awe at sun rays like this. She always says it looks like the Lord himself is going to walk out on the sun beams and rescue all humanity from itself. I think for a moment, I wish Mama could see this. She'd probably faint from excitement, it's so beautiful.

The ocean breeze is whipping up the side of the mountain and swirling around making my sundress flutter. I stand straight up and hold the still-closed Tupperware container close to my chest. What do I say at a moment like this? What *does* a person say when she's about to release her friend's ashes from a Tupperware container off the side of a mountain? I can't find any words, so I close my eyes and think of Evelyn. I think of her laugh. I think of the first time we met. I think of the crease in her brow when something had her worried or angry. I think of her forward way of saying what she thought, but not in a way to hurt someone's feelings. I think of all these things, but I can't think of anything smart, or touching, or right to say.

Suddenly, it's like I hear her again.

"This is Eagle to Sparrow. Come in, girl. Over."

"Sparrow to Eagle. I'm here. Over," I answer.

"You got me? Let's do this," I hear her say in my mind's ear, like I heard her say so many times.

"I got you. I'm going to let you fly now." My voice is cracking in the breeze and my eyes are misting up.

I open the container slowly because I don't want a gust of wind to come and spoil the moment. I open it carefully, and then with the lid completely off, I hold the container out to the wind. I turn it ever so slightly to its side and a little breeze takes the first tiny dusting of ashes away. Then, holding my arm out straight, I turn the container a little more and move my body in rotation. The most perfect breeze comes along and picks up Evelyn and as I turn my body in rotation, I swear I see her ashes making a circle around me, spinning and swirling around before they take off in all directions out over the water, over the rocks, and down the mountain side.

After I set Evelyn's ashes free, I stand there for a long time, just staring out over the water, not saying anything. I stare at her ashes as long as I can, until they disappear.

I don't know how I feel right now. There aren't any real words to describe it. I think about how everything worked out so perfectly to chase the people off the mountain, so I could have this moment for Evelyn's ashes to swirl around me before going off with the wind.

Mama would say the Lord God himself made that moment happen. I don't know. I asked God so many times why this all had to happen in the first place. I never got an answer from God, so I just had to figure it out for myself as best I could. So, here is what I reckoned in my deepest of thoughts. I reckoned maybe that night, four and half years ago, Evelyn dreamed herself up some wings.

That's right. She dreamed up some wings and flew on out of that place.

I picture in my mind what it must have felt like to her floating up high, above the red alley way, high above the pink mimosas, above the purple lilacs, until she got up to Heaven and sat there, a lovely angel with great big golden wings.

Afterthoughts and Extras

"I'm sitting in the grass in the backyard with my Walkie-talkie and staring at Evelyn's window. I keep thinking at any moment, her light is going to come on and she's going to flash her flashlight out to me."

"Mama says the doubled-up fence is there to protect people from the elephant, who's a "mighty creature indeed." I don't think she looks that mighty with the way she's like a prisoner behind not one, but two, cages." Laska – Photo by *The Albany Herald*.

"I didn't know I could feel sorry for an alligator since it isn't pretty or fluffy. But I do, especially when I think in my mind what it's like to be one of these here alligators. The sun is burning my skin so bad it cracks and there's nowhere to hide from it." Photo by *The Albany Herald*.

"We see sea cows squeezed into a water tank with no room to swim. There's green stuff Stevie says is called algae growing all on the side of the tank and we're all holding our noses.

'Smells like feet!' Stevie says." Photo by *The Albany Herald*.

JOE'S
CELLAR LOUNGE
300-B N. Washington
Presents
GIGI ROSSE
Lovely Spanish Dancer
POLLY ANNE
And **JAMES LEWIS**
Country and Western
Vocalists
Music By
THE "SEE"
Direct From Missile Club,
Cocoa Beach, Fla.
FREE BIKINI PANTIES
AND CHAMPAGNE
TO THE LADIES EVERY THURS.

"Once she was back at Joe's Cellar, church was out. That's the way it was when she was working there before and then I didn't know why, but now I do, because I'm old enough to know that it's a bar where people drink alcohol and I'm pretty sure it's a sin to drink alcohol. Except it's a little confusing because I know that Jesus turned water into wine at a party once, and wine's got alcohol in it, so I don't know how it can be a sin to drink alcohol when the Lord drank it himself.

I asked Mama about this once and she said she didn't know the answer to that since she ain't a preacher or anything." Photo by *The Albany Herald*.

Isabelle's Bird's-Eye View Sketches

"We spent a long time under the tent, her making birds galore and me drawing all kinds of things from a bird's-eye view. I used up every piece of paper she gave me drawing things like our neighborhood how a bird would see it, the school yard and how it was laid out and even inside our apartments how they would look to a bird if he got in and flew around."

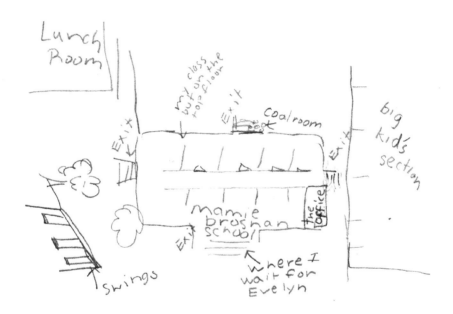

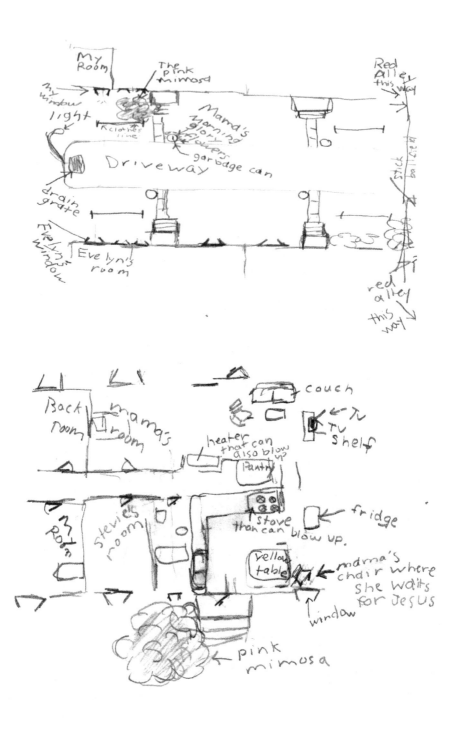

My Room

The Pink mimosa

Red Alley this way

My window

light

Mama's Morning glory flowers

R clothes line

garbage can

Driveway

stick

balloon

drain grate

Evelyn's window

Evelyn's room

red alley this way

Back room

mama's room

couch

TV

TV shelf

heater that can also blow up

Pantry

Stevie's room

my Room

stove that can blow up.

fridge

yellow table

mama's chair where she waits for Jesus

window

pink mimosa

A Word from the Author

Dear Reader,

Thank you for reading my debut novel. I sincerely hope the story leaves you feeling like you have gained something by having read it. If nothing else, perhaps you might feel a mild case of the warm fuzzies to know that a portion of the proceeds from your purchase will go to help fight hunger in the United States.

For every book sold from June 26, 2021-June 26, 2022, $1.00 US will be donated to Feeding America. To read more about this organization, go to https://www.feedingamerica.org/.

As you may have noticed on the copyright page, *Sparrows* is a work of semi-autobiographical fiction. Parts of it are true to the letter. *All* of it was inspired by real experiences in my childhood growing up in a public housing development in Albany, Georgia in the 1970's.

Some of the details of the scenarios are fiction. However, the portrayal of poverty and the intersection of poverty and racial injustice is true.

Every situation depicting the hopelessness of extreme food insecurity is based on actual personal experiences. If you found these scenes to be relentless, monotonous, lingering or painfully slow, that was by design. That is very much the way chronic hunger is.

It is a dream stifler. Having an empty stomach that could not be filled made us feel hopeless. As soon as the hunger was satisfied, a glimmer of hope could return. Thus, we picked ourselves up, adapted, moved on, much like sparrows do.

The sparrow is described by the Audubon Society as tough little birds, "adaptable and able to survive on city sidewalks where few birds can make a living."

That was us, the kids of Society Avenue. (And probably the kids who live there now.) Yes, we were tough, but the shame of poverty impacted us deeply.

Poverty and chronic hunger were like a heavy weight on our tiny wings. In some ways, we were defeated before we could ever learn to fly. And all that any of us really wanted to do, after all, was fly.

If you would like to make an independent donation to Feeding America, go to https://www.feedingamerica.org/ for more information on how. Every amount helps.

I will end by saying thank you for helping fight hunger by purchasing this book. If you would like to make your purchase count more, please consider leaving a review on Goodreads and/or the platform where you bought your book. The more *Sparrows* is talked about, the more sales it will make. The more sales, the more can be donated through our fundraiser to Feeding America.

Sincerely,
Rose Betit

About the Author

Rose Betit resides in Montreal, QC. She has a growing repertoire of published works, including articles, short stories, poetry and now, her debut novel, *Sparrows*.

Her work can be found in the *Montreal Gazette* and various newspapers across Canada operating under the Post Media umbrella, *The Wilderness House Literary Review*, *The Aroostook Review*, and *Brain, Child Magazine*, among others.

Her previous independent publications include *Delicate Bones: 21 and a Half Poems* and *Using the F-word on a Sunday Morning*. She is currently working on a collection of short stories titled, *Sidewalk Stories*.

Made in United States
North Haven, CT
23 May 2022

19448950R00261